AKINIWAZISAGA
Into The High Places

Book Three

LAND OF THE SEVEN FRESHWATER SEAS

AKINIWAZI

DEDICATION

To all the members of Realm Makers

Who showed me I am not alone in this literary journey

LINKS & SOCIAL MEDIA

If you enjoyed the book, the best thing you can do for an indie author like myself is leave a review from where you purchased the book and any other social media outlets you enjoy. Let others know what you think, including the author. Your reviews are appreciated.

For news about Akiniwazi and other projects of M.D. Boncher, you can find updates, communication and news at:

http://www.akiniwazi.com

or at my Discord channel: Resonant Point
https://discord.gg/jeyp6B6

BIBLIOGRAPHY

Akiniwazisaga

A Light Rises in a Dark World
The Inheritance Thieves
Into The High Places

Into The High Places

Encyclopedia Akiniwazi

2 Samuel 22:33-35

God is my strength and power: and he maketh my way perfect.

He maketh my feet like hinds' feet: and setteth me upon my high places.

He teacheth my hands to war; so that a bow of steel is broken by mine arms.

KJV

1. BEYOND THE BOUNDS OF LAW

Brother Finn looked back through the branches of the forest and down the path they had climbed to leave the Eitrfjord. Far in the distance, the last sliver of Lake Wanashiabinoogi shimmered, begging him to turn back. Finn stared at the bright shimmer on the deep blue of water, palms sweating and his heart began to pound for a brand new reason.

"Just one more step, Bergie," Finn muttered.

"All it would take is one more step, the lake would disappear from sight and my skoggang breaks," he said to his ever faithful companion who only panted in reply. "I would become fredlause, you know? Unprotected by the law, any man who desired to take my life could do so without fear. Just like a wild animal… no reprisals… no feud… no trial. Only justice served."

Glancing farther down the trail at the small ad hoc company with whom he had thrown in his lot, Finn was still astonished with his reasoning. He gave Bergamot, his mastiff, a bittersweet smile. She waited patiently under her heavy packs.

"Such is my life," Brother Finn said with a small snort. "Why should I even care about breaking my obedience to the Kyrkja so much? They were the unjust ones, but yet I remain chained to their ideas and authority regardless of its perversion," he complained.

11

Misty sunlight sliced up the shade of the thick forest into glittering magical shafts. A still voice whispered in his mind, "The needs of the Forsamling are far greater than claims of the Orthodoxy. The purposes of God are grander than the vision of a few petty men in comfortable palaces."

Brother Finn nodded a few times with the wise words that came from somewhere deep within, drew a cleansing breath through his nose and resolved to serve both his Lord and his Tign. Turning his back to the lake, Finn began descending the deer trail. The act completed his disobedience to the laws of man. His fate rested in the hands of God and Visekonge.

Far down the slope the group headed toward the sound of a babbling brook. No one had noticed Finn's personal struggle or failure to keep up. Their long climb out of the Eitrfjord made them grateful to have a downward slope that quickened their steps. Finn could no longer see the rest of the party through the foliage but heard their voices echoing through the trees. They were much too loud for Finn's comfort. Who knew what else could be listening among the curtains of green? He and Bergamot rushed to catch up. As the slope grew steeper, gaps in the canopy showed they were rapidly descending into a series of interconnected valleys. The white and gray peaks and palisades of the Ondeaandkorgfjall fanned out before them, ominous and beautiful.

A branch cracked above and to his left. Finn had just enough time to see Friar Amr flying at him from out of a dense cluster of spruce with a bloodcurdling grin on his face. Brother Finn could not bring his harpoon to bear on Amr's attack in time and was bowled over with a loud whoof.

Thyrnir charged out of some dense brush, barrelling down the grade. Bergamot wheeled on Thyrnir and growled, intercepting the other dog's attack, knocking him down with her superior size, using her packs like armor.

The two dogs tore at each other in a frenzy, while both their masters slashed and blocked each other in a blind tangle. Friar Amr's strikes with the barb of his harpoon missed by a hair's breadth but struck soundly with the blunt end. Brother Finn fought to gain distance from this savage attack.

Then just as quickly as it began, Friar Amr and Thyrnir vanished!

"What? Where?" Brother Finn sputtered, finally in a good defensive stance, head reeling from a slap to his temple.

Even Bergamot could not understand how her enemy disappeared.

"You are slow and sloppy, Finn," Friar Amr said coming out from behind around a large tree. "How you will survive a Skaerslinger attack, I do not know. I am still astounded you survived Athrvorthfestning, if the reports I have read are even close to true." Amr laughed. "Let us hope your ability to fend off fell magic or demons is much stronger than what you just showed me."

Now feeling the blows that he had taken, Brother Finn winced. They had all been to the softer parts of his body. None left a mark, but for the pain. Every blow to his face had been with an open palm that pushed more than struck or was hidden by his thinning hair. Bergamot fared the same. The sound and fury of the fight was more like roughhouse play than an attack, but Thyrnir bore a small cut on his left foreleg.

"Your companion plays too rough. See that you keep her away from him," Amr chastised with a silken smile and then began to descend to the rest of the group, whistling as he went. Brother Finn followed in a frazzled state, still unsure what Amr had done.

"Is everything all right?" Declan called back.

"Everything is fine, Meisteri Declan! We were just testing our readiness for the Skaerslinger should they attack. Bergamot plays a little too rough though. We will have to keep an eye on her. Not very dog friendly, it seems."

Brother Finn held his tongue as he slowly caught up to the rest of the group who had stopped near a thin trickle of a stream in the small but steep valley. Friar Inge walked back to his friend, saw Finn's expression and grimaced.

"God's hairy armpits, Finn. You know better than to be alone with Amr near, and that is just me taking your word about him," he said standing close.

Finn did not answer, as he fought to steady his wobbly steps.

"Are you hurt bad?" Inge asked.

"No. My belly aches and my pride is inflamed."

Inge was not satisfied.

"You look dizzy, too. How many fingers do you see?" he demanded softly holding up three close to his chest."

"Three," Finn said with a cranky grimace.

"Where are you?" Inge demanded.

"Trekking through the Ondeaandkorgfjall protecting the Tronerving and his sisters on some foolish march that you concocted through these demon infested mountains to escape those tjovekjakji rebel jarls who trapped us behind their lines," Finn hissed at Inge. "And doing all this with the one man who wants me dead more than any other in the world."

"Greithr, greithr," Inge said with a relieved smile, now confident Finn was not seriously impaired.

"Oj!" Finn growled and gave a frustrated snort. "Breaking skoggang distracted me. I hesitated at the top of the ridge. It was a stupid mistake but that does not matter now. If Amr breaks his word to Leif about my pardon, I need to be ready for it. At least it is clear what he is capable of."

Finn patted Inge's chest. "You must watch your back too, my friend. I may be protected by his oath not to treat me as a fredlaus, but you are not, and in a reckless gambit like this, there are many ways he could cause you to have an accident."

"That is why I stay on the opposite side of the group or behind him. He is too strong for me physically, but I think I have an edge on him in other ways," the portly friar said folding his hands in prayer.

"If God be on your side, jah jah," Finn breathed letting Inge believe his illusions.

"Friar Inge!" Leif called back. His fingers tapping rapidly on his sword's hilt. "Where do we go now?"

"I believe we need to follow this trickle down to a small set of falls and then I will be able to check my bearings again. If memory serves, the last farmhold is going to be north by northwest from the falls," Friar Inge said trying to see through the trees.

"Dearest Lord Jesus, please guide my memory and sight to find it," Inge whispered.

"I have faith in you and the angels whom you command, my friend." Finn bumped his fist on his friend's shoulder.

Amr was already walking point on the eastern side of the stream, just out of the thick ferns and brush. The Kronadottirs followed behind with Declan and Leif.

"I suppose I should lead from the front," Friar Inge said and hurried off to lead the company.

Finn looked down at Bergamot as she leaned against his leg. She was shaking.

"It will be greithr, Bergie. Sooner or later, he will go too far. Just like before." Finn patted her tenderly on her shoulder.

The two started off again and caught up with the party, lest they be caught alone by something far more vicious than Friar Amr.

As the morning went on, the stream quickened, biting hard between the rocks as the soil drew back from the bones of the mountains. Long bare slabs of hot stone opened them up to the bright blue sky. The splashing water, not yet able to cut into the stone, broadened into a shallow sheet that rushed on toward a set of falls not too far ahead.

15

"I suspect we will have a better view once we pass the next line of trees and then we can see where we are going," Inge encouraged.

"Good. I hope we can reach the farmhold before sundown," Declan complained. His distaste for marching showed.

The Kronadottirs groaned under their packs. The sun's heat reflected off the rock and sapped their strength even more.

"When can we take a break?" Solveig whined.

"Jah, I need a rest," Mirjam chimed in.

Leif scowled at his sisters' weakness.

"When we get to the falls, we can stop and have something to eat if we must," he said.

"My Tign, you are pushing too hard," Amr cautioned.

Leif gave the older man a sharp look, and Amr quickly gave a subdued bow and scrape saying nothing more.

When they reached the edge of the treeline, another long flat slab lay before them, rolling down to the edge of a small cliff. Cracks shot through the rock but nothing grew out of them, almost as if they had been picked clean by gardeners. They walked toward the edge, where the brook plunged down a few dozen yards into a small pool and piles of eroded rock before it continued on.

The whole of the valley spread out before them as a small river began to form. Its ribbon flashed in the sun as it wound away into the dense pinery.

"That is what I was looking for!" exclaimed Friar Inge, as he pointed off to the north northwest. "See the circle of cleared land? That is it. Those are the fields and pastures."

"But where is the farmhold?" Leif demanded impatiently.

"In the copse of those trees in the middle I suspect," Friar Inge said.

"Look at the size of them! They must be more than a ship's length tall," Declan said in admiration.

"Jah, it makes me wonder what is hiding among them," Brother Finn said as he puffed from exhaustion and Amr's beating.

"Quite a good question," Inge said and smiled. "God's rosy red blisters, I do not remember this for the life of me! Perhaps they have improved their farmhold since I was last there."

The group sat down, broke out their supplies and began to eat and drink.

"How far away is that?" Mirjam asked.

"I do not know," Leif answered around a mouthful of dried bison.

"I would guess we could make it there by sundown, but it might be close," Declan said wishfully.

"We should," Friar Inge agreed but frowned, and pointed off far to the east. "I came up the valley the last time from that way and remember it is deceptively big."

After a short rest, they descended the cliff by using a steep, switchback path. When they reached the river, Brother Finn looked up at where they had rested and his blood ran cold.

"Inge, come here please," he said softly. His friend came up to him and saw what startled Finn before another word was said.

"God's bloody knuckles! Is that-?" Inge gasped.

"I think it is, and we walked right through it." There was a small note of fear to Finn's voice. "Nothing that looks sacrificial or like an altar, so I pray it is only a territorial warning."

Behind them, the cracks in the stone formed an effigy of a giant wolf visible only from along the river. At every corner of the design, a small pile of rocks marked it plain. The largest pile made up its malevolent eye, watching the river. Watching them.

"Should we tell the others?" Inge whispered.

"No. Let us not worry them. Just, be on our guard in both fronts, greithr?" Brother Finn said and patted Inge's shoulder before they turned their backs on the reminder that they should never have come here.

2. PLANNING THE CORONATION

Visedronning Marianne sat before her late husband's Privy Council. Together they had held the Statsraad at bay for a month, and the epistles demanding to reconvene were becoming insolent. The danger of recalling the jarls and reassembling her parliament was still far too great. Leif had not returned and she was at a loss as to when, or if, he and her daughters would come home. She dared not entertain the question of whether or not they were still alive. That dark thought constantly threatened to destroy her sanity.

Ironically, a new source of strength had been discovered in her subjects. Were it not for the splendid loyalty and prayers of the Sveinnaettir and the outpouring of support from the Forsamling at large, the Halmarpakt and the Union would have already crumbled.

Crown Chaplain Thulrsson had been a great support to her in these black days, ministering almost constantly at first, but now as she strengthened in spirit, he only checked in for daily mass.

With none of the wives of the jarls in the city, she had no peer to speak with, save one woman who visited as often as her duties to the Kyrkja would allow- the Lendmann Mother Ulla Mogrensdottir Asbjornaettir. Their dark night in the chapel together had given the two a deep empathy for one another, and allowed for very frank discussions about what should be done next to keep the angry jarls at bay.

"My Tign, if I may?"

"Go ahead, Chancellor," she said. "Though I suspect I know the question."

"Of course, my Tign." The chancellor gave a quick sad smile as he stood and walked from his chair to stand before her. Seeing her sit in the Visekonge's high seat was painful for him, but she did retain her rights, and this time of transition was one of them.

"Just after the funeral, you tasked me to find anything in the law or the Halmarpakt by which you could delay the Statsraad from reassembling against your will," he cleared his throat, "and reinforce their abolishment till the Tronerving could be returned to us for coronation."

"I did," she said in a mere acknowledgment of what she had commanded.

"Your order to abolish the Statsraad and send the jarls along with their retinue and huskarls home was legal and valid. Most of the jarls went without a grumble. Some have even sent notes of full support. Others have protested vociferously."

"I am aware. I signed the decree," she said. "What about my order binding them to their lands? Forbidding them contact with one another?"

"That has not been met with as much success. Most have been getting around it by the use of factors and spies. Rumor has it that on two occasions jarls have personally met, but we do not have enough evidence to act," the chancellor apologized.

"Why do we need evidence? I am Visedronning, am I not? It is within my right to protect against sedition against the Halmarpakt," she demanded petulantly.

"The law of the Halmarpakt protects the jarls' rights just as much as yours, my Tign. We can trust the testimony of those who claim to have witnessed these things, but that is where we begin to enter the realm of politics. The accusation of a common karl is not equal to the word of a peer," the chancellor hedged referring to the Hird's innate rights, superior to those of the common man in matters of law.

She arched a delicate eyebrow. A hint of a frown line could be seen on her brow.

"Most of the jarls are content to wait for the Tronerving's return. Others are demanding habeas corpus. Produce your son, or assume he is dead on whatever errand the Visekonge sent him. Since the story about your children being with relatives in Silenoeyaneland was proven false, they have legal recourse to demand this."

"The Tronerving will return when his mission is done for the Visekonge, and not a moment sooner," she said, irritation leaking into her crisp words.

"Jah, my Tign. The point of contention is we have only your word and the Minister of the Wardrobe's on it. Vouchsafing for each other in the Privy Council only carries so much weight outside these chambers," the chancellor explained. "Realize, I believe both of you. Rumors of this testimony as to their whereabouts persisted long before you both confirmed it to us, the Kyrkja and the Statsraad."

She drummed her fingers on the armrest of the high seat.

"The point, my Tign, is that the people will be mollified for only so long. We must gamble and set a date for Leif's coronation despite the risk. That would at least give us some time to plan in case..." The chancellor looked at the floor, unable to say the words they all feared.

"In case he has not survived or was captured by our enemies," the Visedronning finished. Her words were bitter ice. After a long moment of holding back the avalanche of emotion this statement contained, she spoke again with brittle words. "Do you have a suggestion?"

None of the men answered.

"You are my council now," she commanded. "I expect an answer."

Coroner Storisson stood up and walked slowly forward. Fingers twiddling in front of his rotund belly. He gave a skittish glance at the others.

"Wh… why not tie it with a h-holiday, my Tign," he stammered.

"You mean like Gildithokk?" the chancellor blurted. "That is only a few weeks away. We need something further out, but not too far."

"Gregor's passing in such a manner has kept the peasantry on your side, keeping the jarls from moving openly against you, but this will not last," the coroner explained." You need something for the people to rally behind and look forward to. I agree that Gildithokk is far too soon, but it must be before the snow comes and sympathies wane. By tradition you may have a year to mourn, but that does not matter to the hearts of your people who have lives."

"Do you think we could use Christmas?" the Minister of the Exchequer suggested.

"Too late. Winter will be fully settled in and the Kyrkja would not stand for it," Father Thulrsson said with a severe shake of his head. "The Bishopric would never tolerate any intrusion on that holy day."

"That leaves only Allehelgensdag or some other minor feast day that only the Kyrkja follows," the Visedronning said.

"That could work," the coroner mused.

"Is that too far away to satisfy those who are rabblerousing against me, Chancellor?" the Visedronning asked.

"I think they could be persuaded to tolerate that much," he answered, stroking his chin.

"Reverend Father Thulrsson, would the Kyrkja begrudge me a coronation on the first of November?"

The Crown chaplain stood up as he was addressed.

"It would irritate the Cardinal, to be sure. He would have to conduct services here instead of Ulfshaugrstrond, so there would be some grousing from that alone. Not to mention many of the Bishops will detest travelling so late in the season. If they are forced to winter in the capital, expect them to be trouble come spring," the Crown chaplain said and sat down.

"What if Leif returns earlier than that?" she asked.

"Then we either hold the coronation immediately, something I would recommend, or we wait till Allehelgensdag and do it then," the chancellor said, a relieved smile spreading on his round cheeks.

"There is also the benefit of quashing further complaints from the jarls. You can put forth an edict to recall them for the festival and coronation. The Forsamling would be looking forward to that date and, God willing, everything would go according to plan. The Tronerving's reign would be off on a good start with support from his subjects."

"Excellent," she said, a slight but genuine smile came out as the two men sat back down.

"My Tign," the Minister of the Exchequer said meekly.

"Come and be recognized," she commanded.

The clean shaven man walked forward.

"Assuming that the Tronerving is successful in his mission, may I propose we bestow the lesser peerage in the Union with a small gift for celebrating your son's coronation? It would also make it harder to sway the peasantry away from the Crown."

The Visedronning toyed with an earring for a moment.

"Could we give it to them in trotes instead of gold and silver?" she asked.

There was a sudden murmur from the men. Trotes were looked down upon as a lesser trustworthy form of currency. They were paper certificates used to barter in large scale with the Crown's banks, using the physical wealth they had on hand as collateral. It helped smooth trade and kept the handling of livestock and other unruly merchandise to a more manageable form. It also meant that the Crown could control when the banks redeemed them for gold and silver. The system worked well in the far reaches of the Union where the people were cash poor but rich in agricultural or mineral products or other valuable crafts.

"It could..." came the slow response from the Minister of the Exchequer. His smile growing. "If you issued them in certain products, like for food or essentials for a festival. Consider lamp oil and paper. Those could work very well. The perversion of their intended use would go down some. And although it would anger the jarls by bypassing them, it could divert some of their subject's deeper loyalties to the Crown. It would be wise to over-issue trotes in this manner if we do take this option. You can never be sure of factor exchanges and hoarders."

The minister of the exchequer sat down absentmindedly, smiling and tickling the air as he calculated the risks.

"Stallare Marshal. Admiral. I suppose that leaves only your reports to me," she said. "How stand we against a rebellion?"

The stallare marshal stood up and marched to the center of the arc of council chairs. Admiral Sverirsson moved as if waking from deep sleep, unable to look directly at the Visedronning.

"My Tign, our intelligence on the loyalty of those jarls who have not reinforced their pledge to Gregor and Leif, and by extension to you, is very light. It would be wise to coordinate with the chancellor and send spies into these jarls' forces. We need more of their activities as soon as possible. For now, we are well protected in the capital, and the loyalist jarls have been made aware that there is sedition afoot. In either case, the fear of false accusation should help slow this from spreading throughout the peerage. Of course, I always advocate swift and merciless action to any svikari caught in our midst. Be quick with the axe and cut off trouble before it bites our bottom." The stallare marshal's broad smile gave quick confidence to her.

"Admiral?" she asked. "Are you well?"

"My Tign, I am fine. My kapteins and commanders have reported increased viking activity in the far reaches of the lakes. Nothing that cannot be handled," he mumbled through a billow of heavy drink.

She frowned. The admiral had been walking around in a daze ever since Gregor died. Perhaps the man was taking the loss even worse than she was. The notion almost made her laugh. That she, a woman, could be handling the loss of her husband better than one of his servants.

"Very well. I believe we have several things to put in motion. Reverend Father Thulrsson, if you could stay behind and help me draft a letter to the Cardinal, I would appreciate that. The rest of you are dismissed with your duties."

The men stood and bowed. "My Tign," they all said, then quickly dispersed throughout the Kronapalasset to do her bidding.

From the shadows above, in the court's balcony gallery, Lendmann Mother Ulla smiled, and quietly disappeared into the shadows.

3. UNDER THE LOWERING SKY

Rain had blown up the valley shortly after noon and the mountains became smothered in thick clouds. The constant drizzle grew colder as the day wore on and the world filled with the dripping hiss of rain falling through the forest canopy. It would be wet and dripping for days. Everyone was soaked to the skin and shivering.

"Friar Inge, I thought you said this was the way," Leif barked.

Night would be falling soon, and they had yet to arrive at this farmhold Inge insisted was close.

Hurt and frustrated, Inge replied, "I am certain those were their fields we saw from the waterfall. It is hard to hide acres of farmland, particularly in the thick forests of these valleys. I know for a fact they are not up above the treeline."

"Because you have been there before?" Leif snapped again as he slipped around some muddy rocks.

"Jah, because I have been there, and cleared fields cut out from the pinery are rather obvious from a mountain," Friar Inge quipped, forgetting his place.

"Leif," Mirjam said, "I cannot stop shaking. Please let us take shelter and make a fire?"

He looked at his sister who was in a terrible state. Her lips were blue with the cold. The cabinboy clothes she wore were made for warmer days, not this sullen misty weather. Solveig was not faring much better, but Declan had given her his bear shirt, wearing only his Gambeson and mail.

"It is not safe here. We must find this farmhold or someone else who will put us up. I know it is hard, but we must press on." Leif wrapped an arm around her and gave a comforting squeeze. He wanted to give in to her desire, but the need for safety overwhelmed the need for comfort.

Ahead, there was a crashing in the ferns. Someone, running quicker than most would dare in this tangled wet wilderness, was coming. Before anyone could react, Friar Amr burst into the open on the deer path ahead of them, back from scouting. Thyrnir loped out of the brush, covered in burrs and mud. Hot blasts of breath came out of the dog's mouth like a locomotive, tongue hanging out at an angle. The mastiff was enjoying the weather to its fullest, unlike his human companion. Bergamot, although warm under her crammed full packs, did not look to be enjoying the journey nearly as much.

"Did you see anything?" Declan called.

"No. The clouds are too low over the trees." Amr waited for them to catch up. "I am sure we are almost there. We must have faith in Friar Inge's memory."

Finn was unsure if that was a genuine compliment and Inge looked too distracted by his own worry to care.

Then Amr saw Mirjam.

"My Tign!" Amr exclaimed. "Here, take my cloak."

"But you need it too," she said through chattering teeth as he shucked off his cloak in a swift move and brought it to her.

"That may be, but you need it far more than I do. Take off your pack," Amr ordered. She refused.

"I will be fine," the lie transparent.

"Mirjam," Leif said in a sharp voice, "this is no time for bravado. He is trying to protect you."

Amr helped her slip off the heavy pack.

"Even if only protecting you from the cold and damp," he said with a smile. The cloak was too big but settled on her shoulders with a comforting weight. It was soaked through, but warm from his body. Steam rose from the friar's shoulders as the cool rain chilled his flesh.

Mirjam pulled the hood up, gave a sigh of relief at its warmth and reshouldered her pack. Her shivering seemed to transfer to Friar Amr who bore it in stride.

"There, much better. Declan?" Amr asked. "Is Solveig greithr, too?"

"She is well enough for now, but I agree we must take shelter soon. Night will come early if the clouds do not break."

The rain swollen stream they had followed was getting louder up ahead as another slope promised to take them down to the bottom of the valley. Brother Finn kept watch from the rear of the group. He could not help the deep resentment towards Amr as he continued to ingratiate himself to Gregor's children.

"Is everything greithr for you, Finn?" Amr hollered back as if he could read his mind.

"Everything is fine here. Nothing is following us," Finn replied.

"Good. The last thing we need is Skaerslinger running us down," Amr chided.

"I am more concerned with demons than with Skaerslinger," Inge pointed out. "Remember where we are."

"Jah, jah. The Ondeaandkorgfjall. Demons, demons everywhere," Amr dismissed, reshouldering his own pack. "We are three Havarians. All experienced in spiritual warfare! What could possibly come against us and triumph?"

Finn fought hard to suppress the derisive snort.

"Move out," Leif ordered. "Mayhap we find this farmhold in the next hour or so."

The small party began to trudge down the slope. Friar Amr and Thyrnir stayed close to the Kronadottirs, while Leif walked in front with Friar Inge. Brother Finn wondered how it had come to this. He felt as lost in the spirit as they were in the pinery, praying that Inge was right on his bearing and they had not gone off course. At least for now, they could not go in circles. The stream and grade made sure of that.

Mirjam slowed down and drifted back to Brother Finn as they walked. Amr stayed focused on Solveig, talking to her quietly as they went. She laughed at something he said, and Finn gave a poisonous glare to Amr's back.

"Brother Finn?" Mirjam asked.

"My Tign?" Finn snapped back to his surroundings.

"Why do you hate Friar Amr so much?" Her boldness caught him off guard, but Finn had long expected these questions from the children.

"It is a personal matter from long ago, my Tign. Now is not a good time to talk about it." Finn's eyes turned hard at the memory.

Mirjam gave a mischevious smirk.

"He said you and he were the personal guards to a Curate when you were younger. He said you betrayed both him and your Herre. Is this true?" she asked, refusing to back down. Finn could see he would have to satisfy her curiosity.

"From Amr's point of view, I suppose I did betray them both." Finn's eyes were sparking like flint against iron.

He saw her stunned expression that revealed she never expected such candor. Clearly she enjoyed making the pompous squirm by nitpicking their words, but had not planned for Finn's candor. He turned to look back where she had stopped.

"My Tign?" he invited with an open hand, encouraging her to keep walking.

"Oh," she started, smiled an apology, and caught up. The rest of the group was getting farther and farther from them.

"Were you expecting me to deny his claim?" Finn asked as he quickened his pace to try and catch up to the rest.

"I suppose so," she reasoned. "Most men refute such a charge. They do not want to look less of a drengr."

"Not I. My value as a man is not tied to the opinions of others. If it had been, my life would be far more comfortable right now. To answer your question, I will go so far as to say that I did not betray the Kyrkja or the Crown. In the end, only a few men escaped the justice they deserved. Amr was one of them."

Finn held out a hand to help Mirjam over a log. Once across, Amr's cloak that she wore brushed Finn's thumb.

There was a prickle on the back of his hand like spider legs crawling up his arm.

In shock he jerked his arm away, slapping at his hand as if a deadly insect was there, but found nothing.

"What?" Mirjam exclaimed watching his frantic reaction. "What is wrong?"

Finn looked again at his hand, and arm. Nothing was there, but the memory of that sensation remained.

"Demons are nigh," a voice whispered close to his ear. He turned around, looking for the speaker that could not be there.

"Brother, you are frightening me," Mirjam said. "What is wrong?"

Ahead, they had lost sight of the rest of the group, and were alone in the green and gray wilderness.

"My Tign, we must pray right now. You and me both. Something is happening or about to happen. Perhaps we can head it off," Finn half explained.

"Greithr," the girl said, confused.

Brother Finn fumbled in his hip bag, searching by feel as his eyes swept all around but kept returning to the cloak she wore. He handed her his harpoon as he dug deep to find what he needed. He drew out his anointing oil, pulled the cork with his teeth and poured a liberal splash on his hand. Before Mirjam could protest Finn drew a cross on her forehead.

"In the name of the Father, the Son and the Holy Spirit, I seal Your child and call upon Your Link Angels for Mirjam's protection. Let no demon touch her, body, soul and spirit," he said around the cork.

"Take off that cloak, my Tign," Finn ordered as he too helped her with the pack, careful not to touch Amr's garment.

"What? I thought we were to pray?" she protested.

"Do it!" his voice was not loud but so sharp it could split rails. Startled, she sloughed it off and held it out to him. Finn refused to touch it.

"What is-"

"On the ground."

She let it fall between them. Once there, he drew a cross in oil on the garment. A sting shot through his fingers. He jerked back, shaking his hand.

"Demon, I command thee out of this cloak in the name of Jesus!"

"Brother, this is silly. Friar Amr gave-" What Mirjam saw made her tongue go dead in her mouth.

The shadows of frightening insects crawled off the cloak and ran under the ferns. Mirjam's eyes became round with terror. She looked at Brother Finn who was glowering at the cloak.

"He..." she started to say but could not finish.

"Jah, he gave it to you but may not have known."

Mirjam shook with rage.

"I want him dead," she hissed. "Giving a Kronadottir a cursed item? How dare he? Cut him down and chop him into pig food! I order you to do this!"

"No, my Tign. I will not, nor will you say a word," Brother Finn's voice was deadly serious.

"What? You dare refuse?"

"I dare, because we must for now," Finn said shaking his head.

"Must? Must what? What are you talking about?" she demanded, her frown now askew.

"My Tign, do you realize how precarious a situation we are in?" Brother Finn asked sternly.

"Jah, of course I do," she protested.

"I can see in your eyes you do not. Right now, you are angry, and deservedly so. You have been betrayed by someone who claims to be a man of God. He may very well be. Or was a curse put upon him by something else? An imp along for the ride literally on his coattails. It would explain the weather suddenly going sour, among many other misfortunes that have happened. Our lives may depend on him being another body between us and a fang or axe, so it is best we keep him there, and never forget that he cannot be trusted."

"You honestly think he is still a man of God? A man wearing a demon saturated cloak?"

"If the demon had legal right to be there according to the laws of Heaven, jah, it could be Amr never knew. But I will never trust him. Nor should you."

"Because you believe he murdered this brother monk of yours and for your past together which you keep silent about?"

Brother Finn nodded and picked up the cloak. The rough wool was scratchy but no longer felt of horrible crawling things.

"I will tell you when the time is right, my Tign." He held out the garment for her to put on. Mirjam was already shaking with the cold.

31

"No," she refused. "No. I will not put that thing back on."

"You must, my Tign. It is safe now and so are you," he shook the cloak again. "You are freezing to death and need this. Put it on. Then we will pray and go catch up with the rest.

"Why must I?" Mirjam whined with fear.

"Besides succumbing to nature? If you do not, he will know something happened between us. If the demon on this was there with his knowledge or was his minion, then he is already aware of what we have done or may believe I have turned you against him. That is also part of his gifts. He reads people with uncanny skill. It is what made him so good at his job. I suspect it is what aids him to this day in serving his masters, whomever they really are."

"Greithr, but will prayer help?"

"Of course. We should start. What I am about to teach you, say it twice every day. You are the best person to stand up and ask God to protect you, and if you never did before, now is the time to start."

The cloak now wrapped about her again, she sat on the log while Brother Finn knelt down in the mud.

"Dearest Lord God, King of Heaven and earth, we beseech thee for Your aid and protection in this journey you have sent us on. We put our trust in You, Lord Jesus, and ask you to show us Your path. Guide our feet, and expose all evil raised against us. Grant us the truth of Your wisdom and let no deception lead us astray."

Mirjam blinked at the personal nature of the prayer obviously used to rote recitation. She had never experienced such an appeal directly to God before, and it fascinated her.

"Lord, we cast down our vain imaginations and take every thought captive to the obedience in Christ. We ask you, Lord, for a renewing of our minds."

Some of the clouds of fear began to dissipate from Mirjam's thoughts.

"We ask the Holy Spirit to seek your will in all things and for Jesus Christ to intercede to you on our behalf," Finn continued.

"We put on the full Armor of God, including the Helm of Salvation, the Shield of Faith, the Breastplate of Righteousness, the Sword of Your Word, the Belt of Truth and the Sandals of Peace."

Her whole body began to tingle in reaction to the prayer, feeling fortified and confident.

"We plead the Blood of Jesus over us and our families, and place our feet upon the rock of Your Word, and our backs against it as well."

For the first time in weeks Mirjam felt as safe as she did in the Kronapalasset, and breathed a sigh of relief. Can a prayer really do this, she wondered? She had heard it spoken of, but never experienced it for herself.

"Grant us, Lord, a new anointing this day," Finn went on.

An anointing, she wondered? She had never been given an anointing till now. Her fingers went to her forehead feeling the oil still there.

"Place around us Link Angels and a ring of fire."

That image blinked into her mind. Angels towering over her on all sides, swords drawn with their backs to her. Then it was gone like lightning.

"We break all hexes, curses and spells cast towards us and our family."

Mirjam gasped. From all over her body, the sensation of teeth being pulled out of her flesh could be felt. The feeling left her light headed and her shivering stopped as a warmth built up from deep within her chest. Little lights floated in her vision.

"And we ask You, Lord, to cancel any prayer prayed towards us and our families if they do not come from a position of love, and if they are not in the name of Jesus Christ. Amen."

Deep inside her spirit, tethers stretched and snapped like ropes under too much strain. Then everything seemed brighter somehow. It was then she realized she was smiling and silent tears ran down her cheeks.

Brother Finn remained kneeling for a while longer, praying in tongues. When he looked up at her, she only smiled, unable to voice her jumbled emotions.

"No one has ever prayed for you like that before, have they, my Tign?" Finn guessed.

She shook her head, snuffled and wiped her eyes.

"You have been under curses and spiritual oppression for quite a while now it seems. Let us continue this as we travel. For today though, that is enough. Tomorrow, we will pray together again."

Bergamot woffed at the two from far ahead, guiding them to where the rest had gone.

"Come, let us catch up before we are lost," Finn encouraged Mirjam, and the two chased after the rest of their company.

4. LIKE SHEEP TO UNCERTAIN PASTURE

The setting sun fringed the last retreating shreds of clouds with gold as a crystal clear sky was left in the storm's wake. The thick forest was bathed with the soft light of evening while the rag-tag band kept trekking toward the promised sanctuary of Friar Inge's memory. No one relished having to stop for the night exposed in these mountains, so they pressed on past when they should have stopped to make camp. The prospect of traveling in the pitch black of a moonless night felt like lunacy. Perhaps the auroras would come. If those heavenly lights cast down their ethereal wash they could keep going, but who knew what else would take advantage of the illumination.

At the base of the valley the smoothly rushing river began to slow and wind through marshy lands. Ponds appeared, and fens became common, full of thick choking grass surrounded by rings of dead trees, forcing several detours. They judiciously walked around them. Despite seeing moose and deer rummaging in their waters without a care, none of them felt safe. The birds began their evening songs, and the crows began to gather for the flight to their rookery.

"You said we should be there by sundown, Friar," grumbled Leif.

Inge had been expecting this rebuke. The strain of the day had been plain to his eye for hours. That was still thin comfort.

"Perhaps this valley is wider than I thought. God's fluffy beard it is easy to misgauge distances out here, you know," Friar Inge said with a banked temper.

"Mind your manners, Brother," Friar Amr barked. "You said by nightfall, and here we are, nightfall. We cannot even tell where those fields are anymore thanks to these trees blocking our sight."

Amr held up his fingers to the angle of the sun as it touched the mountains, measuring time. "And we have possibly an hour and a half of light left. We may have no choice but to hunker down and wait for morning," he said rubbing Inge's nose in his looming failure.

"There is no definite time table in the pinery!" Inge defended himself tartly. "What are you expecting? A train schedule? We are trusting my memory, gambling we will find a place of safety and avoid your certain death, my Tign! I know we are all cold, tired and angry at not being in a warm bed with goosedown blankets pulled up to our eyes. I cannot help it if these worthless tambakkji distances are longer than I remembered."

The outburst shocked everyone. Inge had done well to hide his own strain, but now it had gushed out like a lanced boil. He stood there, at the front of their band, panting, red-faced, but certainly not sorry for letting his temper fly.

Leif opened his mouth to rebuke the friar.

"No, my Tign," Inge interrupted. "I am sorry. Sorry beyond my ability to express." He swallowed hard, his mouth dry. "But I know we must be close! This was always going to be a risk, and I may have guessed wrong. I am doing my best," then gestured to the rest of the band. "We are all doing our best to keep you three alive."

Seeing the disheartened man crumble under impossible odds cooled his anger. He now recognized how hard they were all pushing, and this was still only their first day on their own.

Leif held out a hand, "Greithr, Friar Inge. Greithr. We will get through this. I see you are just as bad off as I feel. Let us push on for another hour and perhaps we will find it." Leif soothed. Inge scratched his scalp and nodded.

"I suppose another hour will tell," Friar Inge said looking at the blackening trees and the peaks turning red. "But we will be hard pressed to make a good camp where we can light a fire."

"I am willing to take that risk to prove you right," Leif said.

Inge smiled. "It should not be far now."

The words brought a thin chuckle from the rest. And with that, the little column began moving forward again.

Solveig had heard her father's voice in Leif, and drew a deep sigh.

"Declan," she whispered, "do you think Friar Inge is right?"

"Skatten min, I do not know, but I have faith that God put him here for this," Declan said in a low voice.

She smiled at his pet name for her.

"Meistari Declan," Brother Finn said as he came up behind the two giving both a jolt. "I need to talk to you alone, please."

"Of course, Brother," Declan agreed.

The two dropped back a little from Solveig and Mirjam while Amr and Inge stayed with Leif in the front. Finn gave Bergamot a hand signal to keep with the Kronadottirs. With a jaunty jingle she trotted up to them, much to their delight.

"What can I help you with?" Declan asked.

"First, it seems your burns are healing very well for such a short time. No blisters or cankers, I see."

"God has blessed me," Declan said, proud of his constitution.

"Have you taken account of our defensive situation?" Finn asked.

"How do you mean?" Declan was curious what he meant.

"Friar Inge and I have our harpoons and knives, you have your axe and shield and that dagger. Leif has his sword and a tomahawk. Amr has a bow, a saxe and possibly some other knives, but the Kronadottirs are unarmed. Beyond these weapons and our encumbered dogs, we are unprepared to respond to a threat such as a band of Skaerslinger or a pack of wolves." Finn brushed aside a low branch for them as he finished his point.

"I should be able to protect Solveig and Mirjam without issue," Declan said, a little insulted. "You have seen my prowess."

"And what of Leif?" Finn asked. The pointed question caught Declan off guard.

"Ah," Declan said, subdued.

"Precisely. You cannot be two or three places at once. You will have to choose, and although I have faith in my own skills as well as Amr's, Inge has not been in battle for a long time. Although he was capable then, his heart and belly are softer now. More for study and brave enough to row into a storm, but not so much for using his harpoon to kill."

"What do you suggest?" Declan asked.

"Do you have any monies for trade on you? When we arrive at the farmhold, we must see if we can acquire weapons for the Kronadottirs. They need to learn to defend themselves. We also need winter clothing. This rain proved how ill prepared we are. If we do not improve our situation and Ogimaak Mikwam blows us a snowy kiss early, we could all die of illness or exposure."

Declan did not like the idea of perishing to an enemy he could not fight. Even the most terrifying demon or hellspawn was preferable to something as insidious as cold, disease or starvation.

"What kind of weapons would you want for them?" Declan asked. "They cannot swing an axe or use a spear well."

Finn thought about it for a moment as they walked soundlessly through the edge of a thicket dripping with lichens and moss. The trees were beginning to blend together in the shadows. They might not have an hour left before darkness forced them to stop.

"Ideally, crossbows or spring bows and a tomahawk as backup. It is not much, but if we can give them basic instruction on how to shoot, a crossbow would bring down most Skaerslinger, and it is not hard to use a tomahawk, as long as they do not throw it. Perhaps a saxe, for anyone can swing one of those."

"They are of noble blood, do not assume they have ever done such before. Despite spending the last few months as cabin boys, they are more refined and not like lesser members of the Hird," Declan reminded.

Finn chuckled at the thought.

Bergamot and Thyrnir both froze in mid step, ears pricked up and both looked off to their northwest.

Everyone stopped, listening for anything out of the ordinary.

The birds kept singing their night songs.

Frogs croaked.

Fireflies blinked.

Nothing came.

"It must be a deer or ram. A moose maybe," Amr whispered, bow at the ready.

"Maybe," Friar Inge said. Declan and Finn closed up behind to protect the Kronadottirs.

The dogs slowly relaxed and began to walk again. Everyone else took that as their cue to continue on, but no one spoke. Eyes sharp, ears pricked up and searching for any strange movement.

The dogs froze again, but the travellers heard nothing but crickets.

"What is it?" Solveig asked too loudly.

"Shall I go find out?" Amr asked.

"No. Stay with us," Leif ordered.

"But I could-"

"I said no," Leif hissed, not used to men questioning his orders.

"I obey, my Tign," Amr apologized.

Again, nothing moved.

Then the far-off rattle of a bell could be heard.

"Oh-ho-oh-hey-yih!" The voice floated through the trees. A woman was calling.

"Skaerslinger?"

"No," Inge said. "God's beautiful dimples, it is the farmhold! That is a Kulning call, bringing their animals in for the night."

"What would be allowed to range free up here?" Leif asked.

"I have not the foggiest idea, but it would have to be something that could thrive," Amr said and took off to scout ahead with Thyrnir at his side.

Leif spread his arms in futile frustration at Amr.

"What did I just say?" Leif snapped but was ignored.

But the two were already gone into the brush, moving fast.

"My Tign," Declan said as they all bunched up, "we need to make haste for that shelter."

"We have no idea who they are," Leif protested as Inge started moving out after Amr as well.

Another sing-song call echoed from the northwest.

"They are Forsamling. We can worry about whether or not they are friendly when we arrive. Come, My Tign," Brother Finn said ending the discussion, gently urging the Kronadottirs forward toward the promise of a safe, warm night."

5. THE LAST FARMHOLD

Friar Amr's silhouette bounded ahead while the rest of the band struggled against the grain of the land toward the unseen woman's voice. Like a siren calling to sailors, it drew them to safe harbor as night closed in. Clothes snagged on branches and boots tripped over unseen rocks. Pine boughs slapped at them with an eerie willful nature. It became harder and harder to follow Amr as he blazed a trail through the increasingly thick pinery. Declan and Leif chopped at the thick brush that blocked the way, trying to clear their path. The Kronadottirs' long straggling hair came undone and caught several times forcing Finn to cut them free. From the roots to the leaves, nature had declared war on their progress.

With a flurry of hacking, they finally burst through and into a clear pasture of purple twilight. Ahead of them stood a copse of impossibly tall trees snug against the foot of a cliff. None of them had ever seen conifers like this before. Behind the stand the peak vaulted up and up in sheer rock faces, split and stacked as if by the hand of God. Its majestic peak catching the last little sliver of red sun on its white cap. Between them and the gigantic trees, sheep, alpaca and llamas ran before them like little wind whipped white and gray clouds, disappearing among the titans of the forest.

"Is this the place you remember, Friar Inge?" Amr asked. He had been standing partially hidden just inside the brushline.

"No, but there are Forsamling here, and we are in no position to be picky on the sanctuary the Lord provides," Inge said, gasping for breath. He was bleeding from several cuts and scratches. Save for Amr who looked untouched, the rest had fared about the same. Finn emerged from the trees and gasped in awe.

The voice ahead changed, but kept calling.

"Come on!" Leif ordered, fearing they would be locked outside by the farmhold.

The battered party ran across the well-grazed pastures that surrounded the copse, hope rising. Just as they were about to leave the pasture a new voice called out.

"Halt!" shouted a man from high up in the trees. Try as they might, they could not see him. They were not sure if it was a bandit or shepherd who commanded them.

"Bless all those who come in peace!" the man shouted.

The Havarians smiled at the challenge, while the other four looked at each other in confusion.

"May the Lord bless all those who live in this place!" all three brothers shouted back.

From above, they heard a surprised snort disbelief, then a response in Latin.

"Which sect do you belong to?"

"Havarian!" shouted back Friar Inge.

"You three are a long way from water, Brothers. Who is with you?" the man's voice continued in the same tongue

All three paused.

"Do we tell them?" Inge whispered.

"Do we have a choice?" Finn said, keeping his voice low as well.

Amr did not bother with counsel.

"We come with the heir and daughters of the Visekonge in need of sanctuary for a night or two," he shouted back again in Latin.

No response came down from the blackened canopy of the trees.

"You told them who we are?" Leif hissed at Amr.

"Oh! You speak Latin, my Tign?" Friar Amr was genuinely shocked.

"Of course I do," he sneered. " I am an educated man!"

"Huh!" Amr blurted, thinking hard for a moment. "Good to know," he added with a queer smile.

"Will you grant us sanctuary?" Brother Finn asked.

"Those are the children of Gregor Sveinnaettir?" The voice was positively transparent with incredulity.

"Let us meet face to face and you can see for yourself," Amr shouted back.

More silence. A few pinpricks of light moved among the branches. Several men with hooded lanterns were moving about. A loud bray of shocked laughter came out from deeper in.

"Greithr, my friends. Come through the trees." The unseen voice could not hide his amusement.

"Follow the flocks," the voice commanded. "But hurry. It is best everyone is out of the meadow soon."

The party entered the copse. The trees were so large it would take twenty men or more to encircle them. Their thick powerful shafts came up half the height of the cliff above and gave the thin outer ring of normal trees a shrub-like appearance. Inside the savanna of these giants of the forest, soft beds of needles cushioned their walk, and the path of the animals was plain to see. Passing to the edge of the other side. Above, an intricate webbing of ropes and planking created a hidden battlement. Wooden hoardings and bridges allowed fast movement a hundred feet above their heads on which moved a dozen or so armed men as they watched, bows in hand but not at the ready.

43

As the group came to the other side of the copse, they saw a thin rope bridge leading into a rock face then disappearing into the cliff above. A hundred feet before the natural battlement was a clearing filled with large blocks of talus and small shrubs pushing through the rubble.

To cross this gap and into the mountain, a long ramp descended, suspended by a complex set of ropes, chains and winches. It was wide enough for two men abreast and long as a ship. Ahead, the last of the llamas went over the lip of the ramp and into what lay inside the mountain.

"We are going up there?" Mirjam asked in surprise. She was out of breath and trembling in exhaustion.

"That is where our sanctuary is, so that is where we must go," responded Leif. "Let us worry about who they are once we are safe from the dangers lurking in these mountains."

They began to climb the sturdy ramp that now could be seen for what it was, a drawbridge. As they reached the lip, they saw a gentle slope lead down and into a small rock cut that preceded a lit tunnel leading further into the mountain. Midway up the cut, a series of chains and stone pillars with greased wheels sat waiting. The network of ropes was an ingenious winch and crane system that raised and lowered the ramp allowing it to slide to its resting place above the path and through the stone gap, hiding everything from view save for a few hard to see ropes to their tree forts.

Attending the ramp were a dozen men and four oxen while the defenders returned from the copse of trees along the thin and precarious rope bridge to the tree hoardings.

"Astounding," breathed Friar Amr as he came to the top. "This whole thing slides up over those smooth skids and levers down to the edge of the copse."

With that observation, a teamster shouted at the oxen, and they began to pull the whole contraption up. With a great rumbling and squealing of wood and rope, the ramp slid up and over their heads and into the rafters of the cut, secured till it was needed again.

"I wonder why they are so heavily defended. Why does no one back in Dyrrvatn Kastali know of this place?" Declan mused aloud.

"Because we belong to no jarl or bandit," a new voice declared defiantly. "Welcome to Saelirskjol. May you find safety and rest in this place."

Coming out from the tunnel, a bear of a man walked towards them. His cloak and hood were a bison hide worn over black robes with a trim of white and crimson. His hair was drawn back into a yard long blond ponytail, and his goatee was in two braids on either side of his chin. An empty but ornate scabbard for a sword on his hip. Next to him came a whip thin woman with a plain face. Lines cut by great loss and hardship making her look old before her time. Her eyes were expressive betraying a keen intellect. She wore blue, purple and red robes of the Taitians, but carried a superbly crafted sword in a poorly tooled sheath.

"I am Ansgar Valrsson, Curate of Saelirskjol and Ragnarite Paladin. This is my sister, the Reverend Chorister, Edda Gerdasdottir. I am told that my Tign's son is here?" Behind him a ripple of snickers came up from the assembled men.

Leif bristled and stepped forward to berate them when Friar Amr took him by the elbow.

Surprised, Leif readied to unleash his ire at the monk.

"My Tign," Amr whispered so only Leif could hear, "Consider where we are and how fantastic your arrival is to anyone ignorant of your... ahem... previous travel arrangements."

As his irritation abated Leif nodded, shrugged to regain his composure and jutted out his chin. "I am Leif Gregorsson Sveinnaettir. Tronerving of Akiniwazi. These are the Kronadottirs, Solveig and Mirjam," he said gesturing toward his sisters, "and these four men are our escort. We ask for your hospitality, Reverend Father Valrsson." Leif stepped forward, took hold of his sash and twisted it around. The gold broach of the Sveinaettir Crown seal glittered in the torchlight as it was exposed for all to see. There was a collective gasp and every man of Saelirskjol dropped to their knee or bowed before Leif.

"My Tign, I could not believe it was you. Forgive my men. How could they even know it was..." The Reverend Father stilled himself, then continued, "We welcome you and are thankful for your visit here. Our farmhold is yours."

"Greithr and thank you," Leif said like he was greeting a favored courtier. The simple gesture made the rest of the Paladin's men smile. It seemed his father's lessons on how to treat karls and kerling was good advice after all. "If we could retire to your hall, we have desperate need of fire, food and a place to bed for the night. There I can explain what has happened."

Nearly all of Saelirskjol's turned out as they walked up the rising tunnel for the news of their arrival had spread faster than they could walk. An annoyed racket came from the flocks of animals as they were disturbed from their evening routine by the large group walking by their underground stables.

"Is this all hewn out of a mine, Reverend Father?" Mirjam asked the Ragnarite.

"No. This was dug years ago," he answered, a smile in his voice.

"Years ago?" Behind them they could hear the teamsters fussing with the riled animals as they walked past, following the lanterns as they went. "How long has Saelirskjol been here?"

"We do not know. It is a blessed refuge and so it was named thus. How else could you explain a ready-made town and fields safe from threats in the side of a mountain?"

"Who found it?" Leif interjected.

Reverend Father Valrsson chuckled.

"Jah. We still do not know who built it, but many thoughts exist on the matter."

The tunnel opened into another deep cut after minutes of walking up its grade. People crowded around the railing that had been built around the cut's edge and murmured in giddy curiosity.

"You will not be able to enjoy the view tonight, but if you do choose to wander do not go past the brushline. It is a very long drop, and the rocks are sharp," Chorister Gerdasdottir warned.

"I promise you, dear Dame," Leif answered, "none of us are interested in exploring. We may just fall asleep in our food!"

Several of their growing entourage laughed.

As they rose out of the ground in the last dim strains of evening, the farmhold came into view. The deep blue of the sky separated by a ragged edge of brush and low trees that disappeared into the black mountain silhouettes. The wind was fresh and gave the sensation of sailing on the lakes.

They saw no longhouses here. Nor were there any round or pit houses, only a hall, a few stabbur for grain and other stores. Carved directly into the cliff were the houses. Big blocky homes stacked and connected by stone stairs and ladders before becoming solid rock again which rose up a few dozen yards to the next plateau. Warm light leaked out of shuttered window cracks, and people poured out to see the visitors.

There were dozens of men, women and children of all ages, maybe hundreds. Children ran about like a pack of happy pups. Some older boys and girls bowed and showed deference to the Visekonge's heirs.

Many of the younger children wondered out loud why they had to be respectful to these travelers.

The scene bothered Brother Finn as he watched the children. A few women took the youngsters in tow leading them back to the cliff homes. There were Skaerslinger children mixed in! The epiphany was startling. This was an orphanage! A blessed refuge for much more than what was implied!

The whole experience was both wondrous and disconcerting to Mirjam and Solveig.

Mirjam looked up toward the peak. Several gargantuan shadows loomed over Saelirskjol and danced with malevolent glow of firelight. The figures were taller than any giants she could dream of, thirty, forty feet tall, visible across the whole alpine valley. It was impossible to tell how many were there. Four? Eight? Fifteen? They jumped around and back and forth.

"Oh!" she shrieked and clapped her hand over her mouth, certain these were more shadowy demons. Mirjam's startled cry made everyone jump. Sword and axe were instantly out, ready for a fight. The men of their band sprung to defend them, sword and axes drawn. Everyone flinched back, children squealed in fright. They gasped as they looked up to see the top of the mountain.

"My Tign!" Chorister Gerdasdottir sang over the commotion, hands high. As swiftly as the chaos began, it was over, every eye locked upon the woman. She began the lullaby tune again:

"All is well! All is well."
Listen and you will know.
You are safe, you are safe,
Allow God's peace to grow."

There was a collective sigh of relief as curiosity and wonder came over the tired band. Chorister Gerdasdottir closed her eyes, laid a soft hand on the girl's shoulder and breathed deeply, and willed everyone in her aura to do the same, and to breathe out slowly. Like a conductor, her hands began to sway and from the heavens a voice came in song:

" In Domino speravi quomodo dicitis animae meae transvola in montem ut avis."

The voice was in reality an intricate braid of many voices. The polyphonic nature made it sound as if it came from everywhere, soft but clear on the wind. The chorister's hand swayed like a reed pushed by the breeze of the song. The sound swelled in chords as it reflected off the arc of the cliff above.

"How? What...?" Leif sputtered in amazement at the beautiful sound.

"In the LORD put I my trust: how say ye to my soul, Flee as a bird to your mountain. The tenth Psalm, and very appropriate," Friar Inge translated as the melody continued.

"The cliff's shape amplifies song," the chorister explained. "From there, a good strong singer can be heard over the entire valley when the wind is right. It is from there you heard the Kulning earlier. Now we all can hear the Vespers service hymns and songs. Spoken voice does not do as well it seems, but song..." she opened her eyes again.

"And with that, we keep the Skaerslinger and manitou out of the valley for our animals. They hate praise and scripture," Reverend Father Valrsson added. "Psalms most of all."

Friar Amr looked distinctly uncomfortable at the sound, staring wide eyed at the titanic flickering shapes. He seemed to writhe despite not moving a muscle, desperate to run away. Brother Finn saw the look in Amr's eyes and felt a small spike of joy. It was good to see someone like Amr so distraught.

"That is impressive, I must say," Amr swallowed uncomfortably, "but why do the Skaerslinger not come here and attack? They know where you are with that display."

"From what the children say, the Skaerslinger believe the shadows and songs to be powerful manitou, so they come near only in the direst of circumstances to where this farmhold used to be. They actually leave children and offerings of peace there. That is why we light a bonfire at night. Speaking of which, there is a roaring hearth fire for you inside," the Reverend Father goaded. The company of weary travellers began to move again, but continued to look back at the singing shadows on the mountain face.

"The children?" Brother Finn asked.

"Jah, the Skaerslinger's children. They leave them behind for us from time to time and we raise them," Chorister Gerdasdottir answered. "Many were made orphans by their wars, or thought too unworthy to live. The Skaerslinger expose their unwanted children like our own custom, you know." Her hatred for that custom was as plain as an open wound. "Life for them is not easy or kind."

"The Skaerslinger... are friendly here?" Leif asked, his astonishment nearly an insult.

"I would not say they are friendly, but they are not unfriendly. They have spent years sharing lands with the Saami, and so have become..." the Reverend Father searched for the right word, "gracious? That is almost the word I want. Like the wolf tolerates crows picking at the carcass after it has eaten its fill. We have our roles, and this has become one of ours."

"You raise them as your own children? As Forsamling?" Friar Amr said, his distaste also too strong to be completely hidden.

"We raise them for the Lord." The edge of warning was subtle in the chorister's voice, but sharp like a razor.

"But not like the Kyrkja schools, of course. We would never do that to them," Father Valrsson's words were bitter and clipped.

Behind the rest, Friar Inge and Brother Finn grew broad grins. This would be a very interesting education for the Tronerving and the Kronadottirs who were raised on a strict diet of Orthodox teaching.

Leif, stared at the straight black hair and ruddy complexions of the children's faces, and at some who were of obvious mixed race in the crowd. His face froze into a diplomatic smile. Solveig and Mirjam adopted the same polite yet unreadable expressions and remained silent, subtle glances back and forth between the two the only indicator of their feelings.

Finn gloated at Amr's growing discomfort. In that moment, he realized what he was doing and it became clear his nightly prayers were going to be a lot more complicated. The amount of spiteful pleasure he took in the misery of his poor misguided brother surely was not something he should be enjoying.

"Here we are," the Reverend Father said as he opened the door for them. "Now come inside and tell us your saga."

6. WHERE A CLANDESTINE RENDEZVOUS OCCURS

Solveig was no longer able to hold onto sleep as dawn began to break. It was not the unfamiliar surroundings nor the prickly mattress she lay upon that bedeviled her, it was that Mirjam had been so wrong about everything. Her sister's promise of an exciting adventure and romantic trysts with Declan never materialized. Months of tedious hard work and humiliation were Solveig's reward for giving in to her lusts and agreeing to her sister's plan.

Upsetting decorum and irritating Mother and Father might be fun to Mirjam, but never did she seem to consider the consequences of her scandalous pranks. What these antics fed in her sister's soul was beyond Solveig's understanding. But then again, was Mirjam not suffering the consequences this time along with her? Could it be that this prank went awry?

She definitely enjoyed the game right up until they were caught and she was made to serve as a cabin boy. Stripped of her privileges and forced to serve like a thrall, that humiliation seemed to have broken Mirjam's spirit. Little jests and jabs at authority ceased to be fun while the threat of flogging hung over her head.

Even memories of Declan's tender affections were tinged with frustration. If only, if only, Solveig bemoaned, regretting her part in inspiring Mirjam's plan that brought her to this place. Perhaps there was a nugget of truth in her expressed desire to be patroness of Solveig's romance, but the rewards never came. Those golden promises were just as ephemeral as the moonlight during the feast of Klarrvatn.

Lying there she prayed earnestly for God to help her deal with the pain and guilt of what she had inspired thanks to her sinful lust. She folded hands as she lay on the lousy mattress, her thoughts were but clumsy groanings of the heart without real understanding only desiring the removal of the shame she now felt. Maybe absolution could be granted from her Havarians escorts. She shuddered. How could she confess such delicate things to them and have them pray for her? There must be a way to pray for herself without involving another soul, she thought.

Perhaps her faith was not strong enough. Then came the terrible idea that she had come out from God's protective grace and the monastic prayers that served as her family's divine covering. Could her disobedience and lust block all those monks praying for her safety and well being? Was she now beyond redemption? A panic began to grow in the recesses of her mind.

In the end, Solveig began silently moving her lips in the worn confessional penance, repeating Hail Marys and other recitations as if she had been given them by Reverend Father Thulrsson.

As light seeped through the window shutters, she rose from a bed inappropriate by any royal standard, restless and dissatisfied. Were it not for the terrible weariness that took her last night she might never have slept upon it. The aches in her muscles and torment in her spirit made it clear there was no chance of sleep returning. Had it only been one day since she was sleeping in a hammock aboard ship? That felt a lifetime ago, and yet so recent.

Solveig dressed and without waking Mirjam slipped past the snoring chorister and her husband who muttered in his sleep. She supposed she should feel more gratitude for the two who had given up their own bed, but could not. Quietly, she ventured out of the block-like house and into the cliff alcove and terraced fields of Saelirskjol.

The morning star was bright in the sky and the pale blue dawn colored the east, while drifts of low fog clung to the damp fields. An ox bellow echoed faintly from the tunnel they had walked through the night before as the animals were being made ready to work. She walked by a field of rye almost ready for harvesting and could hear the farmers assembling to begin working their strips. The mountain air was cool but not discomforting. Desiring to see the lauded view, Solveig headed for the treeline that marked the edge of the terrace. Perhaps she would see the path they took to come to Saelirskjol.

Her feet were soaked and chilly by the time she pushed through the brush and found a safe rock to sit upon that provided a view of the valley filtered through the branches. As she sat contemplating, a few armed men walked across the rope bridge to the east of her and into the hidden tree fort. The foot-thick ropes looked like glistening spider silk at this distance, and she was able to look down upon those same giant trees which stood hundreds of feet tall.

As the first hints of red came to the sky, the faint rumble of the ramp was heard as it extended out, then levered downward. Two by two, the grazing herd ventured out. First the llamas, then the alpacas and vicuna, then the sheep. The alpenglow making them all but glow on the dark pasture of late summer.

"Solveig?" a whisper came to her from behind. She started and spun around only to find Declan crouched between some low bushes.

"Declan!" she gasped. "You gave me such a fright!" The thrill in her stomach came back strong as ever, the shame incinerated. "Is anyone else awake?"

"No." Declan emerged from his hiding place. "Leif is still counting playful nymphs in his dreams. The Reverend Father kept him up later than me last night talking about courtly politics and the position of the Crown with the Kyrkja. I think the priest is worried that now that they are known to Leif, there will be problems. There is more here than just an orphanage for Skaerslinger. It was so boring, I fell asleep." Solveig patted the rock she was on, and Declan slid up next to her. She leaned into his warmth and sighed.

"So the children and intermarriage in this place does not bother you?" Solveig asked after a long moment.

"Why should it?" Declan said.

She looked at him with squinted eyes. Did he not understand?

"Kjaere kvinne," Declan said tenderly, "I have fought alongside and against enough Skaerslinger to know it is not the skin that matters, but the heart. When you spill a man's blood, you come to know him better than all others, and that means I know an army of men. Some good, some bad. My enemy is the man who picks up the sword to do harm to you, your aettir, the Crown, my family, my friends or myself. Be they Forsamling or Skaerslinger. If any of them dare wish you harm, I will split them like kindling or die trying."

Solveig considered the object of her affection, drinking in his devotion, savoring it. The power of a veritable force of nature in a man's body, hers for the commanding, brought a tingle throughout her soul and a faint smile to her lips.

"I see that you would," she said playfully.

Solveig wrapped an arm around his waist, hugging him close. His arm draped around her shoulder.

The two sat on the rock, looking over the valley, watching the animals graze as the light started to yellow and the peaks began to turn bright orange with morning rays. Deeper in the valley, the low clouds clung to the swamps and stands of pines.

"Do you think we will survive this trip, min kjaeraste?" she asked.

"No question, elskling. You have four men devoting their lives to keep you safe. Three of them priests who can fight. I am certain the angels swirl around us, keeping the Ogimaak Nichiiwad, the Storm King and all his minions away. The only thing I worry about is how fast we can get home, lest your brother need to wage war for his crown," Declan assured her, tightening his arm around the young woman's shoulders.

Solveig kept silent on her worry that her and Mirjam's weakness would be what slowed them down in the end. Despite becoming stronger from working for the last few weeks as cabin boys, it might not be enough.

Solveig brought his hand to her mouth and kissed it. Letting her lips rest on the warm flesh. She felt surprise and thrill surge through his body.

"At least Mother will not be pushing me into any political marriages anymore," she sighed.

"Then, after Leif is crowned, you can be my wife," Declan whispered. He turned his hand around, lifted her chin and kissed her. Solveig's eyes sparkled with tears of happiness at those words. The passions of sensual desperation washed over them, demanding immediate satisfaction. There was nothing left to prevent them from being together anymore.

Solveig felt the thrall's collar of her duty to the Sveinnaettir fall from her throat. No longer bound to the needs of her father's politics.

Declan felt the intimate mastery of a man loved by a beautiful woman who desired him in kind. A simple karl who rose by force of arms, became a warrior, earned the title of Berserker and then won the heart of the Visekonge's daughter. The life of a hero's saga burned in his veins with each hot kiss.

The fear of tomorrow's dangers, and the strain of yesterday's hardship, was overcome and lust blew open the battlements of restraint. Her kisses came more and more frantic, clutching at him, desiring him. Declan began to strip and she followed his lead, lips hardly leaving the other for a second, exploring the gifts of their youthful bodies. The closeness of death and calamity if discovery was like thrilling bellows on the fire of their lust.

And then, alone and in love, bare before one another.

"Elskling," Declan whispered.

"Min Kjaeraste," Solveig breathed.

Hidden away on the edge of a cliff in the first rays of golden morning sun, Solveig and Declan gave themselves to one another.

7. RISING FOR PRIMAE

Mirjam, the Reverend Father and Chorister Gerdasdottir exited the mouth of the tunnel as they ascended the long spiral up through the mountain toward the kyrkje at the top of Saelirskjol. Along the way, several of the residents stopped and paid silent deference to Solveig as well as to their farmhold's leaders. Mirjam was jarred at how much she had missed this common courtesy for her position. Being sunk to the lowest level of a ship's crew doing the work of a boy had been more humiliating than she had realized. The sensation left her feeling uncomfortable and resentful of a bitterness that now stung her ego for enjoying this proper recognition which was long overdue.

Her aching legs reminded her what she had endured with every step up from the back of one alcove of cliff houses to the next terrace, passing through in one continuous succession. Each alcove grew smaller and the tunnels now went at angles and curled around to the cliff faces.

"Did you cut these tunnels? Or were they here before you came?" Mirjam asked.

"They were here beforehand," the Reverend Father answered. "Though our ramp, the hordings and our little outpost in the trees are our creations. This place was abandoned by a people long since dead who left little evidence behind. Perhaps victims of the Skaerslinger."

Mirjam nodded. The oddity of this settlement was confounding, but if its former residents had been slaughtered by Skaerslinger, it no longer seemed quite as safe .

The chorister's sword beat a dull ringing tone against her leg as they walked up a steeper portion of another tunnel.

"Why is it you wear the sword, but he wears the scabbard that is clearly its mate?" Mirjam asked.

The Reverend Father grimaced and sighed.

"Ansgar does not like to talk about it," Chorister Gerdasdottir answered.

"Then why does not a Ragnarite wear it?" Mirjam persisted.

The chorister glanced at her brother who resigned with a shrug to the telling and trudged along like a petulant ox.

"Ansgar and myself are from a small aettir that lived among the islands of Lake Ninabimnibo. We were not even among the Sivuaettir. No crest, no colors, no page, no number to list us in the official Bok av Familier. Our parents sired a large family. Father was a peat cutter, and mother was a skilled weaver. Fourteen children later, the ability to feed the family was difficult. Our priest said we were blessed many times over for not one of us died from the same ills that plague most families. Many of us were given away to guilds or in Ansgar and, in my case, the Kyrkja.

"We were sent to the school in Ulfshaugrstrond to be raised up in the priesthood. Both of us showed strong gifts for spiritual warfare and for music. When we completed the Trivium and the Sectarian Council met, the Ragnarites and Taitians fought hard for both of us. One of the scribes who witnessed the deliberations claimed that the arguments almost came to blows, and both clergy had to be restrained and eventually expelled for the rest of the deliberation over our fate. The remaining five sects decided for them, and came to a conclusion that made neither the Ragnarites or Taitians happy."

The Reverend Father's pace slowed again with the weight of the story.

"Most of all, we were not happy." His sister placed her hand on his shoulder.

"Ansgar is a sensitive soul and his heart was for inspirational music." Edda smiled at her brother who snorted a laugh. "Mine was for war, but the lots were cast, and our fates sealed."

"Edda went to a Taitian conservatory to learn music and art for the glory of God, and I was sent to a Ragnarite Mission to complete my Quadrivium," the Reverend Father added.

"We never struggled in our studies as God blessed us for both, but our hearts and souls chafed under the yoke of our servitude. The Taitian's choir masters choked on songs I wrote praising the same God in the language of crusaders and berserkers, while the Ragnarite krigsprests spit blood over Ansgar's use of song and word to demoralize and manipulate the enemies of God."

"It was laughable to see how they spoke out of two mouths. They wanted me to immortalize their exploits in saga and ballad, for I could do it better than any of them, but when pushed into the battle, they claimed I was distracted and risked lives with my lack of focus," Ansgar said, kicking a small rock to the side of a tunnel.

"After the two of us served the required four years for our sects, we were given the chance to stay. Both of us spurned them and quit the priesthood. They were unhappy-"

"My sister is given to understatement here," the Reverend Father interrupted.

"But..." His sister threw an irritated glance at him. "They could do nothing to stop us and therefore sent us on our way with a small stipend for our service." Edda shook her head at the vanity of it all. "I could see the anger in my own choir master's eyes. In the most civil of well wishes, he pronounced a curse on me. I knew the man was conceited and hidebound, but to be that petty ensured I would never change my decision."

"My war priest was perfunctory but my comrades were less interested in holding their tongues while they thought I could not hear their bitter words. They viewed me as a coward and traitor to the Kyrkja and the Union, more interested in foolish frippery." Ansgar's words were poisonous. "With nowhere else to go, and no idea that both of us had done the same thing, we returned home." Ansgar pointed an accusatory finger at the invisible Kyrkja. "There we shared our sagas, and learned how poorly both had been served. We both loved the Lord, but hated the people in charge of his Kyrkja. Even the village priest considered us to be a blight on the island. A couple of diseased sheep to be driven from his diocese lest they infect the rest of his flock."

Edda nodded as they came out onto the sixth terrace. Only a few cliff homes remained. The rest of the buildings were grain storage and weavers' cottages. A large cistern of water gurgled from the snowpack runoff in lieu of a field. Beyond, the mountain valley dazzled in the morning light. Mirjam became aware of how much she was puffing for breath, making her glad she was not the one talking.

61

"The priest was unable to drive us out, because we did nothing wrong, but our family was still large with too many mouths to feed, and we had no place to live or work. It was the Armann for jarl Olinaettir who commanded us to leave for our village priest had poisoned his ear against us," Chorister Edda explained.

"To be fair," Ansgar interjected, "he did offer us a chance to stay."

"Ha!" Edda scoffed. "Some chance. He wanted you as a common guard and me for a bard in his meadhall. Your public oath to never wield a sword again ended that discussion. I am certain there are those who still remember your skalding words."

"I emphasized my refusal by marching down his dock and throwing that sword into the lake," Ansgar admitted, pointing at the one on the chorister's hip.

"I dove right in and swam out to retrieve it before the blade touched the bottom. The thought of letting this weapon fall into unworthy hands was unbearable. An actual sword of such refined quality? No one should be able to consider leaving it!" Edda was still angry about the incident. "Since he swore that oath, I could not give it back, therefore I claimed the sword for myself and swore my own oath."

"Against her better judgment," Ansgar fired a brotherly barb at his sister.

"That I would die with this blade in my hands before anyone unworthy would pick it up for themselves."

"Then why did you not take the scabbard?" Mirjam asked.

"It is a symbol of what I was and a reminder of my oath. I am a man of peace now," the Reverend Father said. "Nor would I let her take it," he added with a smirk.

"I think part of it was to spite me for my own oath. For a man of peace, dear brother, you are still quite the man for Glimma," his sister jibed back about his wrestling prowess.

"Glimma is sport, not combat. There is nothing wrong with it."

"A wrestling priest," Mirjam mused. "Why does this seem appropriate?"

"That is why I made my own scabbard. As I am no leatherworker, it is ugly and haphazard, but it is functional, in the manner which God made me. Therefore it is perfect. I said before, my heart is for war. I took the sword laid down by another, made it ready to shed blood for God's glory. If He so chooses, I should draw it in His name."

"Thankfully, that has been a rare occurrence," Ansgar teased back.

"Does it have a name?"

"Inkjenamn," Edda said. "Ansgar would not name it as is tradition, so I christened it 'No Name'. It has had little chance to earn a new one in my hands, but that may change some day."

"Heaven forefend," Reverend Father Ansgar shook his head with a smile.

"So we left our home together and wandered till arriving at Fjellporten. There, we were treated badly by the local clergy who did not trust anyone who would think of leaving the Kyrkja. They were worried that we would start spouting some blasphemy or who knows what. Once you are labeled a pariah, it is hard to change minds," Ansgar agreed.

"There, we learned of Kynligrspiejl. A place for outcasts and exiles of the Kyrkja. They took us in but encouraged us to go farther and help the farmholds and mining villages around the lake as itinerant priests till we found a new home." Edda's voice swelled with pride.

"I do not understand why you were put in sects that were not proper for you." Mirjam was angry that the Kyrkja would do that. The rebellious spring deep within her soul began to run clean again after being repressed for so long.

"It happens more often than you think, my Tign," Edda said.

"How?"

"The politics of man are not always the will of God."

"But they are the Kyrkja! They are bound to obey God." Mirjam's voice held a frantic tint. So many beliefs of the nature of priests and the Kyrkja had been shaken in the last two days.

"They are men, my Tign. They have desires which defy our Lord and follow their own consciences rather than waiting on Him for guidance." The pair stopped, Chorister Edda's voice was low. "All men fail, but worse, all men sin. Not even the Cardinal is immune from it."

"But-"

"No, the only exception is Christ."

"Then how can I trust my priests?" Mirjam whispered, feeling adrift.

"You should never trust one person's interpretation of Scripture, or Tradition. When at all possible, read and know it for yourself." The Reverend Father's voice was grave.

"I am a Kronadottir. I am to focus on other things rather than prayer. It is the duty of the Kyrkja to tell me truth."

"My Tign," Chorister Gerdasdottir said after a pause to consider the counsel she was giving, "with that belief, you will be forever at the mercy of your inferiors. The worst sinners and liars in the world are those who believe they are doing good in the name of God. Their desire to use power for the benefit of all can lead to the greatest of evils no matter how royal or holy they may be."

Mirjam was repulsed by the notion.

"Let me give you an example," the elder woman said. "See the top of the steps and the tunnel mouth?"

"Jah."

"How would you describe the light coming from there?" the chorister asked.

"Bright, maybe. Warm."

"That sounds inviting and good, does it not?"

Mirjam nodded.

"What if you had not been here to see that light right now and relied on me to tell you about it? What if I described it as blinding and painful?"

"That would be a lie." Mirjam denounced the idea.

"No. That would be someone else's opinion. To my eyes, that light does hurt. It comes with age. Your young pretty eyes have not seen enough yet to hurt at such a brilliance."

Mirjam was pleased by the comparison but was not comforted.

"The same can happen with scripture. One person may interpret the Word of God one way, while you would see it differently."

"So who is telling truth?" On one level, Mirjam knew she had to trust those who knew more, but on another, the illusion they could be trusted without question was vexing.

"Being that you are an educated woman who can read, let alone read Latin, this is for your own heart to decide." The Reverend Father was solemn.

"But are not priests the ones who decide what the Word of God means?"

"Jah, many believe that is the exclusive authority of the priesthood, but in our experience, you should be careful about blind faith. Those who prove their words with actions are the most trustworthy. In the end, you must have your own discernment. That is a gift that God Himself gave to Solomon, and you, as a Kronadottir, should pray for it in abundance if ever you must give counsel."

Mirjam assented despite the scowl on her face.

"Come now, Primae is about to commence and we need to be there," the Reverend Father said and quickened his pace up the steps to the last terrace. Mirjam and Chorister Gerdasdottir followed him out into the light.

8. A TROUBLING NEW INSIGHT

Despite the bone weariness Brother Finn felt, he woke with the first verse of the dawn prayer song lilting on the air from above. He lay there listening to the hymn amazed at the power he felt from the voices. There was much he wanted to ask the spiritual leaders of Saelirskjol. Bergamot snored peacefully beside him, her jaw lying dutifully on his thigh. He drifted in an out of sleep with every blink. Each one shorter than the last till he was awake. When the morning service completed, the sun was up and pale blue light filtered through the shutters of his room.

As she rose off the mattress, Bergamot stretched and let out a loud ear flapping shake. A low groan told the rest. Finn dressed as quickly as he could, assessing all the scratches and bruises from their frightful trek yesterday. A full bowl of clean water was left by his host in a green copper basin for him to wash. He did so, tending to his wounds as well as Bergamot's. It did not take long, and he felt so much better for it. No other noise came from the rest of the house nor did he hear the sounds of farmhold life at dawn. Everything was tranquil.

This home was strange. Three square rooms carved out of rock and filled in with brick and wood attached with curtains on the doors. He stepped into the bedchamber of his host, hoping to wish him good morning and offer his blessings on his home, but found no one there. Confused he passed through to the next. Again no one was there, just neatly made beds and long snuffed candles on the bedstand. His body was still complaining bitterly as he moved about. He dipped into his hip bag and pulled out a short strip of white willow bark and began to chew. The bitter taste would soon do its work on the pain.

Bergamot gave another low whine as she looked up at Finn. He could use the relief too as he had not located a chamberpot. Passing through the main room and around the softly bubbling pot of pottage on the hearth, his host was nowhere to be found. He walked out the door in search of a privy.

The direct light from the late summer sun as it came over the peaks was a powerful yellow shock to his eyes. The sky was pale with haze and the breeze was pleasant. Everything was coated with thick dew and he finally saw the nature of Saelirskjol's land. It was a man-made terrace, ringed with short dense trees that obscured direct sight from a distance and rendered the entire bank of cliff houses invisible from the valley. Only from certain peaks on the other side could you chance to see it, and deep shadows hid the rest. No wonder they felt secure here, Finn thought.

The terraced field was narrow but long and curved around the side of the mountain. Several men were working the harvest farther down the land, out of earshot. Oxen pulled carts loaded with maize and gourds to raised stabbur for winter stores.

On the end, where the tunnel rose up from the copse of coniferous giants, women worked with children in strip gardens full of herbs. Here were also a few other storage barns, the main hall and a large sauna next to a cobblestone stream channel. After finishing his morning ablutions he walked over toward the hall which leaked smoke from its thatched roof.

Next to the swiftly rushing stream he saw Declan and Leif, like him, investigating their new environs.

"Good morning, my Tign," greeted Brother Finn, "and to you, Meistari Declan."

"Good morning, to you too, Brother," Leif replied, but his expression was distant, not focused on anything in particular in the calm morning. "How are you feeling today?"

"Better than expected," Finn lied. "Ready to go again as soon as we can. It is too bad we wasted so much sunlight."

"We needed the rest. I believe my sisters are still asleep," Leif said. "Besides, it is inadvisable to go today. Being women, we must consider their frailty."

Declan nodded in agreement. Brother Finn smiled. They were young women of royal blood. They could not be expected to be as hardy as the kerling working in the gardens and fields here. The common life was a strain for them, though they had toughened up some working on the Silfryxen.

"My Tign, we must make sure to have them eat more. Both look gaunt," Declan advised.

"Forgive us, Brother," Leif said watching the fast rushing water of the stream so narrow you could hop across. "We had just been discussing their health when you arrived. Declan is of the opinion we are pushing them too hard and they are wasting away from the strain."

"I understand, my Tign," Finn said. "I am not familiar with the Kronadottirs' constitution, so I cannot offer much advice. I think our biggest concern is how to stay warm and dry. Yesterday proved we need better clothing for what is to come."

"Agreed," Leif said. "If we can keep them warm and dry, we can move faster, too." He blew on his chilled hands to warm them. "How far do we have left to go to get to the sea?"

"I do not know," Declan answered.

"Nor do I. It will depend on what we find to help speed our passage, but if we are forced to walk, it could take almost a month in this terrain, assuming we all stay unhurt and unnoticed by the Skaerslinger, manitou or demonspawn." Brother Finn was glum with the thought. He now saw that, without help, there was little chance of reaching Dyrrvatn Kastali, let alone the Kisiina Sea before the arrival of Ogimaak Mikwam, the Ice Queen, and winter made the northern passage impossible.

"God's little blue toes, Finn! How are you not desperate for that sauna there?" Friar Inge said in greeting. Then sketched a bow, "My Tign. Meistari."

Declan smiled at the salutation. "I believe they are about done heating. I woke briefly during the night and saw a fire was going before dawn."

"Good, good!" My bones ache, my muscles are tight, I am phlegmatic and chilled to the bone," Inge said. "Do not grow old, my Tign. It is not as splendid as some may have you believe."

"Did you sleep well?" Leif asked.

"Jah. I slept fine, when my body let me. Oh, I wish they would hurry up," he said pointing to the object of his obsession.

"I think we could all benefit from a good sweat," Leif agreed.

The four men fell silent in the still morning.

"My Tign," Brother Finn began delicately, "may I ask you something of your religion?"

Leif cocked an eyebrow and turned his full attention at Finn.

"Jah?" His tone warned Finn to tread lightly.

"I noticed your reaction when you realized there were Skaerslinger children and intermarriage here," Finn started to say.

"Was there something wrong in it?" Leif said, his voice barbed.

"No, my Tign. It was very diplomatic, but in the short time I have known you, it seemed surprising that you should harbor such sentiments against Skaerslinger. Perhaps I was putting some of my own disposition on you."

"Is this why you were given skoggang?"

"Among other reasons, jah. I disagree with Cardinal Klaus on several points. One of the most glaring ones is his declaration that Skaerslinger are not human, but akin to the Nephilim and therefore outside of salvation."

There was a hint of disappointment in Leif's eyes at Finn's admission.

"What is your reason for thinking so?" The Tronerving's question pushed hard at the edge of civility.

"As you no doubt know, Nephilim by their very nature are damned and cannot stand up against their demonic masters, correct?"

"This is true."

"I have fought a demon with a Skaerslinger man at my side who was a more powerful warrior in the spirit than several Ragnarites I know. We stood together, with angels, on the island of Neinnvanbjarg and drove out a demon of exceptional power from a small boy under my protection."

"Perhaps you did this in spite of this man's involvement."

"Absolutely not. This man not only healed in Jesus' name, but named the demon we faced again, and helped bolster the angels with his prayer."

"Absurd," Leif scoffed. He had heard of such things, but for a Skaerslinger to have any sort of authority like a Ragnarite Paladin or Exorcist was beyond polite dismissal.

"I can vouch for his testimony, my Tign," Friar Inge interjected. "I have read the report of his trip and it was verified by the Kyrkja, including a very testy interview with Herre Aske, the Skaerslinger in question."

"I see," Leif considered. "What are you asking of me, then?" His words taking on that chilly diplomatic tone Finn heard the night previous.

"Consider for a moment that these Skaerslinger are not your enemy, though they may not be your lineage and skin. Much like the crusaders of old wrote about the dark skinned Arabar in the Holy Land, many came to Christ in those days. Entertain the thought, that if the Skaerslinger can come to the Lord, that they may not be inhuman, and therefore could become your allies, or someday perhaps, your subjects? I do not ask this of you now, but to just consider that the Cardinal is a fallible man who on this singular point is wrong."

Leif's face was a diplomatic mask. Brother Finn knew the Tronerving was young and trained by the best Kyrkja tutors in the Union. All of whom would have been Orthodox by Finn's reckoning. The tie between the Kyrkja and the Crown was tight enough that he may have signed his own death warrant despite the pardon bestowed upon him days ago. But then, a small twitch in the corner of the eye happened.

"Greithr. I shall consider it a possibility, but only that. To imagine myself as Tign of Skaerslinger! Absurd!"

Yet, there was an intoxicating amusement buried in those words, Finn noticed. Was something deeper stirring? Emboldened, Finn risked another point.

"My Tign..." he began cautiously, "point in fact, what you see here in Saelirskjol proves you already are."

Leif's face drained of color. Finn saw a fracture forming in the keystone of Leif's Orthodox tutelage. Perhaps there was a purpose beyond what Finn could see. In supplicating himself to God's will, risking his life and taking the Tronerving back in defiance of the Kyrkja, he was granted a chance to change the next ruler of the Akiniwazi Union's mind. That one sentence may have been worth the price of his own life in the end.

Only time would tell.

"Brother Finn," Leif said, voice stiff, regaining official capacity, "thank you for your counsel. I shall meditate on it in due course. In the meantime, I believe we must focus on the immediate needs of our trek, not the spurious philosophies of religion."

Brother Finn and Friar Inge looked at each other in confusion from the sudden change in topic. Then Bergamot began to growl.

"Good morning all," Leif said past the two Havarians, and they turned.

Behind them the rest of their band approached with the Reverend Father and chorister.

"Good morning, my Tign," the leaders of Saelirskjol bowed. "Are you all awake enough to talk about your plan?"

"I believe so," Leif replied.

"Good!" the Reverend Father exclaimed. "I took the liberty of having the sauna readied for us after Primae services. Let us go in and talk in private."

9. PALLIATIVE HEAT & THE ROAD AHEAD

Friar Inge sighed as he lay on the top bench of the sauna, absorbing the heat like a soft rag drinks in water. The small rawhide windows let in enough golden light to make for a comforting glow. A whoosh of steam met everyone's approval as Chorister Gerdasdottir poured another dipper onto the red hot rocks. Everyone sat or lay upon one of the three sets of benches. Without clothing, jewelry or heraldry to denote their position, the illusion of equality came among them.

"Saunassa ollaan kuin kirkossa?" Mirjam read the carved words on the rafter above the door. "I do not recognize the language. What does that mean?"

The Reverend Father looked up and smiled.

"It is an old homily from the Gamlehaven," he said. "One of our long passed members who knew the lost tongue said it meant "One should behave in the sauna the same way one behaves in kyrkje."

"An excellent sentiment," Friar Amr sighed, a linen cloth draped over his face as he lay sprawled on the middle bench and fumbled for a vihta below him. The heat drew the aches out of his stiff joints from yesterday's exertions.

"It helps to have it up there and remind the young and new to our community of expected behavior," Chorister Gerdasdottir added.

"If this place is a refuge, I imagine many do not know how to act. Some people just cannot behave themselves in our Adamic state," Amr added.

"The Skaerslinger have something similar to our saunas and steam baths, but they are used more for religious than medicinal purposes, I believe," the Reverend Father explained.

Solveig became conscious of staring at the chorister. The older woman was so thin and wiry muscled. Very much like a man. Solveig was much more conscious of her own body this morning. It maturing into a woman's was weak and lush in comparison, though stronger than it was a few short months ago, compared to the chorister's.

Gratefully, Declan sat behind her. Outside, they could hear some of the younger children playing with Bergamot while Thyrnir lay at guard outside the door. The dog had made it clear to the children who ventured too close with a terrifying growl that he did not play.

The conversation wafted to more particular details of how they found Saelirskjol and where they must go from there. Reverend Father Valrsson was disturbed to learn they could not go back to Lake Wanishinabinoogi thanks to the growing rebellion and blockade. He was horrified at the possibility of another Aettirkrigen, the war that forged the Union, brewing. That had not been a proud time in the Forsamling's history. Murders in the middle of the night. Ambushes and fires by the light of the moon, families destroyed and bloodlines severed forever. These were the hammer and tongs that forged the nation.

They talked equipment and the need for haste. Clothing and shelter for cold weather, packs and food were the easy part of the discussion. Both dogs could be used as pack animals, and there were some spare weapons available to purchase with enough skilled men-at-arms to help train the Kronadottirs to defend themselves, leaving the rest to the Havarians and Declan to refine as they travelled.

Ultimately, the problem was time and distance. Every day not spent on the move was a day closer to war. Over one thousand miles from home, getting there in a month or two would be impossible on foot. Even sailing the length of the Kisiina Sea along the shore would be difficult as no steamknarr dared travel those dangerous waters, only sail. To be efficient in that passage they would have to sail far enough north where the winds flew to the east like the falcon. But at the edge of the world, they would have to brave killer icebergs and floes along with frequent blizzards no matter the season. Only the craziest and most desperate of whalers dared take their ships that far.

But what other chance did they have if they wished to arrive before the snow flew? If winter came early, it would be springtime, perhaps even next summer, before they would make Mannvoenlandnam. A winter trek by sleigh or dogsled through some of the most dangerous territory in the land could only be described as suicidal. All this still required a three hundred mile or so tramp from Saelirskjol to the coast through the northern fjords of the Ondeaandkorgfjall.

Then again, there was the proof it could be done, for the Saami not only met the challenge, they conquered it every year with the caribou migrations as they drove their herds south out of the mountains to their southern pastures. That was the slim hope. If they could link up with a migrating Saami aettir and get close to the coast or hire a guide to take them the rest of the way, their gamble showed real promise of success.

"Is there any other way to get out of the mountains and go north from here?" Friar Inge asked. "I could have sworn that merchant caravans came up here to trade with the Saami."

"Not anymore. The Skaerslinger have stopped all that. There are at least a half dozen tribes in the area preying on the caribou not marked by the Saami," Chorister Gerdasdottir said sadly.

"The Skaerslinger respect the Saami's property?" Leif was incredulous.

"Most certainly. The Saami are similar to the Skaerslinger in their customs for they have chosen to preserve their ancient ways. Both are nomadic and live in harmony with the land. This engenders some respect between the two. Of course, the Saami are Christian, but worship in a much more primitive way than even what you could call Low Kyrkja. They take God in the natural state of the world. It is almost as pagan as the Skaerslinger themselves. Maybe you will see this when you meet. Right now, they are one of your only chances for success."

Everyone fell into silent contemplation, with only the sound of Friar Amr flagellating his legs with a vihta.

"There must be a faster way to travel in the mountains before the snow comes," complained Leif.

His frustration getting the best of him. "The Skaerslinger seem to have no problem with traveling fast in this country. What do they do?"

"Canoes!" Declan said as if waking from a dream. "I remember from when I was a boy, the Skaerslinger travel long distances up and down the rivers and streams a man could straddle on canoes that are so light they can easily portage them over land! Is that possible here?"

"All the rivers and streams on this side of the mountain range drain into the lakes. You would have to cross two valleys to find a river that goes out to the ocean. But we have no canoes and carrying one that far would be a backbreaking effort. A portage of ten miles is possible, but not a hike through the mountains like this. Not even Skaerslinger try that as far as I know."

"Would the Saami have them?" Leif asked.

"No. They stick with their herds, traveling overland," the Reverend Father replied.

Everyone deflated with the thought. Riding in a canoe would be much easier.

"You said that there were at least a half dozen tribes in the area and they use them. Are you on friendly enough terms to trade?" Finn thought aloud.

"On this side of the mountain, we are. But on the other, once again, we are the crow to their wolf. Get too close and we may be the meal. Therefore we give them a wary distance."

"How about stealing them?" Friar Amr offered. "We four are easily a match for many a tribe's best warriors. Meistari Declan might be able to wipe out an entire village on his own." Declan gave a tight smirk and looked at the floor with the compliment.

"You vastly underestimate their prowess. They are not stupid, only different in what they know. Besides, it would take two of you to carry one effectively, and something as valuable as canoes would be guarded or in use. They do not craft to excess, only to meet their needs. " Reverend Father Valrsson shook his head sadly. "You will not just steal them in the middle of the night and scamper away. No, they would come down on you with the fury of an angry beehive and pursue you into the ground."

"Besides, are any of you skilled at using canoes?" Chorister Gerdasdottir's rebuke was firm.

Silence was her answer. "I thought not. Therefore blood would be your only route, and killing a few hundred Skaerslinger is more risk than anyone should even consider, particularly with what is at stake."

"Hold one moment, Edda," said Ansgar. "He is right on one point. The Elk tribe might be willing to trade for a pair of their canoes in the Djuprgil. They are friendly with the Saami enough that a stranger from here might not be killed on sight and possibly helped if they have anything of value to trade. Assuming you can find them."

"That is reckless, even by my standards!" Chorister Gerdasdottir snorted, pointing a sharp finger at her brother. "You know where that river leads, thu vethr! It may not be as full of rapids and falls till leaving the mountains, but what is in the middle, hmm?"

"Blothugjokull," Reverend Father Valrsson muttered. The name brought gooseflesh to everyone despite the rich heat.

"Why do you call it Bloody Glacier, and why should we fear it?" Mirjam asked.

"The glacier bleeds. Somewhere deep within its length, blood rushes down and bursts out of its crumbling face, running through its debris, bright as a slashed throat. The lake beneath it is the color of a giant scab as it goes down to Thrjujokulldalr. A valley of many glaciers that twine together and cover the river in places before you escape those mountains," Chorister Gerdasdottir explained.

"One year, I was with a mission to rescue some Saami who became separated from their aettir as they searched for a herd of prized caribou that wandered off. The fogs were bad that season, and as the search went on we, too, became lost. When the clouds lifted we found ourselves on the shore of that cursed lake beneath that... horrid..."

She paused in her recollection, girding herself. "We were miles from where we thought. As we fought to reorient ourselves, it became clear we were not alone on those shores. Covered by the shadow of the glacier, several Wendigo rooted around in the sand and gravel. When they found something important, they would give off a lamentable howl that to this day I cannot bear to describe. As if a song from hell itself."

No one dared breathe as they waited for the saga to continue.

"I kicked up some gravel to see what might be so important in the beaches of that foul place. Glittering among its rough gray sands were nuggets of refined gold, glass beads and even jewelry of some kind. I had never seen its like before and have no idea who made it. But I do know it was not by Forsamling hand, and the Skaerslinger show no aptitude for metalwork. I dared not pick any of it up. If Wendigo wanted it, there was good chance it was cursed."

Chorister Gerdasdottir crossed herself, hands a bit shakey.

"Praise the Father, Son and Holy Spirit that we went undiscovered by those giant cannibal demons. The pinery was dense enough that we made it back without any trouble, but the missing Saami were never found. If we tracked them true, they found that lake, greithr, but never left its shores. Maybe those demons on the shore were them," she whispered under the strain of the tale.

The brave woman fixed them all with a glittering eye, her voice regaining strength.

"And if you manage to survive going beyond Blothugjokull, the river threads its way over and through the Thrjujokulldalr. One minute you might be riding the water on top of a glacier, the next you could disappear into a crevice, never to be seen again. Dozens of rapids and ice dams from collapsed faces weave back and forth in water as cold as the ice it melted from. Can anyone survive that trip?" Chorister Gerdasdottir concluded.

Brother Finn swallowed hard as he tasted bile, mouth tight.

"I am sure people have if they made portages in the right places," Declan insisted. "You did."

The chorister gave the suggestion a dismissive wave. "My band was not foolish enough to try. We surveyed it from a safe distance away."

"God's curly nosehairs! That is what we have to brave to make it to the coast?" Inge lamented. "Oh, dearest Lord, why did this have to be so laborious?"

"All is not lost yet, Inge," Finn consoled. He turned back to the Reverend Father. "Is this the fastest way or is there another route to take where we might find canoes?"

"If you desire to take the sea, no other method would be faster," the Reverend Father explained. "Granting your success, I suspect you could find a Saami tribe in two or three weeks at most, or perhaps find a fjord and use that to sail out. There are a good many whalers or seal hunters who dart in and out of these fjords from time to time. They could have you in Mannvoenlandnam and the Sumarpalasset in a week or so with good wind."

"Who will guide them to the sea, Ansgar?" she demanded returning her attention to her brother. "No one can know from one day to the next where those Nomads or hunters would be for it can change daily," Chorister Gerdasdottir's animated warning was tinted with a respectful fear.

"What about Gunnar?" the Reverend Father suggested. "He knows their favorite camps."

Edda scowled.

"Who is Gunnar?" Leif asked.

"A Skaerslinger trapper. He works throughout these ranges of the mountains. Comes and goes as he pleases for a few months at a time, but is due back any day now. If anyone knows the way to the sea from here, he is your man."

"Would he do it?" Leif insisted.

"Knowing his distrust for Forsamling, it will be a tough request."

"I suppose we must pray for the Lord's provision on that," Reverend Father Valrsson admitted.

"We could be home in a month!" exclaimed Solveig hopeful for the end to this ordeal. "It is only a day's journey by train from Mannvoenlandnaam to Dyrrvatn Kastali!"

"But first, we must find the Skaerslinger camp in the Djuprgil. That might take time and a nimble tongue," Leif reminded his sister.

"Five weeks then!" Solveig's hope refused to be deterred.

"This is not like walking down the boulevard to Domkyrkjeplassen with your handmaids," Leif scolded his sister.

Solveig pouted at the rebuke.

"This all assumes everything goes right. No one gets sick or injured," Amr reminded as he sat up with a groaning sigh.

"It is either that, or we brave many of the same threats through the pinery, on foot for two months or more to get to the shores of Lake Ogimaque, and pray we find our way through the blockade somehow," Brother Finn said rubbing his sweaty face. "Before winter comes."

He stood up and walked to the back door of the sauna. "I do not see how we choose any other course. Time is of the essence. Let us pray that Gunnar is willing to be our guide."

Having said his peace, Finn slipped through the door and jumped into the cistern of snowmelt water with a splash and a shout of happy surprise from his shocked chilled body. The rest took this as their cue and joined.

10. PATIENCE IS A VIRTUE OF GREAT VEXATION

"I see the anger in your eyes, my friend," Urban said at long last.

"Then you know me better than most," Aske replied in that same careful emotionless manner that veiled his counsel.

As they walked through the packed city streets, the calm day left the banners hanging lifeless from shops and taverns, flags drooped on their hoists with barely a stir. Thick warm mid summer air had settled over the city like a heavy quilt. Above, the last cherry tones of sunlight faded from tall thunderheads slowly approaching from the east.

"What is it that frustrates you?" Urban pried.

Aske's eyes mocked him but said nothing.

"I want to hear you say it."

After a few dozen paces Aske let out a sigh like a frustrated bull.

"I feel wasted and useless. Were it not for my faith that God wants me here, I would have left after meeting the Factor Soliaettir. I do not know why God answers my prayer with the same verse," Aske said in a rare burst of complaint.

"What verse is that?" Urban asked and gestured to turn back toward their lodging in the Truartorg neighborhood.

"Cessate et cognoscite quoniam ego sum Deus exaltabor in gentibus exaltabor in terra," Aske repeated.

"Be still, and know that I am God: I will be exalted among the heathen, I will be exalted in the earth." Urban sucked his teeth and shook his head with a smile. "I hate that response too."

"So I obey. Just as you obey," Aske said.

"Are you sure this is also not about your wife?" Urban hazarded to guess.

"Of course," Aske growled.

"When is she due?"

"Sometime before winter. We could not be sure of the date of conception."

Urban chuckled at that.

"Happy wife, as they say."

"Happy husband to be true," Aske gloated a little and Urban snickered.

"You married well, Herre," Urban agreed.

The shops and merchants now clearing the streets for the night made the city feel empty for the first time in weeks. The Visedronning's order kicking out the jarls to their own capitals and disbanding the Statsraad till the coronation had been draining the excess population, but the city was far from back to normal. It seemed several people used the funeral as an excuse to migrate for good, hoping to find work and abuse their Hird's generosity regarding travel. How many trains and steamboats filled to overflowing had come in recent weeks?

"If only we had a person to track or sign to follow. That I understand," Aske groused again. "Nature is much more honest."

Urban's eyebrows shot up in surprise.

"But we are able to track, as it were. We are tracking through other types of sign. Herr Tandri gave us much to work with."

"I know nothing of that fashion of tracking."

"We are tracking the nature of men now discovering what they do," Urban explained. It felt good to be able to teach someone a little of his own craft. The fact it was to a man who could appreciate it was even sweeter. "When you track an animal, you look for things in the way it may have disturbed the land, greithr?"

"Jah."

"What else do you try to know?"

Aske thought for a while.

"You consider the nature of the animal," Aske said.

"Exactly!" Urban exclaimed. "And if you have no physical sign, you follow the nature of the beast. You learn its habits and think how it must feed, where it would sleep. Men act in similar ways. You know that."

"I think you are better at that than I."

"Years more practicing and praying," Urban said.

"Do we even have quarry to track?" Aske wondered.

"Why do you say that?" Urban was taken aback.

"We no longer have the ring. Which means, without proof, we have no reason left to be here. What are we tracking? Why hunt?"

Urban frowned. A lamplighter was refilling one of the lamp posts with oil at the edge of the Truartorg. The pedestrians had thinned out as all took to their houses and the thin streets became too dangerous to walk without a lantern.

"It is true," Urban considered slowly, "that we do not have evidence linking the dead body you found to any aettir. Factor Soliaettir lied to us. Herr Tandri made that clear and put forth some ideas why."

"It is not our business. Our duty ended when Factor Soliaettir took the ring. He is Hird. There is no reason for us to go on," Aske said referring to the disappointing resolution of their vigorous chase the day the jarls were expelled from the city.

"And yet?" Urban prodded.

"God tells me to stay, and be patient," Aske mumbled.

Urban felt sympathy for his friend.

"It is because your view lacks context about the bigger tapestry of our society," Urban said. Aske had the common courtesy enough to not roll his eyes, but listened respectfully.

"You are a member of the Fourth Estate. A merchant by way of your wife. But you came from the peasantry, the Third Estate, adopted into it by the Ragnarites taking you from your dead village. From this you joined the world of common peasantry and became a karl of your jarl. His subject, destined to labor." Urban paused for a moment. "Huh. If you think about it, you almost were First Estate but you rejected joining the Kyrkja when given the chance. Plus you are grounded in a culture outside the one you now call home, for the feet of a child often keep a similar path to their blood."

Aske nodded, but scowled. "Those are pretty words with little meaning."

Urban laughed. "Greithr! To my point. As I am a member of the Kyrkja and a Ragnarite and an inquisitor, I have a different view. It is my responsibility and duty to help keep the devil's corruption out of society. To keep the faith pure and safe. God, through the Kyrkja, has granted the Hird the right to rule, but we must keep the Hird true to their oaths to the other estates. In a way, the Kyrkja are the spirit of the Forsamling. When something is amiss, we must follow it to make sure it is not a threat, like a dog following an unfamiliar scent."

Aske seemed to understand Urban's meandering big picture reasoning, but was still clearly unhappy with it.

Urban continued embellishing. "Men do things for reasons. Sometimes sinful reasons are the cause more often than we desire to believe. That is why we persist. There is something far more nefarious going on. The Soliaettir by reputation are a tricky lot. Prone to feuding and used to getting their way. That is part of their character. The factor lied about knowing who the body might possibly be and stole the only piece of evidence that tied his family to the body."

"The body was eaten by a bear, so it is my word versus his. No Domari would care. Nor would any Thing take my word. Even if it was a karl," Aske muttered in a rare sign of self pity about his skin. Urban realized the strain must be powerful upon his friend's humors.

The Blessath Borth Inn glowed merrily as they arrived. It attracted visitors like moths from the darkened neighborhoods as night lay claim to the small alleys and streets. The thick air started to lose the day's warmth, becoming sticky but cool.

"That is because I remember some things you do not," Urban said hoping to grant some solace.

Aske scowled at Urban. "When were you going to share this with me?"

"I was hoping after we heard from Father Tuajaksson and learned about the gold ring."

Aske looked stunned.

"How could I have forgotten? Again! The ring with the seven arrows around a hollow circle," Aske breathed.

Urban frowned.

"I think there may be a demon attached to that ring which protects it from inquisitive minds. That then begs the question of why was such a ring made, and why would a dead man have it on your island?"

Aske sat down on the edge of the square's fountain, like he was resting from a heavy load. Astonishment that he may have been under the glamour of a demon left him shakey. Urban prayed silently for his friend, then reached forward and held Aske's shoulder.

"In the name of Jesus, demon of forgetfulness, I demand you come out of Aske this moment, bound hand, foot and deed. You have no further claim over him for I break the binds you have placed upon his mind. I command the scales to fall from his eyes and for him to be free of your evil deeds. Do this now in Jesus' name. Amen."

Aske felt like talons were releasing his mind and eyes, and then the pressure was gone and a lightness remained. He blinked at Urban for a moment in wonderment.

"I-" he began to say and sneezed. The explosive sound rang off the walls of the buildings in the square, doubling Aske over with the force. Then he sneezed again and again, leaving the man dazed.

Aske looked up at Urban in shock, so unsteady by the exorcism that Urban had to hold him upright.

"How could this have taken hold of me?" Aske grumbled, blowing his nose out with powerful snorts, one nostril at a time, as if determined to get more out of his head.

"Easy, my friend. Easy," Urban assured him. "These things happen. You have been touching an unclean object for months and neither of us realized it was dangerous till now."

"That is how you knew this was a bigger mystery?"

"That and Herr Tandri reminded me of the Giptumathr. He said that the relative of the factor got on and went to Ulfshaugrstrond so long ago. It all ties together with your island."

"It does?" Aske was confounded again.

"The Giptumathr is the key. She went to Ulfshaugrstrond in July two years ago with a murderer on board. That same month, the Giptumathr sailed from Ulfshaugrstrond and was attacked by vikings. She put in to Tryggahveneyer where one passenger, Brother Finn, put ashore and a curate abused his authority and pressed Brother Finn into service. He ordered him to take seven children to Saint Martin's Academy in Tungloddr despite Finn's protested, but obeyed. A trip that was renewed on the steamknarr Heijl's Valor with a new sailor they hired on at Meidrhvall. A sailor who was, in truth, an assassin sent by someone from Ulfshaugrstrond to kill Brother Finn. He made his attempt while the Heijl's Valor was at your island, repairing its boilers from a storm. The assassin failed, but before he perished, he summoned the dead to finish his job. Brother Finn and the boy Reimar escaped the draugr by means of a large fire. That fire burned the body of the assassin, but not all of it."

Aske recalled the cries of alarm in the night and the clang of the cookhouse flat iron. The dull orange glow over the trees and billows of smoke and spark. Then a man and a boy staggering through their fields, caked in mud and blood, covered with wounds and stinking of draugr.

"The Heijl's Valor, you may not know, went aground on Ogimaak Mikwaam Island several days later. Thanks to the greed of her kaptein, Brother Finn, the seven children and six sailors escaped the wreck only to be caught in the middle of the Battle of Athrvorthfestning where they had taken refuge. After the battle, Brother Finn was able to complete his passage thanks to the arrival of none other than the Giptumathr which took him and his wards as far as Tungloddr." Urban was constantly amazed every time he considered this chain of events, going through them like a perverted rosary.

"That ship was the key to realizing there is something far bigger going on. It ties to Brother Finn and I intend to learn more, for if my suspicions are right, there is a plot afoot far greater than the misdeeds of the Soliaettir."

Aske's face lifted with the knowledge, then fell with the meaning.

"Jah... now you see it all. And..." Urban said stabbing his finger to emphasize his point, "all this is tied back to jarl Olinaettir and this mysterious woman who took a disobedient son away from his family and when he came back, he was an assassin and practitioner of black magic!"

"My God! This is the root of evil?" Aske breathed.

"A poisonous tree, growing right in the middle of the orchard and bearing fruit."

The square was empty, save for a few tables of the night's drinking public under the awning of the Blessath Borth Inn.

"What can we do?" Aske breathed.

"Keep digging up the roots till the tree comes down." Urban's face was hard set against the harrowing task he was about to take up. Aske fought to clear his mind.

"Come," Urban said, offering Aske a hand up. "Let us get several horns of brennevin. We both earned them."

Aske nodded and the two walked slowly over to the inn and began drinking till late into the night hardly saying another word.

11. OATHS, THREATS & HONOR

For a week the little company of necessity prepared their traveling kits and trained the Kronadottirs how to use spring bows and tomahawks. Much to the amusement and surprise of the community, both girls were passable archers, and adept at using the crank to reload. Their use of tomahawks to defend themselves was less noteworthy despite their spirited effort. The preparations for their grand enterprise built up their strength for the trek into the Ondeaandkorgfjall. Their nights were filled with feasting, sagas and songs, growing their confidence with every tale.

Friar Inge prayed ferociously for hours every day asking God's blessing on their odyssey. He was at every mass. Both the Reverend Father and chorister felt shamed at the man's fervent devotion and wrestling with God. In the depths of his impassioned pleas, he would roar. His prayers escaping the confines of kyrkje, echoing against the cliff's walls like a whisper on the wind. He had grown even more lean since arriving, sustained by the power of God's word, losing much of his plump physique, but not wasting away. It was as if God was toughening him like a tanner making leather, till he rose, knowing it was time to go feast and celebrate before the hard journey began.

Only Gunnar, their promised guide was notably absent. The Chorister heaped praise upon him and told many stories of his exploits. Enamored with the tales, the party could not wait to meet him. Hope continued that his arrival would be any day, as their planned departure came closer and closer.

On this night the feasting was a wonder to behold, for tomorrow they would begin their adventure as Gunnar had been spotted in the valley below with his llamas piled high with furs. The music and ballads so rich and full. The sagas of great achievement drew cheers of excitement and fired the blood of all those attending.

Amr's head was swimming, for he had imbibed, by his estimation, a bath of mead. How else could he explain why he was swaying to winds that did not blow? Everyone was drunk as a viking jarl as they looked forward to a great future.

Amr laughed at a joke overheard from someone he could not see and staggered up to the dais where others had been swearing oaths. Something deep in his besotted brain knew it was the right time to make a proclamation.

"Everyone!" he bellowed. "I want... I want to declare my o-oath!" Some cheered and raised mugs and horns, others ignored him.

"Listen!" he said trying to make the crowd take him seriously. The hall quieted a little, expectant. With a suppressed belch through his lips, he continued.

"I swear my oath that on pain of death that I will see my Tign, Leif Gregorsson, and the Kronadottirs, Mirja... Mirjam and Slovic... Solveig to their home unharmed! So I have said it, and as all of you are my witness, I pray that God helps me keep it."

This brought shouts of approval and laughter from the crowd. A few faces frowned in befuddlement. Perhaps they were too simple to understand, Amr thought.

Declan, who had become close with Amr as they had trained and worked together, reclined with other farmholders. He pursed his lips at Amr's oath as his pride goaded him. His new friends helped him up, he stood and took several careful steps to the dais. With his bear cloak, he exuded a primal aura that awed many.

"I, too, wish to give my oath." Declan's voice was soft and clipped with the effort to be clear. He looked down at Leif who sat with the Reverend Father and Gunnar.

"My Tign," he began, blinking hard with emotion and focus, "I pledge to you my life and my eternal friendship and to serve you all the days that I am permitted to be in your service. May God help me keep this vow." His drunken smile made people wonder if he was joking, but his slow, careful words seemed proof of his sincerity. To the cheers of the rest, he staggered off the dais back to where he had been sitting.

Brother Finn, who was far from drunk at this bacchanalia had enjoyed the fact that no one had asked him to repeat any of his sagas. It was more interesting to watch the festivities and well meaning, if not over-the-top, gestures be given. He was only worried that one of their band might make a foolish gesture or promise.

Leif slapped his thigh and stood up a little too quickly. He laughed as the others steadied him, then walked up to the dais as well. The room became hushed as he stood waiting in silence for the attention of those in audience. When all was quiet he began.

"People of Saelirskjol, I wish to thank you for all you have done in service to me, my sisters and my retainers. We came to you as lost sheep, and you brought us into your fold like so many others before us. When we were weak, you strengthened us, and to that we are all thankful. My father once told me to be gracious to those who you lead. They owe you their safety and fealty, but you owe them your honor and your strength.

"Therefore, I pledge to never forget the kindness and grace you bestowed upon me, your Tronerving and future Visekonge. When the crown rests upon my head, I will reward you for all you have done. May God help me keep my oath."

Leif had expected a roar of approval from the farmhold.

None came.

He looked out over the audience perplexed as to what was the matter.

The Reverend Father was the first to act and he walked forward and knelt before the dais.

"My Tign," he uttered, head bowed.

Like a ripple turning into a wave radiating out from his bent knee, the rest of the farmhold did the same, echoing the humble words of their leader. Friar Amr came over as Leif stepped down, puzzled.

"My Tign," Amr said in proud low tones, "that was a masterstroke."

"What? Why?"

"You have the common touch like your father. This is a rare thing among the Hird. Bel-believe me when I say that most jarls have no interest in the problems, let alone recognize the blessing, of their karls.

"I only said what I felt. They have done all these things, and it is true, jah? I did not speak idle flattery." Leif was too drunk to make all the connections Amr saw, and the noise of the feast was rising again.

"Jah, all true, but they are never told such things from the likes of you! Your father would be proud for you have created loyal subjects for the rest of their lives, if not this farmhold's existence. Well done! Well done! You are truly a Sveinnaettir!"

Leif's brow creased, still unable to grasp how he had impressed the monk so.

Frustrated with the young man's inability to see through the alcohol, Amr gave a dejected wave and grunt of disapproval then walked away. Irritated, Amr went outside to cool in the night air and clear his head. He was tired of being drunk.

Small clusters of people were outside, talking quietly and looking up at the sky. In the mountains the stars were even more brilliant, and the auroras were beginning to swirl in green and yellow billows around the edge of the mountain. Thyrnir drew up behind him from where he had been laying outside the hall and came to heel.

Amr listened to snatches of conversation. Some about their journey to come, but most about life in general.

"...Most of the stabbur are full, and we have half the fields of maize left to bring in..."

"...Twenty seven alpacas in an hour? I could..."

"...We only have a few more hours, then they will be gone and we will be safe from the Sveinnaettir again..."

Safe? Amr wondered. Safe from the Sveinnaettir? Who said that?

His attention wheeled from group to group, trying to listen in and find out why that was said.

"Lord and master, hear my prayer," Amr muttered in prayer, "clear my mind and show me the one who is hiding a secret hatred of the Sveinnaettir. Grant me the oracle I seek."

It felt as if the alcohol was trickling out of his skin and his senses became sharp. He now walked with steady step through the chattering pockets of people.

There was a smell. A stench of guilt that hooked his nose. He followed it to three men talking next to a low fence around the herb garden, large horns in their hands. He had not seen them before. Had there been enemies in their midst the entire time? Were they the jarl Vilhoaettir's men waiting to inform on their Tronerving? Were they traitors to Leif so soon after he lauded them all? A resentful hate began to grow.

"What do you want?" One of the men demanded as Friar Amr came up to them.

"Safe from what?" Amr demanded.

"What are you talking about?" one of the men demanded. He was of mixed race. Amr felt his gorge rise, but kept tight control.

"You said you were safe from the Sveinnaettir. Why?"

"I am not talking to you," replied the man who stank the most and turned his back dismissively. Amr's rage began to dance and crackle like a fire.

"To whom are you loyal? The Visekonge or one of those treasonous rebel jarls?"

"Get away, Havarian. Mead has taken your senses."

"We pledge loyalty to no jarl or the Visekonge. We are free men of Saelirskjol and servant to none," the third one growled and took a step forward.

Thyrnir's hackles were up and a low rumble came out of the mastiff. The other two men fled.

"Whom do you serve?" Amr demanded taking a step forward, menacing over his challenger. "Tell me!" he snarled through clenched teeth.

"That is enough!" a voice barked and Amr was knocked to the ground like he had been butted by a ram. When his head cleared, he saw a giant man standing over him and the man he was interrogating ran away as fast as his legs could carry him.

"What do you think you are doing? Interrogating people like an inquisitor or a Domari," the newcomer demanded.

"It is none of your business," Amr groaned, slowly getting up.

"Do you think it funny to accuse free men of treason?" Amr's attacker growled.

The argument had begun to attract the attention of others.

"Do you serve jarl Vilhoaettir?" Amr asked, assessing what he must do to prevent this from spiralling out of his control.

95

"I have never seen your face before. That makes you the stranger here. Who do you serve? Your eyes show me you are hiding something." Like a wolf, the man circled Amr slowly. He outweighed the Havarian by more than fifty pounds, and looked to dwarf even the gargantuan berserker.

A circle of curious onlookers hoping for a bit of sport had surrounded the pair. Expecting another drunken fool to be thrashed. Amr's gaze flitted over the growing crowd. He had to act.

"You tjovekjakji! You told the jarl's men? When will they be here?" Amr yelled.

"What is this you say?" the man was dumbfounded at the wild accusation.

"Lying bacraut! You are a spy for the Vilhoaettir! I heard you!" Amr pressed his narrative, relying on the drunken chaos of the feast. "You sold out this farmhold for harboring the Tronerving and now you seek to turn him over to the rebels for gold? How could you do this to these people?"

"That is a lie!" the man was incensed, his ruddy skin flushed even darker with fury.

"No! That is the truth! I have not seen you since I arrived and you accuse me of being the stranger? Where have you been? Off spying for the rebels, I wager! There is only one way to stop me from revealing your treachery, you hrodinefr! " Amr spat.

The childish taunt was the right sting to make the behemoth charge.

Amr deftly dropped to a knee and parried the outstretched arms. With a loud shout, he punched upwards into the now exposed throat. The giant Skaerslinger went face first into the dirt thrashing in a spasm as his crushed Adam's apple strangled him. A horrifying death rattle escaped his lips.

The crowd of witnesses gasped as Amr delivered a merciful killing blow to the back of the dying man's neck. The left leg twitched for a few seconds, slack fingers trembled and then the giant became still.

"What have you done?" shrieked Edda.

Amr turned to look at the hysterical chorister. "I have saved the life of our Tign. Like a Judas, this traitor had a plan to betray us to jarl Vilhoaettir."

"But he was your guide!" Edda wailed.

Amr looked down at Gunnar's body.

"A part of his plan," Amr said, his voice calm as a morning pond. "Who better than to betray us? He planned to take us to a secret place and turn us over. He could make up any story he desired, and no one could contradict his tale."

The Reverend Father arrived from the mead hall with Leif in tow. He had heard half the story as he had rushed to the scene.

"Gunnar was going to betray you? How do you know this?" the Reverend Father demanded, having heard Amr's claim to Edda.

"He admitted it just before he attacked me, Reverend Father. It was his hope to cover up my discovery with murder. As a wandering trapper and Skaerslinger, he had no real ties anywhere. Why else would he leave and come back all the time? He sold you out to the rebels who surely would have revenged themselves upon you."

A low murmur went through the crowd. Amr's instincts were correct. The farmhold did fear jarl Vilhoaettir and enough distrusted Gunnar to believe the tale. He stood and composed himself again.

"Ask anyone who saw, it was a fair fight. No weapons used, but he wished to kill me for finding this svikari out," Amr attested. His eyes scanning the crowd for anyone who dared call him on his version of events.

"Gunnar attacked me first, and I defended myself after determining he was a rebel spy and acted accordingly. I am sure our Tign would agree this is the proper punishment for traitors to the Crown," he repeated, reinforcing his view of the fight.

Leif looked at the body. What was done, was done and no witnesses contradicted Amr for defending himself. Brother Finn gave Amr a hard look, jaw tight. Amr returned it in kind, daring him to say something. Finn held his tongue.

"Reverend Father, do we have another person who can guide us? Leif asked.

"Jah," he sighed. "One."

His fearful eyes slowly drifted up from Gunnar's body and came to rest on his sister.

12. PLACING THE BIT IN THE MOUTH OF THE WILD

The Blawisflojt slid past like a sheet of black glass while the thick summer clouds promised a day with heat but no rain as soldiers marched in formation on the lawn under the imposing bulk of Barskaborg. Farmers and traders moved back and forth across the fortified bridge.

The tall walled fortress loomed over a thin section of the river as an inspection and tax collection point for all ships entering or leaving Wanashiabinoogiland and subject to jarl Vilhoaettir's power. In a compromise with his neighbor, the two jarls shared in the revenue, though it was manned exclusively by the Vilhoaettir.

jarl Jakob was wroth. He stood on the tall battlements of his fortress glowering over the river.

"They should have found or captured the Silfryxen by now. The vision said the wolves would run her down and then I could go collect the treasure and put the crown on my son," he growled to himself and gave the stones a hearty thump with the fleshy bottom of his fist.

Birgr stood with him oblivious to his father's mood. He was busy watching the soldiers spar in the courtyard below, wishing to be among them, showing who was the greatest warrior in the land.

"Where is she?" jarl Jakob growled.

Birgr turned to look at his father.

"It will come soon enough. The vision foretold, therefore it must come."

"Do you not understand the nature of visions, boy?" The jarl wheeled on his son. "They are not prophecies! Nothing is for certain! They warn or counsel, portents of things possible. If you play the game right, God will hand you the world!"

"Were you not just grousing about the vision not coming true yet?" his son's tone was insolent and smarmy.

"Taken to mocking the man who will make you Visekonge?"

Birgr shrugged and went back to watching the soldiers below.

The jarl ground his teeth in frustration at his son. A karvi tied up to the taxman's dock by the bridge. A man stood by the rudder, waved and bowed to the jarl.

"Then trust all will be as God designed," Birgr dismissed. "Pity if it does not come about. Solveig looks like she would be a good lay. Nice hips."

"Those hips, as you have indelicately put it," jarl Jakob ran his hands through his hair and scowled, "are the key to your future. Not just your wealth and continued comfortable life." The jarl was seething, giving full vent to his disgust for Birgr's obsession of sport, hunting and sparring. "If the Tronerving somehow makes it back to Dyrrvatn Kastali with that fortune, your prospects of a future that does not include the axeman's block are limited indeed! I have wagered everything on this gambit, and need you to get your mind on that wager as well!"

Birgr glanced back for the briefest moment before returning to the sparring below. jarl Vilhoaettir was flummoxed. Birgr smirked to himself as he heard his father's angry step. It was expected.

"Gentle, Jakob," the graded gravel voice of Jarl Ofbradh Evinrudeaettir soothed. "The scope of what is in motion lies beyond the boy's comprehension."

Birgr turned to face the new voice.

"Ofbrahd! When did you arrive?" Jarl Vilhoaettir said in happy surprise to his peer's arrival. The Jarl Evinrudeaettir was dressed more like a ship's captain than his actual station.

"Around noon, Jakob. I took the train to the rail head, and a carriage brought me the rest of the way. I did not want to wait for a tug to pull my ship up from Lake Ogimaque. Your men are doing incredible work out here."

"Civilizing the waste is difficult," Jarl Vilhoaettir agreed.

The two men shook hands, speaking brief pleasantries about family and aettirs, forgetting a moment about Birgr or the Visedronning's prohibition of the jarls coming together till Leif was crowned. Birgr turned away more interested in some mild excitement of a farmer at the bridge tollhouse who was being roughly inspected by the tax collector. He smiled at the abuse of the petty functionary doing his job with enough malicious enthusiasm to make sure the local karls did not forget their place in the world.

"Can we have a frank discussion?" Ofbradh's words caught Birgr's ear. He did not bother to look, but paid closer attention.

"Of course. He best learn the full nature of this," Jakob said.

Ofbradh came up close behind Birgr.

"Do you realize the risk that I have taken to speak with you?" he asked the young man's back.

"Should I care?" Birgr dismissed with a wave of his hand. His eyes focused on the men below.

"You are that sure of your strength and prowess in battle that you think you have nothing to fear from me?"

Birgr gave a snort of spoiled contempt.

"I see," Ofbradh said, his voice bitter. "Your father is risking much on your behalf. He desires much for you despite such a boorish nature. Do you understand that?"

"I do. He wants me to be Visekonge. Claims it is my destiny for I am the most deserving to wear the crown. To be honest, it seems to be a big quarrelsome mess to me. Other than all the bedroom perks," Birgr said, bored.

Ofbradh smiled and shook his head in that same bitter manner. Holding up one finger, he stopped the father's intention to intervene.

"No, Jakob. I will deal with this."

Birgr turned around to face the older man who was clearly half his weight and had not swung an axe in years. His well tailored clothes were common but too new to be anything but from the wardrobe of a man of wealth. His posture stated plainly he was his superior in every way.

"Deal with?" the youth sneered, now even more insulted at the sight of the man. "How do you propose to deal wi-"

Jarl Ofbradh was against the young man's sloppy wide open stance in a blur. A small hooked knife between his legs pressing just hard enough to let the young cockerel know what was in danger. His other hand he cupped around the back of Birgr's neck and pulled the startled man forward.

"You whelp. I need you to pay attention to your betters... very careful and perfect attention, and quit thinking with your wedding tackle. Before you try to overpower me, consider, I have a needle filled with poison ready for your neck. It will not kill you, but will make you waste away till you are a feeble old man in six month's time, incapable of walking, let alone lifting a sword. You will be left an invalid, requiring a wet-nurse to change your diapers.

"If that is not enough to convince you, that sharp prick you feel against your loins is a simple cobbler's knife. One swift pull and it will geld you before you can even act. I may not be as strong as you, but I know where and how to strike, so I do not have to be."

Birgr stood on his tiptoes trying to escape the terrifying touch of the knife. Sweat bursting out.

"Jakob," Ofbradh said over his shoulder, "the others have sent me to see why promises have not been kept. You promised us messages proclaiming your success. Messages now overdue. The others are anxious to make good on their part of the bargain. At this point, we would all prefer to murder your wife and put you on the throne rather than this thundering bacraut." He emphasized the statement by increasing the pressure to Birgr's loins.

"No," gasped Birgr. Ofbradh turned to examine his face, tilting his head and letting out a faint smirk.

"When will this be accomplished?" the Jarl Evinrudeaettir insisted.

"Soon! It will be any day now," Jarl Vilhoaettir's voice was robbed of all strength by the fear for his son's life.

"Good, my friend. Forgive me for putting you through this. You know how much I care for you, but there are bigger things at stake than just your ambitions and your son's coronation. If we fail, the Union will fall into a civil war that could kill all of the Hird and the Skaerslinger will wipe away the rest of the Forsamling with a bloody rag."

Jarl Ofbradh turned his attention back to Birgr who was whimpering softly.

"Now that I understand you are controlled exclusively by your lusts, allow me to explain something more to you, boy." Ofbradh's voice was just above a whisper. "You will ascend to the Crown only because we jarls allow it, not by your own will or entitlement. That means you will also be compliant to our... needs."

The older man's hot breath was in his ear like a flame. Birgr felt faint, the strength was leaving his ankles as he tried to remain on tiptoes and away from the knife's sharp point.

"You are not the master of your fate. Not now, nor have you ever been, nor ever will be. You are our pawn, and you need to get your head off the sparring ring and women's skirts and into where the real battle is. A fight of wills, not blades or fists. We will teach you this, but the choice to accept must be yours. You have the potential, like any sword, but till it is drawn by a practiced hand, it is only dead iron weight."

Birgr looked at the canny jarl, eyes frantic. The point of the knife would soon draw blood, if it had not done so by now.

"I am willing," Birgr gulped.

The knife blade between his legs came away and Birgr settled back to solid footing, grateful his wobbly ankles did not fail.

"These better not be words to save your skin for now or you will regret it. We will not invest in your future for vanity's sake." The subtle tapping of a finger on the back of Birgr's neck reminded him of the poison. Birgr was not safe until the jarl chose.

"I will submit to your teaching, Deres Naade."

The hand came away. Jarl Jakob gave out a long sigh. Birgr blinked hard to fight back tears.

"Splendid!" Ofbradh said giving Birgr a chuck on the shoulder with his fist. "I was afraid for a moment that you were going to prefer castration."

Birgr gave a weak laugh, bracing himself against the stone crenelation.

"Do not suppose it is out of the question if you fail to stand by your commitment." Ofbradh's voice was dark as the grave and Birgr's laugh died.

"Was all that necessary?" Jarl Jakob sulked.

"It was. You are too soft on the boy, for you hit him in the wrong places. We need him to get in line with our plans, and time is short." Ofbradh turned his focus to Jakob. "You are not out of the trees yet, either."

"After all these years, you speak to me in this manner?" Jarl Vilhoaettir was shocked.

"Do not misunderstand. I come not for my sake, but as the face chosen to deliver a message from those making your dreams possible. Your bargain requires you make their dreams a reality too, and also those for your son. Currently, these allegiances are in good faith and without coin. This waiting threatens those desires and, just like you, they do not like their desires threatened."

Below them, a tax collector finished assessing the fee to the karvi and they made ready to pay and cast off. A few other longboats were rowing up to the fortress from Lake Ogimaque, and the drawbridge began to rise. In the distance a steamknarr chugged and whistled at some obstacle blocking her path.

"Let us go to my hall and enjoy the hospitality of the fortress, Ofbradh. I wish to put this all behind us, and to talk of better things," Jarl Jakob said, trying to erase the shock of the last few minutes.

"I would enjoy that. Then in the morning, Birgr and I will depart for his instruction.

"Depart?" both father and son blurted.

"Jah. He is going to be instructed on how to be the Visekonge and readied to take the Crown. It is clear this cannot be done here. You are too distracted by your love for him, and honestly do not have the skill necessary to teach him what he must know.

"Where will he go?" Jakob asked.

"Do you really wish to know if the worst should happen?" Ofbradh put the question back on him.

Jakob struggled with his pragmatism and fatherly desire to keep his son near.

"Of course!"

"He will stay with a trusted friend of yours, skilled at teaching the young what must be known about being a ruler. I am sure you know who I am speaking of?"

"Lendmann Mother Ulla," Jarl Vilhoaettir breathed. Always back to her it seemed.

"Precisely."

Jarl Vilhoaettir looked over the battlements one last time down at the karvi departing the dock. The crew waved, some bowed. He gave a half hearted wave in reply as he left to go down to his hall.

Once through the arches of the Barskaborg bridge and around the first bend, Kaptein Gramrsson, former master of the Silfryxen, disguised as a filthy fisherman, breathed a sigh of relief as Friar Inge's risky plan bore fruit.

13. A RACKET IN THE TREETOPS

"I think we have come far enough for today," the Chorister Gerdasdottir, or as she preferred being called, Edda, announced as they came to the crest of a steep rise.

After the death of Gunnar, no one questioned why Chorister Gerdasdottir stepped up without being asked by anyone to replace him. Her course north then northwest had been easy to follow through the first two valleys and the group passed without incident or hardship through the mountain passes. She knew where the caribou migration paths might take them to the Saami. So far, God had not seen fit for them to meet. Ahead was the thin pass that led into the Djuprgil where they might be able to trade for canoes and Blothugjokull lay near the valley's northern mouth. The stone was a deep gray with streaks of pale rose, and purple shot through the thrusts of rock. Sandy soil glittered with quartz crystals through the detritus of leaves and needles.

The August wind blew strong and dry under a hazy sky. Clouds streamed over the peaks, letting only a faint glimmer of sun through. Trees were thinner here as low grasses and brush became more prevalent among the rocky soil of the deep Ondeaandkorgfjall.

Although the sun was going down before Nocturn and coming up after Primae, no sign of autumn was yet showing in the trees.

Everyone was puffing hard and several times had to resort to roping together and to pull the dogs up the steep trails as they were laden down with heavy packs. The view was breathtaking as spots of sun cut through the clouds here and there speckling the valley and black water lake beneath them. Far off, an elk, the "Ghost of the Mountains," bugled its chilling mating call reminding all of how fragile they were in the wilds.

For all his life, Brother Finn thought no one could live so deep in these mountains, but yet, here they were. How deep could one go before those beliefs came true? For ten days they had trekked into this high frontier without calamity. The Kronadottirs were doing well, weathering the forced march with little problem. The week of rest and feasting seemed to have helped.

Finn spent most of his time walking the point with Chorister Gerdasdottir. Declan took up the rear guard with Solveig and Mirjam between, springbows in their hands, barely talking as to save their breath and keep up the pace.

"We could make camp in those trees and have a little shelter from this wind. See how the ones higher up the pass have flagged branches, all pointing the same way? That means high winds are common. If it worsens overnight, it could be real trouble. Besides, I want a fire, and the whole valley need not know about it."

"Amen to that!" Friar Inge agreed.

They found a suitable spot to make camp in a thicket of balsam and firs that was dense enough to cut the wind with a melodic soft sigh. Declan set to work digging a pit for the fire in the rocky soil while Finn and Amr took the loads off Bergamot and Thyrnir. Leif went looking for firewood with Solveig and Mirjam while Edda began setting up a bivouac over low branches.

By the time the mountain's shadow rose up from the valley to cover them, a cozy camp had been built. The fire was hot and meat roasted over the coals as they all pulled up close on their furs. The wind sighed, and the trees groaned and squeaked.

"Tomorrow," Edda began as they ate, "we enter the Valley of Blothugjokull. The upper river is where one or two tribes of Skaerslinger may be passing through, or have summer camps. I have to go by what I have learned me over the years." She sent a nasty glance at Amr who returned a hurt expression back. It was impossible to tell if he was mocking her or whether he truly believed himself to be the aggrieved party.

"How will we gain the canoes we need?" Finn asked.

"My Skaerslinger is poor, but good enough to communicate for trade," Edda said blowing on a chunk of hot caribou balanced on a barley cake. "I will try to trade for them, if we have anything they would want. What moneys do you have, my Tign?"

"I have some gems, a little gold and silver."

"Essentially a fortune to a Forsamling," Amr said, shaking his head in disappointment. "These primitives would probably bargain for something inconsequential to civilized people, like beads or mead."

"You forget how similar our two people's are," Inge interrupted, insulted at the insinuation.

"What is that supposed to mean?" Amr said with a snort.

"They are tribal. We are clans. They organize around their faith. So do we. But much like the beaten wife, they cannot seem to leave a faith steeped in blood and human sacrifice to idols and demons."

"You cannot possibly-" Amr was cut off.

"Inge is right," Edda snapped. "Every tribe has a ruling manitou. That manitou controls the shaman. He is just like our priests, save for whom he serves. Their oppression is what has reduced them to this state. You would know this if you were not too busy feeling superior to them, and everyone else in this world. My God! How are you even still a priest?"

"Fy da! Watch your mouth!" Amr exploded at her blasphemous attack.

Leif watched their back and forth with intense interest.

"Everyone... calm down. We need not be at our throats when so much out here desires to do it for us," Finn soothed.

"My point was that starting tomorrow morning, we must be much quieter and work harder to pass without a trace lest we bring an ambush upon ourselves before we can reach a camp to trade. A Skaerslinger hunting party, or worse a war party, could spot us, and then we would have real problems," Edda pointed out.

Declan got up and adjusted his belt and bearskin."I think I will take a walk around. Make sure we have not attracted any attention," he announced.

"May I come with you?" Solveig asked. "I would like to learn more on what to watch for."

"Good idea," Edda said.

Declan hesitated for a moment and looked at Leif.

"It would be my honor," Declan agreed.

Solveig went to her springbow, made sure it was ready. She smiled at the bemused look on the faces around the campfire. Mirjam's eyes twinkled in a conspiratorial expression and gave the most imperceptible of nods.

Once they disappeared behind the screen of trees, Inge shook his head and smiled.

"Why do you smile, Friar Inge?" Mirjam asked, eyes a little too wide and skittish.

"Infatuation is so easy to see," Inge explained, putting butter on a chunk of bread.

"Infatuation? What?" Leif's startled words were sharp.

"Is it not obvious to you, my Tign?" Inge said around his full mouth. "She has a little crush on your berserker."

Inge saw Mirjam pale and appear as though she were about to vomit.

"If it were not for their stations, I would worry about those two going off like that. Clearly she is just trying to impress him." Inge licked butter from his fingers and rubbed his hands clean of crumbs.

From the fringes of his vision the friar could see Mirjam breathe a secret sigh of relief.

"I suppose so," Leif begrudgingly admitted. "Declan is drengr and a good friend. I cannot imagine him doing anything that could harm me."

"Of course not," Amr interrupted. "May we return to the issues of tomorrow in regard to obtaining our canoes?" His snippy words irked everyone at the fire.

"As I said, the gold and silver may be enough to trade with. Possibly some cut gems. Do not be surprised if they demand our swords in payment." Amr's words were horrifying to hear.

"Are they mad?" Leif exploded.

"Swords are easily the most valuable things here, and the Skaerslinger do not forge metal," Edda explained. "You cannot have forgotten that a flint or an obsidian edged war club is an imposing weapon, but cannot stand to an iron blade like ours."

Leif picked up a clod of dirt from the leaf litter and launched it out of the camp.

"What happens if we cannot trade for the canoes?" Leif asked.

"The obvious answer," Amr's voice was grave. "We take them by force and kill all that we can. If they will not agree to a good trade, we will not steal them unawares. They would suspect such kind of trickery."

"That is too risky," Leif shook his head. "We need a better solution."

"I am open to any better suggestions," Edda grumbled, exasperated at their predicament.

"Listen to that wind!" Mirjam said, looking up at the still treetops.

"The timber will groan tonight," Inge answered.

Declan and Solveig pushed backwards through a low branch of needles into the camp.

"You are back awfully quick-" Amr started to say then stopped as he saw their white faces.

"What is wrong?" Mirjam asked.

"The trees," Declan said, looking around.

"Jah, the wind has a good hold of them," Edda replied, pleased her instincts were right on taking shelter.

"You do not understand," Declan said. "The wind has stopped."

Mirjam froze. That was what fascinated her about the trees and all the loud sounds they were making. Though they rattled and moaned, they did not move.

Edda slid Inkjenamn from its sheath, while everyone else crept for their weapons.

"What is up there?" Finn asked.

"I do not know, but I doubt it is good. We are in the Demon Basket Mountains." Edda's voice had the grim determined edge of a battle hardened warrior.

"My hands will not stop shaking," Solveig said.

A dark shape lept from branch to branch above them, twirling around branches like a fur covered serpent and vanishing into the leaves and needles. Then another. Every time a shape moved, they heard the groaning of the trees. A fetid smell wafted through the camp. Like toadstools, mud and slugs on a rotted log.

"Uffda!" Inge exclaimed.

"What is that?" Amr sounded sick.

Both Bergamot and Thyrnir were caught somewhere between growling and whining. Tails between their legs and backing away from the strongest smell. Whatever this was, they were terrified of it too.

A sudden snap of a branch, a squeal of wood and a loud thump came from a pile of dead leaves that had drifted against a pine's drooping branches. Solveig let out a squeal of surprise and fired. Her bolt smacked into the trunk of the tree, unbloodied.

The leaves began to shuffle and hump, like something was under them. Everyone took a curious step forward to see better. A noxious eye-watering wave of that smell came out from the pile, and then an amazing thing happened.

The most adorable head of a giant weasel popped out, eyes bright and curious, like a pet desiring to play!

"Awww," Mirjam sighed at the creature, melting with its adorable countenance. "It is so cute!"

The weasel sniffed the air, and ducked under the leaves again, scurrying to the other side of the tree under the cover of the noisy sienna carpet. Claws scrabbled up a hemlock till the cute furry head poked out and looked down at them. It chittered a sound that was more akin to a handful of dry twigs breaking.

"No!" Edda moaned upon hearing the creature make that sound.

"What?" Leif said, his fear ratcheting up a notch.

"Treesqueaks!"

"Treesqueaks? What kind of a haensafretr name is that for a lort'e weasel?" Leif shouted in frustration as his fear poured out, no longer recognizing the cute animal as dangerous.

"Look at it!" his tirade continued. "It deserves to be walked by my sister on a leash, not a terrifying threat. The thing is so disgustingly darling, I cannot stand it!"

"Shh!" Amr hissed. "I have heard of these monsters. Like giant otters of the trees that come out only when they wish to be seen.

"Otters?" Leif said trying to pick the reference.

"Do you know what a family of otters can do to a lake? Clean it out, and treesqueaks are not even that picky about what or who they eat."

"Or... who...?" Solveig moaned.

Trunks began groaning and crackling with the weight and movement of a dozen or more agitated treesqueaks.

"Be ready..." Edda's commanded preparing to call the charge.

Declan began to growl, shield and axe at the ready.

With the sound of shattering tree trunks, the racket of treesqueaks burst out of the branches in yard-long streamers of fur, claws and fangs. The rotten musk smell was almost visible it was so thick.

They hopped among the humans like they were at play, but every nip and scratch drew blood. Emitting squeals like an old wood floor, they would hop back as a blade or bolt sliced through where they had been a split second before.

Some began to grapple with the men. One clamped its teeth onto Declan's forearm after he missed with a powerful swing. It wrapped its long body around the berserker's arm and began gnawing his Gambeson jacket, digging its claws in.

Another jumped onto his shield and clung with playful desperation as Declan waved it about trying to throw the creature. He shouted in pain as the teeth punctured the thick cloth of his armored jacket. Adding insult to injury, the treesqueak swatted Declan in the face with its fluffy tail, smearing its musk in his face.

The reaction was instant and Declan vomited.

As the berserker bent double, the treesqueak released Declan's arm. He faltered from his body's sudden weakness. The creature lept for his eyes, only to be cleaved in twain by Leif's sword. The fatal wound sent it thrashing to the ground making an incredible variety of sounds, akin to a ship breaking up in heavy seas, and then lay still.

Mirjam put a bolt through another.

Bergamot and Thyrnir attacked, but after killing one, Bergamot began foaming at the mouth from the treesqueak's flavor which she could not abide. She fled and was pursued by a small pack of the weasels. Thyrnir seemed to ignore their defensive odor and tore through them like a terrier on a pit of rats.

Another treesqueak jumped on Amr's back and viciously clawed his kidneys and bit his neck, trying to get a killing bite. The friar plunged his dagger through the side of its neck killing it instantly.

Solveig missed another shot, as the beasts leaped from leaf pile to tree, shrieking their strange cries as they went. She gave up on the springbow, dropping it to the ground and pulling out her tomahawk. Frantically, she chopped at any that dared come near her or Mirjam. he treesqueaks came steadily closer.

Leif's swooped in with vicious slashes that drove back the monsters that swirled in a deadly vortex around them.

Finn and Inge gave a valiant fight to keep the racket of treesqueaks away from their food, but there were too many. Within a few seconds, the dog's packs were in shreds and the dried meat was dragged away into the trees beyond their reach. Then the cheeses, fish, eggs and breads.

And as suddenly as they came, the treesqueaks were gone.

A ring of the dead weasels lay about their camp.

It was a despoiled mess. Everything reeked and what food that survived the ambush was not fit for man or beast.

"What in the name of God's hairy bacraut just happened here?" Inge shouted. "How can those things do so much damage and look so innocent? What kind of abomination are those things? Dreamt up by Beelzebub's toy maker?" His combustible language and ranting was just as foul as the stink and went on till he ran out of insults to hurl at the creatures.

Bergamot came out from behind a cluster of low ferns slicked in the blood of her victims. Finn went to her and found several bites and scratches. She might limp a little in the morning, but without a heavy pack, it was not a worry.

"I hope they choke on our food!" Declan spat. He had stopped vomiting but was still weak.

Edda wiped the foul blood off Inkjenamn and put it back into her scabbard, surveying the wreckage of their camp with an expression that could only be described as irritated and amused.

Mirjam and Solveig were shaken but not given over to hysterics, and Amr examined Thyrnir who seemed to come through unscratched.

"Quiet. Everyone," Finn admonished. "Right now, I believe we should all get down on our knees and give thanks to the Lord we were not killed. Those creatures found us too tough of prey to bring down and fled before more died. If they had kept at it, or went for us over our supplies, we would probably be dead."

"Praise God for an animal's instinct to cut its losses," Leif agreed.

"We can be glad they did not act more like wolverines," Declan said and retched again, then rinsed his mouth with some water and spit, trying to get the foulness out.

"Be thankful? When did starvation become preferable?" Mirjam demanded on the verge of tears as the grave nature of their plight became clear.

"Perhaps this is God's way of telling us we forgot to trust in Him?" Edda asked to no one in particular. She picked through the shreds of her bivouac. The blankets and furs were beyond repair, and they were a long way from any fresh water.

"Perhaps, but for now, come. Everyone. Let us give thanks, pray and then set an extra person on watch from here on out. We are in the enemy's land."

Somewhere miles away, an elk, possibly the same one, bugled again as if mocking them.

14. A CASUAL SUNDAY RECREATION

The leather ball hung high in the scorching air, traversing its arc to the roaring of men in pursuit. To Aske, the ball floated like a cloud down toward him, as a rare smile crossed his lips. With a graceful step, he swung his Knattleikr bat, and the wall of charging men raised their own, made from old paddles and oars, to block his action.

The ball cracked off his modified axe handle with a joyful snap and all heads spun to watch its flight. The roar became a groan as it soared through the upper goal... again.

Aske's team shouted their triumph as they scored another triple off his bat. A shirtless Tandri lifted Aske up in celebration as the stevedores continued their domination of the sailors, much to the crowd's delight in a home team's winning.

"Five! I have never seen the like before!" shouted Tandri setting the big Skaerslinger down again as the other men crowded around their sporting gem. Aske was dominating the game, scoring twenty points on his own, and running up the score thirty-seven to twelve.

"Wish I had placed a wager on the game," groused one man.

"Glad I did!" said another rubbing his good fortune in the other's face.

The sailors grumbled and pushed each other back in line reminding their pitcher to keep the ball away from Aske.

Urban slapped his friend on the back. "Are you sure you want the rest of us on the field?" he joked.

"If I miss." The rest of the team burst out laughing.

"Ready?" the call came from the other side of the Knattleikr pitch. The stevedores quickly took up position on their quarter line to either side of Aske who stood like a confident general leading his army.

He raised his bat over his head.

"Ready!" Tandri returned the call, and the ball was airborne. The arc was low. Aske counted in his head assessing whether it was a legal pitch.

One...

Two...

The ball was almost to him. It was not good.

"Fault!" Aske shouted and held his bat over his head.

The charging sailors did not stop.

"Skeiturhuth!" One of the charging men screamed. Aske realized what was about to happen a split second before the scrum of men collided with him. It was instinct that drew his bat down in an attempt to parry the lead attacker's cut down oar. There was not enough time to do more than divert the wooden shaft from striking his exposed throat, smashing it into his chest instead.

The man's bat splintered against Aske's chest throwing him backwards like a rag doll as the rest of the sailors piled on top. Urban, Tandri and the rest dove into the scrum that formed on top of Aske and a twenty-two man brawl broke out on the pitch.

Under the pile, Aske curled into a ball, shielding his vitals from elbows and knees. Shins and thighs protected his body while his forearms cradled around his head and throat. Yelps of pain and rage rang out while epithets were growled into his ears. Aske peeked between his wrists and saw the face of his attacker, filled with black hate and trying to get at his face with torn fingernails. Another tried to pull his thick legs away from protecting his groin. A squeal issued from the pile as someone got his testicles twisted hard by another man sick of this foolishness.

A finger slipped through toward Aske's eyes. He writhed and the finger found his mouth instead. Furious at the attempt to gouge him, he bit down.

There was a meaty crunch and a shriek of horror from the sailor. Aske shook his head from side to side like a wolf and the would-be gouger strained to escape. As the scrum was untangled there there was a set of tearing snaps as the sailor who started it all was dragged off by Urban and Tandri. The enraged stevedore promptly punched the sailor in his exposed gut hard enough to make the others flinch, and threatened to start the brawl up again.

Aske stood up, face smeared with blood, his lips a cruel slash open to bright pink teeth.

With a snot-filled inhale through his nose, he spat out the other man's middle finger he tore free. It flopped onto the hot sandy beach.

Everyone took a step back from the big Skaerslinger, his ruddy skin even more striking with the blood covering his bare chest. The sailor, bereft of breath and short a finger, crawled away from the man he sought to maim not a minute before.

"Are we sportsmen, or shall we do war? Who's body shall the dogs drag off?" bellowed Aske.

No one dared answer.

"Which will it be?" Tandri added, ready to kill the perfidious sailor who tried to harm his friend.

"Nephilim," screamed another man. "Demonspawn! Using black magic to cheat!"

"Aske is good drengr!" shouted Tandri back at the crazed sailor. "You backwater bacrauts would know that if you remembered where we are. Do you think a demon would be tolerated here? In this city? This man is no more drengr than any of you baksteypir! Thu vethr!"

The large crowd swelled at the edge of the pitch, the locals and shipmates ready to join the fight.

"Oj!" shouted Urban, laying a hand on Tandri's shoulder who ceased his profanity laced torrent, but remained ready to lay into these out-of-town upstarts. "Any man who does not wish to play against our team, because they do not approve of men we stand with, walk off the pitch now. Otherwise, let us get back to the game, or you forfeit the match." Urban's authoritative tone cooled the hottest desires to fight into a sullen hate.

The sailor who made accusations of black magic helped his wounded crew-mate walk off the pitch. Then, one by one, the rest followed till only the Stevedores remained.

"I suppose we won?" Tandri said and shook his head as the visiting team walked back to the canal and their ship in the docks. "Why does it feel like we lost?"

"Because everyone did," Aske said, picking up the finger he bit off and walked toward the sideline of the pitch.

Some of his teammates spoke sympathetic words, then went down to the beach to cool off from the hot July sun in the cold water of the Dyrrvatn.

Aske walked over to the fire pit where they had been roasting meat and early sweet corn.

"Are you done cooking here?" he said to the man tending the coals.

"I suppose so."

"Good. Do not cook anything else in this pit tonight," Aske said and tossed the finger into the flames where it would be reduced to ash.

Tandri came up to him. "You know we do not think of you that way, right?"

Aske said nothing, but gave a slight nod.

"You have more than proven yourself while working and praying with us." Tandri's eyes searched Aske's face for what he was thinking.

Aske nodded again.

Tandri looked ready to say something else but stopped short. He then smiled and nodded toward the water. "You look a mess. Go clean up."

Aske nodded again and went to get the blood off him. Urban, dripping wet from his own dip came over to Tandri.

"How well do you know that crew?"

"Not at all. First time that ship has made port here that I know of."

"Where are they from?" Urban persisted.

"Vithrflojtdalland," Tandri said.

"Are they part of Jarl Sutcliffaettir's household?"

"Could not say," Tandri shrugged. "It does seems odd. Some of these Sunday matches have been much more tense of late. A lot of rough customers coming into the city more anxious to fight, and always from places I do not normally see around here. Seems like all the mourners are being replaced by pilgrims of some sort, but they are angry pilgrims. More like river vikings than citizens and merchants," Tandri observed, seeing a knarr flying a Tusundfelland banner as it made her way for the docks in the soft breeze.

"How are things with your wife and the Olinaettir household?" Urban changed the topic. Tandri barked a laugh.

"The cat is away," the scrawny man implied, putting on his shirt. "She did mention one other thing that was unusual to her. Means nothing to me, but to you, who knows?"

"What is that?" Urban prodded.

"There are lots of men showing up. They are doubling and tripling up in the rooms too. She says it is busier there than when the jarl is in residence with his whole family."

"Uffda," Urban exclaimed considering the workload of the servants.

"She also said it seems like no one is in charge in the house, but the men are well behaved to some extent. Acting more like soldiers and huskarls, than courtiers, and their clothes are from all walks of life. It is almost a boarding house."

"Are they all the jarl's retainers?"

"That is what makes it even more strange to her. Their heraldry comes from all over the Union nor are they kin or of the same aettir."

"How many men are there?"

"Two or three score. They even share with the in-resident servants. My wife is plenty glad she lives outside the mansion," Tandri said.

Aske, content with his washing, came out of the water and rejoined the two as they spoke.

"Ready to eat, or shall we go somewhere else?" Urban asked his friend.

"I came to have sport and eat good food with friends," Aske said. "I have had one, now for the other."

"Then let us be about it," Urban laughed and the three men went to the tables set up on the edge of the beach to relax in the shade of the trees and consider the things weighing on their spirits.

15. QUID PRO QUO

By sunset on the next day, the discouraged band of travelers was half way down into the Djuprgil. The incredible land was sprinkled with a series of small lakes in a large basin ringed by another range of mountains that disappeared over the western horizon. All that could be seen of the other side of the valley were the faint white peaks above the curve of the Earth. The view was awe inspiring and heartbreaking at the same time. How could they ever find the right Skaerslinger tribe in all this wilderness, let alone any friendly Saami who would guide them. Edda called this the caribou's western feeding grounds, for this is where several aettir of Saami drove their herds. Beyond that far off line of mountains, no Forsamling dared to go. Not even the Saami would chase their lost animals up there. Even the Skaerlinger refused to enter those mountains, for it was land given over to devils.

The fire was low, but it was big enough to cook on and provide a little warmth, but they dare not make it large enough to shed much light. To the north, the Aurora swirled in green and blue waves, and a crescent of the waxing moon rose.

Finn stood watch with Edda. Bergamot snored peacefully against his legs. Although unencumbered by most of her load, she was showing the signs of her age. He rubbed her ear and sighed.

"Ask already," Edda whispered. She had been sitting across from him and hummed off and on as was her habit. The lullabies had been soothing.

Finn stared at her, curious.

She arched her eyebrows in resigned encouragement.

"I suppose..." Finn started to say, and moved over to her as to not wake the others who slept under a rapidly made lean-to covered in needles and leaves. "Why did you decide to become our guide before anyone asked you to serve as such?" Finn shrugged.

Edda smiled.

"The Lord gave me no choice, I suppose," she sighed. "I had been given a dream that I was going back into the wilderness. In the dream I was looking for Jesus to give him a crown. I do not claim the gift of prophecy, nor the interpretation of dreams, but I do recognize one that is significant. My husband..." she trailed off at the word.

"He, um... he interpreted the dream for me after I told him. Eirick was a regular Joseph." She gave a small laugh, remembering her husband. "He said, 'Edda, if this is where God wishes you to go, not a single force in the world can stop it from happening'."

Brother Finn nodded, remembering how true that sentiment had been in his own life.

"But then Gunnar returned and I thought I was saved. He had only come back to Saelirskjol, and was busy with his pelts at the tannery." She rubbed her chilled nose and blew through her hands.

"I thought this was God's provision. He would step up and take the challenge. It was just the way Gunnar was. Impulsive as the wind and often just as fleeting. I was so happy that the cup of suffering would pass from me, that God had meant this dream for another purpose. But..."

Edda choked on what was next. Her eyes shimmered with tears that welled but refused to fall.

"When I saw Gunnar lying dead at Amr's feet, I knew then Eirick was not wrong." She drew a deep breath, reinforcing herself. "He was not wrong," she whispered.

Finn nodded in sympathy to the woman's pain at losing her friend and leaving her husband behind.

"And here you are," Finn said in kind.

Edda nodded. After a long moment, she sniffed and looked at Finn and Bergamot who had come over and laid down on his lap, fast asleep again.

"How about you?" she gave a faint grin. "How did you come by this happy circumstance?"

"Oh..." Finn also smiled, but was much more wistful. "I suppose you could say I was pressed into service by God in the same way. Given a choice I could not refuse, despite it possibly meaning my death."

"Death?"

"At the hands of Cardinal Klaus. Executed for violating my skoggang."

Edda's eyes were wide with surprise.

"Do the rest know?"

"Oh, jah. They know thu vethur. Amr dreams of my death many times over. I can see it when I catch him watching me."

"Why did you come? I mean if it meant your death, and you are now a Fredlaus."

"I felt there was no choice. You have seen how our Tign's children are? Competent, but in such circumstances," he paused and shook his head. "

"They never would survive all this on their own. What other choice did I have? Though, I would not have come if it not were for securing a pardon out of the Tronerving and his forcing Amr to abide by it as an oath. He has already proven once that he will walk right up to the edge of his word and look over the drop. If I die in mysterious circumstances, it is certain his hands are behind it," Finn concluded.

"Why does Amr hate you so?" Edda asked.

"We were once as brothers in thought, word and deed. We served together in Mestrflosslidhaland for a bishop, as his bodyguards. Amr had been there a few years before me, and it was my first assignment. What halcyon days those were." Brother Finn felt warmed by memories of his youthful seasons in the sun.

"But..." she coached, suspecting what was to come.

"But..." Finn continued with a tip of his head. "This bishop was a corrupt and base man. He employed several pardoners among the sects of his land. Pardoners whom he encouraged to get the most money possible from the suffering sinners in his midst. Overselling pardons from Pergatory, or inflating the prices of the indulgences. The money was then skimmed and every corrupt conspirator involved received a cut of the excess profits while the Kyrkja got their proper share and remained none the wiser. Amr and I were the two sent forth to collect the sin money. We each had a lockbox that the pardoner would fill, along with a receipt of the indulgences bought."

Finn looked over his shoulder at Amr. His breathing was slow and rhythmic with a light snore.

"One day, we had a problem. Bandits robbed one of the pardoners, but did not touch the money for the indulgences. Amr did not believe the pardoner, accusing him of hiding his true accounting. He furiously beat the man within an inch of his life and ordered me to search the house for the rest of the Kyrkja's money." Finn hunched his shoulders in a quashed bitter laugh. "The Kyrkja's money was all there as I considered the receipt and estimated the coin we had received for every indulgence. That was when I figured it all out." Finn grimaced at his foolish innocence up till that point.

"To make matters worse, Amr found the excess money hidden away above the flue in his fireplace. There had been no bandits."

"What happened?" Edda breathed.

"He burned the pardoner's house down..." Brother Finn took a deep breath.

"With everyone inside?" she asked.

"Even his infant daughter in her crib."

"Oh, no!" Edda breathed.

Finn crossed himself and nodded.

"Why is he not dead for his crime? Surely some aettir swore vengeance on him," she whispered.

"They did... they did. Nor did I keep silent. I took this immediately to my bishop whom I originally thought innocent of such a corruption. When he then took pains to cover everything up with the Kyrkja, I realized what a fool I had been. He had been running this syndicate of graft for years if not decades. He was publicly one of the most respected and senior bishops in the Senate of the Diocese.

"Then he tried to bribe me. It was too late, of course, for my testimony made it to the ears of an honest Ragnarite inquisitor who forced the issue all the way to the Cardinal. They held a trial at the Keldathing and found him and his conspirators guilty.

"I am certain several other bishops and curates voted to convict just to cover their own sin in this matter. If one was doing it... one so senior, many others might have been doing the same," Finn said.

Edda shook her head in disgust. "I expect no less from that pack."

"By this time," he continued, "I was disillusioned with the Kyrkja, but not completely turned against it. I saw that it was only a few bad men, not the institution as a whole."

Edda scoffed.

"Amr and the bishop were arrested and taken away with several other priests and pardoners. Amr swore eternal vengeance against me. The bishop was tortured to repentance as an example of the Kyrkja's justice then granted the blessing of the pyre. Amr and most of the pardoners and priests under him were given skoggang for twenty years to life. Somehow, Amr must have found his way back into the good graces of 'Mother' Kyrkja." Brother Finn gave a wry grimace and shook his head. "What miracle he must have performed to do this is beyond me."

"What happened to you?" Edda asked wrapping a blanket around her as the chill in the air was enough to see their breath now.

"I was sent off to a Havarian estate for a few years. Once the stink of the scandal had blown away from the halls of Ulfshaugrstrond, a curate requested my services. I am sure many a bishop cursed my actions and hoped I would die in a storm. So, off to Manitouland I went to serve." Finn made a shadow puppet gesture of a bird in flight. "The whole experience let me know there was something deeply wrong with the Kyrkja."

"I learned that too." Edda sympathized.

"So you left your comfortable and safe home in Saelirskjol because God gave you a dream?" Mirjam said. The two jerked to look back at the Kronadottir. The girl's eyes were wide with astonishment at the two.

"Erm..." Brother Finn cleared his throat. "I, uhh... I-"

"How much have you heard?" Edda asked beckoning the girl over.

"Enough, I suppose." Mirjam walked over as quiet as one could on a carpet of leaves and twigs. None of the others stirred. Edda and Finn offered her a place to sit between them in front of the fire. An act so common, but shocking if decorum and precedence was considered. The daughter of the Visekonge realized this and she accepted the invitation. Their time together in the pinery had bred a familiarity and familial comfort unheard of in her life experience. They were her subjects, but at the same time, she was torn. It was an even more powerful sensation than what she and her sister had experienced with her nursemaids and governess.

Mirjam snuggled in between the two. Once settled, Bergamot who had risen again to accommodate Mirjam chose to use her for a pillow instead. The three smiled at the innocence of the dog.

"Why did both of you join us if you knew the dangers?" Mirjam asked. The question had never entered her mind before. It was always the duty of the Forsamling to obey. Both Edda and Finn had volunteered without question and she assumed it was thus for the priesthood as well. To learn that they had a choice made their decisions all the more admirable to her. It was clear now that without the help of these four priests, they would never survive the plans of the rebel jarls.

Finn closed his eyes and quoted "What doth it profit, my brethren, though a man say he hath faith, and have not works? Can faith save him? If a brother or sister be naked, and destitute of daily food, and one of you say unto them, Depart in peace, be ye warmed and filled; notwithstanding ye give them not those things which are needful to the body; what doth it profit? Even so faith, if it hath not works, is dead, being alone." He smiled at the girl, like her father used to.

"I... think I see," Mirjam said, squinting at the understanding. "You did this as a representation of your faith, not because you were bound by law to obey."

"Your brother never asked me to join, but I needed his protection to do so, otherwise without his pardon, I am a fredlause. Friar Inge did so because it is the right thing to do. I have no idea why Amr joined, but doubt I would believe any explanation he could give," Finn explained.

"And I also was never asked. Not even by my brother on your behalf," Edda added. "I volunteered, as you well overheard." Edda gave Mirjam a playful poke at her waist, causing her to give a squeal and giggle.

"By faith, we joined you. Not because the law compelled us, but because the law was written on our hearts by God. It was in alignment with His desires for you," Finn said.

"But the danger..." Mirjam protested. "I guess I never would have risked my life like that."

"That is because you have rarely lived for something greater than yourself or your family," Edda said. The words were not meant to be a rebuke, but they cut Mirjam's spirit for they were true. Even more true for her than the rest of her siblings. Leif had to live for her father. Even Solveig had to live for the Sveinnaettir. But she was not as important save as a political marriage some day. But now, even that was gone. Leif was the one that must be married, as the bloodline would go through him, and there was little to no chance of her being compelled to shoulder the burden as Visedronning to a suitable husband. And even before her, Solveig would be the one chosen.

"Perhaps that is why?" The question was but a whisper, aimed at herself, as Mirjam contemplated her own nature.

"My Tign?" Edda inquired.

"Just..." Mirjam considered revealing what she just discovered about herself. The need behind the pranks. A longing, if only on a spiritual level, to be relevant and influential.

"What little secret are you willing to tell? Edda pried.

Mirjam thought for a while.

"I was the vessel for the Holy Spirit that warned us about the rebellion," she admitted, pushing those thoughts deep inside for later reflection.

Finn nodded, remembering being told about the heaven sent warning.

"Actually, there is something about that message you may be able to help with, Edda."

"What is that, my Tign?"

"A word, given through me that no one else knew. Perhaps you know it since you speak Skaerslinger."

"Not well, mind you."

"Better than the rest of us I would suspect."

"The word was..." Mirjam concentrated in an effort to remember it correctly.

"Baasadinaa Animaazakonenjigebizo. That was the word, or words rather."

Edda thought about what she just heard. Her brow furrowed and she frowned.

"Is it Skaerslinger?"

"Jah. It most certainly is. Give me a moment.

The two waited, listening to Edda repeat the words.

"Valley... Drives evil..." Edda struggled.

"No, wait. Drives evil away with light?" Edda's countenance lifted. "The valley that drives away evil with light. I think that is what it means."

Mirjam's face fell. "But what could that mean, and why would the Holy Spirit give me a word in Skaerslinger."

"Perhaps it is a place with no Forsamling name?" Finn suggested. "Therefore God used the name they gave it?"

"I have never heard of such a place, and why would there be a place with a Skaerslinger name like that? We know the only things they seem to name are lakes, rivers and mountains. They certainly have no cities," Edda considered.

"Another piece of the puzzle found, but more questions remain," Mirjam sighed.

"Well if neither of you are ready to sleep, I am going to take the opportunity to do just that, if you do not mind," Finn said.

"Good night, Finn. May God bless your sleep," Edda said.

"Good night, Brother," Mirjam added.

"Good night and God bless you both," Finn said with a yawn.

Finn and Bergamot went back to their shelter, tucked in among the rest under his fur and blanket that still smelled of the treesqueak musk. Bergamot curled up at his master's feet and both drifted off to sleep.

16. AMONG THE WOLVES

"Over there," Amr said pointing through a gap in the thick shoreline brush. "Just beyond that stand of aspens."

There, the rest saw it. A thin wispy curl of smoke twined among the trees on the other side of the small lake.

"Let us pray that they are on friendly enough terms and my skill with their tongue holds out," Edda said.

"I hope we can trade for food as well," Solveig groaned.

"Agreed," Friar Inge added.

Their supplies had dwindled dangerously low, and they had been left to rationing pemmican, cattail root and whatever else they could grab in a few minutes of rest before pushing on. Although their stomachs growled, starvation for the time being was not a threat, but it was growing.

Solveig and Mirjam had struggled with the lack of food and the pace of their march. At first, there had been subtle complaining to each other, but never to the men. They felt the weight of being out of place among them, and saw how Edda managed to stand up to the punishment.

The older woman was a rock, honed by a much more difficult life than they had faced, and although they knew intellectually that had much to do with it, they tried to use her as a role model for how they, too, should act. By the time they were ready to complain openly, exhaustion stole the strength to do so.

The lakeshore was marshy so Edda led them up to higher ground before making the push toward the Skaerslinger camp. It meant they walked farther, but they should arrive just after midday and the trek would be much easier. The air was warm and cloying with biting midges and mosquitoes constantly around them. Clouds from the southeast promised rain was on its way. After a run of nearly two weeks of dry weather, it seemed their luck was about to change. The mountains were no place to be when the sky turned sour.

To the north, the entourage crossed a small stream that rushed through the rocks and reeds.

"Let us make this a rally point should anything go wrong at the village," Declan suggested. "If we must run, scatter in any direction you can, and work your way back here to hide. From here we will work out what must be done next."

"Agreed," panted Finn. He had been having a hard time with the thick air and heavy brush.

Rounding the west side of the lake, the excitement turned to unease. Edda noticed it first as they approached the smoke. There was no sound of birds or animals in the trees. What had been a near constant twitter and call had vanished. Even squirrels stopped arguing with bluejays and the chipmunks had disappeared from the ground litter. Their pace slowed as unease gave way to dread. No one dared draw a weapon, but everyone was ready to pull one at a moment's notice.

Ahead came the smell of meat on a fire and the soft sounds of people talking just beyond a line of brush. As Edda was just about to lead them through what appeared to be a gap in the sumac, a small boy burst out wearing a breech clout and moccasins, chased by three others of similar age. They saw the party and froze.

Edda motioned for everyone to keep still and prepared to greet the children when one of the boys shrieked a warning cry and ran. The two others followed, leaving one boy alone to face eight Forsamling standing at the edge of their camp.

"Hello," Edda greeted the child in his tongue. The boy gaped as she spoke their words. "Go get father your." Edda said mixing up her words. "Wish trade. Peace. Stay here, us."

"The boy gave a distrusting look and turned to run when a band of Skaerslinger burst through the brush. The men wore no paint, but had warclubs, tomahawks, and knives at the ready. They hooted and gave startled cries at who they saw. The boy turned to them and repeated Edda's request, though far more articulately than she had.

"The paleflesh devils wish to be at peace with us and trade?" a strapping young man said, astounded. He was covered in ritual scars that Edda had never seen before. Another young man wore a chestplate made of bones and painted rawhide. The paint and dyes on it looked recent, and the scars seemed to cover old marks. The boy verified Edda's claim.

"You are not our foolish brothers, the Sa'ami!" the warrior shouted at them. "They have at least some good sense to share the ways of nature. But you have the stink of cities on you! The filth of the false god comes with you." Warriors yowled in angry agreement.

"We wish trade, leave land on peace," Edda petitioned again. The warrior flinched as she spoke to him and took a few angry steps forward, knife in hand. Behind him, many figures could be seen in the brush line. Some watching with bows in hand, arrows nocked, but none yet drawn.

"A woman speaks for you?" the warrior demanded, offended.

"Him-they speak your tongue not," Edda said. "I speak for."

The warrior raised his knife over his head.

"I am No-Star. War Captain for the Wolf Clan, second to Chief Bitter Fang."

"Me Chorister Edda Gerdasdottir. Second chief of Saelirskjol. We Skaerslinger friends. Take orphan children for the Elk and Raven Clans in east. Friends."

"That is how you know our tongue? You trade with those weak blooded clans?" No-Star spat. "We kill their men and take their women for thralls. Leave their worthless spawn to starve." The growing clan cheered at the claims. The thought of more slaves and hunting range exciting them.

Edda swallowed hard, realizing who had been victor in at least one recent war which had given them so many to care for.

"Wish only trade. Much respects to Wolf Clan. Leave soon as done."

A stirring came from behind the crowd of Skaerslinger which now encircled their band. Everyone had fallen behind Edda. Leif, Solveig and Mirjam in the center of the four men. No one drew weapons yet, but the urge was powerful.

From behind the wedge of warriors, an older man walked out. He bore the marks of many battles, as well as what looked to be fresh ceremonial scars burned on top of familiar Wolf Clan markings. He had put on his paint and mantle of office before coming out to see who had come to his camp. He walked like an old wolf, cautious but confident in his steps.

"I am Bitter Fang," the man said and gave a threatening smile of sharpened teeth. "Bring me your real chief." His eyes locked on the bearskin cloak of Declan. When Edda called Leif forward, his face clouded with a perceived insult.

"I said your chief, not some young whelp who's teeth could not hurt a hare!" the chief shouted. "Him!" He pointed to Declan who looked at the angry chief in surprise.

"My Tign, come up here with Declan, please," Edda called.

"Look, the she-wolf calls," one voice mocked.

"Paleflesh does not understand proper mastery," quipped another as Leif and Declan came forward to stand beside her.

"This is the Chief of all Forsamling. All paleflesh," Edda explained to Bitter Fang gesturing to Leif. "This champion. Great war captain."

Bitter Fang laughed out loud.

"You have a chief that is not ready to stand and be chief? How can your people survive with such weakness leading you?"

Edda translated as best she could. Leif's face burned bright red with the insult.

"Look at the pup!" Bitter Fang mocked. "He knows truth when he hears it!" he shouted to his people. They joined in the mockery. Edda and the rest kept silent. Bitter Fang held up a hand, and the clan settled down.

"My pack obeys me because I am strongest. I am wisest. I know what is best for my pack."

"You trade, we go?" Edda asked, testing whether that door was closed.

"No. It may be better to kill you and take what we want from your bones."

The warriors gave a new howl. Something primordial that made the hair stand up on their necks.

"I challenge you!" Leif shouted at Bitter Fang who was letting No-Star and his warriors strut around like wolves on a helpless moose, taunting and readying to attack. Letting terror soften their prey while eyes were focused on their chief.

"My Tign, no!" Declan said, taking his shoulder. Leif shrugged it off.

138

Bitter Fang looked at Leif.

"What is the whelp saying?" he demanded of Edda.

"Challenge you." she translated. "He win, we trade."

"I will kill him and then you will all die," Bitter Fang threatened.

Edda jutted out her chin, defiant. "He accepts," she said to Leif. "I hope that there is a ceremonial precedent for them."

One of the warriors ran back to the camp after getting his orders.

"My Tign... Leif... you are mad. Do not do this," Declan implored.

"It is done," Leif said cutting him off. Fat warm drops of rain began to fall. He looked up at the dark clouds overhead. "Perfect," he said in sour complaint.

"The risk to you is too great," Declan fought against the hysterical desire to fling himself into the tribe and release his berserker strength like Samson on the Philistines.

Leif turned, fixing Declan with an angry glare. "It is done, I said. There is no way to back out now."

"He is right, Declan," Edda chimed in. "They are Wolf Clan, so they think like wolves. He must take the challenge and win it." She turned to Leif. "But do not kill him.

"What?" Leif said in shock.

"Do you want to negotiate with No-Star? He is wild. Blood crazy. Or possibly their shaman wherever he is? The fact that he is not around worries me, so do not kill Bitter Fang. Force him to surrender. Dominate him. Because he is trying to kill you, he may adopt a tactic you can exploit."

A large ring began to expand and a few children came forth to separate Leif from the rest. He allowed himself to be moved back by children into the ring. They were surrounded by more warriors. The rest of the camp formed the outer ring among a few trees.

The warrior returned with an onyx black warclub. Razors of Obsidian glass and flint arrowheads studded the paddle-like shape.

"Are you ready to die, whelp? Is your mother whimpering for her dead child yet?" Bitter Fang sneared.

He looked to Edda and nodded. She just shook her head at the taunts.

"He ready!" she shouted to the chief as Leif drew his sword.

As if watched by the Storm King himself, a low grumble of thunder came out of the mountains and signaled the start of the trial by combat.

Bitter Fang circled Leif, watching the young man carefully. He gave quick darts in, seeing how the boy would react. Leif fought to recall all his training in single combat, keeping his feet moving, responding to Bitter Fang feints in confident steps.

The first blows came sizzling in with terrifying howls that made Leif's hair stand on end. He blocked the blows with ease, but the power was unnerving. His sword rang and the sting of the impact went through his fingers, slowing his counterstrike. Bitter Fang saw Leif shake his off hand and gave another sharp toothed sneer.

Again, the chief jumped in, landing powerful blows and knocking Leif sideways with the flat of his war club. A quick slash from the ground prevented a powerful overhand blow from ending the prone Tronerving's life right then. He laughed and his pack howled in delight.

Muddied, Leif picked himself up. Bitter Fang wasted no time in pressing another attack. Leif parried and dodged the blows in a frenzy. Obsidian razors shattered on his iron blade, and a counter slash clipped a bone on the chief's breastplate. It was clear that the Skaerslinger chief was not even trying hard. Years of fighting duels to stay on top of his pack had trained him to be a deadly foe.

Leif was not used to the jumping, snapping style Bitter Fang employed. Like a wolf, the Skaerslinger jumped in, bit, saw what he could come away with and hopped back before the return strike came. And always turning, turning, turning. How did a deer escape a lone wolf, or more accurately, how did a hunter catch or kill a wolf? Leif thought as he struggled to keep his feet moving, and cut off every attempt Bitter Fang made to get behind him.

Wolves were caught by trappers, the realization came. He needed to lay a trap.

Another powerful overhead strike drove the flat of his sword into his own face. He kicked out where he thought Bitter Fang was and hit nothing. Blood flowed from a cut under his scalp. The Skaerslinger chief was too fast and powerful. Another lunge from the wiley old chief, and the blunt head of the war club was thrust into his belly, knocking the wind out of him. Leif went to his knees.

Amr made a covert sign. A slashing motion across back of his thigh. Leif rolled backward as the war club whistled through the space where his head had been.

That was when he saw it and and realized what Amr was hinting at. Bitter Fang was light on his feet, and he should go for his strength like a trapper catching his prey by the leg.

Leif was allowed to gain his feet again, much to the amusement of the pack. He stood there, both hands gripping the sword, guard low, panting and exhausted. Bitter Fang continued his confident prowl, driving Leif back against the ring which now pushed at him to get in there and fight their leader.

Leif was not sure what cued him in. Perhaps his sister's screams or possibly instinct. He spun, sword making a low slash behind him as he turned. The blade caught the warrior in the thick of the calf as he was poised to kick him. The wounded Skaerslinger went down with a surprised scream.

Leif finished the spin by going to his knees as the war club again went through where his head should be. Left with no ability to carry the movement forward, Bitter Fang realized too late he over-extended his attack.

Leif brought his sword into a downward chop towards the exposed thigh. The chief mustered his strength to bounce back away from the spinning sword a fraction of a second too late. The slice missed its intended target, but clipped off the tip of Bitter Fang's moccasin, two toes still inside!

Bitter Fang let out a grunt of pain at the sharp tug on his foot, and saw the tip of his moccasin laying in the mud and needles of the trees. Leif picked himself up as the pack went silent in shock.

Bitter Fang stared at his severed toes for what seemed an eternity. Leif could see his opponent was off balance now. The chief hopped back, getting distance for a moment. He no longer had the same spry gait. Blood spattered heavily in the needles and mud. Leif saw something in Bitter Fang's face as he shook the foot. That confidence was gone. Perhaps that was his opening to end the fight without further bloodshed. What kind of action would a man who took wisdom from an animal respect? How could he convince him that it was no longer a fight he could win? Leif risked another glance over to Declan who towered over his sisters in a protective stance, eyes wide in wild hope that Leif would win.

Bigger. He must get bigger!

"Yield!" Leif commanded in a voice befitting the title of Tronerving despite his weariness. "I have no desire to kill you."

Edda translated his words. Bitter Fang glared at her then back to Leif who now stood, no longer looking winded and tired, sword rising to a high guard above his head. He saw Amr clench his fist and mouth a shout of joy, eyes blazing in a paroxysm of victory.

Bitter Fang's snarl revealed he could not fight for much longer. The blood flowed quickly in the rain. Leif could see the Skaerslinger considering the cost of victory in this duel. It would either be his own life in trade, or Bitter Fang would fall very soon to the next war captain that desired to be chief like every old alpha.

"We came to trade, not to fight. Not to be enemies," Leif gave the entreaty again, and Edda repeated it. Bitter Fang gave a sigh blended with anger, sadness and exhaustion, the war club slumped tip first into the mud and the defeated chief leaned heavily on it. The pack gave a horrified gasp as the braves began to swirl with angry mutters. No-Star's eyes burned with the blackest hate toward his chief.

"Never before has anyone matched me in combat. Like the wolf, I know when a prey is too strong and will go to lick my wounds," Bitter fang declared.

The pack sighed with disappointment.

"We will trade."

17. A DANGEROUS ACCORD

Considering that he had just lost two toes, Bitter Fang's hospitality was peculiarly gracious. Leif was escorted into the chief's longhouse. Only Edda was allowed to accompany him and both were grateful to be out of the rain. War captains grumbled till a backhand to No-Star's face brought an end to the murmurs.

Leif started the negotiation while the rest of his companions were milling about the camp at their pleasure. Always attended to by at least two Skaerslinger observing their every move. Some watched with naked interest, others were covert. It was surreal for six Forsamling to be wandering in the camp at large. They were treated like odd but harmless animals wandering around their lodges and longhouses. Most of the camp was bemused but uninterested. Their focus seemed to be far away.

The thunder came in gentle growls and the other side of the lake faded in and out with the drifting curtains of rain. The downpours were a mixed blessing for they washed much of the remaining treesqueak musk off their clothes and meager gear, but it was going to be an uncomfortable and damp night.

Inge, Finn and Bergamot huddled down near a cooking fire sheltered under a canopy as the warm rain wavered between light sprinkle to drenching downpour. Amr tried to learn some of the Skaerslinger tongue while Thyrnir ranged around him, sniffing all the new scents. Declan wandered all about the camp. Solveig and Mirjam remained all but plastered to Declan who took full advantage of his freedom to move about, satiating his curiosity despite the weather. Mirjam was just as curious as Declan, but Solveig was always looking over her shoulder, keeping an eye on the rest of their company.

Of them all, only Amr looked comfortable in camp. This disturbing realization was reinforced as Solveig watched Thyrnir. Normally, the hostile dog would never allow anyone but Amr to touch him, but the Skaerslinger were able to touch and pet him. The dog even wagged his tail and accepted food offered from their hands.

A Havarian mastiff was alien compared to the wolves and sled dogs in the camp that weighed in at less than half his size. If such a thing was possible among dogs, the pack rendered worshipful reverence to Thyrnir. Thyrnir held his head high as if all this deference was his rightful due. The Skaerslinger seemed to think him to be of some sort of familiar for their gods.

How was it, Solveig wondered, that in such a place, among these people, Amr could be so comfortable? A quick look showed Finn and Inge felt the opposite. Their body language openly revealing they saw threats from all quarters. Perhaps it had something to do with their Reformist beliefs, but if they were wrong with God, would they not be more at ease among the Skaerslinger?

Inge and Finn took off their rain cloaks just outside the sheltered kitchen while they enjoyed the warmth and watched the women who chattered as they worked. The men seemed more content to stand in the wet weather laughing at them. Finn suspected as to why. Unless they were a chef for the Hird or there were no women available to do the job like a timber camp cook, only old men, servant boys and thralls were found in a Forsamling kitchen. The same seemed to hold true here for there was only one thrall slaving away in the Skaerslinger kitchen doing heavy tasks.

The boiling stew and roasting meat smelled tempting. Soon, Finn could not resist asking to have some rather than eating a small piece of their own pemmican. Perhaps it might be considered an insult, but the smell was overpowering caution. He made a motion asking if he could have some roasting meat. The women yelled at the thrall who obeyed her commands. It was clear who was in charge of the kitchen, not the other women and their enslaved servant.

The thrall came over to Brother Finn and knelt down next to him. His fine golden beard and violently curly blond locks were bedraggled. His clothes were a mismatched combination of Forsamling attire and Skaerslinger repairs. Like the other hunters and braves he wore a breechclout and leggings but kept a light woven tunic made from dirty gold and white hemp. His face, haggard and his arms and legs revealed the scars and burns from obvious beatings and torture.

"May the Lord of Hosts bless you, my son for what you have endured," Finn whispered.

"My suffering is immaterial, Father, for my time is short and I go on to my reward."

Inge opened his mouth to give him encouragement, but the thrall gave a faint shake of his head, as if knowing what he was going to say.

"There is nothing you can do for me, but I can serve you. Please listen. My dame says you can eat when trade is concluded and not till then. You may have water if you wish. I will have more to say when I get back with your drink."

"Is this their custom in trade?" Inge asked.

"No. With what has happened, all their customs are broken right now. Your leader's victory was just the final straw of what is to come," the thrall said. He then stood, told his dame where he was going and rushed off into the rain.

"Something is not as it seems here," Inge said quietly, as the women chattered loudly, watching the priests.

"I agree," Finn said. "Their shaman is missing, for which I am thankful. Praise you, Jesus, for that."

At the sound of the name of Jesus, there was a loud pop and hiss as a knot in the fire exploded and sent a shower of sparks toward Inge and Finn. Chunks of hot coals struck their clothes. They steamed and sizzled as the two men brushed them off while the women laughed hard at their misfortune.

"It seems demons reside even in the fires of this place and hate that name," Inge said in sour reproach at the flames.

Through Edda, Leif laid out the desire to purchase two canoes, resupply their food and a few blankets. Bitter Fang listened to the trade proposal without a word as they sat inside his longhouse, attended to by his wives, thralls and a medicine man. After the medicine man uttered an incantation that caused Leif and Edda's hair to stand on end, the chief's two missing toe stubs were cauterized with a hot rock. The freshly severed toes had been sewn into a medicine bag packed with herbs and some other powdery concoction then hung around his neck. The Skaerslinger gave no impression of being in pain save for a flaring of his pupils in the dim light of the dwelling.

"You ask much for a little gold and gemstones," Bitter Fang said at the offer. "They may impress women, but men have little need for these. How can you do better?"

"What could you value more than gold and gems?" Leif asked.

"Iron," Bitter Fang said and pointed to Leif and Edda's swords.

"No," Leif and Edda said in unison. No-Star was so tense with his fury that he was shaking.

"What else can you offer that we would want?"

"Have not I spared your life?" Leif asked.

Bitter Fang pursed his lips at the reminder.

"You have. That is why we are speaking. I am paying my debt to you by keeping No-Star and the rest of my warriors from killing you all. Our courtesy to paleflesh comes with a price. I choose to repay it in this manner."

The thought had not crossed Leif's mind, but a glance at Edda confirmed she had been considering it. Right now, they were all vulnerable, scattered about and constantly watched.

"Perhaps one of your women. Not her, but the young ones? They could make good wives for a warrior." Bitter Fang's suggestion infuriated Leif. Were it not for Edda's hand being placed on his shoulder, he would have drawn his sword to kill every Skaerslinger in the longhouse.

Made dumb by rage, Leif shook his head. The memory of his father came upon him, and he drew a deep breath, letting it out slow and quiet. His father knew how to handle hostiles in negotiations. Would he be able to live up to that legacy?

"Then there is nothing more to speak of. We desire iron, thralls or wives. Both dogs would be a proper trade too. Canoes for dogs. Will you do that?"

"I cannot trade those, they belong to my escorts," Leif said.

"What sort of chief must respect the property of his people?" Bitter Fang scoffed. "They are part of your pack, and that means your right to anything for the sake of the pack. They serve you. You paleflesh do not understand the world. How you came to be given so much power is crazy."

"I have an idea," Edda said to Leif. "We have some iron we can give them." She turned to Bitter Fang. His smile revealed he knew his position.

"We have little iron we can trade, but only if you trade us some in kind weapons too," Edda began.

"What are you saying, Chorister?" Leif hissed.

"Trust me, my Tign."

"I am interested." Bitter Fang leaned in.

"We have two water-spears. Many saxes. You make new spears and javelins from them.

"But no swords? No axes?"

"Never."

"You would give away the Havarian's harpoons and most of our saxes to them? They will never stand for it." Leif was incredulous.

"What of your strange metal bows?" Bitter Fang said after No-Star reminded him by sign.

"Our spring bows? No. We must have them, too," Edda said. "Besides, you could not make more bolts or fix them if they broke."

Bitter Fang scowled for a long moment, then nodded.

"In return, you give us war clubs, flint spears and maybe javelins and other weapons, they will-" Edda began but was cut off by Bitter Fang.

"Two canoes and paddles, and a spear for a spear. A knife and tomahawk for a saxe. For your gold and gems, we will give you food too. Is this a trade?"

The woeful blond thrall returned with cups and spring water that quenched Inge and Finn's thirst.

"There must be something we can do for you," Inge said to the thrall.

"No. You are not here for me. There is nothing that can be done for my sake. I have been here too long, and only wish to return to my herre when the time is right."

"When will that be?" Finn asked, getting an eerie feeling from the young man. He noticed he wore a belt with a fawn tanned leather thong that used to hold a sword's scabbard.

"Very soon," he said with desperation. "Promise me three things before you go."

"Of course, my son," Inge said.

The thrall's dame started shouting at him, clearly upset he was dawdling with the paleflesh.

"Do not eat or drink anything from their hands. It is cursed. Do not come back for me when you leave and lastly, pray for me that I have the strength to finish my duty."

"What duty is that?" Finn asked.

The thrall smiled but did not answer.

A hot rock hit the back of the thrall's head knocking him down into the priest's laps. The dame of the kitchen cursed at him in the most foul terms she could muster. Finn and Inge helped the man back to his feet as he bled from behind his ear.

"We will do as you ask. What is your name, my son?" Inge asked?

"Daniel."

And with that, the thrall ran into the rain to do as his dame commanded.

18. TWELVE FINGERS

As the air cooled and the clouds broke up, mist rose off the lake and the camp began to get quiet with the onset of evening.

"What have you been looking for, Declan?" Solveig asked, sick of aimlessly meandering about the camp. To her, he had been looking at various things without rhyme or reason.

"Their totems," Declan answered. "Edda said these Skaerslinger are Wolf Clan. That means they should have plenty of sign of their ruling manitou here, but I am not seeing any.

"Oj," Solveig and Mirjam softly breathed in tandem, eyes getting wider. His aimless rambling was not so random after all.

"I have only found this stick figure of a man, open mouthed with antlers, fangs and two war clubs. In all the camps I have seen at war, I have never seen its like before among the spoils of battle."

Mirjam shuddered as she looked at the symbol closely.

"Perhaps Edda knows about this sign," Mirjam suggested, tearing her eyes away.

"I was hoping that too, but till she returns..." Declan trailed off.

Out of the corner of his eye, movement caught Declan's attention. He saw happy squealing children at play, pulling at a hunk of ratty deer hide with someone on the other side of a lodge. He walked around to see Thyrnir playing tug of war with them, with Amr laughing at their antics. The dog that was so completely standoffish was playing with these Skaerslinger children?

Declan's blood ran cold.

"Solveig?" Declan said softly.

"Jah?" She turned to look at what he saw. Amr was now putting a child onto the back of the mammoth dog to ride.

"Promise me to stay away from Thyrnir from now on."

"Why?" Solveig looked at Thyrnir,

"Those children belong to the wolf manitou. Who did the children of Saelirskjol belong to? Do you see it now?"

Solveig swallowed hard. Thyrnir had snapped at the children of Saelirskjol, but with these boys and girls... he played like a puppy. That must be the missing piece, she thought. Could a dog be possessed?

"You will never have to remind me again, thu vethur," Mirjam said.

Her eyes went to Friar Amr who was now returning their stares. His expression was unfathomable. Something deep inside the friar was being torn asunder as his mood seemed to fight for a balance between happiness, anger, conspiracy and fear.

"Let us go find Brother Finn," Mirjam said, turning away and walked to the center of camp hoping Finn and Inge were still there. The rest followed under Amr's unsettling gaze.

The door of the chief's longhouse opened, and Bitter Fang, No-Star, Leif and Edda walked out. As the commotion of their exit spread throughout the camp, Leif and Edda made straight for Finn and Inge.

"We have a trade, but you will not like it, I suspect," Leif said with a grimace.

"What did they demand?" Finn asked.

"Iron," Inge said seeing the look on the Tronrving's face, "as predicted."

"Jah, so I gave them what we could spare," Leif confirmed.

"What could we spare?" Finn, asked softly.

"Your harpoons and all but three saxes. But I saved the swords, springbows and Declan's axe."

"God's bristly armpit!" Inge exploded. "Why not send us forth with a teacup and ball of yarn to hunt bears?"

"They will give us spears in exchange for your harpoons, and flint knives and tomahawks for your saxes. They would not make the trade otherwise. We also get food for a month for a handful of gold and gems."

Brother Finn blanched at the statement.

"Food?" he all but stammered

"Jah! No more worry about starvation," Leif said with great relief.

"My Tign," Brother Finn said, looking back at what he had been calling the kitchen. "We have been warned by a thrall to not eat or drink anything given to us. It is cursed."

"What is cursed?" asked Mirjam. Her hopes of a good meal dashed.

"All the food and drink. Take nothing but water. Their thrall warned us."

"They have a Forsamling as a thrall?" Leif asked startled. "We must liberate-"

"We will do nothing of the kind," Finn cut him off. "Inge and I have promised to not try. That is his wish. Leave him for what he must do. I think he is dying from the way he talked, or intends to give his life to some purpose." Finn's low voice was hardly needed.

Sounds of happiness and outrage traveled throughout the camp as the news of the deal spread and small knots of Skaerslinger talked frantically about the decision.

"But, our business is complete. Bitter Fang is happy with the trade," Leif reminded the rest.

"My Tign," Edda said, "that is because you do not speak their tongue or know their custom. There is a power struggle happening. Look." Edda gestured toward an angry pack of warriors. "No-Star is livid. See him in counsel with those warriors? You must have noticed how he has been since you beat Bitter Fang in combat. Something is spreading and has the portent to get even worse."

"Twelve Fingers has returned!" a Skaerslinger boy shouted from the shore. "He is coming! Twelve Fingers is returning from the gods!"

The camp breathed a collective sigh and went quiet with awe.

Out on the water, a large canoe, like one Brother Finn had seen off Ogimaak Mikwaam Island as he and another group of terrified travelers rowed for their lives, approached in silence. Its dark ominous shape cut through the steaming glass-smooth water in the evening light.

No-Star let out the first howl, and within a second the whole pack began howling. Even Thyrnir joined in as Amr trotted up to the others. There was a quick scuffle as Bergamot snapped at some curious sled dogs who followed Thyrnir and ventured too close. Finn pulled her back to his side, but she never stopped watching his back as the pack now kept a much farther distance from them all.

"This could be very bad, jah?" Amr said.

"Where have you been?" Leif asked as he saw Amr's strange countenance.

"With the children, playing. Since we were trying to be friendly, I thought it good to show we could be trusted with their children."

Finn and Inge hid their disbelief. Solveig did not bother concealing her contempt. Amr looked her dead in the eyes, his expression challenging her to denounce him. Leif shoved between the two and glared back into Amr's stare.

"I do not appreciate you looking at my sister that way."

"Your pardon, my Tign," Amr said and ducked his head, backing away from him with a bow. "This place disturbs me, and I long to leave."

Solveig was open mouthed at his claim. He rolled his eyes away and gave a pantomime turn toward the water. "Perhaps we should be more worried about who this shaman is?" Amr asked pointing an open hand at the canoe about to make shore.

"Twelve Fingers is not a very reassuring name," Inge moaned.

"Something about it worries my spirit, and not just because I know he is the demon's representative among the tribe," Edda agreed.

The camp turned out en masse for the return of their shaman. They flooded the shore cheering. Leif and company stayed back but under the watch of No-Star and his warriors. Bitter Fang limped forward to greet his pack's spiritual leader.

In the bow of the canoe, a Skaerslinger with patchy frost white and dark red skin stood proudly. The man was over seven feet tall! Trophies from a dozen animal parts were woven into his long red hair, his face in ceremonial paint that gave him the look of a skull. His body was laid waste by rot, but rebuilt by something else just as quickly as it was destroyed. Despite this illness with no name, his power was palpable.

The shaman stepped out of the canoe as it struck the sandy shore. His devoted coming to escort him to his people.

"Has anyone ever seen a Skaerslinger with red hair?" Inge asked.

"Never, but I have heard rumor of half-breeds with captured Forsamling women," Amr answered.

A spark of memory came to Brother Finn.

Suddenly, he was back in the library at Kynligrspiejl a lifetime ago, reading the forbidden book of Enoch. A tome that was secreted away by those who denied the Orthodox position that all books not in scripture or written by the Kyrkja were apostasy, designed to lead them astray. An idle curiosity to see if he could learn more about God. Most of what he learned left him with doubts on whether to believe these extra canonical books or not.

"Twelve Fingers..." Finn muttered.

"What?" Inge said, unable to look away from the shaman.

"No... this must not be true." His voice was a fear induced growl as he moved back and forth trying to get a better look at the shaman.

Sigrid's face flashed before his eyes. Dear Sigrid, he thought, remembering her in the dungeon on Athrvorthfestning. He had always prayed she was exaggerating. That what she claimed was not true.

"Count the fingers on his hands!" Finn hissed to them all, terrified at the answer.

"I cannot see them. They are under that shawl thing he is wearing.

"What is the matter with you?" Leif demanded of Finn.

Finn did not answer for the short conference between Bitter Fang and Twelve Fingers had concluded. The shaman strode through the crowd toward the fearful company of Forsamling, like a horrible predator sizing up his prey. The wounded chieftain following as fast as he was able, and No-Star's warriors spreading out behind in the same predatory fashion that they used before the challenge.

"I have been told you have come to trade peacefully with us, Chief of the Paleflesh," Twelve Fingers said in accented Norroent. They were all taken aback. Even more confusing was his lips did not match the sound of his voice.

156

"You speak our tongue?" Edda asked timidly.

The mammoth man looked down on her.

"I do." Again, his mouth moved one way, but his voice another.

Leif straightened himself, cleared his throat and stepped forward.

"We do come in peace, Shaman of the Wolf Clan. Your chief and I have struck an accord, and we will honor it and leave your land immediately."

The shaman gave a slow smile and looked back at Bitter Fang. The languid glance was so cold and alien that the powerful chief paled.

"Then let us complete our trade and part as brothers. Prepare your goods, and I shall ready the ceremony to finalize our barter."

"As you wish," Leif responded, attempting to sound more confident than he felt. He held out his gloved hand. "To conclude a deal, this is how we Forsamling show intent," Leif said. Twelve Fingers looked down at the gesture.

The shaman's hand came out from the covering and clasped Leif's in his own.

He had six fingers.

With the briefest of hesitations, Leif shook his hand thrice, and Twelve Fingers looked amused at the custom.

"Tonight, we shall conclude our deal like real men," Twelve Fingers promised. "In blood."

19. SACRIFICES

Finn did not believe for a moment this ceremony was for the conclusion of their trade no matter what assurances were given. With no idea where to sit and wait for Twelve Fingers to give his blessing, they stayed near the shore and the canoes. Throughout the late afternoon two excellent canoes were prepared, loaded with dried meat, fish and much to his distaste, more pemmican. The scent from their kitchen had become unbearable. All were hungry and drank only from their waterskins when necessary.

Keeping to Daniel's warning irritated the Skaerslinger women who now offered food or a broth of some sort in curious shallow dishes. Although insulted, they did not make a large show over the refusal. There was an undercurrent of disappointment, like someone gave away a secret and their plot had been thwarted. It was particularly difficult for Solveig and Mirjam to refuse. They were incredibly hungry, and the women kept tempting them. The Kronadottirs struggled against their diplomatic tutelage which insisted they accept offers of food despite the nature of their hosts and take it graciously. The dissonance caused by their hunger and being rude roiled their emotions.

Shortly before sundown the camp began to empty as the Skaerslinger disappeared into the pinery.

"I think it is time for us to pray," Edda said. "Something is coming and we best be ready for it. Finn, will you lead us?"

He nodded.

All but Finn and Inge dropped to their knees for prayer.

"Up, up!" Finn commanded looking at their minders. "We cannot let them understand what is happening. I do not know what the demons will stir up if they see this, so, Lord Jesus, blind their eyes," Finn ordered, his eyes scanning the remaining Skaerslinger to see if they had noticed. "I have been praying for the manitou to be silent since we arrived, but dared not do much else. It is time to put on the Armor of God, and be ready to stand firm."

He ushered them to come close together, bow their heads and clasp hands.

"In the name of the Father, the Son and the Holy Spirit, we beseech You, Lord Jesus, to lay Your protective hands upon our lives. To You, oh Lord, we offer ourselves up for Your service and ask for Your protection and grace. We cannot see Your will for what is about to happen, and ask that Your glory be done. Let Your enemies be brought low, and your children come out from among this evil land to safe pastures. In the name of Jesus, I command that no demon cause harm to any of us, nor afflict us in the spirit or flesh.

"Grant our petition, O, Lord, to keep all profane things from our touch or lips. Help us to come away with what is needed for our journey in safety. The fate of Your people, the Forsamling, and all those who would come out of darkness to You hangs by a thread if seen through the eyes of man, Oh Lord. But You, who are just and righteous in all things know what is to come and what you desire to be."

"If we have allies unknown to us, let them be blessed and go forth to do Your will. Let all your enemies fall into the pit they desired for us. Grant us, Lord Jesus, the discernment, wisdom and strength to follow You even if it costs us our lives for your greater glory. Place around us a host of angels, and deliver us into Your loving arms."

"Amen," everyone uttered, keeping their heads bowed, following their own conscience in silent prayer.

Edda began to sing softly in tongues. A delicate sensation of peace came over them like far off birdsong. Inge began to feel the familiar weight in the spirit of angels surrounding them.

As her song trailed off an unknown time later, Finn looked up, drawing a deep breath through his nose. As he let out a long peaceful sigh he saw a figure dart out of Bitter Fang's longhouse, a flash of silver in his hand. Before he could register who it was, the person was gone into the trees.

Mountain shadows crept over the camp. With them came a company of Twelve Finger's acolytes to collect the small company, instructing them to follow.

Their guides seemed to meander through the dense trees till they were thoroughly lost. Soon they heard chanting and dancing drifting in the darkened pinery. Edda did not understand the words being spoken. They were primordial. Guttural. Nothing about them felt like an intent to invoke brotherhood or friendship. Their guides stopped and they stood silently in the dark listening to the Skaerslinger's ritual, their fear growing into a deep dread.

Then with a loud shout of joy the drumming and jangling bells ceased.

"Bring forth our new paleflesh brothers and sisters!" commanded Twelve Fingers from somewhere ahead in the dark.

The acolytes began to chant low and reverent. They guided them by hand around a hidden corner where a dark gap entered a small knoll. Little fires at their feet lit the way through the narrow chasm that was hardly more than the width of Declan's shoulders. From behind, hissing was heard as the little fires on the ground lighting the way were doused. The crevasse opened, revealing the entire pack. The Skaerslinger sat on the ground along the ring of eroded stone. Two small fires burned at the corners of a pale stone altar in the center, lighting Twelve Fingers from below, decorated in his full shamanic glory. Pockets of luminescent fungus along the rock walls and from under the altar provided a dim glow. The light was refracted by strata of white quartz crystals, bathing everything in a blue green light.

"It is so cold," Mirjam whispered, clouds of breath hanging in the air.

"Be brave," Solveig encouraged though she too was shivering in terror.

"I hope God listened very close to our prayers. I see no way of getting out of here alive if things go bad," Declan muttered to Edda.

"His will be done," she whispered back. "His will be done."

They stopped before the altar and waited.

The chanting ceased.

"We welcome you, Chief of All Paleflesh into a pact of brotherhood with our pack. You who have come in peace and shown your worth will now prove to be a man of your words," the shaman said, his lips still moving in conflict with what their ears heard. "You have seen us honor our words on the beach, giving you what you desire. Bring forth your trade and place it between the fire," Twelve Fingers commanded.

Finn came forward and placed his saxe and harpoon on the ground. Inge did the same. Amr produced his dagger, and Solveig and Mirjam left their tomahawks. Leif came forward and placed a stack of golden Oere coins and mixed gemstones next to them. Some were cut, others were raw. An acolyte came forward, and chanted over the items, waving smoke over them with the wing of a bird. A tension in the air began to build along with the incense of the smudge pot. The thick smell of ozone mingled with the smudge and the pack sighed like the wind.

Once complete, the drummers began again in a soft beat.

"Leif, Chief of All Paleflesh, come forth and we shall seal our friendship forever in the blood of those who would feed our peoples," Twelve Fingers commanded.

"Please, no. Do not go," whispered Mirjam. Solveig grabbed the back of his sleeve between her finger and thumb.

"What choice have I?" Leif muttered.

"Eat or drink nothing. No matter the cost," Inge warned.

Leif stepped forward. As he did, from behind Twelve Fingers came the sound of some heavy wood groaning and a light grew from the ground as a new fire was uncovered.

Heralded by a chorus of creaks and pops, Bitter Fang was raised up from the ground, lashed to a rack of wooden beams slicked with dried blood.

His limbs and body bound in the same pose of the totem man Declan had seen earlier. His jaw torn wide, splitting his cheeks, and stuffed with a mouthpiece of false teeth made from the fangs from many animals. Antlers of a deer had been attached to his bloody skull. His legs bound, forever dancing, and in his hands, the shiny white femurs of a man!

Solveig and Mirjam's scream of terror that was drowned out by the terrible predatory howl of the pack rejoicing at the display.

"Behold! The way of all prey!" Twelve Fingers shouted. "They shall become the meat of Gakina Giiwioswinini! Hunter of All!"

With a long obsidian knife, Twelve fingers stepped to the bound chief and, with great expertise, cut out Bitter Fang's heart.

"The old and weak must perish to feed the young and strong! This is the way of all flesh! All life serves to feed the hunter. Gakina Giiwiosewinini!"

Leif could see the terrified eyes of Bitter Fang grow dim as life fled his body. Twelve Fingers stepped forward and poured out the blood from the heart into a bowl, offered the organ to the sky and then took a bite.

The chant began from the pack and all realized the horror that they faced.

"Wendigo...

"Wendigo...

"Wendigo...

"Wendigo!"

Twelve Fingers held out the heart to Leif who stared at it in complete revulsion.

"Feed and become our brother," the shaman commanded. The words contained such pressure Leif could feel them pull on his soul. His hands trembled at his side as he fought against the urge to take the bowl. Against his will, they rose. Frost began to form a rind on the lip of the bowl of blood as he watched, the steaming liquid rapidly chilling.

"As winter extinguishes summer, you must hunt or perish." The shaman's words floated in the air with the steam of his breath, the dim blue of his eyes glowing in the dark. All around him, the pack's eyes reflected the hellish expectation. Finn's fears were true. This clan of Skaerslinger had become corrupted by an even more powerful demon than that of the wolf manitou.

"Join the hunt. Choose to live!" The voice was so seductive and Leif's hands began to rise. No one could move to stop them.

As Leif began to step forward and take the bloody trophy, a figure landed between him and the altar. The impact threw Leif backwards to be caught by Declan. A flash of light came from the figure's hands and split the heart in half, shattering the stone bowl with a loud bell-like clang.

Daniel stood before the altar where Leif had been just a moment earlier, sword still ringing like a tuning fork. Twelve Fingers tripped backwards and saw what stood between him and the paleflesh.

"You dare thrall?!" The power of the voice strong enough to deafen the sturdiest of ears.

"I dare in the name of my herre, the Lord Jesus! Lord of Hosts! Konge of all!" Daniel shouted back defiantly. In his hands he held a sword of silvered iron. A sword Finn had seen in his dreams a little under two years before. Daniel turned back to face the startled Forsamling as the roar of the outraged pack began to rise.

"Flee for your lives!" Daniel commanded. "This is a foe beyond your power!"

Edda drew her sword, and Declan his axe. Amr and Inge shielded Leif with their bodies and together they wheeled around to escape through the darkened gap of rock. Their blades cleared the path of startled acolytes as they fled.

Behind them, it was as if the sun had dawned. Mirjam turned as she ran and saw the divine standing against the infernal.

Daniel was radiant. Wings of light and a sword of fire as he translated into his heavenly form. Before him, the fleshy disguise of Twelve Fingers burned away and the screams and howls of pain from the Skaerslinger began.

What rose from the charring, suppurating flesh of the shaman was a skeletal figure twice his size, with a bloody antler rack, and a mouth of fangs surrounded by tatters of lips. Its eyes pinpoints of icy fire. The flesh pulled away from its rib cage like starvation in the depths of cruelest winter. Inside beat a glimmering heart of ice.

And then it was gone, out of sight behind the rock walls of the knoll, but its hellish screams drove them on.

They fled pell-mell into the dark. Behind them, the light grew even stronger, illuminating the low clouds above, providing them with a forest fire glare to see by. Shafts of brilliance cut through the trees. As they ran, the group began to scatter among the trees and bushes as they searched for their way back to the camp.

"Where is the lake?" Amr shouted, nearly out of his mind in fear.

"Is it not this way?" Leif yelled.

The light from behind began to fragment and split into rainbow shards as the two celestial beings clashed with the sound of a sword smashing against rock and bone. The shadows of Skaerslinger trying to run down the escaped Forsamling could be seen running between trees as well.

"God's blessed elbows, I am just as lost as you!" came the panicked voice of Inge.

They did not stop running. Behind them the roar of the Wendigo made the leaves quake and the light faded away like a snuffed candle. Everyone fumbled in the dark, looking for each other but seemingly unable to regroup as confusion controlled their eyes and feet.

"Over here! Edda shouted. "I see a light ahead!" It did not matter if anyone was left at the Skaerslinger camp. They must fight their way out or meet their doom.

As they ran toward the light, she began to sing the Twenty Third Psalm, guiding the rest with her voice. Tripping and breaking the tangles of vines and branches, they converged on her song till they burst out of the forest among the longhouses and spied the canoes on the beach.

The remaining women and children fell upon them with demonic savagery as they ran through the camp, slashing and stabbing but not staying to finish of their opponents.

"To the canoes!" Finn shouted.

Using his martial prowess, he disarmed one old warrior and took his spear before running him through. Thyrnir and Bergamot ran along with their masters, attacking Skaerslinger like coach dogs running along side carriages. Biting legs and dashing to catch up, helping to shepherd them to the water.

A thick fog was rising up from the lake while the sky above was clearing fast.

"Get in, but be gentle! The bark is only so strong," Declan cautioned as they reached their goal.

Leif took the bow of the first while Edda helped ease it into the water with Amr and Inge. Finn, Solveig and Mirjam got into the second as Declan pushed them off, then went back.

"Declan!" Finn shouted, not understanding what he was doing. It became quickly apparent as the berserker, angry at having run from a fight, took out his frustration on the remaining canoes, thrashing them into shreds.

"There!" he shouted triumphantly. "Let us see them follow now!" He sloshed through the shallows and with great care, Declan levered himself over the lip of the canoe at the stern. Carefully, he traded his axe for a paddle and with powerful strokes they pulled away from shore to vanish into the low fog of the night.

20. REFORGING BAD IRON

The lightly covered coach pulled up in front of the unassuming mansion off the Domkyrkjeplassen. A Koenraadian banner fluttered in the hot gusty breeze promising a summer storm. Birgr Vilhoaettir stepped from his father's carriage as the skies began to darken and the smell of rain wafted down the street. Two men dressed like valets, but moving like huskarls, jumped down from the back. The pair of guards at the entrance came to attention when they saw the young man get out. As he walked up a few stone steps to the entrance, the door opened, and a pageboy came out.

"The Lendmann Mother, Ulla Mogrensdottir Asbjornaettir, welcomes you to her home, Din Naade Birgr Jakobsson Vilhoaettir." His bow was deep. If it were not for the fact his body blocked the door, Birgr would have gone right inside ignoring proper custom. He stopped short and gave a sniff of irritation.

"Before you enter," the page said, "you are unarmed?"

"Of course. These two made sure of that," Birgr groused and hooked a thumb at the two valets. They nodded, verifying his words.

"Thank you. You are now permitted to have your audience with the Lendmann Mother." The boy stepped out the way.

Birgr felt the sting of that statement, as if he was the inferior here. To a Lendmann?

Birgr followed another servant, who stood just inside the foyer, at a slow and deliberate pace through the manor and back to the atrium. The rain scented air was thick and uncomfortable. The Lendmann Mother sat in her ornate wooden chair in front of a small low table packed with delicacies and drink that were beyond Birgr's simple palate. She stood and gestured to the much less ornate seat in front of her.

"Welcome to your new home, Deres Naade. I hope you will be happy during your time here," she stood to greet the petulant jarlsson. Despite being on a step higher than him, they remained eye to eye. Birgr made a strained and barely tolerable gesture of greeting and sat without a word. The Lendmann Mother gave a tight smile at the young man and sat as well.

Now he remembered her. She had been among the Visekonge's guests at Klarrvatn, when his appetite for the flesh of young maidens of the Hird was thwarted by his mother's hovering and that Pandora of mischief, Mirjam Gregorssdottir. Mirjam was worse in his mind, for she had not even left hope behind.

The sheltered garden behind the Lendmann Mother was lush with late summer flowers that gave off an intoxicating perfume on coy puffs of wind. Around the atrium courtyard, servants were closing windows and balconies before the rain began.

"I see you are not happy with your father sending you to me."

"I do not appreciate it, no," Birgr mumbled, turning to look at his two escorts who were standing by the entrance to the manor with her two Kyrkjaguard. "I see the trust is lacking, too."

"That is not by my choosing Birgr, but a necessity for the time being. You are too wild for the circumstances that surround you. This could cause you to be harmed, or worse. I seek to prevent this for the sake of your father, and all of the Union," she said with a twinkle in her eye. "Many people are counting on you to behave for they depend on you playing your part," she tut-tutted and wagged her finger at him like a disobedient child.

"Now see here, my Grevinne Ulla," he began in the most polite tone his offense would allow. His eyes wandered his surroundings evaluating all the threats he could see. Taking on four armed men would be a hard fight, and probably not worth it in the end, to beat this woman senseless. "I am ready to sit on the throne. I do not need all this supposed training and refinement that you think is necessary. Finishing school is for women of feeble blood and no control. Politics is for men too weak to pick up the sword and do the right thing!"

"Calm yourself, Deres Naade. Peace be with you," she soothed ignoring his insult. Something in her voice drew the anger out of Birgr, like a poultice.

"You must be hungry after your long ride. Please try some of the morsels. My cooks are very good."

Birgr looked down at the table and saw pickled vegetables and fish, cold roast meat with cheese and fruit. An enthralled servant, delicate silver chain jingling as she walked, appeared out of nowhere and poured a small goblet of aquavit for him. Birgr looked at the girl, who was exquisitely groomed and smelled of exotic blooms. The Lendmann Mother watched his reaction at the delicate flower of womanhood. Birgr grinned like a wolf.

"I see you approve of my serving thrall?"

"Jah..." he drawled out. "I do indeed." The word "thrall" made Birgr even happier.

The girl returned a tantalizing expression and vanished behind a large corner pillar much to Birgr's disappointment. He picked up the small glass and drank it all in one gulp, in hopes that she would be back to refill it. The girl did not return.

The Lendmann Mother cleared her throat, and Birgr's attention snapped back to her. She shook her head slowly.

"Your reputation, it seems, exceeds the reports I had been given about you."

"What reports?" Birgr questioned a little too loudly.

"That you cannot control your wandering eye, and that is something I cannot have in my house." Her voice was neither angry nor sad, but disapproving in a way Birgr could not comprehend. For the first time in his life, he felt shame at failure. How could the temper of her words crush his soul like that? The fighting spirit drained from him.

"May I have another drink?" he asked, hoping to restore himself with the beverage.

"No, I believe you have had enough. We have much to do, and I need you in a more cooperative mind." The Lendmann Mother's voice had a timbre to it that Birgr could not place. It was as if something else was speaking through her with an authority his soul could not resist.

"What do you plan to do with me?" Birgr asked with thick words.

"Birgr," she said, dispensing with his title. "You are like a lump of iron in the hands of a blacksmith. Jarl Ofbradh has already gotten you hot on the way here, so to speak, but now-" a roll of thunder punctuated her point, "I see I cannot take the hammer to you... yet."

"What does that mean?" His anger felt stunted and weak. Two sensations he had not felt since he was a little boy. With every sentence from her lips, the sensation grew in intensity.

"It means I am worried that the iron of your spirit is of poor quality and I am going to have to melt you down again and skim off the dross of your pitiful character before you can be reforged and I take the hammer to you. For now, you are a weapon incapable... unworthy to be used in battle."

Birgr's sight was getting blurry, a ringing grew in his ears.

"What is worse, is that I do not have enough time to do this properly, so I must take drastic measures to remake you. Then you will become the weapon our friends need. You know of which friends I speak, jah?" The Lendmann Mother stood up over Birgr who now slumped in his seat. He slurred a sound of acknowledgment for it took all his effort to focus on her. The strength was fleeing his legs and arms. A sweat broke out on his brow in the damp air. Lightning flashed and the Lendmann Mother glowed with Saint Elmo's Fire.

"Therefore I apologize to you now Birgr. This will be the only time you will hear me say it. I do not enjoy this method of training you, but we cannot have an oversexed, self-centered lout romping about with no concept of the political, let alone spiritual battle he has been chosen to lead."

"Why... muh legss?" he mumbled, his face slack. The smell of petrichor was overwhelming.

"Just a little dram to make you more attuned to what is about to come. Relax and let it happen. It will be less... terrifying."

Birgr's eyes closed and he began to slide out of his seat, only to stop when his knees bumped into the table before him.

The Lendmann Mother gave a sigh and nodded before looking at the four men who had kept watch over the whole incident.

"Leave us. I have much work to do."

They left with a quick bow, closing the door behind.

A little silver jingle was heard over the sweep of rain as it began to patter heavily into the atrium garden.

"Mother, I did well?" Matilda asked, a hopeful smile on her lips.

171

"Jah, Matilda, you did excellent." She opened her arms to receive her disguised daughter. "I now know the depths of his depravity and what must be beaten out of him."

The Lendmann Mother hugged her daughter and kissed the top of her head.

"Now, to work," she said and walked around behind the unconscious Birgr. Matilda stripped off the padded dress, returning the straight lines of her young figure and walked into the rain sluicing into the atrium. She let it wash off the simple cosmetics of eye kohl and lip rouge, enjoying the feel of the storm. Her face clean, Matilda removed the dainty ankle chains and shackles from under her hangrock dress, as her own house thrall came out to wrap her in a robe and take the girl to change for dinner.

Matilda spared one last glance over her shoulder toward the unconscious Birgr. In the dim light of the storm darkened courtyard, she could see pale blue light come from between the fingers of her mother's hands as she laid them on him and prayed.

21. HOPE FROM AFAR

With the banishment of the Statsraad, the halls of the Kronapalasset were eerily silent. Visedronning Marianne had taken to sitting on the throne in an empty hall, watching the hearth fire burn and Olivr amusing himself with toys he brought from his chambers. Once a day the Privy Council would come and deliver the most basic of news and needs that must be attended to by their monarch.

Without a new Visekonge on the throne and the Visedronning paralyzed by mourning, what could they expect? Or so the gossip of the Forsamling went. The fabric of the nation was tearing, or was it?

Steamknarr still came and trains continued to run on time. Life went on strangely unabated. The Hird had not openly mobilized their men-at-arms any more than before, and the leidangrs had not been called to serve.

The one surprise was the sudden outpouring of treasure from the Crown to all the lands in preparation for the Tronerving's upcoming coronation. Trotes flowed into the Hird banks and people were able to start preparing for the feasts only a few months away like it was a second Christmas.

This helped leaven the mood of uncertainty that had pervaded the people. A worry dampened by greater abundance of drink and food.

All eyes had turned to the capital curious to see what was to come. But Dyrrvatn Kastali was a city of secrets. Outside the palace walls, the city held its breath and placed little trust in the rest of the Union. The Cardinal had been given a cordial but firm summons for the planned Allehelgensdag coronation. This did not please the Cardinal who stoked an ill temper in Ulfshaugrstrond among the clergy, becoming less and less charitable towards the Sveinnaettir. As for the Tronerving's whereabouts, there was much speculation. The story of visiting relatives had fallen apart, but no popular theory had become the favorite replacement in the minds of the Forsamling. Several of the lesser families in the Sveinnaettir began dusting off their genealogies to see if any of them could step up to the throne if the worst should occur.

The one thing no one dared say out loud was that Leif had perished somehow and that his death was being held secret till some clandestine negotiation was concluded and someone new would ascend to wear the crown. Of course, that idea fell apart when people considered the absence of all the Statsraad and jarls in the city. There was no one left to negotiate with. All the jarls held their tongues, too, for time was their friend as well as their enemy.

The Visedronning watched her son play his simple games with his wooden caribou. He was having another race with them galloping around the hearth fire, cheering them on. His play was the only thing that kept her thoughts from obsessing about the rest of her children or Gregor. From time to time, it seemed he was engaged in play with some other child that she could not see, but this did not worry her. Lacking any peers, his penchant for imaginary friends was a constant.

A loud knock came from the entrance to the hall, and the herald rushed in, sprinting up to her.

"My Tign," he whispered, looking wild eyed, "The Athrhuskarl of Djevleportfestning has come with prisoners. They claim to have a message which they will give only to you in person."

"Prisoners? What is this?" she demanded, startling the herald. "When do we give in to demands from prisoners?"

"He would not give any more details, my Tign," the herald added with an extra bow of humility. "He said that there was evidence that proved the need to entertain their request."

She thought for a moment, watching Olivr who had become very interested in the hushed meeting.

"Nurse," the Visedronning commanded, "Take Olivr to his chambers. Herald, call for the Privy Council. When they arrive, show them in and then bring me the prisoners and their captors."

All was done as she asked. Like the wind, the herald and nurse departed on their missions. Within minutes the Privy Council rushed into the hall, confused and fearing the worst. Before any could inquire as to why the sudden summons had been given, the Herald opened the main doors and six prisoners entered, chained together and surrounded by eight huskarls, with the Athrhuskarl in command of the Djevleportfestning leading the way. All who came forward, rendered obeisance to her and the council. She set her stern eyes on the commander.

"Report."

"My Tign," the Athrhuskarl began, "I bring word from the Silfryxen."

"What!" she exploded, launching herself off the throne and down the dias to the armored man. "Who brings this message to you?"

"He does, my Tign." The Athrhuskarl pointed to a bedraggled man at the front of the chain of prisoners.

"Why is he under arrest?"

"They did not arrive on the Silfryxen and were carrying a secret cargo of this." The Athrhuskarl pulled out a small bag from his hip and offered it to the Visedronning. She held out her hand. Into it he emptied cut amethysts, rubies, diamonds and golden coins of various denominations. She gaped at the wealth that dripped from her fingers onto the floor.

"Where did you get these?" she demanded of the lead prisoner, her voice shaking with a myriad of emotions.

"My Tign, these are from your son, my Tign, Tronerving... I meant, the Visekonge... Leif Gregorsson.

"He is returned?" Coins and gems flew as she reflexively put her hands over her mouth.

"No, my Tign, but I do have information for your ears alone. I dare not give it to anyone else, or speak of it in their presence."

"Who of the prisoners know of this intelligence?"

"Just myself, my Tign."

The Privy Council was whispering to themselves. The Minister of the Exchequer's eyes were lighting up with glee at the scattered treasure on the floor.

"Get out," she snapped. "Thank you for your service and loyalty, Athrhuskarl, but you, your men and all the rest get out, but do not leave! I will speak to you momentarily."

Within seconds, the man was unchained and left to stand before her, drawing himself up to a more dignified pose befitting a servant of the Crown. The empty hall's door closed with a gentle boom.

"They must stay?" the prisoner asked looking at the Privy Council as they stood their ground.

"They will stay and you will tell me everything. What is your name?" she demanded.

"I am Kaptein Gramrsson, of the Silfryxen. I sailed her under order of the late Visekonge, Gregor, and grieve at what has happened since our departure so many months ago."

"My son? What of him?" her voice quavered.

"Your son is alive as last I knew. Your daughters as well. God's providence smiled upon us in the darkest of hours." Kaptein Gramrsson gave a bitter smile.

"What happened?"

"We were attacked by vikings who were doing so under the authority of Jarl Vilhoaettir. He tried to take the ship, steal your treasure and murder your children.

The news smote her like a fiery dart from Hell, and the Visedronning burst into tears. She slumped back onto the steps before the throne, unable to stand. The kaptein went to his knees on the floor in front of her.

"My Tign, do not be sad. Your children are in the best hands possible considering the circumstances we found ourselves in. As we speak they are on their way here to you. The Lord God provided us an incredible blessing. He warned us of the full danger we faced, and after the enemy fell upon us, we were sent three Havarian priests who came from out of the wild. One had been with the vikings as a spy who turned against Jarl Vilhoaettir. He gave up all he knew of the traitor's plans. There is a rebellion afoot, and that is why Leif could not come with us.

"Where is your ship?"

"Scuttled to the bottom of Lake Wanishinabinoogi, but not before we scattered the cargo among a dozen or more karvi and knarr and snuck it past the blockade at Barskaborg where they were waiting for us.

"Where... is... Leif?" Her voice was a ghastly mix of grief and raw hate. "Where is my son?"

"The three priests and the Berserker Declan took them into the Ondeaandkorgfjall."

"What?!" She could not contain her terror and burst into great wracking sobs that shook her whole body. The Privy Council was in an uproar shouting all sorts of questions at Kaptein Gramrsson.

"Please! Please!" he shouted, begging them to be quiet so he could continue. "My Tign," he pleaded to her, daring to take her hand to make her look at him.

"My Tign, all is not lost!" his eyes shining. "The three priests are expert in spiritual warfare and have fought demons before. The one, a Friar Inge, came up with a plan to not only find an escape for your children, but also deliver your treasure to you despite almost insurmountable odds. They are escorting all three through this dangerous land with your champion. A berserker with no peers. If anyone can get them through to the shores of the Kisiina Sea, they can."

"What good will that do? We have so little time left, and by foot, there is no chance," Marianne sobbed.

"They are going to meet with the Saami, and with them, find passage on a whaling ship or with seal hunters to bring them to Manvoenlandnaam! From there, it should be easy to come south, and no one in the rebellion could suspect it!"

There was a gasp of appreciation from the Privy Council. The Visedronning looked at them confused.

"This... is a good plan?" she inquired as her sobbing stopped and the first smoky wisp of hope was kindled in her.

"If they can avoid the Skaerslinger and the manitou," the Stallare Marshal said, "there is a very good chance they can reach the Saami as they begin their migration to the southwest."

"But if they go to the coast, finding a seal or walrus hunter would be very possible. They like to trade with the Saami as well, and some of those aettir stay close to the coast for longer times," Admiral Svirisson reassured.

"If those priests somehow know the land or the Saami, or at least find a guide, they will have little trouble. Three priests make for a strong spiritual wall against any manitou or shaman that they might come across."

With a sniff and a laugh, the Visedronning dried her eyes with a handkerchief.

"Thank you, Kaptein," she said and pressed his hand between hers, "For the first time since... I cannot remember when... I can dare to believe again."

She stood up with the help of the kaptein's gentle hand, then he stepped back and waited for her command.

"Go, be with your men who undertook this mission with you, and be the Crown's guest for the night. We will talk more later."

"Greithr, my Tign," Kaptein Gramrsson said and left her presence.

Once he was gone, she looked at the councilors and gave them an expression they never expected to see. It was not only hopeful, it was devious.

"Now, my dear ministers, let us consider what must be done to help my son's return for his throne!"

22. AN ORACLE COMES

Daylight came softly through Birgr's gummy eyes. His head throbbed as if from a night of hard drinking. Thick wool wrapped around his memory. What had happened? How had he found himself in this dim bedchamber that smelled so unfamiliar? He looked out his single window set deep into a plain whitewashed wall. Fine mansions that he did not recognize sat across a small square and the bright afternoon sun cut through the pale blue sky. In the distance, he could hear the clatter of traffic on a mighty boulevard, but only birds seemed to be close by, singing lustily at the day, piercing his ears with their song.

He groaned as he raised himself up to sit in the comfortable bed. Mouth thick and sticky, tasting of bitter copper. The blankets were soft and comfortable. Rubbing his eyes, he surveyed the room further. Clean clothes lay neatly arranged on a stool next to a modest sized wardrobe. His vanity held a glistening glazed pitcher and wash basin. The porcelain chamberpot was clean.

Then he noticed the man, sitting in a plush arm chair set for reading, revealed by a dim slant of light. It took Birgr a moment to realize what he saw. The man was lithe, clean shaven and had dark curly hair. His nose was regal and full lipped, his eyes crystal blue. Birgr had never seen a man who possessed such a face. Something different that his mind could not put together. Was he a priest or faith healer? The man remained still, fingers steepled, elbows on the armrests and bare legs crossed in a dainty manner under his unfamiliar plain cream short robe.

"Who are you?" Birgr's voice was rusty.

"My name is Sabino Agustin. You may call me Sabino," the man said. His accent strange and almost lyrical, his speech held an atypical cadence. "How are you feeling, Birgr son of Jakob?"

"Confused. Tired." Birgr still struggled to remember what happened last night. "How did I end up here?"

"I have no idea. I found you thus and waited for you to wake," Sabino said.

"Found me?"

"Jah." Sabino had not moved save for his inscrutable smile.

"Why are you here?"

"To teach you. Guide you. Give you the knowledge and power to make you into the man this world needs in such times as this."

"Are you the tutor the Lendmann Mother hired?"

"Hired?" Sabino laughed and uncrossed his legs to lean forward. "No. I was not hired. I was sent to bring you forward. Give you wisdom and teach you how to use the power you possess within. How to connect with the greater primordial forces found beyond the veil that you, sadly, have forgotten." Sabino's passion for his appointed task excited Birgr. Every point Sabino made was an intoxicating sip of some piquant elixir. Promises to be fulfilled.

"So you are a warrior and scholar?"

"Better," Sabino said standing up and crossing to Birgr's bed. His robe skimmed the top of his bare knees, the wooden floor did not groan under the weight of his high laced sandals.

"I am your personal oracle."

The revelation took Birgr's breath away.

He gulped. "You were sent by-"

"The ruler of this world and lord of heaven himself, answering the prayers of the Lendmann Mother and so many others."

"Uffda," Birgr whispered in awe.

"Time is short and we have much work to do, Birgr, son of Jakob. There is so much to learn and little time in which to comprehend it all before it is put to use."

"How do we begin?" Birgr asked, leaning forward to Sabino.

"We must pray together and you must offer yourself up to your destiny."

"Wait," Birgr said, pulling himself back from the smorgasbord of possibility now placed before him. His mind whirling on what it could all mean. "What about my wants? I never desired to rule."

"That is because you do not understand what it is to rule," Sabino said, sitting softly on the covers next to the young man, barely denting the mattress under him.

"How do you mean?"

"To rule means to be in charge. To have no one tell you what to do. To set your own course in life. To live as you see fit!"

"But Jarl Evinrudeaettir said-"

Sabino waved off the protest with a charming smile and soft chuckle.

"What he said is irrelevant. In time he will fall down at your feet to worship," Sabino's words were like honey.

Gesturing as if plucking succulent grapes, he elaborated more. "What they want is beneath what you will have. They are the wants of men, not the lord of heaven. You are being chosen to meet the lord's needs and he does not mind if you enjoy sport and women aplenty. Those are the rewards for a faithful novice who does well in his herre's eyes. Fear not. Those shall never be taken from you. As for your desire to prove yourself in battle..." Sabino let the words trail off, watching Birgr lean in, open mouthed.

"Jah?" he said, absolutely enthralled.

"There will never be another Berserker more reknown than you. More powerful than you. More successful than you. You will become a legendary warrior sung about in the Sagas as long as mankind has breath left to sing."

For a long moment, Birgr looked into the smiling face of Sabino, weighing his words. Could this man be trusted? Was he a man? Was he even awake?

"Why me?" Birgr asked.

"For you have been chosen. Centuries before even your aettir existed. Before the Forsamling even came to this land, you were chosen for this task. To be the redeemer of Akiniwazi and heal it from its delusions and corruption. The lord of heaven desires for you to be the instrument to usher in his kingdom for all mankind."

"Then I accept," Birgr burst out, hands trembling.

"Good." Sabino patted the top of Birgr's right hand like an approving uncle. "Lie back, close your eyes, fold your hands and repeat after me."

Birgr did as he was told, mind whirling with visions of himself as a fabled king of old. Like Harald Bluetooth and Beowulf rolled together with the berserkers of legend.

"I, Birgr, son of Jakob Vilhoaettir Fritjovsson," Sabino lead and Birgr repeated, "do give my life and soul to the tutelage and command of Sabino Agustin and to the authority of the Master whom he serves. I bind myself to be his novice and pledge my servitude till released at his pleasure. I open up my heart, mind and body, giving them willingly and completely to the lord of heaven and by my own choice, forever more."

For a while, Birgr lay there trembling with excitement of what was to come.

But nothing happened.

His smile dimmed as he wondered if something should happen next. Was Sabino not to guide him?

Again, only the birds outside could be heard chirping their shrill song, irritating Birgr more.

His thoughts turned dark as the desire to kill that singing bird grew stronger. The innocent twittering cutting at him like a string dragged tight against his neck, burning him with every note.

Unable to contain himself anymore, Birgr threw the covers back to rush the window. Before he could complete the act, a set of rough hands with bristly hair and sharp talons grabbed his shoulders and slammed him to the bed. Wide eyed he looked up and saw a Sabino, twisted into a malevolent blackened form, naked as an animal. His devilish face recognizable, but his form warped by malice and hate beyond man's understanding. Fangs and greenish drool dripping down onto his chest and face.

"Waiting always makes this part sweeter..." Sabino said, "..for me!"

The birds fled in a startled cloud as Birgr's screams shattered the air.

23. IN WHICH OCCULT KNOWLEDGE IS REVEALED

For five days they fled in their stolen canoes. When the current was calm they would nap two by two in each vessel, the others keeping a languid pace, never stopping save for nightfall. Once they determined who worked best together, they kept up a good rhythm. The miles racking up and putting a lot of distance between them and the Skaerslinger, fairly confident Declan's impulsive act saved them from a dogged pursuit.

Edda steered the first canoe, with Finn, Mirjam and Solveig rowing. Bergamot did her best to stay still between Finn and Mirjam. Declan piloted the second with Amr, Inge and Leif rowing. Thyrnir sat in the bow, with what little cargo they had.

It had been a very sad night when they tossed all the food over the side. It bobbed in the middle of the lake, taunting them till they moved around a bend. The lightening of the load did help them in crossing land. The portages had been very difficult at times, clambering down around cliff faces to avoid rapids or falls, while others were simple walks across a few dozen feet of dirt before dipping back into the water again.

Almost all their supplies had run out by the third day, but they dare not stop. It was certain the Skaerslinger pack hunted them. Or were they all Wendigo now? No one was sure, and none wished to go back to find out. The non stop rigor followed by uncomfortable sleep had worn any curiosity out of them, though many questions were on the tips of their minds.

"Brother Finn?" Solveig asked as she reclined, unable to sleep.

"Mmm? What is it, my Tign?" he said breaking out of the exhausted repetition of paddling.

"I have been thinking about what happened."

"As have I. What pesters your thoughts?" Finn asked. Perhaps the mental activity would wake him up more.

"Why did you ask how many fingers the shaman had?"

Brother Finn sighed and looked back at her. She had been sitting on her pack, using oilskins to keep it from getting wet in the bilge they were forced to live with.

"It was a suspicion," Finn said, not desiring to pick up this thread of conversation.

"But, it was strange that he did turn out to have twelve fingers, was it not?" Solveig noted, sitting up.

"No," Finn replied and hesitated as he considered how to best answer her curiosity while giving a few more long strokes of the paddle. "A while back I had come across an apocryphal book of scripture that talked about the times of Noah. The book of Enoch."

He heard Edda grunt at the statement, leaving him unsure of her opinion, but knowing she was very interested to hear what he was about to say. She dug her paddle in to get them around a set of sharp rocks in the thin channel.

"In this book, it talked about some of the characteristics of the Nephilim, who were thought to be the children of women and angels. Some descriptors said they were giants and had six fingers and toes. A few commentaries on the book claimed they had red hair, too. This seems to be corroborated in the Books of Genesis and First Chronicles too."

"So that creature was the child of an angel and a woman?" Solveig surmised in surprise.

"In the strictest sense, possibly. I could not know for sure who Twelve Finger's sire was. He must have come from a mortal woman though."

"Where did you see such a thing, Brother?" Edda asked perhaps a little too sharply.

Finn shook his head.

"I will not say, but for this, the Cardinal and those who follow the Orthodox view believe they had destroyed all of those books in the Union. They are wrong, of course. At least one exists, and I have read it. It is an astonishing book that reminds me of Revelation, save for it talks about the days before the flood, not on the return of the Christ."

"Oh," breathed Solveig.

"But why in just the strictest sense of the word, do you say these Nephilim are the children of angels and women," Solveig was entranced with the thought. It both frightened and thrilled her to the quick.

"Consider. Angels are servant spirits of God, greithr? God does not allow His angels to go around taking wives now, does He?"

"No," Solveig said. Mirjam better propped herself up from her nap to listen.

"So an angel who takes a wife or knows a woman would be what?" Finn asked, pushing off from a rock with his paddle before they hit as they eased through a tight spot in the river that was hardly more than a stream.

"I do not know," Solveig admitted.

"A demon," Finn looked back at her with a grimace. "All demons were once angels. Every last one," he added for emphasis. Finn gave Edda a glance. She raised her eyebrows and nodded in sleepy agreement.

"So Twelve Fingers was devilspawn?" Solveig asked. The thrill and excitement at the idea of a divine lover instantly drained from her.

"Correct."

"So the Wendigo are Nephilim?"

"That I do not know. We know that it is a spirit that can control men... possess them. The Wendigo's spirit turns them into cannibals despite having the food. Perhaps it was an unlucky Nephilim, destined to be a man of reknown and legend, like in the times of Noah, but was awakened one by one of the deep evils of the world. Then, in a short time, it spread more of its brothers throughout that Skaerslinger pack. I dearly hope that Daniel slew them all. Lord Jesus, bless him and his act of sacrifice."

"I saw Twelve Fingers transform into a Wendigo. They are real! We were always told that they were just wives' tales and ghost stories. I suspected if draugr were real, so were Wendigo," Mirjam said, then added in a much quieter voice, "I wish I had never seen proof."

"You saw that?" Finn looked back at her, astonished.

"I did. I also saw Daniel transform."

"Transform?" Finn's heart leapt in his chest with a thin thread of hope he dare not utter. "Into what, dear Tign?"

"An angel. He had a sword of flame and wings of light twice the size of his body. That is what lit our way in the darkness, till Edda found the fires of the pack's camp."

Finn dared not look back at them. He was overcome with joy. When he saw the bedraggled thrall, he wondered, but could not dare to hope such a thing was possible a second time. He began to laugh in relief and covered his mouth. His eyes stung with tears that wanted to fall. His prayers had been answered in a way he never would have expected. Did God send an angel, and put him into bondage to demons, for just that moment to help them escape? Did prayer transcend time as well as all the heavens and earth? His head reeled.

"Paddle, Finn. Paddle. The current is slowing," Edda commanded as she saw him shaking, the handle across his lap. With a jerk, he began helping again.

"Brother Finn?" Solveig asked, worried for the monk.

A loud gasp and snort escaped his lips as he fought to regain control.

"Why is this so upsetting to you?" Mirjam asked. "Would not an angel be a good thing?"

"It is," Finn's voice was but a whisper. "Daniel has saved me before. No," he corrected himself. "No, not me, but one of my wards when I was sent to Kynligrspiejl. All this time, I thought Daniel was the boy's... Reimar's guardian angel. Perhaps he is mine instead?" Finn was amazed at his own words. It was common to believe that you had an angel personally assigned to protect and aid you, but was another matter entirely to meet them and know the lengths they would go to sacrifice for you.

"A guardian angel?" Solveig was astounded again.

"He fought the Azhikwe, with six other angels, and stopped that ancient manitou from taking a child's soul. A child under my protection." Finn was back in the rhythm of paddling with Edda. The other canoe had gone farther ahead, and they all put their backs into catching them.

"If the Nephilim were these men of myth in the days of Noah, how could there be one walking around now?" Edda asked. There was a hint of incredulity to her voice as she probed for the truth.

"I learned that there is a plot afoot among the Skaerslinger to bear children who would become Nephilim. The maidens would know a manitou's host and bear a Nephilim child."

The women were dumbfounded.

"That cannot be possible," Edda burst out.

"They assured me it has already happened."

"Lies." The chorister dug in her intellectual heels.

"Twelve Fingers seems to indicate it is truth despite our wishes," Finn's words snapped back at Edda, and broke through her stubborn rejection.

"I concede that... might be true."

"I do not wish to believe it either, Sister, but I will not deny what I know." He let out a sharp sigh, resigned to his explanation. "For a brief period, I was imprisoned with a Skaerslinger ceremonial 'bride' who was captured on her way to a ceremony. During this pagan ritual she was to become the mother to a manitou's child. In our brief time together, I was the means in which God brought her to salvation, and... uh, and..." Finn did not want to finish. The new realizations had reopened the wound of Sigrid's loss, becoming all the more painful to him.

Sigrid had been telling the truth. There were Nephilim walking the face of the earth for possibly the first time since Noah lived, and that thought terrified him. What hope did they have against creatures of such power?

"Did she know you loved her?" Solveig asked softly.

Finn's paddle froze as it dipped into the water. The question would be a scandal for him. Only his dear friend, Inquisitor Urban, had realized it as they stood on the pier looking out over the black waters of Lake Ogimaque, smoke from the funeral pyre scenting the brisk wind of that chilly night. Finn steeled himself and finished the stroke.

"She is with the Lord now. I will see her again one day."

"Did you tell the Kyrkja?" Edda asked, still thinking with the warrior's mind.

"It was all in my testimony to my confessors and sent to the powers that be. Perhaps it even reached the Visekonge's ear at some point."

It was Solveig's turn to fall silent as that wound was re-salted.

Ahead the sound of rushing water could be heard, and Declan put their canoe in to a gravel shoreline. Edda nosed in just above.

"Is this the last set of rapids before the river goes to Blothugjokull?" Leif asked as they got out to stretch their legs.

Edda got out and walked a little farther down the shore, saw a familiar set of falls and returned.

"Jah. I suggest we have enough lead on any pursuit that we can make camp in comfort. Let us portage down, and camp for the night. That will allow us to forage for some food and sleep well. We all need the rest. What comes next may require all our courage and strength."

24. A FOOL NO MORE

The first light of dawn found the homing dove strutting on the ledge of the Towrnvilhoaettir as happy as you please with a blackened message canister strapped to its leg. The finicky fowl gave the birdkeeper a merry chase out on the ledge as it seemed not quite ready to go back to its cage. People fifty yards below on the streets of Fjellporten watched the poor man chase the errant bird on the ledge, gasping at all the close calls.

Once caught and stowed back in its coop, the coded message made its way to the Jarl's Minister of the Wardrobe who decoded it and then himself flew down the hall to his master's apartment in a frantic state. Such was his haste he forced himself past the huskarls protecting the jarl's door and interrupted the jarl in the middle of passionate embraces with his wife. If it had not been for the content of the message, a vacancy would have appeared in the jarl's court.

What followed was a reckless mad dash on caribouback, not carriage ride, to Barskaborg, with Jarl Vilhoaettir's retinue of a full company of soldiers and his personal huskarls struggling to keep up in their chariots and war carriages. His eyes flashed mad as he blew down the road in the misty morning sun, its golden rays slanting through the trees to the Barskaborg, leaving terrified subjects in his wake.

He made the ride in record time, arriving in the mid afternoon a full mile ahead of his closest escort, caribou nearly dead from the pace they had been driven, sides bloody from crop and heel. Such was the jarl's state as he ran to the draw of the fortress that his own men did not recognize him, the guard rushing to bar his way, polearms at the ready.

"Out of the way you fools!" Jakob Vilhoaettir screamed at them. "Call out the Athrhuskarl! I demand he come to the taxman's dock! Open the gate and blockade the river! Blockade the river!"

Ducking his head, he dashed through the bailey gate of the fortress where he threw himself off the dying animal and rushed for the dock, his commanders scrambling to understand why he arrived in such a state.

The confused men, recognizing their jarl's voice, did as commanded. Ahead, a karvi was undergoing inspection, the official writing out the tax bill for the ship to pass, and a sailor standing ready to make his mark and pay the toll.

The jarl's rude arrival caused a stir of curiosity and fear on the deck of the ship as they saw the chain nets drop with a splash on the down-river side of the bridge, sealing off the channel. What could have possibly happened to create such a fuss?

The taxman handed the sailor his bill and excused himself to meet the jarl who rushed down the steps to the stone dock.

"Taxman!" he shouted. "Have you inspected that ship?"

"Jah, Deres Naade," his confused servant sputtered. He was only an armann and knew his peerage resided on giving flawless service for his master. "We inspected the barrels and crates. Salted fish, dried fruit and nuts going to Hitilopt Island in Ishkodeland."

The jarl fixed his mad eyes on the sailor who's hands had begun to shake. He locked eyes and began to walk toward the man, the stride of a beast of prey.

"Bound for Hitilopt?" the jarl repeated heatedly.

"Jah, Deres Naade. That is where I have been contracted for this cargo. Your armann is holding my manifest," the sailor said, pointing a trembling finger to the paperwork.

Jarl Vilhoaettir drew out his sword. The karvi's master gulped in terror.

"Tis true," the taxman whined. "I have done everything you asked as you desired it. I will show you again, if you wish it. The flustered official stepped back onto the karvi. "Please, min Naade, observe what-"

"Shut your incessant prattling!" the jarl barked, without looking at him. On the bridge above, the river was sealed, red pennants fluttered in the breeze. Up and down the river ships dropped anchor to wait lest they be ordered into the dock and get caught up in the drama. Springbows were at the ready, as well as ballistae loaded with harpax.

On the deck of the karvi, several of the crew milled uncomfortably. The jarl watched them for a moment, then looked at the sailor before him with the queerest of smiles.

"Where, pray, did you purchase your cargo, oh kaptein?"

The tone was almost playful and chilled the man's blood.

"K-kynligrspiejl, Deres Naade," the sailor stuttered.

The first of the jarl's huskarls arrived on the bridge, while the thunder of the full company could be heard approaching farther down the river road.

"I see," Jarl Vilhoaettir sighed, his eyes shining with a horrible glint.

"Armann taxman!" the jarl shouted and his servant flinched as if struck.

Deres Naades?"

"Open every crate in this ship. Search every barrel to the dregs. If any man so resists or dares interfere... kill them all."

The soldiers from Barskaborg poured over the karvi, pushing and shoving the sailors till they were all brought onto the dock. Jarl Vilhoaettir watched as they poured out every container into a ruined mess. The thumping of hard dried fish was joined by billows of the bright smell of cherries and apples, and the sharp clatter of filberts, hickory and black walnuts.

Deres Naades!" Came a shout and all dumping of cargo stopped.

There, halfway through the barrels of walnuts glittered shiny gold coins. Oere, and Ertogs. Silver Pennings by the sackful, and a few heavy Marks lay in the pile, a shocked hirdmann looked up at his jarl. The pile of wealth at his feet was enough to feed a city the size of Fjellporten for half a year!

And that was only half of one barrel!

Jarl Vilhoaettir's eyes flashed to the sailor standing next to him, rage curling his lips into a murderous rictus. He drew back his sword to thrust.

"Stop!" shouted another sailor.

The blade held back by the power of that word.

"I am the man you seek. Spare these sailors, and I will tell you what you want to hear." A tough looking man tried to step forward on his own, but was instantly restrained by the soldiers, dragged before the jarl and forced to his knees.

"You are the one responsible for all this smuggled wealth?" the jarl demanded, as he rested his sword on his shoulder. Dismissively, he slowly pushed the sailor he almost murdered backwards into a pair of soldier's who shoved him back him in line.

"Jah. Just me," this new sailor said.

"And they did not have any ideas on what you were smuggling out of my land?"

"None," the sailor said.

Jarl Vilhoaettir noticed that not only did the man fail to obey proper etiquette and deference due his station, but his eyes were aflame with hate and disgust.

"Who are you?"

"Carpenter Bramsson."

"Ahh," the jarl breathed. "Why would a ship of such small stature require a skilled woodworker on board?"

The man did not answer.

"What was your ship?"

"My ship sank in a storm a few weeks back. I found myself in Kynligrspiejl, thanks to the Havarians who rescued me from the wreck. From there, I negotiated passage most of the way back home to Manitouland through service.

"What ship did you say?" Jarl Vilhoaettir asked again in a calm voice that could not cover the violence restrained behind it.

He watched Carpenter Bramsson with such intensity he was sure the intensity of his gaze gave off heat, but the man did not squirm. No. This karl's insolence and hatred for him was bolstering his courage. It did not matter though, thought Jarl Vilhoaettir. Till ice sealed the lake every ship would be inspected from crow's nest to bilge. Their little scheme was thwarted, and the rest would come filtering down and be plucked out one at a time. The jarl looked at all the witnesses on the shore and several curious ships as to what was happening. The word would spread.

But there was no way to warn any of Bramsson's conspirators! The delicious dilemma warmed the cockles of the jarl's heart.

"What does it matter?" Carpenter Bramsson asked. "If I tell all, will you give your word to let these men go free and unharmed?" the sailor wheedled.

Jarl Vilhoaettir smirked.

"You are in no position to bargain with me. Would you prefer to tell me now, or suffer torture?"

"I am not afraid."

"I thought not," Jarl Vilhoaettir said. "That is why you will be forced to watch them suffer for your sake," he gestured with his sword, "be tortured to death in front of you. Then it will be your turn."

Carpenter Bramsson blanched.

"Quartered... crushed..." the jarl knelt down face to face with the now terrified man. "I even have a Katherine's Wheel and Brazen Bull back in Fjellporten. I promise you, every man here will suffer one of these torments, if not more, because of your recalcitrance."

The carpenter shuddered uncontrollably from the thought of the torments.

"I know the Brazen Bull is so very pagan, but every once in a while, you need such tools to pacify rebellious subjects."

"The Silfryxen," Carpenter Bramsson admitted

"The Silfryxen?" the jarl tasted the name. "Another alias could hardly be more appropriate. Where is she?"

"Scuttled. Her cargo scattered through dozens of ships. We were the last and you will not steal any more of what belongs to the Visekonge, Leif Gregorsson!"

The backhand rocked Bramsson onto his hands and knees.

"You lie," the accusation hissed through Jarl Vilhoaettir's lips like smoke.

"Your Tign's treasure has slipped through your tjovekjakji fingers!"

The flat of the jarl's sword bounced off the carpenter's skull, rending the man senseless for a minute. In that time, he paced back and forth thinking. How many ships could the treasure have been spread across? Could it have been stolen by others?

"You have been beaten, Vilhoaettir. Once Tronerving Leif's coronation is complete, your life is forfeit as the rebel and svikari you are," Carpenter Bramsson taunted.

The jarl whirled on Bramsson with an alarming sneer.

"That is where you are wrong. I know where Leif has run off to and am already moving to intercept him. There is no possible means he could employ to stop this counter."

"Liar," the carpenter spat.

"Oh? Am I now?" Jarl Vilhoaettir towered over the kneeling man. "Then let me leave you with this one word to prove I am telling the truth."

The day stilled, leaning in close to hear the word.

"Sumarpalasset," the jarl uttered, and saw Carpenter Bramsson's heart fail with the weighty dread.

With that victory and proof his intelligence was right, Jarl Vilhoaettir stood up, sheathed his sword and walked away. At the bottom of the steps up to the fortress his huskarls waited.

"Impound the ship, seize the cargo and execute the lot in the dungeon. Leave no trace." He looked at his taxman. "All down-river ships will go through complete inspection till the end of the season."

"Deres Naade," the three men agreed with a salute and bow.

The sound of the jarl's feet was lost in the chaos that erupted on the dock. He never looked back and disappeared into Barskaborg to plot his next action.

25. SECRETS FROM THE LABYRINTH

Father Tuajacksson walked back and forth in a reflective pace following the path of the labyrinth to its center. Like many other days before, he had traversed this course several times already. It was impossible for him to explain why he kept coming back here day after day to walk the path after mass, his eyes half closed, mind stretched to the troubling edges of his imagination.

The sound of the laity working on preparations for the Domkyrkje to receive Tronerving Leif for his coronation that felt too soon yet was so far away. Banners were hung on the columns. The altar was decked out in Sveinnaettir burgundy, gold and white. All things were nearing readiness for a grand coronation after months of anxious waiting.

Parishioners and pilgrims sat, praying near the altar. Others could be found kneeling or laying prostrate in front of small chapels to the saints. Above him dangled a gold rendering of the Virgin, beatific and surrounded by a platinum halo. Colored light speckled the floor as the sun cut through the stained glass on a rare brisk August morn that chilled the stone under his feet. A foretaste of winter to come.

He arrived at the center of the labyrinth again, and like the dozens of times before, he took out the golden ring. The seven arrows from the hollow circle shown in the muted light, mocking him. It had not revealed any of its secrets to him yet. All records had come up with nothing like this simple pattern. No aettir claimed or renounced it, nor sect. No clan, no military unit or ship that existed. Not even a factory. Whatever this symbol was, no one had seen it before, or at least not by him or any other protector of wisdom he knew about. It was no letter from an alphabet either. Not even the forbidden runes of the Gamlehaven.

He moved his feet in rote repetition from each of the six lobes of the center of the labyrinth, praying and asking God for a word of wisdom. As always, silence was his answer.

Why did this ring pull at him so?

Why never more strongly than when walking this particular labyrinth? The one in the cloistered garden outside, or even at the university, did not have the same pull as it did here. Something deep kept drawing him back to this spot turning an idle curiosity into an obsession. He wound his way back out on his path, resigning himself to failure once more.

A sharp clattering of metal on stone startled him just as the last turn to exit the pattern was reached. Father Tuajaksson's hands slapped over his heart and the ring dropped making an almost musical ping on the floor. Finding the source that shocked him so, he saw it was just a clumsy altar boy banging offering plates. The realization struck him at what he had lost. He looked down, ready to search and saw the top of a woman's head picking up the dropped ring.

"You lost something, my son," she said, looking at the bit of gold as she stood up.

"Oj! Thank you Lendmann Mother," Father Tuajaksson gasped. "I do not know what I would have done if I had lost it."

"Oh?" She said, voice as soft as a cat in the night. "Why is it so important?"

He paused. Should he take this lady into his confidence? She turned the ring over in her hand and saw the insignia there.

It was a flutter. Less than the blink of an eye. But he saw it as she handed back the ring. She recognized it! But how? And then she smiled.

"I am sorry," she said, voice low as a pack of pilgrims came in to pray. "I see you cannot speak about it."

"Thank you for understanding, Grevinne Mogrenaettir," he said using her secular title. I would like to entrust you with what I am working on, but I do not have permission from the owner of this ring to do so," he stammered.

"I completely understand. With all the political intrigue that is going on in this city, one must be careful regarding who is trusted." Her smile was warm, but her eyes vacillated between hard stone and controlled warmth.

"I can say this much. I have been puzzling over what it means for weeks. I suppose this is just a strange personal design someone made for their own enjoyment and vanity," he said, praying silently she could not hear the tremor in his voice. Her eyes seemed to relax and the smile, though dimmed a little, looked more natural as her eyes now joined it.

"I am sure if anyone could decipher it, you would," she flattered. "Your reputation precedes you, Brother." The unexpected upgrade in status to her equal caused the tightness in his chest to lessen and he breathed easier.

"I wish I had your confidence in my deduction."

"Do be careful to not focus too long on it, lest you see something that is not there. The human spirit is capable of many tricks we would never expect. Desperation can open a doorway for Satan to meddle."

"I have taken extreme precautions with prayer against occult bewilderment and am secure in my safety," Father Tuajaksson said, puffed up a little more at his own diligence.

"So you meditate on it here?" the Lendmann Mother asked.

"I do. When I am here... there is something in this place that I cannot fathom which makes me feel close to unraveling this riddle. But in the end, nothing comes of it."

He tossed the ring gently in his hand, feeling the weight of it rattle between his fingers, and frowned.

"Perhaps you are pushing too hard," she suggested. Behind her, some of her huskarls shifted, their mail jingling.

"There may be some truth to what you say," he said and turned around to look at the labyrinth and then down at the ring in his hand, holding it up, seeing the gold sparkle in the light.

"Sometimes, putting a problem away helps God come in to grant us an answer as we work on another challenge," she offered.

"I suppose..." Father Tuajaksson trailed off.

His eyes locked on the center of the labyrinth. The six bulbous alcoves of the design commanding his attention. A cold electric chill went up his spine. It made the hair on the back of his neck stand up and then dance in the middle of his tonsured head.

"Father," the Lendmann Mother asked, "you were saying?"

"I..." But the rest of the statement did not leave his lips.

His mouth was dry, tongue sticking to the roof. Without thinking he walked toward the altar of the Domkyrkje and turned to face the main portico. He held up the ring, the long arrow now pointing directly at the Lendmann Mother.

The lobes of the labyrinth center matched the arrows. The angles were the same.

The entrance and exit to the labyrinth matched the long arrow pointing out the door!

"Father Tuajaksson, are you well?"

His heart froze in his chest.

The symbol was for a religious sect! A secret order!

But secret orders were forbidden by the Law of the Halmarkpakt as well as the Kyrkja! They always lead to heresy, and then to bloodshed.

And the Lendmann Mother knew what this symbol meant.

Her two huskarls stepped forward from their respectful distance, hands loose and ready at their sides as they saw the priest acting suddenly strange.

His hand shook. Was this a symbolic labyrinth? What were the arrows pointing out from?

An image of his visit to Ulfshaugrstrond and the Sjuheilagdomen and praying at each of the saint's shrines flashed in his mind.. Each arrow would have pointed to a shrine and the entrance matched the long arrow pointing out toward the water.

What did this mean, and why did the Lendmann Mother suddenly terrify him?

"Your pardon, Grevinne," he said abruptly and gave a slight bow. "I must get back. Many of my duties are waiting for me and I need not waste any more time on such foolishness as this silly design."

The Lendmann Mother's face was a mask of sympathy.

"You are right, for my own duties are insistent as well, and I have my penance yet to do."

"Jah, jah. Thank you my Grevinne for your wise advice," Father Tujaksson said and took to his heels fighting to keep from running like a madman out of the Domkyrkje. The morning, although bright and cheerful, felt menacing with its cool bite.

Once around the corner of the Domkyrkjeplassen, Father Tuajaksson slowed. His legs began shaking and he stopped to lean against the wall of a shop.

The ring that he had squeezed so hard left an angry red circle in his palm. It glittered painfully in the sun. He had discovered part of its secret, and in his spirit he felt that whatever was behind the chunk of gold and onyx was angry.

Then again, what did he have to report to Inquisitor Urban and the Skaerslinger? The symbol might represent a secret order inside the Kyrkja? What proof did he have? None. Only his instinct telling him that this was so. Should he report back to Brother Urban and his comrade? No, not yet, he concluded, the comforting door handle of his library in his hand. Not until he had more concrete thoughts on the matter.

"From now on," Father Tuajaksson vowed, "I must be ever more vigilant and pray that is enough."

With that note of caution to himself, Father Tujaksson started walking back toward the university, looking behind now and again, to make sure no one followed.

26. EVERYTHING ELSE WAITS

"Who are you?" Birgr demanded of the young man.

"Ole Olesson Magniaettir from Fotrishkode, herre,"

"Why are you in Dyrrvatn Kastali?" The demand more threatening than before. The young man looked shaken, not expecting the menace.

"Looking for work. I was told by my uncle, I could make good wages here," he stammered.

"Is there no work in Fotrishkode?" Birgr circled the man who stood at rigid attention like he was being confronted by a palace huskarl.

"My aettir is small, and the Herse has taken a disliking to us. Many of my cousins are refused labor there. I have skills as a smith and even some training as an apprentice mason. I know there is always building to be done here."

"You cannot farm?" The voice was mocking and aggressive.

"No, my herre. I was raised inside Fotrishkode's stockade. Fourth son of a merchant. There is no inheritance and the Kyrkja does not want me."

"Have you found work yet?"

"No, herre. I am hoping that will change so I can stay in the city and not be forced to go into the pinery come winter."

"Where do you sleep?" Birgr persisted.

"A poor family. The Gustavssons. They have no aettir, but proudly fly the Sveinnaettir colors. They give me a place to sleep and a meal for a copper penning a day."

Birgr paused his slow pacing around the man.

"Do not embellish!" Birgr shouted. "Embellishments create flaws in your story and you will be discovered!" he whipped a powerful backhand into the man's meaty stomach, folding him over, but he did not fall. "Names give them a way to track you if the worst happens. Playing to sympathies makes them remember you. Straighten up." There was a beat of silence before Birgr roared "Stand up straight!" and jerked the man up to his full height while he coughed.

Behind the subject of his abuse were several rows of similar men. All ready to test their mettle in battle. They had come from far and wide to join up. They learned their legends and, with the help of conspirators in place, began to seed themselves throughout the guards, guilds and other places of authority or essential jobs in the city. The network had grown quickly in the last few weeks.

Every day, small cadres came to this hidden cellar tucked away under a sympathetic inn to spar, train and rehearse the plan. The cellar was originally built for a merchant guild's private meetings. Many of the stonework decorations still adorned the walls. It had a massive vaulted ceiling that was possibly two hundred feet in length, arched lengthwise with thick ribs an eighth of that apart allowing them to practice archery.

Light was provided from large silvered lamp sconces. On one end was the staircase in a small alcove, the other was a storage space hidden behind curtains. Several pews had been pushed to the sides and stacked neatly. At the other end, an altar stood, white stone stained like an old butcher's block and large enough for a man. Above that altar hung a large tapestry of Mary. She was adorned like a Visedronning, but no sign of the infant Jesus as was typical. Instead, she was attended to by six angels. From the moment Birgr first laid eyes on it, it made him ill at ease. Almost queasy.

A small chime jingled from somewhere behind the walls.

"Get out, all of you," Birgr ordered turning his back to them, looking ahead to the altar at the front of the room, trying not to focus on the tapestry behind it.

"Wait in the mead hall. I will send for you when I am ready."

"Jah, Deres Naade," the men responded. There was the sound of weapons and armor being gathered up and feet climbing the flight of stone stairs. Then silence.

In the silence, he remembered Sabino.

Had that been a dream? He remembered the pain of the creature as it entered his body. Soaking into his flesh like water into cloth.

Sabino's laughter and roar of triumph.

The sensation of drowning, breathing something other than air.

The terror of being consumed by a giant beast and then the bliss of oblivion.

A part of the wall slid to the side on a well greased track, only a dim thud of it opening fully could be heard.

The Lendmann Mother entered smiling at him, without thinking he knelt on one knee, face to the ground.

"The training is going well?" she asked, her tone curious, clearly feigning ignorance, walking around the vaulted chamber.

"It is progressing slower than I would like, Grevinne Ulla," Birgr said as he rose. "But we will be ready. Several are in place with the Kyrkjaguard. Others have joined the Leidangr and have reported on their garrison strength. It is formidable, but not insurmountable."

"This is good to hear. How do you enjoy your training space?" She gestured about the chamber.

"It has been excellent for our preparations," Birgr said, his mouth quirked reflexively as he looked at the woven image. The eyes of all eight figures followed him. The angels' coppery hair seemed to flow in a wind that did not exist. He looked away and back to the Lendmann Mother.

"That is good news. It helps quench my mood at the moment," she admitted.

"Something displeases you, my Grevinne?" Birgr asked, as he followed her down toward the altar and the disturbing wall hanging.

"It seems a distinct threat to us has been revealed. Her voice was brittle with suppressed anger, echoing sharply against the wall.

"Someone knows?" Birgr asked, aghast.

"No. A deeper threat has been uncovered." She turned to face him. Eyes burning with a pure hatred that came from beyond the veil. A dim echo of the hatred seen in Sabino's face. A playful thrill of fear skipped up his spine.

"Something that must be addressed. You are the only person I dare trust to deal with it," she said, her voice wire taut.

"Name it, and it shall be done," Birgr whispered, feeling her worry.

"There is a priest who has a ring in his possession. I must have it at any cost." The Lendmann Mother's lips were stiff, twisting the sound of her words.

"It shall be done." He spoke without thought. She must have thought him flippant.

"That is not all, my dear boy." She swallowed hard, a smile fought to cross her lips "This priest must die. It must not arouse suspicions."

"Greithr," Birgr agreed, uncertain of what answer she wanted. "Do you have any desire for how?"

She advanced on him like a draugr, stiff legged and deliberate.

"It must look like an accident, and all evidence of this ring must vanish."

"Where might he keep this ring or his evidence?"

"I doubt it would be any place another person might find it. Go to his home. My suspicion is he would keep it in his chancery. If he knows what he has, he would hide everything there in a safe place close at hand. Bring anything relating to the ring back to me, and I will deal with the rest."

"When must this be done?" Birgr asked.

Behind the Lendmann Mother, the images pretended to move again. One of the angels, with a hand on its sword now gripped it even tighter. There was the faint sound of creaking threads like a distant sail under a strong wind. In the far attics of his mind, he heard Sabino's malicious laughter. His mouth went dry and tasted of copper.

"At once. Everything must wait till you complete this task," she said and fussed with the medals pinned to his heraldic sash.

"Impossible. We have too many ventures tonight that cannot be cancelled. What about-"

The suggestion never left Birgr's mouth.

The Lendmann Mother's hand shot out and grabbed him by the throat with a thick slap of meat. Her eyes now blazed like a fire, a window into hell itself. She jerked him off his feet and he hung in the air, lifted like a throttled kitten.

Terror overwhelmed him but he was unable to scream. With the bang of his metal greaves she slammed Birgr to his knees, her hand clutched hard enough that her nails dug deep into his tender throat and she wrenched his head sideways with a jerk.

"Everything else," her voice growled with chilling power, "waits!"

Birgr grabbed instinctively at her arm. It was like touching a glazer's furnace under her robes. He could not choke or gasp. Not even a gurgle escaped his lips. Only a sickly clicking of his tongue in his mouth.

"Do you comprehend this simple task?" her voice tore at his ears. "You are not your father's pawn anymore. You are mine and you will obey the orders I give you and the tasks I need done or you will never receive the crown."

Birgr tried to nod but could not. Bright white sparkles started edging in on the sides of his dimming vision. Sabino's voice echoed in his mind once again but contained a note of fear toward the being that had Birgr by the throat. "As you desire, my herre," said Sabino through Birgr's lips.

It had not been a dream, and the realization of whom he had chosen to ally himself with was driven home. Worse, it was too late to escape.

The Lendmann Mother released his throat to the sound of a loud gasp as he fell to his hands.

"Now," her voice back to normal, sounding relieved, "Are you ready for your instructions, my dear boy?"

"Jah, Deres Naade," Birgr gasped. He knew better than to try and get up till she gave permission. "Who must die?"

The Lendmann Mother's mouth twisted into the smile of a wolf and she began to instruct him on all he needed to know.

27. BECOMING THE MONSTER

It had not taken Birgr long to find the address, but he found it more difficult to remain unnoticed. Father Tuajaksson had a small three level home, sandwiched in the middle of a row of similar houses, almost touching with their upper floors, but a body could walk in between them. He had watched from the comfort of a tavern as Father Tuajaksson's assistant came and went. A man came to the door after dark, rang the bell. A chambermaid opened the door. Over the boisterous clattering of men drinking and playing Tafl, he saw the maid say something to another person still in the house, then leave with her escort by the light of a swinging lantern. There must be one more person in the house, and therefore his victim was safe. Birgr's temper began to grow hot as the hours crawled by.

As the rain became a fine mist the tavern filled with men who wandered in to escape the miserable night. It was becoming entirely too busy to stay. As he started to rise, he spotted a trio of militiamen. They walked with heavy steps, lacking the discipline to march as was the custom. Their large lantern on a long staff swinging sloppily with their weariness, poleaxes shouldered.

211

They slogged past complaining about the need for more watches, even on nights like this. Birgr waited, heel tapping, as they disappeared down the street. Once certain the militiamen were gone, Birgr took his leave while the taverner was in the tap room and the rest of the inebriates were distracted by the alewife's bawdy antics.

The gentle tapping and splashing from downspouts and overflowing rain barrels made it impossible to hear if anyone was about. Although the deserted street was nearly pitch black, Birgr found his eyesight unhindered by the gloom. He took up a new post to watch in a thin alley across from his victim's house as the fog began to rise.

"It is time to begin, Birgr Son of Jakob," Sabino's voice said softly in his ear. Birgr flinched away from the voice then turned to face it. Nothing was next to him in the thin alley.

Sabino gave a friendly laugh at the fright he had given his novice.

"Listen to your instincts. Hear with your soul, and do what I say."

"What must I do?" Birgr said to Sabino.

"You will come with me," his oracle said. "Lean back against the wall, close your eyes. I will do the rest."

Birgr did as he was commanded, relaxing as much as he could and let out a soft sigh.

There was a sudden jerk, like twitching in bed, and Birgr floated free of his body, Sabino grasping his hand tightly. With a gasp Birgr saw a silvery cord back to his heart from his now separated soul.

"There we are. Now we can work. Our lord will not tarry long. We must not keep him waiting."

"Him? Do you not mean her?" Birgr said, entranced by the beauty of the night that surrounded him.

Through the veil, the night appeared as if it was painted by a master artist, drunk out of his mind. Idealized and somehow exaggerated. His surroundings seemed to throb and breathe with the light of emotion and history. Places and things connected with happiness glowed while sadness and misery were dark but just as lush.

Sabino gave a soft chuckle. "She is only a vessel for our lord. A servant from whom he graces the world with his presence and sends forth his oracles."

Birgr turned to look at Sabino. For a moment, he expected to see the horrifying creature that he last saw.

Instead, he saw a being of light. Refined and vibrating as if a plucked harp string could have color and shape. He glowed softly in concert with the night.

"Remember, Birgr son of Jakob, I am your mentor as well as your servant. But as you now understand, we are all servants to someone whether we know it or not," Sabino reminded.

Birgr nodded like an astounded child.

"Now," Sabino said, pointing to the door of Father Tuajaksson's home. "Imagine yourself at his door."

Birgr did. With a sudden dragging sensation and rush of wind, he stood before the door without moving. When he looked back, the silver cord floated in the air like rope in the water.

"No more! This is too much!" Birgr bemoaned, unable to come to terms with what was happening.

Sabino jerked his arm and snarled at him. "Quit mewling! We have work to do and if you are not about it quickly, I will show you the consequences when you fail in your duty!"

Birgr tried to jerk away but Sabino's vice-like grip prevented it. His soul scrabbled and clawed to escape like a feral cat hung by its tail. Birgr's thoughts expressed instantly to action on this side of the veil.

Sabino flared a terrifying red-beyond-red and grabbed Birgr's silver cord with both hands, twisting and kinking it.

The pain was apocalyptic, drawing a wail and leaving Birgr's soul to float like a drowning swimmer.

"Calm yourself, or the pain will get worse. You cannot hide your thoughts here like you can in your flesh, Birgr son of Jakob. I see you more clearly than you ever could imagine. There can be no lies here, for here, there are no inner thoughts. Here you are your inner thoughts," Sabino threatened and gave an extra twist that left Birgr a twitching ball. From across the street, Birgr's body spasmed and fell over into the mush.

"If I tear this cord, you will never be able to return to your flesh and your usefulness will be at an end, but your eternal torment will begin. Are you ready to obey now?"

Sabino's voice was soft but had the same threat of a punch to the face.

Birgr wanted to vomit, but could not. His revulsion was like a stench on him but he nodded. Sabino released his silver cord and Birgr floated free again, the kinks and twists unwinding in an ethereal breeze.

"Then get up and we shall go inside to prepare the way. Walk through the door and let us see what is there."

Birgr closed his eyes did as commanded, passing through solid wood and iron like they were mist.

Inside, several furnishings in the priest's plain main room glowed with warm light, while others possessed a grime and ichor on them. There seemed to be no rhyme or reason to it. It may be as simple as a cloak on a hook that glowed, or a candle stand that dripped with shadow.

Sensing his question, Sabino answered. "What you see are blessings and curses, and the manitou attached to them. There are angels and demons for more tasks and appointments than you can imagine. Even the stars in the sky have names and sing. The same is true here. Be mindful of what you touch and commune with, for they will be given authority to act in your life," Sabino warned as they passed through the kitchen. An iron kettle off the fire in the small hearth licked with divine flame. From the scullery, dirty pots and pans writhed with infernal spiders and worms. Birgr recoiled from the sight.

"How is that possible?" he sputtered.

"This is the realm of the spirit. The gap between heaven and earth. It is a place of truth."

They floated up like swimmers to the third floor to Father Tuajaksson's chancery which was shoved tight into the gable of his house. They passed through the door and found Father Tuajaksson inside, scribbling notes at a desk that sat beneath the lone arched window, curtains drawn. The walls were covered in curious shelves that held thousands of tomes and angled in with the gable, looming over the priest as if they were ready to fall, enveloping him in their stored knowledge. The ring sat under a small candelabra on the desk, winking with the flame's flicker like a lighthouse in smoke. The sight of it caused Birgr to rear back, face stretched in a horror he could not comprehend from the shadow that lay upon that golden circle. The symbol a cruel spray of seven arrowheads. There was a watchful malevolence to it that had no need of eyes, but knew all that occurred around it. Something so horrible, it did not venture close to this realm.

"That is what she wants?" Birgr asked, desiring nothing more than to flee from it.

"It is, and do not forget the notes."

Behind them, the door opened with a knock.

"Father, I am going home now," an old man said. His body glowed with God's grace. In his wake flowed several small angelic beings like hummingbirds, zipping to and fro. They shrieked at the sight of Birgr and Sabino, drawing little swords, but did not leave the servant or attack, acting like tiny watchdogs barking at a stranger. As the man walked to the father, the small flock pushed back against the man, stopping him a mere step before he touched Sabino or Birgr.

Sabino laughed at the flock who would not strike first, but made it clear they would retaliate.

"See?" Sabino said through snickering. "They are bound by God's laws to their task. They too function only where they are allowed. These little pests can only defend their subject."

"The Lord rebuke you," the little cloud shouted in a chorus of tiny voices. Birgr suddenly felt a sting, like a hot ash falling on his skin and it was gone just as fast. Sabino laughed harder.

"Good night, my son," Father Tuajaksson said, scooping the ring out of sight and turning to face his servant. "May the Lord bless and keep you. May His face shine upon you and give you peace," the priest blessed, finishing with the sign of the cross. Sabino jerked back from between the two, as if he would be struck by thrown axes. The angels around the man flared with light and gave a strange singsong sigh of joy and praise.

Sabino now snarled at them and the servant gave a shudder.

"Uffda! Someone walked over my grave," he said and rubbed his arms and back of his neck. "Be careful tonight, Father. Some ill spirit is lurking about."

"You watch yourself and carry your lantern high," the father said with a smile.

"I will. God bless you."

The servant closed the door, footsteps thumping carefully down the steep stairs.

"Quick, back to your body. Your chance is here," Sabino urged, all but throwing his novice back into his body.

Birgr awoke with a gasp, and in a pool of slime and refuse. With a retch, he stood up. Spitting his mouth clean of the taste, he staggered across the street.

"Quickly! He is leaving by the back door. Get to the alley."

Birgr ran across the street, and slid through the narrow gap that wove between the houses. The lane behind connected a half dozen small courtyards that servants, thralls and delivery men used instead of the main boulevards, helping hide the business that is required for everyday life in city society.

The door opened and the old cook walked out. Birgr was surprised at what he saw. A man in his late years, worn down by a life of hard work and servitude. Frail and forgettable. But what he had seen standing at the edge of the veil burned in his mind. The flock of angelic hummingbirds did not reveal themselves, but he was sure they were still there. The cook took a moment to lock the door, gave a thick phlegmatic cough, and shuffled away, golden light of the lantern swaying as he went.

Birgr slipped up to the door and gave the latch a try. It clicked open.

"I saw him lock it," Birgr thought.

"And I stopped it from latching," Sabino answered. Birgr looked at the lock and saw that the loose bolt had missed its bar.

"Was it always loose?" Birgr wondered.

"What do you think?" Sabino gloated. "Now do your duty."

Birgr made his way through the stairs in the kitchen and pantry. It looked like any other he had seen before. Nothing looked strange or supernatural, but the sight of the scullery made him shudder. After seeing the priest's home from the spiritual side, it was depressing to see such humble accommodations.

He began climbing the steep flights of stairs up to the chancery. The boards creaked and popped under his slow step. How he wished they would be quiet.

"Did you forget something, my son?" Father Tuajaksson said from above. Birgr froze, and did not answer.

"Hello?" the voice held a tremor to it. Birgr could almost taste the fear in it, sharp and salty.

There was the scrape of the chair and popping of floorboards.

The chancery door opened, and the dim light of the candles lit the top of the hall. Father Tuajaksson did not venture any further than the landing threshold. Birgr smiled to himself as he watched from the bottom of the last flight of steps out of sight from the terrified priest. The sensation of power the emotion gave him was like strong drink leaving him giddy and wanting more. The priest closed the door again and with another scrape of his chair returned to his desk. Birgr began to ascend once again.

"Who is there?" came the voice of Father Tuajaksson, enfeebled by fright. "I am armed!"

Birgr fought to keep from laughing out loud as he reached the landing at the top of the stairs.

"I shall call the militia," the voice all but a whisper as Birgr's footsteps came closer.

Birgr turned the knob. With a loud pop as the latch released, the door swung open by its own weight, revealing his filthy, wet appearance.

Father Tuajaksson let out a squeak at the sight.

Birgr walked forward with a funeral pace, elated with the sensation that being the monster in the night brought, luxuriating in the thrill of the hunt like he never had before.

"I have no money," Father Tuajaksson whispered.

"I am not here for money," Birgr whispered hoarsely.

Something in Father Tuajaksson's mind snapped.

"Hail Mary full of grace, the Lord is with thee," he began to chant frantically, hand blindly scrabbling for his rosary.

Sabino cursed. "Now. Now! Before something shows up to interfere!" shouted Sabino from the other side of the veil.

The memory of the little angels and the ash-hot stings of their rebuke came to mind, and Birgr did not wish to experience what a more powerful angel could do.

In a flash Birgr was across the scant paces to the priest and delivered two hammer blows to the priest's chest with his fists. The thick meaty blows were punctuated with the stick-like snap of bones, and the whoof as all the air was driven from Father Tuajaksson's lungs.

Euphoria burst in Birgr's head. He never felt so alive as the priest crumpled in agony at Birgr's feet, unable to groan, heart stopped by the violence of the blow, slowly dying.

For a long time, Birgr stood over the man whose body went into convulsions, jerking him like a fish on a hook, desperate to keep his crippled body alive. Then with a final tremulous shake, all was quiet. Not even a final sigh, for no breath remained in his lungs.

The emotions from taking his first life left him dizzy and unsteady.

The rain had returned, pattering on the roof drew him back to the world from the strange peace he had been drifting in.

"Congratulations, Birgr, Son of Jakob. You have shed a man's blood," Sabino whispered. "Now you understand the joyful experience of it all. The privilege of the mighty and chosen is to take or preserve life as their conscious sees fit. Relish it."

"Is it always this way?" Birgr thought.

"Yes."

Somewhere deep in Birgr's spirit, that answer tasted sour. It troubled him for a moment then was gone as he looked at the journal Father Tuajaksson had been writing in and the other books filled with his study and thoughts on the ring and what it represents. None of it made sense to Birgr, as his Latin was poor and passages appeared to be encoded.

"Do we know this is all?" Birgr thought to Sabino as he emptied a satchel full of books, replacing them with what he needed.

"We did not have time to interrogate him, and his spirit has already been collected."

The Angel of Death had come? Birgr's hands moved with haste. What else might happen? Would other spirits talk? Birgr picked up the ring and looked at it. Now nothing more than a decorated gold band and signet trimmed with onyx. Something any member of the Hird would wear.

He carefully wrapped it in the scrap of cloth that Father Tuajaksson had used and put it in his purse.

With a light grunt, he picked up the corpse of the priest, walked to the top of the stairs. What he was about to do felt crude, making his lip curl. The priest's falling body made a terrific noise as it slammed and slapped down the hard wooden stairs, coming to rest in an undignified heap at the bottom.

"Oj, for a horn Aquavit right about now," Birgr muttered. He picked up the satchel, tiptoed around the battered corpse, and left through the back door, hearing the latch lock behind him.

28. A WILD & PRICKLY SMORGASBORD

It was quite possible Edda's idea was madness, but no one could provide a better plan. Despite the nerve-wracking wait of an extra day to build up their strength before they attempted the plan, their flesh was thankful. The delay also gave the Skaerslinger a chance to catch up, or they could be discovered by the Wendigo at Blothugjokull if they ranged away from their unholy shrine. A shrine they must sail past as fast as they could in the bright of day. Edda insisted the daylight weakened their pursuers, which would make it possible to shoot the rapids into the Thrjujokulldalr and escape before they could be caught.

They made the most of their day of rest and the small company foraged for as big a meal as they could find. The bounty of the land smiled upon them and they would be able to eat better than they had in two weeks.

Several nut trees and a meadow full of berries yielded a delicious haul as well as a half dozen varieties of greens that none of the Visekonge's children had ever considered eating.

Inge found a crabapple tree and stripped of its early season fruit. Amr risked his life collecting honey from a hive. Tea was made from pine needles. From the river, they harvested several cattails and scavenged river clams and crayfish to boil.

Mirjam killed a large porcupine she found lounging in the branches of a tree with her springbow. Finn had assured her the meat was safe, and Edda knew how to butcher it. Her skill yielded a lot of meat and no one was stuck with the quills.

"Where is Declan?" Leif asked suddenly, as the shadows of evening began to deepen.

Edda looked up from the bloody mess of her butchering job.

"He and Solveig went out looking for more food on the other side of the stream," Mirjam added. "Declan found a small pond on the far side. Said it had a lot of watercress."

"I would feel better if we all stayed in camp from now on till we leave."

Amr stood up from the fire, clapped his hands clean of dirt.

"I will fetch them. I know where they went."

"Take care," Leif cautioned.

"I shall bring Thyrnir. The two of us will be fine," Amr said with a smirk and jogged off into the pinery, Skaerslinger spear in hand.

The five who remained watched him cross the river at the nearby ford and vanish.

Finn shook his head. "One of these days that indestructible attitude is going to end him. "The words came out more as a hope than a regret.

"Not before we reach Dyrrvatn Kastali," Mirjam said.

"Of course. My personal feelings aside, we need him. Consider all the good things he has been doing so far," Finn said forcing himself to sound more appreciative, although he questioned why God would have put someone like Amr in their midst.

"Agreed," said Inge. "Just never forget what he is."

"I never will. You can stake your life on that one," Edda said tossing some meat to Bergamot.

"Speaking of Dyrrvatn Kastali," Inge began and sat back on a log they had moved near the fire, "what designs do you have once we get passage on a ship, my Tign?"

Leif crunched a hickory nut with a pair of rocks.

"What I desire is to make it to the Sumarpalasset. There we will find a company of my soldiers and huskarls. At that point, I surmise that our trip will be more about ceremony than survival, as I will be escorted in Sveinnaettir lands all the way up the Athrfljot to home and my coronation."

Both he and Mirjam gave a deep sigh of longing for the triumphal return. She giggled at their synchronous act.

"Then," Leif said with a chuckle, "I will rally our forces and go to war against the Jarl Vilhoaettir and his traitorous allies. His head will be on a spike at the gates of the city for all to see before next year is out, if I have my way. Crush your enemies quickly and decisively. That is the way my ancestors kept the peace for two and a half centuries and I shall do the same."

The casual bloodthirst surprised the others.

"If you depose the Vilhoaettir, who will take their place?" Edda asked, brushing an errant strand of hair out of her face using her wrist to keep blood off her face.

"I have no idea, yet, but if I must I will use the hand of Solveig to find someone more deserving of those lands. It would be best to incorporate them into the Sveinnaettir holdings as we have so much property there. I will have to find a cousin or some retainer I trust well enough to do it.

"The jarls will be wroth if you do that, my Tign," Inge warned.

"If I could trust a Vilhoaettir, which I doubt I can after this, who would I choose?" Leif asked, cracking open another nut and taking a swig of the pine needle tea with a grimace.

"I am just counseling you against upsetting the order too dramatically. Do not plan a war before your army is before you. The Union is in a delicate state. It may never have been in more danger than it is right now. You might have some in your own aettir who will contend against your reign."

Leif smirked and shook his head.

"My kin are loyal, through and through. There is no chance that any of them would turn against me."

Inge was about to push the issue when he saw Mirjam's worried wave that Leif could not see. He gave a faint nod in return.

"It sounds like you are a fortunate man indeed, my Tign," Inge said changing his tone.

Leif considered Edda for a moment. "In fact, I hope to be able to reward Saelirskjol once we have taken charge of this land. For all you have done, a great reward is due," Leif said changing to a happier subject.

Edda paled, meat half skewered for roasting in her hands.

"My Tign, that is quite generous, but not necessary," her voice was faint.

"Of course it is!" he said with a grin. "We never could have made this trek without you."

"Oh, you are being too kind. Really, you must not go to so much trouble for us. We are fine as is."

"But what about the Wendigo? At least we should send up the Ragnarites to clean that out."

Edda's movements were slow and precise, as if to make one mistake of putting the meat over the fire could result in her death.

"My Tign, please. Understand that, for us, it would be the opposite of help. We are fine and safe. Do you not recall our defenses? The Ragnarites would create unexpected turmoil and bloodshed there. Having your soldiers around would put their lives at risk with little gain. We are half a month's travel into the depths of the Ondeaandkorgfjall. None of your subjects live up here, save for the Saami, who wander with the caribou. The winter is long and hard, and the Wendigo are but one demon that infest these ranges. I beg you, my Tign. Leave it the way God intends."

Leif was thunderstruck by her refusal.

"We appreciate the gratitude, and we have been very blessed to have served you, my Tign, but we wish a simple life," Edda tried to explain.

"I do not believe you. What is the true reason why?" Leif demanded, insulted.

Edda looked to Finn and Inge to see if somehow they could help her explain.

"My Tign-" Finn began, but was cut off.

"But he knew about Saelirskjol," Leif said pointing at Inge.

"Jah, I did. But that was before it became what it is now," Inge said.

"There is another reason that Saelrskjol exists in secrecy. We must protect it," Finn tried again, but was ignored.

"And what is it now?" Leif snapped.

"A refuge for Skaerslinger and fredlause. All those outside the law. Those who cannot or will not live like normal Forsamling," Inge said, indelicate as ever.

Edda's eyes pinched closed at the description and let out a pained sigh.

"Tactful Inge," Finn said.

As the words sank in, Mirjam groaned in the realization, shame burning her cheeks.

"Leif, it is more than just an orphanage for children and lost miners looking to get back home. It is a home for the homeless," Mirjam said gently.

"Everyone?" Leif was dumbfounded.

Edda nodded, confirming the Kronadottir's words.

"Everyone there is a fredlaus either to the Crown or to the Kyrkja. If you send in your army or the Paladins come, they will slaughter Saelirskjol, and under our laws would be well within their rights to do so," Mirjam said putting the pieces together. "They are your subjects in name and desire, but not by law. They never can be, nor would you want them all to be anything more than loving allies of the Sveinnaettir."

Edda was unable to look at the Kronadottir who had given her unspoken fears the voice she could not.

"Oh," Leif said, surprised. His brow furrowed.

"My Tign," Edda began, "if you truly wish to honor us, forget that we exist. Keep us close to your heart and in your prayers, but do not send us help. We could not survive it. Know that despite our status, we choose to be your friends and allies outside the law and, as a whole, harbor no ill will against you or the Crown. Although I cannot speak for every individual, as you cannot for your own aettir, I think our actions have proven that beyond question."

Leif nodded, cracked another nut and ate it, mulling over this new information.

"Regardless, I will not be going with you all the way back to Dyrrvatn Kastali," Edda announced.

"Why?" Leif blurted out but then realized the reason was moot as soon as it was spoken.

"Inge and I will escort you as promised till you are safe among your trusted retainers," Finn added. "Besides. Someone needs to keep an eye on Amr. He will follow you till his scheme comes to fruition... whatever that may be."

"What is his scheme do you think? Could he be an enemy agent?" Leif asked.

"I do not know, but it seems that you are at the center of whatever he has planned. Again, my own feelings aside, Amr would never have fallen in with vikings and traitors like that. They are too..." Finn paused, twirling his hand in the air as he searched for the right word, "vulgar. Jah, vulgar is the right word. His tastes and skills are too refined for the likes of them."

"Then what was he doing among such men, I wonder?" Inge conjectured aloud as he gazed into the glowing coals of the fire.

"Whatever he has concocted, it is subtle, and for someone else's gain. Not just his own. Men like Amr are always servants to something of greater power. He is also mercenary enough to change to the winning side without a moment's hesitation or loss of sleep."

"Then why not stay with the Jarl Vilhoaettir?" Edda wondered. "Forgive me, my Tign, but he had you right where he wanted. Till Amr revealed his plans, you would have blundered blindly into his trap."

"Jarl Vilhoaettir is not as powerful man as he thinks he is," Inge said. "And he is crude. Both things are offensive to Amr."

All laughed at the double insult.

"But consider. Status matters," Inge continued. "Your patronage is far greater than the jarl's ever could be. Even if he manages to take the Crown, he is then beneath his son."

Inge saw the frown from Leif. "My apologies, my Tign, but just think about it. No one has more status or stature in the world than you do. That is the orbit Amr craves to be in. He does not have designs on the Crown or political power that I can see. I am not even sure what bishop or curate he serves. It is doubtful he is his own man. The Kyrkja would not allow it, let alone his own ambition."

"Amr is also a zealot. For what or whom I do not truly know. He worships God with some of his actions, but his others make me wonder what God that is," Edda sniped.

"Jah, he has always been zealous. That has not changed over the years. What you see is his fervent belief in the Orthodoxy's infallibility and authority. He cannot be working against God because he is serving the Kyrkja and the Kyrkja is the will of God because universal magisterium is how the world works in his mind."

"You do not believe the same?" Leif asked. Finn thought for a moment, choosing his words with care. The smell of the roasting porcupine was making their mouths water. They had not tasted meat on the fire since before the treesqueaks.

"No. I do not believe in the implied infallibility of man or Kyrkja, even if it comes through the Pope to Cardinal Klaus, and by extension every other member of the clergy. I have seen proof enough in my life that great evil masquerades as righteous authority. That is one of several reasons why I am called a heretic by many. On this truth I shall not recant."

Leif nodded and Inge shook his head in sympathy.

Finn tossed another log of wood on the fire, forgetting there was meat roasting. Edda cuffed him on the shoulder.

"Oj! That one is yours. Just so you know," she said pointing to the roast that was speckled with ash. Finn shrugged and smiled.

"No more than I deserve."

The shadows had begun to blend in the fading evening and the light of the fire grew prominent.

"Leif," Mirjam hazarded to speak.

"Jah?"

"Who are you going to marry Solveig off to?" Mirjam's words were so delicate they seemed to hang in the air like cottonwood fluff, afraid to land.

"I do not know. Possibly to the jarl who's support I most need."

"But you will not have the authority to use me and her as leverage. Neither of us are in line to the throne anymore. What good would that do?" Mirjam protested.

"Ties to power are still ties to power," Inge said as he stared hypnotized into the fire. "You see, my Tign, Leif can still use you and your sister to mollify the more cantankerous jarls. Being that he is now the head of your aettir, this is well within his right."

Mirjam's eyes burned holes through Inge. When the silence became too long, he looked up at the rest and saw the shock and anger on the faces of Leif and Mirjam.

"God's twinkling toes," he muttered, "please forgive me, my Tign. I have been very rude this evening."

Mirjam's hard eyes glistened and a tear rolled down her cheek. She gave a loud sniff. Inge realized how grevious a wound he had caused the girl.

"I am sorry, my dear sister," Leif consoled, "but he is right. I need both of you and your hands in marriage to stabilize this Union."

Tears ran down both Mirjam's cheeks. Unable to speak, she walked down to the edge of the water to be alone with her pain.

Leif gave a bone weary sigh.

"Perhaps," he whispered, "when all is said and done, she will some day forgive me, and Solveig too."

29. THE DROWNED FOREST

Amr returned a few hours later, with Solveig and Declan in happy tow. Although their food collection had not been so robust, they had caught a turtle and several large frogs. The evening disappeared into night with little conversation. Everyone around the fire seemed to be protecting a secret.

They woke at first light, before the trees could even be separated from the black horizon. Rekindling their fire, they ate the remnants of what was foraged yesterday and loaded up the canoes. They had so few supplies now. Long gone were the iron harpoons and saxes. Reduced to using Skaerslinger flint and obsidian was frustrating for those used to the consistency and durability of metal.

Under a crystal clear sky of pale blue, morning mist gave an ethereal quality to the thin river as it glided through the sparsely wooded valley. The long bodies of glaciers flowed down from both sides of the valley and peeked between scattered trees and outcroppings of rocks now and again.

"The last time I was here," Edda said pointing up to a small gap between two peaks, "I came out there. It is a much more gentle grade on the eastern face. The view of the glacier is startling. It is so astonishing, you are drawn to it."

"You were lucky to escape with your life," Finn said.

From behind him, Bergamot whined. She had been laying on the floor in bilgewater for days, miserable. Every day it came in faster due to the beating this trip was giving. It was astonishing how much abuse these light craft had taken so far and still functioned well, but they were no wooden dugout or rowboat. These craft needed better maintenance. Something no one could provide, so they prayed they would hold together just one more day.

Bergamot gave another moan, eyes flicking back and forth over the lip of the hull. Finn absent-mindedly reached back to give her a pat on the head in reassurance.

"Bergie does not like this place," he said, echoing her sentiment.

"Who could blame her?" Mirjam said and leaned forward to pet her lower back. Bergamot started at the touch, but seeing it was Mirjam she turned around and laid her head back down on her paws, continuing her moans.

As the valley became more level, the river slowed and began to widen into filthy marshes and miles of dead conifers.

"This was not here last time," Edda said, looking at the swath of drowned trees.

"How long ago was it?"

"A few years."

The shoreline disappeared into vast patches of swamp that seemed to be consuming the pinery with a voracious hunger. Moss and fungus dripped from every tree branch as the rot took control.

"Where are the caribou?" Declan wondered out loud when the two canoes came side by side as they had trouble keeping to the river channel and drifted among the trunks. "They are not averse to wading. Would they not be here in whole herds stripping this landscape clean?"

As if to answer his question, a chilling cry was heard far in the distance.

"That is why," Edda said, her voice low with fear. "Wendigo would never let caribou survive for long in their valley. It was why we never found any of the lost caribou the last time," she reasoned.

"During the day they act like that?"

"Day and night from what I have heard and witnessed. They are just far more active at night. My hope is daylight will make them stay in the shadow of the glacier panning for gold nuggets and other strange trinkets and ignore us."

"Wendigo," Amr's voice was on the edge of scoffing, "panning for gold? Who could have ever conceived it possible."

"We know very little about these demons," Inge pointed out. "Few survive long enough to learn even as much as we have, and those who do rarely wish to discuss it. Perhaps there is more to these hellspawn than we realize."

They drifted on in silence as the swamp filled the whole valley. The distances to the peaks hinted at their position. They were now so close to Blothugjokull they could even smell the iron tang of the blood in the air.

"There must be a giant beaver up ahead. How high is this water?" Edda grumbled. Every once in a while, a thunderous crack and boom of a glacier calving could be heard as they grew ever closer.

The sun beat down hard and bright, blessing them all with its safety.

"Will the sun really keep the demons back?" Solveig asked Edda.

"Like someone who fears spiders, they do not want to be touched by the sun. It may be in their head, or there may be a divine prohibition on them. No one knows the rules of heaven and hell by which these horrors conduct themselves. I do not plan to stay long enough to discover them."

"Here, here," said Inge in hearty agreement.

A loud clattering and snapping of dead wood from behind caught their attention as they passed through the tombstone-like trees, the channel again no longer discernible from the swamp.

"A tree giving way?" Finn whispered, fear tinging his voice.

"It could be," Edda said.

"That sounded more like treesqueaks to me," Mirjam added with a shudder.

They listened hard, silently drifting on the calm brown water. No one wanted to put their paddle in to make even the slightest ripple.

Another clatter and snap. That one was closer. Much closer.

"It must be treesqueaks," Solveig hissed, more sure than ever.

"Do you hear the wind groaning?" Edda observed. "It is not treesqueaks."

"I smell their rot," she insisted.

"That is just the swamp," Amr snapped.

"What could be traveling through the branches like that?" Leif demanded.

"Squirrels?" Amr said sarcastically.

"Too big," Declan said. "Agropelitiers?"

"Could be, but doubtful," Inge comforted. "Not with Wendigo about."

The canoes drifted to a stop.

"What sort of hellspawn is active in sun?"

"I do not know! I am just accounting for my lack of knowledge. God's plucked nose hairs, you are a finicky lot!" Inge growled.

The tension gnawed at their bones like a hungry dog.

A set of more crashes came from among the dead branches.

"Look," hissed Finn and he pointed to a large cascade of dead leaves falling into the water a few hundred yards behind them.

"Over there too," Edda said as she saw needles and branches sprinkle out of a tree on the other side.

Solveig and Mirjam turned the cranks on their springbows and loaded them. Mirjam's hands shook so badly it took several tries to get the bolt nocked.

"Paddle. Smooth and slow. We must get to the lake and in the clear. It is not far now," Edda ordered after determining their position by the peaks and faint sound of a rushing water.

The canoes began to accelerate toward their goal.

A black spot flew near the sun. A flash of shadow passed between Inge and Leif, and it was gone. Then a loud crash came from a tree only a dozen yards away. Through the branches, they could see a large human shape covered in blood and paint. Its eyes pinpoints of bright blue flame in the dark shadows that clung to it like a cowl.

"The Skaerslinger pack!" Declan shouted. "They have caught up!"

Two springbow bolts snapped and twanged as Mirjam and Solveig both fired in fear.

"Paddle! For your lives!" Finn roared and all backs went to the sole purpose of escape. The girls threw their springbows down and picked up their paddles to join in.

It was just enough speed as another from the Wendigo-possessed Skaerslinger arced high overhead, its shadow barely missing them, and then splashed into the water, disappearing below its sepia depths. Finn could not help but remember the old story about the shadow of the Wendigo. It only need pass over you and the corruption would spread to a mortal soul. He prayed that it was not true of those who had not fully transformed.

The pack of Skaerslinger, old and young, man and woman, were jumping from tree to tree, sometimes hundreds of feet, snarling like animals, their howls now rising up with the success of running down their prey, frustrated they could not get close enough to strike.

Their bodies had become covered with those same strange wasting cankers that filled in with ghost white flesh, lips chewed to ribbons revealing new fangs that pushed out the old teeth. Their eyes glowing that hateful blue fire.

Edda dug her paddle in hard as another reached down from the lower branches of a tree, hanging by its sore covered legs, to slash at them with the bony tips of its fingers. The canoe hooked just enough to keep them out of reach.

Mirjam's heart sank when she saw that the creature was formerly a young boy. Solveig swung her paddle at the possessed child. There was a loud crack as she hit the creature's head. It tumbled out of the tree and sank like a stone.

Behind them as they re-entered the channel of the river, they saw four or five of the possessed trying to swim after them but fail to keep up.

"There is the mouth!" shouted Edda. Behind them a few more possessed Skaerslinger leapt from tree to tree trying to reach them. The branches shredding their flesh more and more as sharp dead wood cut them to ribbons till they no longer bled. Declan realized that these crazed monsters kept up their pursuit despite having exsanguinated.

The valley which had been so broad before now narrowed as it merged into the glacial lake. Just as Edda had promised, the water was like an old scab, mottled and sickening, stinking of blood. To their left, the Blothugjokull appeared as they entered the lake proper.

Its mass had receded several hundred feet away from the shore, leaving the lake free of ice. A crack from the middle of its crumbling face sprayed forth what could only be described as bright red blood, as if the glacier had torn a hole in the mountain's throat. They all gasped, and in spite of their peril, stopped rowing.

At its base, moving in the blood that gushed forth were several giant skeletal figures. Some had antlers on their heads like those of a caribou or whitetail deer. Others the horns of a ram. Their eyes blazed with blue fire, as well as the frostfire of their hearts glowing through the bare ribcages that were always hungry.

A wail of pure malice went up from the eastern shore on their right, only a few dozen feet away. They recoiled at what they saw.

Twelve Fingers.

The newly born Wendigo stood on a small knoll above the rocky beach and out of the sunken trees, with Daniel's sword lodged in his heart, encased in ice. Twelve Fingers had survived, and had come to take revenge!

30. BELOW THE ICE

As the two canoes pulled away from shore, the howls of the Skaerslinger were joined by those of the Wendigo among the sanguine ice and rocks of Blothugjokull. Black shadows against the shocking blue and scarlet wall behind them.

"They cannot swim?" wondered Leif.

"Maybe, but do you wish to wait and know for certain? As long as we have our canoes, we can outdistance them," Inge answered.

Edda looked around at the gathering pack on the shore as they huddled next to their master. They watched with a hunger so terrible it tugged at the eight Forsamling souls.

Amr began laughing in the face of such evil.

"What will you do now, oh great manitou? Eaters of darkness? Thwarted by a mere swim?" he taunted, raising himself up as high as he could on his knees.

"Are you mad?" Edda shouted.

"Sit down and row!" commanded Leif.

"Where to, oh my Tign?" Amr demanded back. Where can we pass out of this lake that they cannot reach first? They can run faster than we can paddle. We are at a stalemate and, quite frankly, doomed. Look over by the glacier. The others come for us. Soon we will be surrounded."

They searched for an avenue of escape as they drifted toward the center of the lake. On the northern shore, a large cliff created a seemingly impenetrable wall hundreds of feet tall. To the west, the Blothugjokull, where one or two of the Wendigo remained and watched the drama unfold. To the east, their escape route down a fast running set of streams, the mountainsides had collapsed, cutting this lake off from a deep valley beyond.

There was no way out.

"But it was open, I tell you!" Edda wailed. "The glacier made the lake, we could have gotten through with but a little portage and then the way was clear."

"That seems to be irrelevant now," Inge observed. "Those exposed rock faces suggest that they collapsed after you were here last, making an even bigger dam. It would explain the flooded forest."

"How do we escape then?" Amr demanded.

From the south shore, they heard chanting from Twelve Fingers, which was picked up by his possessed minions.

"In the name of Jesus, I command thee to be silent, Demon! The Lord rebuke you!" Inge shouted at the top of his lungs toward Twelve Fingers.

The friar's voice compressed the water into a wave that hit the shoreline like a hurricane, blasting the demon over and throwing the Skaerslinger like leaves.

Twelve Fingers picked itself up, sword sliding out of the ground, refreezing as it rose. Once to his feet and minions reassembled, it was more subdued. The manitou stepped to the shore and touched the water with his boney foot. The instant its foot touched, a solid ice pack formed, spreading out as he began to walk toward them.

The rest of the Wendigo began the same slow pace across the water.

"Winter," Mirjam griped. "Of course."

"So much for the sun keeping them bound to shadow," Declan complained.

Paths of ice crawled toward them. Even if they paddled away, they would be cut off in a smaller and smaller portion of the water till there would be no place left to run.

As the slight breeze from the north pushed them away from Twelve Fingers, a flash of bright purple light caught Declan's eye.

"What is that?"

Leif strained to see in the dark rock of the cliff face. Another brief pulse of light mid way up the cliff.

"A slot canyon? Perhaps our way out?" Leif reasoned. "Edda. Does that look familiar?"

She looked to where he indicated with a nod. Perfectly camouflaged in the shadows of the cliff was a thin crack that went right to the water. At the base of the crack, white mist could be seen.

It was a way out! The lake had filled so much it had found a new route through a hidden canyon she never knew existed.

"Go, we have no other choice!"

All paddles went back to work in frantic pulls with bays of excitement from the Wendigo joyfully pursuing. One of the Wendigo from the southern shore launched itself into a high arc attempting to land on one of the canoes. Declan steered hard to the right and the manitou plunged between the two canoes with slashing grabs that just missed the birch bark craft. The splash was so powerful it nearly swamped the trailing canoe. As they slid by the point of impact, an eruption occurred as the Wendigo popped out of the water clinging to the top of an iceberg that grew underneath it.

"In the name of Jesus, come out of him!" Finn commanded. The Wendigo laughed at the order.

"I cannot leave what was always my home, foolish prey!"

"Then in His name, I command thee bound!" Finn snapped back.

The Wendigo's frigid eyes flared in their sockets as the ice he crouched upon for another leap grew up and over his limbs, binding him to the ice, growing till the whole boulder became top heavy and flipped upside down, submerging him. The other Wendigo tried to speed up their walk across the water, but the ice took time to form, and kept them at a leisurely pace. One of the manitou ran back down its path to shore and leapt to get ahead of them. It landed on a boulder and began to freeze the draining water into an impassable plug of ice. Seeing this, the other Wendigo rushed to swarm the gap and catch them like bears snatching salmon on their way to spawn.

"Keep paddling, I shall deal with this," Edda said, her voice strong with her faith. She then burst forth into song. The melody powerful clearly reverberated off the wall of the cliff with a power none of them conceived possible.

"By the swords of the mighty, will The Lord God cause thy multitude to fall, the terrible of the nations, all of them: and they shall spoil the pomp of Egypt, and all the multitude thereof shall be destroyed," she began.

The possessed Skaerslinger could not bear the sound, and began screaming in agony against the words. The little devils in them terrified at scripture being sung against them. Finn had a strange sense of deja vu and remembered the meadow on Neinnvanbjarg. The smell of earth and ash, blackberry brambles and roses. A small boy's hands trembling in the air as if on strings.

Their paddling increased in speed despite Edda focusing on her singing.

"I will destroy also all the beasts thereof from beside the great waters; neither shall the foot of man trouble them any more, nor the hoofs of beasts trouble them."

The Wendigo began to panic and sought to hide from the sound, retreating to the shade cast by the mountains and hiding behind large boulders and trees along the shore. The possessed fled back into the drowned forest. Ahead, the slot canyon could be seen as the base was filled with a torrent from the lake. Dirty brown water spraying into high foaming waves over the broken rock of its floor. The mist of the violent course shot through with rainbows.

"Then will I make their waters deep, and cause their rivers to run like oil, saith the Lord GOD."

With a loud crack, the boulder split beneath the Wendigo attempting to block their way, throwing it into the river where it was instantly entombed in ice. The volume of water down the canyon increased as rock slid out of the channel creating a current strong enough to draw them toward it. Terrified shrieks came from the scattering manitou, who now swatted at the air as if birds were diving at their heads.

"When I shall make the land of Egypt desolate, and the country shall be destitute of that whereof it was full, when I shall smite all them that dwell therein, then shall they know that I am the LORD."

The canoes reached the newly deepened channel and saw what awaited them. The rapids were far beyond anything the canoes could survive in their battered condition, but they had no choice. Everyone began to pray that God would see them through safely. Leif, Amr, Inge and Declan slid through the channel first, followed by Finn, Mirjam, Solveig and Edda.

Twelve Fingers, seeing his prey escaping, leapt after them in a desire to cut them off, if not capture them before they escaped. As the Wendigo's shadow crept toward the second canoe, his triumph seemed certain. Solveig looked at the dark figure about to eclipse the sun over her and bring upon them its demonic curse.

A searing purple light shot through the canyon to spotlight the second canoe, incinerating the shadow as it passed over them.

They looked up to see the purple brilliance, shielding their eyes as best they could. Just as they could take no more, the purple light flicked away, sliding to where Twelve Fingers had landed behind them.

The Wendigo wailed as if it was suffering the agonies of Hell. It began to steam and the ice encasing Daniel's sword shattered. Twelve Fingers turned and jumped away from the light which disappeared again as quickly as it had appeared.

Before they could wonder more about the source of the light, the canoes entered the rapids, and they had to paddle for their lives. None of them had experience shooting whitewater like this. The cascade was a crazed maze of waves. They flew over rocks into horrible foaming troughs, fighting to keep from being swamped or being thrown overboard. Leif's paddle shattered against a rock which saved them from being smashed to splinters, but this spun them sideways in the current as they struggled to turn around and ended up rushing backwards through the rapids.

"Here!" Inge shouted and tossed Leif his paddle, as he was now in the rear, forced to steer them through the watery chaos with no experience.

"Aim for the arrowheads of water!" shouted Edda over the roar of the river. Leif did as best he could, narrowly avoiding snags and finding deeper channels and safe spots over the submerged rocks and logs.

Finn heard a ripping sound behind him as they went too deep in a trough. A hidden branch had sliced through the birch bark hull all the way from Bergamot to Mirjam. The canoe swamped in seconds. There was no way to keep the water out, but they could use the hull to protect themselves.

"Hang on!" Edda shouted to the girls as the river took control.

Ahead, the rapids took a sharp turn to the east against the cliff face from where the purple light had come. As they looked up at the cliff, they saw an amazing ornate temple carved into the rock, much like Saelrskjol. Few terraces, but a steep stone staircase cut into the canyon. In fact, they now saw dozens of cliff houses carved into all sides of the canyon walls all around, camouflaged from the slot canyon's entrance. This was once a city, much larger than Edda's refuge.

"My God," breathed Finn in amazement. "What miracle is this?"

Ahead, Leif had managed to smash their canoe to kindling against the foot of the stairs. Unable to steer herself, Edda pointed to where the others were.

"We have to swim for it!"

Bergamot was struggling to stay in the now submerged canoe as the current fought to tear them all from it. Finn took one of the spears, wrapped his hip bag around it and ran it under her collar, with the shaft back to Mirjam and Solveig. He trusted the bag to keep Bergamot from being injured.

"Take hold and let her pull you to shore! Trust in her!" he shouted.

The girls grabbed the spear shaft. "Keep your feet as high as you can! Now, go Bergie! Go! Farthu til landsins!"

Bergamot, as she had in dozens of storms before, hurled herself out of the canoe with Finn and the three women in tow by the spear. Their abandoned canoe hit a boulder with a loud crunch, becoming a mass of sharp flotsam that would have maimed all who had stayed within.

The frigid, dirty water tasted of iron as the four struggled to shore. Inge and Amr stepped knee deep into the water, while Declan and Leif made a safety line with a blanket to make sure they did not get washed away. As they reached out to catch the others, they saw another Wendigo had started down the canyon.

The purple spotlight blazed forth again, catching the manitou as it landed on a slab of rock overhanging the rapids.

Pinned in the searing light, it wailed in agony, steam bursting from its flesh. Its frosted heart flaring red before it burst in a cloud of snow. The creature fell to the ground and was immolated till nothing but a pile of charcoal remained, vanishing in the breeze. Farther down, the faint figures of the other Wendigo watched.

"What are they waiting for?" Amr marveled, taking Edda's hand to bring her to safety. With a jerk, she drew back and punched Amr hard enough to knock him down on the steps.

"Do not touch me!" she yelled. "Never touch me!"

Everyone stared at her in shock. Thyrnir growled and readied to pounce. Edda drew out her sword and pointed it at the dog. "Call him off, Amr," she ordered.

Amr, holding his jaw, eyes blazing with hate said nothing.

"Call him off!" No one else dared move.

Amr spit out a mouthful of blood. "Thyrnir. Greithr, boy. Stay." Thyrnir's growls subsided and he went to Amr.

For a long time, Edda's sword remained pointed towards the mastiff who's urge to attack was held in check by his master.

Above them a voice drifted down from the top of the stairs.

"Did their shadow touch you?" called a young man, hardly old enough to shave.

Leif looked up at the youth. The voice was accented in a way he never heard before.

"We are all untouched. Thanks to you, their shadows did not land on any of us!"

"Come up then! We have little time to get to safety. The lens is only good when the sky is clear and clouds are coming! Hurry! I will take you to shelter!"

They turned to look back the way they came. Rolling out of the drowned forest the mountain clouds were coming. They passed over the far shore of the lake which vanished into its soft white billows.

With that last encouragement, the young man disappeared into the doors at the top of the staircase.

"What choice do we have?" Leif said with a shrug. They picked up the few belongings they had left and began to climb.

31. IN THE TEMPLE OF AN UNKNOWN GOD

The company of eight lay panting with exertion on the wide temple porch cut into the corner of the canyon walls. Two ramps lead along the stone faces to high terraced fields hidden from every eye save for any that might stand on the surrounding peaks. The porch was framed with four large square columns of cut stone scarred by violence in every spot decoration might once have been carved, giving its own abstract aesthetic of desperation that erased the identity of this temple dedication, yet unable to collapse it.

Above, the sharp blue sky faltered to bright billows of approaching clouds. They seemed to move like an avalanche down the Djuprgil, striking the cliff face and launching upward into an eruption of mist. A black figure, that everyone suspected to be Twelve Fingers, moved in the mist hellbent on revenge.

"I think we best get inside and find the shelter our host has invited us to share," Friar Inge said, as their pursuer vanished into the protective arms of the cloud. All muttered in agreement, picked themselves up and walked into the broad open doorway.

"How will we be able to secure this without any doors?" Leif wondered aloud.

"Perhaps divine providence will block the Wendigo's path?" Mirjam suggested, looking hopefully at Finn.

"There must be something deeper like a vault we can hide in," Finn suggested.

"Or another way out," Amr thought.

As their eyes adjusted to the dark space, they found themselves in a courtyard of sorts. It was clear that this had been a cave at one time and the architects of some people had hewn it out smooth and employed the natural rock to create load bearing statuary to support the mountain top. Altars, long since smashed by the unknown god's enemies, seemed scattered at what may have once been courtyards and alcoves for worship and offerings. The ceiling was carved out into an even smoother dome, and gave off a faint glisten of great ornamentation and art in glaze or polished metal that could not be discerned in the dark or reached by the vandals who had desecrated this place. In the center, a broad staircase descended into the mountain. Its ten foot wide steps gently descending out of sight, a stark contrast to the stairs outside that pilgrims would have struggled to climb.

More worrisome was the dark. There were no lights to guide their way, only the dimming light from the doorway illuminating the top of the stairs.

From behind in the shadows they heard scuffling of feet hurrying down stairs. They drew their few remaining weapons and turned to see the young man step out into the light.

"That is it for the lens. Nothing will prevent that manitou from reaching here now."

"Lens? What lens?" Inge demanded.

"Whoever the god of this place was, he was a god of light." The man pointed off into the dark above the entrance. "Up there is a powerful lens of silver, sunstone and purest amethyst that you can shine down and into the canyon. It must be why this place is not infested with manitou. The superstitious creatures," the man said.

He was Leif's age, possibly younger. Edda smiled when she saw the youth more clearly. He wore an intense blue surcoat with red trimmed waist, sleeves and neck. Under which a white kyrtill was visible. His dark caribou leather trousers were bloused over more matching blue spjarrars and fur lined boots with comically curled toes.

"Brother Saami, we are glad to have found you at last," she sighed happily and sheathed her sword again. The look was one of pure befuddlement.

"Looking for me?" the Saami said startled. "But I was not lost. Just delayed. My caribou are now lost though."

"I am sorry to hear that." Edda sympathized.

"When the river goes down then I can escape. But for now, I wait." He took inventory of his new guests and although it was obvious his curiosity was tempting him, he asked nothing.

"What is your name?" asked Leif.

"I am Feles."

"Why were you up here, Herr Feles?"

"Finding the last of my aettir's lost caribou, but I was too late," the youth said. "Who are you?"

"Leif Gregorsson," the Tronerving answered, not mentioning his title or station. "These are my sisters Solveig and Mirjam. My personal guard, Declan, and these four are members of the Kyrkja. Brothers Finn, Inge and Amr and Sister Edda."

"A far ways away from any caravan route," the Saami ventured.

"Jah. We became lost in the valleys and ended up here by mistake," Leif said.

"In Skaerslinger canoes?" the youth observed. "But, it is no business of mine how you came to be here. What matters is that you are being pursued by those demonspawn, and are no threat to me. We might both be an aid to the other."

"Perhaps when we are safe we can speak more openly," Leif agreed. "Where is this shelter you spoke of. I do not think it wise to tarry here any more than we must."

"Agreed." The Saami walked over to the dark stairs and began to descend, as if expecting the rest to follow.

"Do you have a light?" Amr asked, his voice so small sounding in the cavernous room.

"Where we are going, we shall not need one," Feles' words echoed back as he vanished from sight.

Left with no other option, they joined their guide and went down into the blackness.

As the last of the light from the doorway failed, a new light grew before them. It defined the descent just enough to reveal the steps and the black edges of the walls. The light was a shifting cool glow, blurring between blue, green and yellow yet it's source was indiscernible. They clung to one another to keep from tripping in the dark, when without warning, they reached the bottom of the stairs and there was a feeling of space again after a descent of unknown distance. From either side, they could see green glows in the walls and ceiling, like frozen ripples of water.

"Lord God in Heaven, preserve us, thy lost and sinful sheep!" Inge breathed.

"Amen," came the response from Feles from some point ahead, only his silhouette visible to them. "Turn to your left and walk to my voice," he guided.

"How can you see in this darkness?" Solveig asked.

"You become accustomed over time," Feles said.

"How long have you been here?" Mirjam said.

"I am not sure. More than a few days, waiting till the moon is right, and I may slip away unobserved. Although they do not enter this canyon, they do watch it closely. There are many ways to reach the icefield on the other side of the mountain where I came from."

As they turned and walked to the dim shadow of the man, they found the light grew into another large court. It was like walking among the auroras, cast in stone. Great washes of green ribbons went throughout the inner courtyard.

"Welcome to the inner court to an unknown god."

"You said this was a god of light?" Amr asked. His voice tremulous.

"It is. What else could trap the aurora in a mountain?"

"Nowhere," breathed an awestruck Edda.

"This is magnificent!" exclaimed Inge.

Everywhere they looked, the washes colored the edges in cool green light, but further in was the other source of light. A soft glow that went between blue and yellow, but never green. It ebbed and flowed like waves washing over a placid shore.

"What is that?" Mirjam breathed.

"That is the temple proper and inside there is god's holy shrine." That is where we must go to be safe," Feles explained. "The Wendigo might venture as far as this outer court, but I doubt it would ever risk the wrath of the one this place was dedicated to."

The naivete of the Saami gave Finn a sad smile. Satan's house was not divided against itself. Demons would not keep out demons, would they? Only one thing did that, he assured himself. But if it did not, that raised a very troubling question in the depths of Finn's understanding. Perhaps demons were superstitious of things beyond man's knowledge regarding Heaven and Hell. Was there something else those rebel angels feared enough to engender reverence? Finn shook off the blasphemous thought, unwilling to deal with that question now.

As they walked through the courtyard, they passed an altar used for the sacrifice of large animals. It was split as if beaten with large hammers and defiled by some revolting residue over its remains. They found more piles of rubble from savaged statuary and drifts of textiles long turned to dust. The broken wall mounts for hanging art objects and icons littered the floor, their treasures long since taken or destroyed. The square pillars here fared the same as those without, scarred and indecipherable.

Somewhere above came the horrible snarl of a predator angry at its prey hiding where it could not follow. The snarls changed to terrifying roars that charged down the staircase like a bear at the gate. Solveig and Mirjam screamed in reflex while the rest took a step back and clutched their weapons tightly.

"Sounds to me like it will not follow. Otherwise, it would have come already," Feles said reassuringly.

"You do not know Twelve Fingers. Although we met only recently, it is clear he will pursue us into the arms of Jesus if that is what it takes to enact his revenge," Inge contradicted the young Saami.

Feles gave a grunt.

"You shall see. Come inside and be safe," he said standing at the door to the inner temple, removing his boots before entering barefoot.

One by one, they entered, Edda hesitating at the doorway for a moment more as she was sure twin pinpoints of blue flame were staring back at her from the dark. Then she too entered the temple.

32. THE WEIGHT OF SIN

"Do not be afraid," Feles beckoned. "Come inside."

As they entered the temple for refuge, Finn and Inge began to pray in low voices for their strength and understanding was failing. What they felt in the spirit ran riot against their instincts.

The little chamber was saturated with light. Walls were encrusted with bursts of crystals which made the walls sparkle like rippling water, causing the temple to feel as if it was in motion. Pairs of slim round pillars went down the length of the temple on either side of the doorway arch with shocks of glowing crystal veins. Piles of dark vulgar ruin marred the wonder of the inner temple but could not diminish it. Delicate carvings of precious stone lay crushed beyond recognition and smashed pedestals covered in ash and dust littered the floor between the pillars and against the walls. A tangle of tarnished and melted silver and gold lay in front of the doorway to a light flooded shrine. Its arms and branches twisted into unrecognizable shapes. Crazy scrawls of its remains spidered out from it. A few feet away rags and dirt lay on the threshold of the entrance like ancient drapes or tapestries that once protected the shrine but were torn down and left to molder.

Without a screen, light poured out of this Holy of Holies giving the distinct sensation of fresh flowing water. Their souls felt saturated with its radiance that began rendering the shadows of sin like tallow. Feles looked back, a gentle smile of peace on his lips as he watched them struggle against the light.

"The shrine will test you," Feles said boots in hand, standing before the entrance to the shrine. "I felt the same way when I arrived here seeking sanctuary."

Inge's hands shook as sweat popped out all over his body as he passed the first pair of pillars. The memory of being caught by a thunderstorm as a boy came to mind. He remembered looking up in awe at the beauty of the sky's power, witnessing the dominion and majesty of God echoing through nature.

"Can anyone else feel that heat?" Amr moaned passing the second pair and shielding his face from the light. He walked forward as if in the winds of a gale, fighting for each step.

"I feel nothing," Mirjam said walking past him, approaching the glow. She smelled a breath of fresh air coming from the shrine and smiled.

Amr, Finn and Inge's steps began to falter. The closer they came to the archway into the shrine, the more every unconfessed transgression became a heavy weight and bubbled to the surface of their thoughts.

"So beautiful," Leif gasped.

Leif, Declan, Solveig and Mirjam did not seem as affected and passed the third pair of pillars without noticing anything strange, enraptured with the light, but when they passed the fourth pair, the Visekonge's children discovered they were not immune. They too began to feel the burning convictions of unconfessed sin. A tickle of anxiety became cumbersome regret and then burning shame.

Yet they pressed on.

The light flared bright blue and yellow to their eyes with sparkles of dazzling diamond white drops falling inside the shrine.

"How can we be safe in this horrible place?" Amr grunted. "There is no door to bar or anything to blockade the way. What will keep the Wendigo back?"

"The light keeps them at bay," Feles' voice drifted to them from the shrine. I have watched them come as far as the inner temple arch, but none dared come through, and all fled soon after."

Edda wondered what spirit lived in a place like this, for the light was terrible and wondrous at the same time. Could this be the light of Jehovah? Edda was transfixed just inside the inner temple's entrance. The weight in her spirit overwhelmed her and she was unable to take another step. With a low groan she sank to her knees and began to pray.

"Please, I cannot... go any further," she begged. "My heart will not let me. I will stay here and stand guard." Her voice failed and she whispered her confessions, nose pressed to the cold floor.

No one responded to her plea for they suffered too.

Solveig and Declan now felt a terrible burning cable of shame that strung between them. Both were enduring burning hot coals in their hips and hearts. The foreign sensation of regret and shame surged through Declan and he dropped to his knees on the single broad step that lay in front of the shrine's entrance.

Finn halted there too kneeling before the tangle of metal. Slices of light cut through the bent and dripping arms of the ruined metalwork, providing stripes of cool relief in its shade. He too confessed his sins as Bergamot, unaffected, came to his side and sat patiently watching over her master.

Amr gritted his teeth and sneered a little at Finn's collapse. He continued past as if approaching a smelting furnace. Using an arm to cover his face, his flesh quaked and unbidden tears ran from pain in the flesh and the spirit. He half expected to see his skin start smoking. Amr pushed to the archway with a mania that showed he would suffer any pain to fulfill his goal.

Then it vanished.

Amr felt he was no longer in the same shrine. He was on his hands and knees in the cold March night. It nipped at his bare feet and fingers. The sound of boiling water rose up and he lifted his head to see the flaming statue of Saint Sanaa above him, reaching down in fury to slay him. He began screaming with a terror he never knew possible. The sky rapidly filled with light as the memory of so many months ago was torn away and the phantasm disappeared like paper in a forest fire leaving him standing under the arch to the shrine.

Where Amr found the reserves to continue forward, he did not know, but some force more powerful than himself impelled his feet to cross the threshold. Thyrnir whined and whimpered as he followed his master into the place, using his faint shadow as protection till it vanished inside.

Inge passed through the arch just as Amr collapsed to the floor in front of him. Inside was a natural shaft surrounded by a thin ledge a couple yards wide made of crusty white quartz shocked through with glowing seams of more crystal that seemed to transmit the sunlight deep into the heart of the mountain's rock. Just beyond the entrance, the ledge jutted a little further into the shaft and on it stood a small altar made of a single flat slab of knee high crystal glowing with the refracting light.

Above, the shaft climbed up into the startling blue sky allowing the sun to dip deep into the mountain stopping short of the shrine's ledge. Water dripped through the open air, fine droplets of water twirling in the breeze. They caught the reflected light, splitting it as it fell in a kaleidoscopic display as the droplets passed down their way into the depths of the mountain. Below, a powerful elemental blue light glowed, like dim lightning from behind the clouds.

Inge felt himself laid bare. When he closed his eyes, he was sure the Judgment Seat was before him. Confessions rolled out of him in muttered madness, convicted of all his crimes against God.

Mirjam's head burned upon entering through the arch. The light wresting her memories from their hidden places. All the dirty little lies and games she had played throughout her life were brought to the fore. She felt the pain of every person who suffered by her acts and words in a foretaste of a judgment unknown to her. A low groan of agony began from the pits of her soul and crescendoed in a pitiful wail of anguish.

Declan and Solveig remained prostrate there, too fearful to utter a sound and unable to look at the light.

When Leif entered the shrine the spiritual heat and weight settled upon his shoulders, but he did not crumble. Surprised at his own resilience as the rest were sundered around him, he looked at Feles in confusion.

"The God is dealing with their sins according to their calling and station in Him," Feles explained and tended to the collapsed and delirious Amr, propping him up against the wall of the shrine. Then moving on to the next, keeping them safe from falling over the edge or tripping over each other if they regained their legs. "I lost count of the days and hours I spent in this state before I dared venture out."

There all remained in the light, kneeling or prostrate, nigh oblivious to their surroundings and ramblings of the others.

"If this is... not of Jehovah," Finn choked, "I cannot conceive what manner of spirit this is." He could not catch his breath and stars sparkled in his vision, but the weight had lessened. He had enough mind to remove his boots and felt lighter again.

"Perhaps... we have offended God coming inside this place?" Amr groaned struggling against the incredible frailty he felt.

"The place you are in is holy, that is to be sure," Feles said.

"Is it God or is this the devil's pagan shrine you respect?" Amr demanded to know as he rolled onto his back, panting like an overheated dog.

Feles ignored the insult and went out into the temple to see Edda. He knelt beside her.

"Would you like me to help you inside?" he asked, his voice gentle as if to an infirm grandparent.

"No," Edda groaned, her body twitched with a silent sob.

"You are not safe out here," Feles said.

"I will not go in there. I cannot bear it," Edda's words were tinged with an unspoken agony.

Feles put his hand on her back. She did not move.

"Is it because you feel yourself unworthy?"

"No," she said, but reconsidered. "Yes. But that is not why."

"Why then?" Feles asked.

"I... cannot say."

From beyond the blackened entrance to the temple came a horrifying growl. "Fools. Do not think that light will stop my vengeance."

The words seethed and bubbled with a malice black and cold as a winter's night. Blue fire for eyes, the image paralyzed Feles with fright.

Edda struggled to look behind as Feles lifted her to her feet.

There was Twelve Fingers, crawling forward on all fours, bony talons clicking on the stone as it approached the arch to the inner temple. Daniel's ice encased sword gleaming in the radiance of the place.

"I will have your blood on my fangs before I give you up to this place, for it will surely kill you if I do not!" Twelve Fingers snarled.

With a mighty effort, Edda shoved Feles away from her.

"Get back!" she ordered.

"I can help," pleaded Feles, drawing his saxe.

"If this demon gets past me, then it will fall to you, but do it from in there!" she shouted, thrusting a finger at the shrine's glowing arch.

Feles nodded, understanding. Twelve Fingers now began to pass the first pair of pillars.

"Tell Finn I am sorry I did not tell him all of my dream."

"What?" Feles asked.

"Go!"

The Saami youth obeyed and ran back to their sanctuary. He stood in the doorway to bear witness of what was to come. The Wendigo's voice had startled the others back to their surroundings, and they scrambled drunkenly to the arch where Feles held them back.

Asked to make a stand in faith for God, Edda was resolved with a glad heart. For weeks she had begged God to take this last secret part of her dream from her. But now, as she stood facing down the demon, the love for her companions and theirs for her became an untapped ocean of strength. All was right under the heavens and this was a good day to die.

Twelve Fingers crawled within a few yards, against the power of the light. It looked as if he was being blown backwards, the shadow and frost stripped from the demon's body by a gale. His terrible strength sapped to a fraction of what it was, but still, it dwarfed hers. She inched Inkjenamn out of its ratty scabbard with arthritic speed.

"Greater love hath no man than this, that a man lay down his life for his friend," Edda said as a sense of peace began to fill her as she took a first dip into the power of the Holy Spirit.

"Edda!" screamed Mirjam.

"This is the fate God has ordained of me, my Tign, and I shall give it unto Him with joy!"

"Oh, daughter of man," the demon chuckled, "I shall feast upon your soul for all eternity!"

Edda began to sing a new psalm. Each note opened the floodgates in her ever so slightly.

"Be merciful unto me, O God, be merciful unto me: for my soul trusteth in thee: yea, in the shadow of thy wings will I make my refuge, until these calamities be overpast."

The light from the shrine dimmed as clouds passed overhead but her strength continued to grow, as well as did the Wendigo's. Its fanged and lipless leer drooled blood as it crawled towards her on hands and knees, careful to not graze the ground with the hilt of Daniel's sword. The song stung its ears like a thousand wasps.

"I will cry unto God most high; unto God that performeth all things for me."

She drew back into a high guard, her off hand stretched out before her, the point of Inkjenamn aimed at her foe. Twelve Fingers let out a horrible mocking laugh at her defiance. Behind her, the rest watched on, helpless to stop what was about to occur.

The sun returned and an invisible door seemed to close between the shrine and the lone chorister. The crystals in the temple reverberated with her singing amplifying her voice. The Wendigo roared but lacked the same power as her song. Traces of other beings were revealed as the veil fluxed. An audience of angels and demons seemed to stand around in witness.

"He shall send from heaven, and save me from the reproach of him that would swallow me up. Selah. God shall send forth his mercy and his truth," Edda sang on. If this was her end, she was ready, though a distant piece of her prayed she would survive.

Twelve Fingers clawed within arm's reach as she stood still. A cloud passed overhead and shaded the sun again, diminishing the light from the shrine. The Wendigo rose up and towered over the small woman. Its antlers brushing the ceiling.

"My soul is among lions: and I lie even among them that are set on fire, even the sons of men, whose teeth are spears and arrows, and their tongue a sharp sword."

Twelve Fingers lunged forward and slashed with a claw-tipped hand only to have it slapped away by the blade of her sword.

"Ah!" the Wendigo shouted, looking at the cuts in its flesh that should not be there. A strange vibration began in Daniel's sword as this mortal sang the Word of God, drawing upon the divine aid and grace that poured into her. The ice around the sword cracked in sympathy with her growing song.

"Be thou exalted, O God, above the heavens; let thy glory be above all the earth," Edda sang on, her voice growing in volume.

In a black fury, Twelve Fingers charged, lowering his head to gore her with his antlers. She slipped under the Wendigo's dipped head and slashed up, striking Daniel's sword on the pommel with a spray of ice and sparks. The two swords rang in musical synergy with the song, the force of her blow smashed the ice and split the Wendigo's heart in twain, popping it like a delicate crystal goblet.

The fire in the eyes winked and every shard of shattered heart became a hateful glare that burned the eyes of all who saw. Edda, slid to a halt on her knees facing the corpse of Twelve Fingers, sword clasped in both hands, blade before her face. Seeing her fallen foe she closed her eyes and drew a deep breath and smiled. In that split second, a wave of impending doom made those in the shrine throw themselves away from the archway with all their strength.

The floor jumped as an explosion thrummed the roots of the mountain. Ice filled the inner temple and ruptured the walls of the shrine as the ice expanded outward, slowing to a halt holding the debris suspended in its icy mass over the shaft.

Frozen soot and blood swirled through ice that destroyed the inner temple. In the midst of the immense block of ice, a faint windblown shadow figure could be seen where Edda had been, Inkjenamn gleaming and whole in the wisp of her hand. Spears of the corrupt ice thrust through the door, trapping the rest. The rock crackled and popped under the extreme stress of the manifested ice. Black frost crackled, radiating from the epicenter of the blast. The fissures growing wider filling it with blooms of charcoal ice flowers.

Everyone in the shrine held their breath as the noise of splitting rock came to an end. Silence lay claim again to the remains of the ancient temple.

Leif looked at the survivors of his company along with Feles. The sensations from the shrine of light blinked out with the explosion.

Leif inhaled to speak but the words never crossed his lips. In that instant, the thin crusty balcony of the shrine gave way all at once and they fell into the glowing depths of the mountain's blue glow below.

33. CIRCLING VULTURES

"Brother Urban!" the shout came with the pounding of a panicked fist on the door of his room shattering the peace of his morning meditation. The inquisitor tried to leap up and defend himself, but the shock and his numb legs made him to tumble to the floor in a confused heap.

"Brother! You must come!" came the shout. "Fy da! It is horrible! May the Lord curse this day! O, Brother! Come quick!"

It was Jan Bjornsson, Father Tuajaksson's apprentice he realized as he pulled himself to his feet by use of the bed frame. What could have sent him into such a frenzy? The pounding continued till Jan heard his slow footsteps.

"What has you acting so mad?" Urban asked whipping open his door.

"Come with me! Come, come come!" Jan choked with the horror. "You must see, but they will not wait long. They promised to wait till I returned, but I do not believe them. Hurry!" He seized Urban's hand dragging him away, the door slamming shut behind.

Urban was not dressed to be in public. He had on his undershirt, pants and boots, but no kyrtill or hat. Half dressed the novice pulled him along like a large dog dragging a child on its leash struggling to keep up. The day was already thick and sweltering with late August heat. The rain from overnight left the streets a sloppy mess of muck sometimes a foot deep as they splashed toward the Koenraadian University.

They turned away from the university library where Urban thought Jan was leading him and headed down the winding lanes of the neighborhood that surrounded it, where the doctors of letters and arts lived.

When Jan stopped running, Urban found himself in front of an unassuming row house just like a dozen others on this block alone, it's door atypically wide open. The Koenraadian seal next to the door revealed where he was.

"Did Father Tuajaksson send for me?" Urban asked. Perhaps Jan's excitement was due to a discovery by the father. Jan said nothing, then took a deep breath and sighed. Haltingly, he mounted the steps and ventured through the open door, disappearing into dark interior.

"Novice Jan? Urban called, voice subdued. Again no answer.
Urban followed.

He found himself in the parlor of the thin home. To his right, Jan was rushing upstairs. Urban followed in silence. Upon reaching the second floor landing, he came upon a pile of smashed plaster and broken lathe with a few drops of blood staining the polished wooden floor. Something heavy had struck the wall. The landing opened up into a modest bedroom with a canopy bed and thick curtains. Jan stood before it, waiting expectantly.

"What is the meaning of all this?" Urban demanded, bewildered. "You drag me out of my room and through the fetid streets to here without explanation and... and..." The rusty wheel of suspicion began to turn in Urban's mind again. His avocation springing to life connecting the pieces of the puzzle before he even verified it with his eyes.

He looked at the crushed wall, swallowed hard, and then to the bed where Jan pulled back the curtains. Father Tuajaksson, cyanotic and misshapen from his wounds lay on top of his bed, hands folded on his breast, one eye unable to close.

"What happened?" Urban breathed as he walked toward the kindly priest's body.

"He looks to have fallen down the stairs last night," Jan said, his voice brittle, fighting to keep control.

Urban's face screwed up with bitter disappointment. He took a moment to consider the injuries, the damage to the wall, then nodded. "What ill timing!" he groaned and rubbed his eyes. "He fell down the stairs, managed to crawl into bed where he died of his injuries. Why did I have to hurry for this?"

"I am not convinced it was an accident," Jan whispered.

Urban snorted. "His wounds look like a bad fall down the stairs. Happens all the time. But you think he was murdered? Greithr. I shall look further," Urban said as he examined the corpse. He checked the man's fingers, examined his tongue and smelled his mouth. "No obvious signs of a drug or poison. Nor does he smell of strong drink that might have caused the fall." He looked expectantly at Jan, waiting for the real reason for the suspicion.

"He was working on your ring," Jan admitted, eyes downcast.

Urban's blood chilled at the admission.

"He did not confide in me," Jan's hands fluttered about him, unable to find a safe place to rest. He gave a big sigh, "I am able to read Latin upside down and saw the ring once when he was slow to put it away. Your secret was not betrayed."

"He has a journal of notes?" Urban was surprised the father would risk writing down any discoveries he had.

"Jah, but I have no idea where he hides them here. When ideas struck him throughout the day he would pull a journal out of his sleeves and scratch down some notes. That is why I noticed it. He would take it out and write the thought that struck him and then put it away."

"And your keen eyes read it." Urban's melancholy was palpable. "Do you remember much?"

"It may still be in his chancery upstairs."

"Let us have a look," Urban suggested, walking toward the stairs leading to the chancery. As he began to climb, a strange scent caught his nose. Acrid and rancid at the same time, and gone just as quickly. A familiar scent.

"Jan, does Father Tuajaksson have a cat?" Urban asked.

"Not that I am aware," Jan said following close behind.

"I just smelled cat piss," Urban said.

"Perhaps from outside?" Jan hazarded to guess.

"Not likely," Urban said noting the windows were closed.

At the top of the stairs, there was a short landing before the closed door.

"He lived alone?"

"Jah. His two servants came, an old cook who made his breakfast and dinner. Then there was a maid, but neither lived here, no," Jan recalled.

"Would he keep his chancery door closed?" Urban asked examining the door.

"It was his custom, jah."

Urban gave a sniff and opened the door. Paper and old leather mixed with the scent of bookshelves greeted them. Another faint whiff of cat urine greeted them and was gone.

"I smelled it this time," Jan said.

"And the window is sealed?"

"Could it have gotten on his shoes?

"Possibly, but surely it would have rubbed off downstairs and not made it up here. I did not smell it in his bedroom," Urban muttered. The room felt askew to him. The looming shelves, packed tight with books and papers. Piles of manuscripts and vellum stacked on thin tables down the sides of the long skinny room made to feel all the more claustrophobic.

But there was no sign of struggle. Everything seemed to be packed into messy order just like his desk at the scriptorium. The only sign of violence was the crushed plaster in the stairwell that gave (all) the appearance of an accidental death.

And yet, something in his spirit demanded that Father Tuajaksson be avenged. But why? How can you avenge an accident? Unless...

"Jan, what do you remember about his writing in the journal?"

"At first it was lists of what the symbol could mean."

"You saw more than you are letting on," Urban smiled.

Jan blushed at being found out.

"The father, God bless him, never shared, but I think he knew I was reading."

"Then I suspect he trusted you with it, or did not see a way of stopping you," Urban encouraged.

"Here! Here! What are you two doing in there!" came the wavering shout of outrage. Both turned to see the cook standing in the doorway, eyes red from weeping, face a contortion of grief.

"This is the brother I told you about," Jan explained walking toward the exhausted man. From below heavy footsteps of several men could be heard climbing the stairs.

"I went to the undertaker and the landowner to deal with his tenant's demise," the cook explained. "You cannot leave a dead body alone like this. No you cannot. Bad for the soul. Bad for the house. What if he started walking again?"

"I sealed the body," Jan pouted. "As if I would overlook such a thing!"

"Could you wait for a little while? I need to make an inquiry into the death of Father Tuajaksson," Urban asked without preamble.

"Who are you?"

"I am Brother Urban av Hitilopt."

"A long way from Hitilopt Island, Brother," the cook said with a wary eye. "What authority do you have here?" Just below the landing, the landlord stood with what looked like three sturdy sons, the undertaker behind them, looking on curiously.

"I am an inquisitor, but currently on sabbatical," Urban said, his posture more formal with the title.

"Therefore no authority," the landlord said.

"Not in any official cap-"

"And that means these are all my chattels for me to sort out with the Kyrkja when they send their factor around to deal with it, and you are just a pirrahndi ahorfahndi with no business here."

Urban bit his tongue at being called a pesky onlooker. How could he say he had legitimate business without giving away the possible cause of Father Tuajaksson's death?

"The father, God rest his soul," Jan butted in, "was working on a project for Inquisitor Urban and had some of his property."

Urban smiled at Jan's defense, crossed his arms and leaned a hip confidently against a packed table.

"Then you and I will sort it out later once I take stock of what is here and what is the Kyrkja's. Once that is done we will talk," the landlord huffed.

"Are you laity?" Jan demanded, striding right up to the larger man, fists on hips, puffed with indignation.

The landlord flinched a little. "So what if I am, you little gobermouch?" the landlord snarled at Jan.

"Then you are bound to obey him, not the other way round!" Jan snapped shoving a sharp fingertip into the man's rotund belly, making him take a step back in surprise.

"He is away from his parish! He has no authority here!" the landlord exploded.

"Regardless, he is an inquisitor! They go anywhere the Kyrkja goes. Their power does not wane over distance! He could be from the Gamlehaven and his authority would still be enforceable!"

The landlord bumped Jan back with his belly, now spoiling for a fight. It was like watching a courtier's delicate cat and a sled dog go at one another.

"You forget, novice," the landlord snapped in apparent triumph, "the honorable inquisitor is on sabbatical. That means he has set down his office for the time being."

The smug tone caused Jan to wilt.

"Then I choose to pick it up again, and shall start with a thorough investigation of this death for I suspect the evil one's hand is involved in these circumstances," Urban announced.

Jan's smirk returned while the landlord's wilted.

"You cannot-" the landlord never finished his protest.

"I cannot?" Urban sneered. "You seem to forget your place, landlord. I have papers stating I may end or restart my sabbatical as the needs of the Kyrkja, Crown or I see fit. Therefore, I order Jan here to stand watch over his mentor's property and see that not a single item is removed till such time as I have investigated it thoroughly and am satisfied that murder has been ruled out and the suspects have been exonerated or convicted."

"Are you willing to pay the rent till this is done? I have many people who could live here starting tomorrow if I so desire."

"I suspect your contract with the Koenraadians renders such a claim false. You are more caretaker than landlord if what I suspect is true. The university decides who lives here. You undertake the menial tasks like collecting rent and making repairs. Furthermore, I suspect that you are also here with your sons to see what choice items you might glean as windfalls of the father's bad fortune. Or do I miss my guess?"

The landlord cringed, and his sons blushed and squirmed.

"Hah!" shouted Jan with a clap of his hands and jabbed his finger at the landlord in time with his words. "Now begone, and I will come collect you when the inquisitor allows you to come back. Then you may take up your duties again." He crossed his arms, blocking the doorway to the office with his whole body.

The landlord turned and angrily shooed his sons down the stairs, vanquished. Just before the landlord's head disappeared from view, he turned.

"This is not finished between us," he growled. "You wait. I will retake my rights, even if I have to call a Thing to have it done. Mark my words, Inquisitor," and he vanished down the stairs leaving squeaks and groans of the floorboards in his wake. Once the front door slammed shut, Urban and Jan breathed a sigh of relief and triumph.

"It will take weeks to investigate everything in this room alone," Jan groaned.

"That is true, but we must do what we can." Urban looked around, then threw open the curtains to look out at the blazing hot day, seeing the distant thunderclouds breaking over the horizon. "I suppose the best thing for me to do is get myself fully reinstated by First Inquisitor Skaersson."

The name sent a shudder down Jan's neck. The First Inquisitor of Dyrrvatn Kastali was known locally as "Gud's Gud's Pisk," and when it came to crimes against God or the Kyrkja, he lived up to the title as a whip of God. Seeing the alarmed look on Jan's face, Urban smiled.

"I have met him a handful of times. Do not worry. Though his reputation is deserved, he is a man you would want in such a position. As just and merciful as a man can be."

Jan nodded, unconvinced.

"Wait here, and keep watch that nothing save for the remains of the poor father are removed. I will be back and with Herre Aske soon enough."

Urban clapped a hand on Jan's shoulder, gave it a confident shake and descended the stairs. There was much to do and several sleepless nights to come.

34. THE BURDEN OF THE SWORD

With great haste, Urban returned to the Blessath Borth to find Aske waiting, much to the ire of the innkeeper who Aske ignored. He was reclined on a bench in front of the building having tea. Most of the passers-by made a point to greet Aske as he had become something of a local celebrity among the boys and some fathers for his prowess at Knattleikr. Aske saw the dark look on Urban's face and his somewhat disheveled appearance, slurped down the rest of his tea and rose, ready to move.

Urban held up a hand to bid him patience. "Peace, I need to change and will be out presently," he said and passed Aske into the inn without slowing. Aske scowled and cocked an eyebrow for a moment. A small boy holding a ball laughed at his expression. Surprised, Aske looked down. Then realizing what the shy child had wanted, Aske crouched down holding out his hands to receive a throw from him. The boy's mother, over at the well, watched, shook her head and smiled.

Urban emerged from the inn a short while later to find Aske playing catch with a few of the boys who had joined in. Aske made a sign he had to go and gave them an extra high throw, to their delight, as they scrambled across the small square to catch the ball.

Urban was dressed in his full Ragnarite regalia. The sharp black and white uniform with scarlet trimmed trousers and sash were a strong contrast to what they were accustomed to him wearing. His sash bore his military medals as well as the Kyrkja honors.

"Your sabbatical is concluded?" Aske questioned. His expression was inscrutable to most people, but Urban saw right through it. He was ready for action. For too long Aske had little to do. Even working with Tandri as a stevedore to make extra money and keep busy had not been enough.

"Not by choice. By necessity," Urban said, his black and silver scabbard swaying on his hip as he walked. Aske fell in and marched next to him. Their focus acted like a plow parting the crowd. Anyone who was in their path briskly moved out of the way. As they walked, Urban filled his friend in on the events of the morning.

Overhead, storms began to roll in overtaking the sun. The city began to move with a more frantic pace. Despite the heat, people hurried to get their chores done and finish business before the rain fell. By the time the pair reached Ragnarplassen and its thick-walled mission at the center, they were in a thorough sweat. The headquarters of the sect reminded Urban of Athrvorthfestning. Low, squat with reinforced stone walls. Halls were built in controlled squares and courtyards while the plassen was an extra large trelleborg. Instead of berms and stakes, the walls were lined inside with shops and other attendant services with the ability to use the roofs as battlements and portcullis gates that could control passage despite never having been closed in their lifetime save to keep them functional. Unlike the Koenraadian university where they had grown accustomed to people who wore browns and greens, the population here wore the iconic black and white with splashes of red. There were few people with a casual purpose, and they moved along with the flow of a military garrison

A small round building in front of the gate off Halgon Ragnar Boulevard served as the factor's chancery for the mission. The pair of Paladins at the doors snapped to attention as Urban and Aske went inside.

A central fire was banked low in the center surrounded by small chambers for the monks who handled the accounting and dissemination of reports. It was a quick reminder to Urban that this was the Kyrkja at war. The mission in Ulfshaugrstrond was the heart of this fighting body, but this was its brain.

"May the Lord bless those who come in peace," an attendant monk greeted them.

"May the Lord bless those who labor in this place," Urban returned.

The monk bowed gently.

"How may I assist you, Inquisitor...?

"Urban av Hitilopt. I am here with my comrade, Herre Aske Rekkersson av Neinnanbjarg. We seek an immediate audience with First Inquisitor Skaersson, please."

The monk frowned sadly.

"Forgive me, Inquisitor. Herre Skaersson is called away to the Kronapalasset and may not be back till evening. Is there someone else who might help you with your needs?"

"Is there a chance he will return sooner?" Urban asked, frustrated.

"Of course," the monk said with a beatific smile. "Do you wish to wait?"

Urban paused and looked the question at Aske who knew his mind regarding the importance of what must be done. The Skaerslinger expressed an ironic shrug with eyes and lips that seemed to say "What can we do but wait."

"We shall wait. It is critical we speak to him as soon as possible no matter the hour," Urban said with a sigh. "May we do so in the south chapel?" Urban added.

"Of course, it is not closed to the public."

"We thank you, Brother," Urban said bowing, and the pair of men went to wait for their audience.

Urban and Aske prayed and talked in the chapel about what must be done. There was a twinge of regret for leaving Jan to stand watch over Father Tuajaksson's home without further instructions, but Urban could not miss speaking to the first inquisitor and needed Aske to be there as well.

The storms passed with the hours and the last waning rays of sunlight peered over the retreating clouds, washing the chapel in bright orange shafts of light through its plain windows. It had been relatively quiet save for when the citizenry and fellow clergy came to escape the heavy rain and hail that fell earlier from the thunderstorm.

Behind them the large door of the chapel opened with loud pops from the hinges. Urban turned to see his superior walking down the aisle. He stood, stiff joints protesting the sudden act. His heart now beating a rapid tattoo in his breast. Aske stood as well. As the first inquisitor reached the two, both bowed low.

"First Inquisitor Skaersson, thank you for taking your time to see me," Urban said, surprised at his emotional turmoil. His superior put his hands gently on the top of their bowed heads."

"The Lord bless and keep you both, my sons, and drive the evil one far from your body and soul," came the blessing. Urban felt a chill shoot up and down his spine at the words. "What is it that you must see me about?"

"Two things, Reverend Father," Urban began, standing at attention. "First, I wish to end the sabbatical granted me by my superior at Athrvorthfestning. You are my direct, well, my ultimate superior in Dyrrvatn Kastali. Odd circumstances necessitate me requesting reinstatement here, and under you."

The first inquisitor nodded, stroking his thickly bearded left cheek that hid an old scar.

"And the second?" he said thoughtfully.

"I wish to deputize Herre Aske under my authority so he can function on my behalf as well as extend the protection of the sect over him when he acts in my stead."

The first inquisitor's eyes narrowed in regarding Aske.

"What does he know of the Ragnarites?"

"First inquisitor," Aske said, "Ragnarite Paladins saved me as a child. I was raised at a mission deep in the pinery of Manitouland. For six years I lived as Ragnarite laity then I was given my choice to become one of the sect, or leave in accordance to Kyrkja laws. I chose to leave, but have maintained the Ragnarite ways, and live to make my saviors proud."

Aske looked deep into the eyes of this powerful man of God.

"That is an odd request, my son," the first inquisitor said, his voice revealing no indication of what he was thinking. "It is not often that a member of the laity is given the opportunity to become a proper Ragnarite, let alone one with the responsibility of an inquisitor. Even more surprising is that you turned down this life previously. What caused that decision?"

"I fell in love," Aske said.

The first inquisitor's let out a breath of surprised pleasure.

"And you felt you could not give your duty just priority?"

"Jah," Aske replied.

"You are still with her?"

"She is with child. Our first. I would prefer to be with her, but God sent me forth with Brother Urban on this quest."

The first inquisitor gave a slow nod.

"Are you willing to take the oath of office, though it may only be temporary for the needs of my trusted son?" Urban felt a flush of warmth toward the first inquisitor with such praise.

"I am pledged to see this affair to the end," Aske vowed, voice low, humble. "I pray that I will return home in time to see my child born."

The first inquisitor stood and closed his eyes as if listening to a trusted counselor whispering in his ear.

"Then come before the altar and kneel, and I shall commission you both accordingly."

The two walked around and knelt on the first step before the altar.

The orange light dimming by the moment into dusky purples and blues, leaving them in the soft glow of the eternal flame hanging in the apse of the kyrkje.

"My sons," he began, once more resting his hand lightly on top of their bowed heads, "like so many who hear the call of God to right that which is wrong, I bestow upon you a blessing and a duty. Neither may be shirked by the hand or thought of man. You are hereby commissioned to take up your calling with all your body, soul and spirit and to do so for the greater glory of the Lord God, Judge of all things. Are you willing to pledge yourself to such a calling?"

"I solemnly swear," Urban said.

Aske repeated in kind.

"Let your minds be clear and discern rightly according to the understanding given to you by God. Let not haste nor the world cloud your judgment. Be sober and merciful in your meditation on the troubles you must face. In all things listen for God's voice which will guide you while you choose to remain obedient."

"Amen," both agreed.

"In the name of the Father, Son and Holy Spirit, pick up the Sword of the Word which rightly divides soul and spirit, joint and marrow, and divines the intent of the heart."

"Amen."

The first inquisitor took out a small bottle of oil and poured some onto Urban's head and placed his hand on top.

"Urban av Hitilopt, Inquisitor of the Kyrkja, you have pledged your life to seek out the enemies of the Faith and threats to His people, the Forsamling. I call thee from thy time of rest to pick up thy calling. Come forth and obey."

"I shall," Urban agreed.

The first inquisitor now anointed Aske's head.

"Aske Rekkersson av Neinnvanbjarg, beloved adopted and prodical son of Halgon Ragnar and those who carry on in his name for the glory of God, you have been called forth to engage in battle with the enemy of all God's children. Come forth and shoulder the burden and blessing of this calling."

"I shall," Aske replied.

"Then as God is your witness to your pledges and oaths, I bless you both in His holy name," he paused again listening in the spirit.

"As it is written in Isaiah 42: 'Behold my servant, whom I uphold; mine elect, in whom my soul delighteth; I have put my spirit upon him: he shall bring forth judgment to the Gentiles.

He shall not cry, nor lift up, nor cause his voice to be heard in the street.

A bruised reed shall he not break, and the smoking flax shall he not quench: he shall bring forth judgment unto truth.

He shall not fail nor be discouraged, till he have set judgment in the earth: and the isles shall wait for his law.

Thus saith God the Lord, he that created the heavens, and stretched them out; he that spread forth the earth, and that which cometh out of it; he that giveth breath unto the people upon it, and spirit to them that walk therein:

I the Lord have called thee in righteousness, and will hold thine hand, and will keep thee, and give thee for a covenant of the people, for a light of the Gentiles;

To open the blind eyes, to bring out the prisoners from the prison, and them that sit in darkness out of the prison house'."

First inquisitor Skaersson took his hands off the men's heads, and drew his sword, making the sign of the cross in front of them.

"In the name of the Father, the Son and the Holy Spirit, hold these men to their oaths and grant them the office and authority in accordance to your will, Oh Lord. Amen."

"Amen," Urban and Aske said. The first inquisitor resheathed his sword. The sound of metal on leather echoed in the silence of the chapel.

"Unless you have other plans," the Reverend Father said by way of invitation, "please come dine with me and tell me more of why the Holy Spirit was insistent I grant your petition."

35. ASHAMED BEFORE THE CROWN

There was a pounding on his bedchamber door. A thundering that splintered his sleep and dragged him back to the bright and painful world. It mirrored the thudding in his head as Admiral Sverirsson thrashed between his thick down comforter and sheets, slick with alcohol laced sweat.

"Admiral?" a voice came barging into his room. The velvet steps of a pageboy thundered into his room and gently whipped back the curtains around his bed.

"What?" he demanded with all the hospitality of a cat dangling by its tail. A thick glass bottle rolled out of the bed, chipped itself on the floor next to several others and clanked against his chamberpot.

"The Visedronning demands your immediate presence in court," the boy seemed to shout in a soft voice at the sight of the admiral's state of intoxication. The admiral whipped off the comforter, and the cool air of the late morning caused his damp body to shiver. His night clothes stuck to his body.

"Fetch my uniform and help me get ready," he snarled in agony.

The page obeyed and fetched the admiral's uniform from a disheveled pile on the other side of the bed. The master of the navy picked through the empty bottles to find one that contained a little hair of the dog and drank it down to stave off the rising hangover.

He had no memory of how he came to end up in one of the guest apartments at the Kronapalasset last night. There had been a meeting with several of his kapteins, including the Visedronning's new favorite, Kaptein Gramrsson. There was a good chance he would be saying "Jah, Herre" to that upstart who never served in a battle before, if his eye was able to still spot a sea change.

Of course, she probably knows that he is responsible, the admiral thought bitterly.

The chill from the air sliced all the way through him with the memory of that day.

But you are responsible, Admiral Sverirsson reminded himself. You tried to kill that child and missed. You missed because God wanted you to miss. Or the devil, maybe. It does not matter, you killed the Visekonge. This must be how Judas felt afterward.

He gave a silent bitter laugh. Yet I used a piece of silver as the instrument of destruction which will become my own. With that thought he drained the bottle dry, but his own personal hell remained unquenched.

"If only I could unwind the skeins of fate," the admiral slurred to himself.

There was not much the page could do to get the admiral presentable for meeting with the Visedronning. His hair was a bird's nest and his beard looked like a mouse had taken residence. He did not smell of strong drink, he stank of it. It took all the decorum the boy had to keep from gagging or grabbing his nosegay as he dressed the admiral. After departing the drunkard's presence, the page rushed to the kitchen to shove a whole clove up each nostril.

When Admiral Sverirsson entered the Court of the Statsraad, he found the rest of the Privy Council already standing at attention and irritated by his interruption. The ceremony ground to a halt as he took his place next to the Stallare Marshal.

At the head of the court, standing on the dais, was the Visedronning Marianne. To her right, the Minister of the Wardrobe stood at graceful attention with the Sveinnaettir sword and scabbard in his hands awaiting use for ennoblement of her subject as reward for his actions in service to the Crown and Union. On her left, the Crown chaplain awaited his turn to anoint the men as reward from the Kyrkja. At the foot of the steps Kaptein Gramrsson and several other officers from the Silfryxen and its crew waited. The chancellor was presenting the sailors with medals for their mission on behalf of the Crown and service to the Union.

The chancellor began again, handing out medals of heroism and valor, shaking the hand of each man in turn. Once complete, he returned to stand behind his Tign.

The Visedronning took one step forward, her ceremonial gown jingling with the bead work and jewelry sewn into the train. It had been her wedding dress, but as a woman had never made such ennoblements before, no one knew the proper protocol, and in a pique of frustration, she chose the most impressive gown she could think of. Her ladies-in-waiting had rushed off to the chapel and cut it out of its cage, where it had been displayed along with the uniform Gregor had worn.

"Even after his death, you served your Visekonge with distinction, ingenuity and great bravery. Thanks to your planning and foresight, you salvaged half of a mission beset on all sides by treachery and deceit. Through it all, you remained true to your positions and Tign," the Visedronning declared.

"On behalf of a grateful Crown as embodied by myself Visedronning Marianne Ostensdottir, the Sveinnaettir, and all the United Jarldoms of Akiniwazi, I thank you for your service. Now come forth and receive your investiture into the Hird."

One at a time, from lowest rank to highest, they climbed the few steps to kneel before her. She drew the Sveinnaettir sword and gently tapped each shoulder of the man, before commanding them to rise with their new title and station. Most of the men were Fellesaettir, with no registry in the Bok av Familiar. They were promoted to Sivuaettir and their families given their recognition with a medallion bearing the page and line where their descendants would be able to look up their lineage from that day forward. One had come from a minor Fargeaettir , and wore his teal and white colored baldric proudly. His deeds were added to that of his aettir, and his descendants would be given a small fiefdom on one of the lakes to be decided later.

Then it came to Kaptein Gramrsson, without whom the execution of the plan would never have happened. He was made Farageattir and allowed to choose the new Gramraettir's colors. The kaptain burst with pride as he was given the title as Hauld Dyggvi Gramrsson.

The ceremony completed, the Visedronning returned the sword to its scabbard, and dismissed everyone save for the Minister of the Wardrobe and Admiral Sverirsson. A cold hand gripped his heart with icy talons as she descended the steps to the last one. He stepped forward to the place of audience before her and bowed low.

"Admiral, I have been hearing scandalous talk about you lately. Are you familiar with what is being said about you?"

"No, my Tign. No such talk has reached my ears. Not even from my friends."

"I am not surprised," she said sharply. "In fact, I have been informed that many of your subordinates have been complaining that you are failing in your duties since the Visekonge's funeral. Discipline has declined, the spirit of the Navy is breaking, and you wallow in drink like a sow in a mire!" Her voice built to a piercing crescendo. "What have you to say about this?"

Admiral Sverirsson stammered a nonsensical reply.

"And now, you come in here, drunker than a beggar on a bender, smelling like the gutter and interrupt my ceremony."

"My Tign! I came as soon as I was summoned!" he pleaded.

"Jah, I summoned you, but did not expect to receive unto my court a trainwreck of a person as you have presented yourself!" Her words were a poisonous fume, eyes cold. "You know better than to come to court in such a state," she huffed, and waited to see if he had anything to add. After a few moments of silence, she continued. "Very well. You are in disfavor in my court, and I am of a mind to banish you from it and seek your replacement! Do you have anything to say for yourself?"

Something in the admiral's head snapped. The irony of it all. Here they stood, three people in an empty room capable of holding several hundred. This offensive tirade was too far for his blood and he would no longer allow himself to be talked down to by a woman who sat upon that throne as a formality till her son, the rightful occupant of that high seat, returned. He would be well within his rights as admiral to strike her down right now and be done with it all.

"What court? You have no court! You have banished them already, my Tign! Half of them are in open rebellion against you and seek to put your head on a pike at the city gates! It is through people like me, as broken as I am that you have a phantom chance to keep your dynasty!"

283

Almost before the Minister of the Wardrobe could register the act, the Sveinnaettir sword was in the Visedronning's hands. The gold and bejeweled scabbard flew across the room and he gasped in shock, sprinting after it without thinking. She did not run but took three large steps forward with a scream of rage, ready to hack the contemptuous man's head off where stood.

"Jah! Do that!" he shouted back at her. "Strike me down!" He jutted his neck out obscenely, baring it to the naked blade that was drawing back to slice him down. "Do God's justice!"

That strange choice of words made the fatal sweep of the blade pause.

"What are you waiting for, woman?" His voice cracking off the stone and glass walls.

"What are you playing at?" she demanded in return.

Admiral Sverirsson's bloodshot eyes urged her to strike him down.

"I am your Visedronning! Your life rests in my hands. It is mine to dispose of as I see fit!" she stated in a tone of hammered iron.

"Then do it! Strike me down!" he shouted.

The sword wavered, wanting to slash down and be done with it but stopped by some unknown conflict.

"Finish me!" the admiral's voice broke hysterically.

The sword still did not fall. The tip began to dip as it grew heavy in her hands. What was stopping her? His Tign's demeanor changed from fury to pity then to disgust. The spirit of suicide attempted another tack in the admiral's head.

"I killed Gregor! It was me! My fault!" he shouted and crumbled to his knees with a wretched sob. "All my fault."

"How was it your fault?" Her voice thick as her emotions drew and quartered her.

"I threw the coin that Olivr chased. How could I have known my Tign would run after him? How could I have known?" The admission gushed out of him like a lanced boil and Admiral Sverirsson fell to his face. Visedronning Marianne swayed, sick with the revelation.

"You... threw... that coin?"

His hands covered his head as he was face down on the floor at her feet.

"I did," he gasped. "I threw it."

From somewhere above him, he heard the strangled fury leaking from her lips, but the blow still did not fall.

The Minister of the Wardrobe came beside her, the scabbard retrieved, then moved to stand between the admiral and his Tign.

"My Tign," he whispered, "do not stain your hands with his blood. Can you not see his torment?"

"But he killed Gregor while trying to kill Olivr," she snarled. "This has threatened everything! A two hundred and fifty year dynasty... my children! A million lives are now in the balance thanks to him!"

"And it is destroying him," the minister said. The admiral's wretched sobs were horrible to hear, even to the disconnected part of his mind that seemed to look on from outside himself. "If you slay him, he is free of responsibility and there is nothing he can do to help salvage what we can out of this disaster." The minister paused. "The sword is in your hand, My Tign, and you will answer only to God. Are you ready to accept this?"

He glided out of the way of his Tign, again revealing the ruin of the admiral to her eyes.

Visedronning Marianne regarded her trusted servant for a long time. Sweat rolled down the minister's sallow skin, and he looked ready to vomit in fear.

For all her position's power, she had never killed herself, despite feeling ready to. Her eyes returned to the broken man at her feet. The man who murdered... no, not a murderer. It was still an accident that took Gregor's life. He attempted to murder Olivr, and failed.

The sword drooped to her side, and the Minister of the Wardrobe held out the scabbard with the slightest of trembles. She slid it smoothly back into its proper place.

Admiral Sverirsson remained on the floor as his Tign stood imperiously over him.

"Admiral, are you still my loyal subject?" she asked as if prodded from someone else.

Admiral Sverirsson's quiet sobs ceased with the first pale light of hope.

"Jah, my Tign," he said, his eyes raising up to see the hem of her gown.

"Do you wish absolution for your crime?" The words were drawn from her by a will more terrible than her hatred for him. A forgiveness that she did not want to give but could not help but offer.

Still on all fours, he whispered, "Jah, my Tign."

"Do you believe with all your heart that my son, Leif belongs on this throne behind me and is owed all your love, blood and life if he so asks for it?"

"He is God's chosen to sit upon the high seat, my Tign. I never thought otherwise."

He dared not look up.

Like a man waiting to be hung, Admiral Sverirsson stayed motionless unable to guess how long he remained in suspension till finally, with a delicate voice she pronounced sentence.

"Until I decide to take your life, I have another task for you. If you wish to gain some form of redemption for your part in the death of my husband and attempting to assassinate my son, you will succeed in this duty. If you fail and survive, I will find the most horrifying punishment possible that will not kill you. Do you understand this is a command of the Crown?"

"I do, my Tign," he said, pushing himself up to a kneeling position before her. The sight of her towering over him terrified him. The stained glass windows high above her silhouette gave an aura like flame.

"You will take the Sjovinna, a small flotilla of steamknarr and ten thousand men at arms with their attendant Ragnarites, Anjars and Taitians north to Mannvoenlandnaam. There you will meet the Tronerving and Kronadottirs and bring them to the Domkyrkje for his coronation. If my husband cannot have the throne, my son will, and you will make sure this happens."

"As you command, my Tign."

36. AMONG THE ROOTS OF THE WORLD

Mirjam awoke in a purple and blue world. Pain pulsed through her veins as she coughed till her vision sparkled and she tasted blood. She was face down on a smooth crystal slab next to a blue glowing lake, a warm pair of hands patted her back, making her cough more till the gasping and rattle in her lungs ceased. She rolled over and saw a singular bright white light sparkle several hundred yards overhead, like a far off star in the colossal hollow of the mountain.

The walls of the cavern were interwoven with lightning bolts of stone that glowed a deepening red from above, and an eerie blue from below. Monumental pillars went from floor to ceiling throughout the massive lake that was as large as any they had seen in the pinery, shot through with trees of crystal that either glowed from inside, or glowed like a mineral rainbow from the light below.

"Praise God! You wake!" Friar Inge shouted. "Thank you, Lord, for returning her to us!"

"Was I asleep for long?" Mirjam muttered, her head throbbed like a rotten tooth. As she sat up, her ribs ached.

"You hit the water hard and we thought you had drowned, but Feles was able to coax you to breathe again." Inge sounded drained from the ordeal.

Solveig hugged her sister with careless force, crying in relief.

"I was worried you had passed on from this world," Amr said with a thin but genuine smile.

"Where are we?" Mirjam asked.

"Deep inside the mountain, I suspect in a place no man has set foot before," Feles said.

"Now that we know you are safe from danger, my Tign," Inge added, "we can begin searching for a way out while your sister tends to you."

"How far did we fall?" Mirjam asked and suffered another wracking cough.

"I do not know, nor can anyone else recall. We lost track of time," Finn said, shaking his head. He was putting away some belongings that had been in his hip bag and managed to survive. He grimaced with how few were left. "I only remember falling a long way and passing through the opening up there, then into all this," he said and gesturing to the root like lattices of stone.

"It was a shock to the dogs," Leif observed.

Mirjam looked at Brother Finn's companion who stood watch over them all. Thyrnir lay next to the elder dog like a frightened puppy.

"I remember the ledge in the shrine collapsing, but then nothing more till I hit the water," Declan said.

"It is the screams I remember," Amr chimed in. "Surprise, then terror."

"God seems to have struck the terrible experience from our memory leaving only what we can tolerate," Inge said. "I, for one, am grateful. No one struck the walls and we had water to land in."

"But it is glowing blue!" Mirjam exclaimed and began coughing again. More water came out of her lungs.

"Shhh, now dear sister. Relax for the time being. We can talk more later," Solveig soothed.

Leif came over to Mirjam, knelt down and kissed her on the top of her head in the tenderest of ways.

"Listen to your sister," Leif soothed. "We must learn where we are. Although I doubt anything could have followed us into this misfortune. I am certain that even if we could climb out, our way remains blocked by ice."

As if to emphasize the point, the water splashed underneath the opening. More ice and rubble plummeted down. The stones sank deep down into the endless blue glow of the water till they vanished as if into a mist deep below.

"Greithr," Leif said as he took account of their situation. "We are far below the surface, with only an axe, a sword, a saxe, and maybe a knife or two. We have no food, no extra clothing, nor blankets or supplies for travel. No one knows the way out, and starvation is only a few days away. Thankfully, the water is at least clean if we must drink." He scratched at his drying hair as he thought. "Let's search for a way out. We can search for exits in three directions from the lake, praise God. Therefore, we shall go in pairs, and see what exits we can find and where they lead. Solveig, you and Mirjam remain here as our camp."

The men were all in agreement. They had to find their way out and quickly.

"At least we do not need lights here," Declan joked grimly.

"Do not count on it to last," Inge cautioned.

"Who will pair together?" Finn asked.

"You and Inge follow the passage along the lake to our left. Declan and I will go straight away from it, while Amr and Feles, take the remaining route angled off that way, to the right."

"Jah, my Tign," Inge said. Feles gave a strange look at him, but said nothing.

"Do not forget to mark your passing somehow. Scratch an arrow on the rock if you must. Anything to help you get back. Think of this as a maze," Amr pointed out.

"Do not be gone too long," Solveig fussed.

"We shall be back before you even know it," Leif said, smiling.

The men split up and went their separate ways, leaving Solveig and Mirjam alone on the shore with a single saxe to defend themselves if the need arose.

"Solveig?" Mirjam asked. Her voice was still soft and rattling from her near drowning.

"Do not talk," Solveig begged.

"No, I need to tell you something."

"And I, you, but now is not the time for it."

"I do not know if we will get another opportunity," Mirjam said, craning to see if Leif and Declan were out of sight. "It must be now."

"Greithr. Go ahead."

"Leif intends to use you as a political marriage once he is crowned," Mirjam said. Saying the words felt like dropping a hot rock. She had been forced to carry this secret for days, and it had been tearing her up all the while.

Solveig's face turned white as cream.

"He..." she started to say. "To whom?"

"Whomever he feels will bring the greatest political advantage for him." Mirjam could see her sister's heart break. "On a happier note, I doubt it will be Birgr Vilhoaettir. I think he plans to behead him and his entire family once he ascends the throne."

"Small comfort," Solveig whispered, her head bowed, silent tears flowing.

"Ohhhh... what? What?" Mirjam comforted, and went to hug her sister. "What is so horrible? You are dodging the worst possible husband in that pig."

For a long time, Solveig did not answer, and Mirjam did not press.

"I love him," Solveig said once she had calmed.

"Who?" Mirjam asked, not getting the context. Solveig jerked her head up to glare at her sister for being so thick. "Ahh... Declan. Sorry for being forgetful. Are you sure?"

"Jah," Solveig moaned and fell backward to lie on the smooth stone, looking up into the false sky of crystal lightning and stone stars. The red had faded from above, and now the world was filled with the bluest of blue light, coming from below and all around. Flecks of incredible colors speckled the ceiling and walls between the natural columns.

"I guess you have always loved Declan," Mirjam said after a while. "I knew that deep down."

"No," Solveig groaned. "I mean, jah, but that was not the only reason why I said that."

"Then why?" Mirjam asked.

Solveig did not speak her answer but merely looked at her sister and waited. It did not take long.

"Oh? Oh!" Mirjam gasped, hand flying to her mouth. "Oh no! No, no, no! You did not!" She spun to face her sister fully and knelt next to her. "You bedded Declan?"

Solveig nodded, her expression was miserable, tears began to run.

"Leif will kill me!" although soft, the words contained a wail of anguish.

Mirjam was stunned. Although for months she had goaded and teased her sister about giving in to Declan, she never believed in her heart that her sister would do it. She was too pure as compared to her own desires. Previously, she would have enjoyed the irony that her sister had a rebellious streak just like she did, but not now. Absolutely not now.

"He could not. Not Leif."

"He would if I ruin his chance to make peace with the jarls. Oh, God! Oh God! What have I done? Not only once but twice!" Solveig began to panic, eyes frantically rolling in their sockets.

"Solveig. Solveig!" Mirjam shook her sister. "Leif is not going to kill you. No one is going to know. I will not say a word. We need to make sure Declan does not say anything to Leif either. We can do this. We can get control back. Just calm down now," Mirjam said, uncertain if they really could accomplish this, though it felt the right thing to say. "No one is going to know. And if they demand a test, we will deal with that then."

Solveig's breathing slowed and the tears stopped.

"We just have to tell Declan to be quiet about this," she said, testing Mirjam's words in her mouth. Getting comfortable saying them and trying hard to believe them. "No one says anything about this. Not you, not me, not Declan."

Mirjam nodded. "And then all will be safe. You enjoyed your lover, and now it is time to think beyond that, for all our lives." Mirjam sat back clutching her knees to her chest. Solveig sat up and leaned against her sister's shoulder and stared out into the blue.

37. LINGERING DOUBTS

"You have been far too quiet, Inge," Finn said.

They had followed the crooked crystalline shore looking for an exit as the light from above dimmed away, and the blue glow drifted up from the deep.

"I am sorry. A lot has been on my mind since Edda was slain," Inge admitted.

Finn was surprised that her death had affected him so deeply. Inge stopped to think a moment. "No, it is not her death, but that temple."

"I have felt it too," Finn agreed. "What did we experience there?"

"I imagine I know what the sensation was. When I was young, I imagined that was how the high priest felt when entering the Holy of Holies in Jerusalem."

"But was that God?" Finn countered.

"It may have been. I cannot imagine anything else giving me such sensations. Never in any experience I've had close to God's power or in the presence of His angels on display. Not even in all the exorcisms I had performed, and all the demons I had faced was there ever such a sensation of complete... nakedness before that light."

"But down here, I do not feel it," Finn added.

"By Go-" Inge stopped his words in his mouth with a low grunt. "That is strange," he tried again. The memory of his burning tongue still fresh.

"Perhaps something good will come out of the experience," Finn said with a wry twist of a smile. Ahead he could see a cave that lead out of the main cavern that served as their cage.

"Perhaps that is our escape?" Inge wondered.

"We can only hope," Finn replied.

The two angled away from the shore and began to climb up a difficult embankment to the chamber exit.

"It is still sad that she died," Inge said. "Giving her life for ours and destroying a Wendigo and Nephilim in the process? I think that could be considered a good trade, and a manner in which she would have wanted to give up her life." Finn gave Inge a queer look. Inge blundered on again without noticing Finn's reaction. "After all, she seemed unable to approach the shrine further. Perhaps there was something in there that she either could not tolerate or would not let her in."

"But why would God not let her in?" Finn demanded, voice testy.

"Do we even know it was God?" Inge asked.

"How can we assume it is not?" Finn snapped back.

Inge looked back and saw the irritated Finn standing, hands on hips and glaring up at him.

"And that is my real confusion on the place. How was it that Edda could not come to safety and Amr, who I am at this point assuming to be under the influence of something demonic, managed to drag his carcass into there easier than we could? God's flaky dandruff! I have no good answers either, Finn!" Inge burst out.

"Forgive me," Finn said as a smirk came to his lips. "It seems your tongue still has the knack."

"Bacraut," Inge sniped and offered his hand to Finn then both pulled Bergamot up. "Speaking of whom, have you noticed anything different about Thyrnir?"

"Jah, he does seem a lot milder in temperament. Like a whipped puppy," Finn agreed.

The cave ahead was poorly lit as compared to the main chamber they had been walking in, but they could still make their way. The cramped spaces pressed in on them as they walked on, but no shafts or branches were found.

"Ahh..." Finn breathed suddenly. "That is what I was sensing. Perhaps it is a natural reaction from such a fall. But what if there is more to it?"

"Let us make an assumption," Inge said. "For the sake of argument, let us assume that the shrine was a temple dedicated to Jehovah. Let us also assume that the fall did not do something natural to Thyrnir as much as something was done by the shrine. Perhaps a demon that had been in Thyrnir was driven out? What do you think of this idea?"

Finn considered it as they walked farther into the narrowing passage.

"It could be, but that is also worrisome. For what happens when a demon is driven out and the Holy Spirit does not take up residence?" Finn said?

"The demon wanders in the dry places for a time till he returns to his home and finds it empty and the place swept and clean. It then takes up residence again, and invites in even more of its friends leaving the person worse off than before." Inge paused walking as he thought. "That is worrisome."

"Jah. If there was a demon in Thyrnir, something I absolutely think is true, it has been driven out, and we need to seal him before it returns with friends and becomes even stronger than before."

"But that refers to men, Finn," Inge reminded.

"Regardless, we do not know how the demon was put into Thyrnir."

Inge nodded, and stopped, pondering the pitch black passage ahead.

"It seems we have run out of light, making this a dead end. Only the Lord knows what lurks farther in." Inge slapped the smooth crystal wall. "I for one do not want to get lost in that."

"Let us go back, and see if we can find a different way out the cavern," Finn agreed. The two priests turned around, shoulders brushing the walls.

"I think we are coming to the end of a fissure anyway."

"Who can tell?" Finn said with a shrug.

The walk back was easier, for they felt like they were walking down a subtle grade.

"Suppose you are right," Finn said, "and the shrine was to God. Suppose that light drove out a demon in Thyrnir, and there is also one in Amr. Would not the light have driven a demon out of him?"

Inge made a wary mewling sound at the thought, struggling with unpleasant ideas.

"Jah?" he said in a guarded whine. "A priest of God, possessed by a demon? That seems rather impossible."

"Oppressed by a demon. Seduced perhaps? We are still sinful men, and you know as well as I that offers a doorway for manitou to take up residence. Like having a bandit in one room of the house, but cannot get into some other locked rooms."

"Then there is a chance whatever is oppressing Amr, to use your term, could have been driven out," Inge posited.

"That is a hopeful thought," Finn said.

"Huh," Inge exclaimed, "I never thought you would feel that way toward your nemesis."

"Amr is not my nemesis," Finn said with a laugh. "He thinks I am his, but if I want to be truthful with myself, I would delight in his turning from whatever dark path he took to come back to righteousness. I think somewhere deep in our past something was wrenched in his spirit and he became twisted. Something perhaps that can be made right, if any demons involved are shoved out of the way."

Inge and Finn made it back to the main chamber and climbed down the boulder. "This assumes that Amr does not want to be evil," Finn cautioned.

"Shocking to think of a priest as evil!" came Inge's stark reply.

"Do you not remember my encounter with Abbot Kennetsson? How he tried to roast me alive in Athrvorthfestning's dungeon?"

Bergamot found it easier to get down from the boulder at the cave's entrance and joined the brothers. She was as exhausted as they were.

"Finn, the thought makes my stomach churn," said Inge, voicing his discomfort at the thought of evil men in power. It was plain he was not so innocent as to ignore that corruption was a real danger to the priesthood, but to suggest it like Finn did was a disturbing admission.

"At least we have not eaten in a day. Nothing to vomit up," Finn teased.

"Starvation," Inge said with deep scorn. "Thank you for reminding me about our lack of food. That means barring the ability to escape this cavern, we can starve to death in a week?"

Finn gave a bitter laugh. "I am sure one or more of us will turn to cannibalism before that happens," he said, regretting his words the instant they came out of his mouth.

"Might we not conjure up that terror, please? Escaping the physical manifestation of starvation and cannibalism is a little too fresh in my mind."

"Forgive me," Finn said, shaking his head hard in an effort to throw the image of Twelve Fingers out of his mind.

"Perhaps we should go back and check on the Kronadottirs before looking for another way out," Inge suggested.

"Agreed," Finn said, as he reached down and patted Bergamot before returning to the girls.

38. DASHED DREAMS

"Perfect," Leif complained and threw a chunk of broken rock out into the dark shaft. The glowing crystals seams had gradually become fewer and fewer till only one thin lightning bolt shaped seam was left, revealing that the chasm their tunnel ended in was impassable. The crystal struck the opposite wall and fell into darkness. No impact was heard.

"I suppose that is why we felt air currents from this giant stale pocket of air as old as the mountain," Declan agreed.

Till this moment, both men thought they had found the way out. A steady climb and the illusion of a fresh breeze giving them false hope. Leif sat down on one of the natural steps of rock to catch his breath. Declan joined him. Although he was in better shape, the lack of food and tight squeezes from time to time drained him more. His clothes fit poorly now, and he relied on his belt and baldrick, and his few remaining pins and ties far more to keep them in place. Even his bear fur cloak felt like a burden.

"I wish we were home," Leif complained again. Declan nodded, agreeing with his leige's frustration. "I wish we had never had to leave the Silfryxen and could have sailed back without any of this catastrophe."

He slapped his knees and spread his arms wide. "There are times I wonder if Friar Amr lied about everything. Did any of us witness anything more than those vikings? No. We did not. We were so rattled, we took Amr's word for it. A man who reveals more and more that he may be the crazy and untrustworthy murderer that Brother Finn warned us of."

Declan did not know how to respond and decided to act like a Stallare who pitched a fit and then stared straight ahead, to not offer any reaction to it.

"Did I really make such a fatal error?" Leif moaned and rubbed his face as if to take the sleep from his burning eyes.

Neither knew how long it had been since they had slept. Every muscle ached, Leif's stomach complained endlessly for food, and he was careful to slake his thirst with only a little water. Both men distrusted water that glowed.

"No," Leif concluded more to himself more than Declan. "I cannot have made that level of mistake. There is so much that seems to back up Amr's statements. God has not abandoned us."

"My Tign," Declan hazarded, "I am sure one of the others found a way out."

"Of course, you are right, my friend."

Declan felt the warm glow of the recognition.

"When we get back, we will either know the way out or have a better idea of which direction to look."

Declan then thought of Solveig. He had been desperate to be close to her ever since they fell. If only he had been allowed to stay with them as protection, but Leif spoke before he could suggest his plan and he could only obey. "And we can check on your sisters."

"That was a close call," Leif breathed. In a flash he relived the frightening possibility of losing one of his sisters. "Thank God for Feles. I am very thankful to him that both survived," Leif said. "Otherwise, I do not know how I would solve this political crisis."

Declan's heart froze. "How so?" he said with the careful steps of a cat slipping by a sleeping dog.

"I am going to have to buy peace somehow."

That statement began to squeeze Declan's chest, crushing the air out of him.

"How is that?" Declan fought hard to keep his voice normal. "Neither daughter will lead to the Crown anymore."

"Oh, but they will be of great value. Not to that tjovekjakji Vilhoaettir, no, no. He has a date with the axeman when I catch that svikari fubrande. I think I will leave him on the rack for at least a year till he begs to have his rotting limbs cut off." The thought of destroying Jakob Vilhoaettir offered Leif a much needed boost in energy and he sounded more confident.

"But if you plan to kill all the traitorous jarls, why do you care who your sisters marry?"

"Gifts must be given to my most loyal supporters. New alliances forged ever stronger. Otherwise what is to stop this from happening again?"

"But surely-" Declan tried to respond.

Leif yelled. "I am now the head of the Sveinnaettir! I must lead and secure our future!" Then in a calmer register, "That means I am Tign of every soul under me just like my father. That includes my uncles and grandfathers, my cousins their wives and children. All those who are of Sveinnaettir blood or claim fealty and protection under my banner. My own mother is now subject to me."

Declan knew how dangerous a path he was taking, but could not resist asking more.

"But if they cannot have the throne through Solveig-"

"And Mirjam. It would be wise to marry both of them off," Leif added.

"How does that secure cooperation and peace with the rebellious jarls?" Declan asked.

"When I die or abdicate, barring my own progeny, they will become the bloodlines to gain the Crown," Leif explained. "That is why my sisters still have value. Mother can no longer have children, and Olivr is a dead branch to the family. That means if I do not have children, for whatever curse that might befall me, the children of Solveig and then Mirjam have precedence in the order of succession. After all these years of serving me, you did not know this?"

"No, my Tign,"Declan said, his emotions roiling in his breast. "None of us like to think on the death of our Tign. We know you are mortal, but I expect to die in glorious battle long before you do."

The suggestion of his father dimmed Leif's fire and both men fell silent.

"Who would you give Solveig to?" Declan asked.

Leif looked at Declan with a curious expression. The words coming out of the powerful berserker seemed delicate and timid.

"How would I know at this point? The one who would be the biggest political coup or provide me with the best military advantage. Trust me, my friend, we are going to war once I get back and those filthy bakstypir kjettarhunds are going to bathe in the blood and ashes of their loved ones before I am through."

In that moment, where Leif began contemplating revenge on his enemies, Declan could almost see the spirit steal upon him. Something deep inside his Tign became hard as iron and poisonous as a viper's fang. He had seen it before in men who had lost all they loved, but never in someone who had yet to experience real loss, and it unnerved him.

"I must say, Declan, you have been acting very odd about my sisters as of late. What ails you?" The way Leif looked at the berserker now in reference to Solveig and Mirjam caused Declan to break into a cold sweat. Had he figured out their affair? Had they not been discrete enough? Panic was rising and he prayed to keep it out of his words.

"Nothing, my Tign. Nothing. They were not made for such rigors and it pains me to see such delicate women suffer like this. It is like watching the Crown's coach being used to haul manure. I find it deeply offensive. You have seen how frail they are. I come from a world of strong men used to such hardships. Not women, no. They have no business being out here." Declan knew he was rambling and fought to hold his tongue. "I... my Tign, they should not be here. Not like this." Declan felt like an idiot. Why could he not have kept silent?

Leif looked hard at his trusted protector and champion, then stood up, and brushed himself off with a brusque swipe of his hands.

"It would be advisable to not worry so much about them tolerating the hardships of this trek. They are of the same stock as me and will rise to the challenge," Leif declared, his voice clipped and tight. Declan slowly stood up with a new caution for his Tign who, without waiting, began walking back down the passage they had come.

"Furthermore," Leif's voice echoed back to him, "I would advise you not to fall in love with either of them. It would be a tragic end for you."

"Jah, my Tign," Declan said and followed after, certain that Leif knew.

39. IF GIVEN THE CHOICE

Amr had not felt so rattled in years, decades maybe. Something deep and terrible had happened to him in that shrine, and he was at a complete loss as to what it was. When he closed his eyes, he saw a giant open wound in his soul, as if a tree had been forcibly yanked from a mire of red clay, roots tearing out of the wet smooth mess, leaving obscene gaps and holes that ran throughout the entirety of his being. Thyrnir acted very much the same way, skittish and unsure.

"How came you to be all the way out here?" Feles asked. "I know you are not merchants or miners for you have no stock, and you are dressed for travel not business."

Lost in his own thoughts, the question caught Amr off guard.

"Uh, no. We are traveling up from Lake Wanishinabinoogi."

"Odd. Why do something like that?" Feles asked. Amr gave the youth a perplexed stare. Why he was interrogating him about such things? With a start, he realized Feles had no hidden agenda and was attempting to make friends, nothing more.

"Our reason is our own," Amr said hoping to dismiss the line of inquiry. Feles obliged. This end of the cavern was filled with many false tunnels that went into the rock latticework of the glowing crystals a little way and ended after granting a hint of hope only to betray it. But that was not what Feles was watching. His eyes were steadfastly on the ground.

"What are you looking for?" Amr asked.

"I am hoping my luck holds and I find running water."

"Like a drain?"

"Jah. This is a cistern. Water is coming in from somewhere outside. I could taste it when I swallowed some when we fell into it."

"You know what the water from outside tastes like? Go on!" Amr mocked.

"I live in these lands. We drink the water and this water is snowmelt. How is it getting in and if it is getting in, this chamber should be flooded-"

"Unless there is a drain!" Amr exclaimed catching on.

"Exactly," Feles said with a grin. "We Saami use caves from time to time, and wet ones like this have lots of stalactites and stalagmites. This one has hardly any. This means that the water here is recent. Just like the lake was recent, and came from a glacier far above us."

"You are suspecting that this cistern must be draining out to keep this depth?"

Feles tapped his nose and smiled. "The water level must have been much higher at some point because we have not seen any signs of it going down on the walls."

"For a man from an aettir of nomadic caribou herders, you sure know a lot about caves."

Feles only chuckled.

They reached a part of the shore that was much rockier likely from a ceiling collapse.

"This does not bode well," Amr moaned as he saw sharp crystalline shards mixed with dusty blocks of dull gray stone.

"I agree, for it means the rock is unstable and loose, but if you listen..."

Both stopped moving on the clattering rock.

The faint trickle of water could be heard.

"Ah hah!" Feles said and scampered over some larger boulders, looking down to see thin rivulets of water cutting between the rocks that braided together and trickled down a passage just out of sight.

"That is the way out, I suspect. Let us just hope the water does not fill the tunnel and we have to swim our way out, or that it becomes too deep."

"You are sure?"

Feles laughed. "Of course not! We must go and make sure."

Amr hesitated, wondering if this was the right choice, or whether to wait for the rest and let Leif decide. Feles did not bother waiting and went into the fissure alone.

A bubble of fear filled Amr. Deep recollections of abandonment boiled up from the deep water of his spirit.

"Wait!" he shouted and scrambled after Feles, Thyrnir an afterthought.

Once inside, the tunnel turned out to be broad and heavily marbled with the glowing crystals. The little trickles of water became a steady stream the length of a man wide, and over two feet deep. It moved at a rapid pace, zigzagging across the base of a tunnel like a slithering snake. The glass like crystal was impossibly slick as it glowed beneath the water.

"I think we should go back," Amr suggested. "Surely you are right."

"Not till we know," Feles refused. "The last thing I want is to discover this just leads to a lightless cistern deeper in the mountain where we will all die."

"That is not the sort of thoughts I desire to have right now," Amr complained. His eyes darted about, following shadows that only he could see. Feles walked on as if he was crossing slick ice. Amr imitated his little marching steps and they continued to follow the water's flow.

"When you were in the shrine, what was God dealing with in you?" Feles asked.

"What? Why do you ask that?" Amr started with the question, irritated that Feles could even consider something other than where to place his next step.

"I assume that you had a lot of sin to ask forgiveness for by how you rolled on the ground."

"That is none of your concern," Amr snapped.

"Perhaps this is why you seem to be so... shaken right now."

"What? How would you know such a thing about me? We only just met."

"It is amazing how little time it takes to get a sense of someone. Particularly when you had spent days in such a place as that shrine. You become sensitive to others pain."

"Pain?" Amr was incredulous.

"Oj! You are in a lot of pain right now. Perhaps confessing it would help," Feles pried.

"I will not. Do you realize how rude you are?" Amr snapped. The retort had no effect on the lackadaisical nature of his companion.

"Rude or not, talking to a stranger is sometimes the best way to heal wounds of the soul."

Amr gaped openly at Feles. Here he was, being preached to about confessing his sins to a layperson and stranger. What madness was this?

"When I was told you Saami were more... primitive... in your understanding of religion, I was maliciously under-informed. No. No. Priests do not confess to layfolk. The ordained confess to other ordained, and there is a hierarchy we must mirror in the manner of the celestial order."

Feles slipped and fell on a slick bit of crystal with a splash in the warm water.

"I wonder how this water became so warm?" he laughed before standing up. "At least that was pleasant."

Amr was too busy concentrating on keeping his footing while Thyrnir continually bumped into him for the dog's footing was even worse. His claws were wearing down as he continually used them to try and keep from sliding.

"Perhaps that is your problem, oh priest," Feles observed. "You think there is a hierarchy and need a religion between you and God. A superior you must appeal to and grasp at the crumbs of their goodness which frequently never comes. Out here, there is no need. It is you and God together."

"Hansafraetrs. Now you sound like one of those fool reformists."

"You cannot blame me for trying to help you. Despite your prickly demeanor."

"Insufferable. Just insufferable," Amr grumped.

A blast of cold came up the tunnel shocking them both. The smell of ice and dead leaves reached their noses.

"Hah!" Feles shouted. "I knew it!"

Thyrnir's footing gave, and the large dog fell into Amr's legs knocking him down and the two slammed into Feles. As a pile, they all began to rush through the now black tunnel.

They howled and shouted with fear in the dark for how long they could not tell before launching into the cool morning air and crashing into a frigid pool of water a few feet below. They found the pool was quite narrow and felt fortunate to have landed where they did. A few feet either way, and the water was no more than a yard deep and filled with sharp rocks. They clambered on top of a pile of dry rocks and looked around. Both of them screamed in triumph at what they saw and embraced each other, thankful to be alive.

On three sides, they were surrounded by glacier that had ground into the mountain till it cut a hole into the lake inside that mountain and the water rushed out, melting the ice back to create the grotto they now found themselves in. Above them were stars sparkling in the pre-dawn sky.

"That explains why we are so tired," Feles said as he pointed to the morning stars rising in the east.

"Jah," Amr agreed as he looked up to the waterfall's peak. They had fallen another three or four yards into the pool. "Now, how do we tell the rest?"

"You and Thyrnir help me up and I will bring them. You wait here-"

"I think it would be best if I went. I know my Tign better," Amr said exhausted.

"Tign?" Feles blinked at the use of the word.

"I mean, my herre," Amr tried to cover.

Feles shook his head. "Why did you call him your Tign?"

"Do you wish me to wait with Thyrnir? I doubt we could convince him to go back up there," Amr demanded.

Thyrnir cowered on the side of the cliff. Falling twice seemed to have broken something in the dog's spirit. Amr tasted bile as he looked at him.

"Jah. Keep him here, and I will be back soon," Amr said.

"You would leave your own animal like this? What kind of a man are you?" Feles looked at Amr in disgust.

"A man with bigger priorities than a useless dog!" Amr snarled.

Feles looked at Thyrnir for a long moment then nodded his head as if agreeing to an unheard voice.

"Sell him to me. How much do you want?"

"What? Are you insane? That is a Havarian mastiff! The best dog breed in the land! They are never for sale."

"You said he was worthless. I have met a few Havarians in my day, and none of them ever talked about their companion with such disdain as you do. Its spirit obviously broken, and no longer good for your work, but I can give him a good home. Perhaps he will make a good guard dog. Something that big will keep the tipi warm at night."

"No! You cannot have him." Amr felt as if the whole world was spinning.

"You do not want him. It is only fair," Feles persisted good-naturedly.

The image of the torn open red clay flashed in Amr's mind again. The holes where the roots had been were filling up with black sludge.

"I would rather kill that mutt than give him to someone else," Amr snarled.

Feles took a step back from Amr, surprised at the hateful power in his voice.

"What sort of monster are you?" Feles gasped, clearly realizing there were sinister forces at work here.

The question echoed in Amr's mind, throwing him out of the world to a place inside where he understood the image of the red clay. It was his soul. Something wicked had been growing in it and the shrine had torn it out, but the ground of his soul was poisoned by something deeper that could not be ripped out. It salted the earth of his being. Time seemed to flow backwards in Amr's mind as he saw his father casting salt upon the wet clay, leaving deep footprints. His father, Vraethur was a fredlaus and a bandit. He had taken his mother from her family and made her his thrall. Amr was raised to help his father's banditry till caught by the militia and Vraethur was hung for brigandage. Unable to find his mother, they threw young Amr into an orphanage where he suffered the torment of unwanted children. His life would have ended in a short and brutish fashion if not for a passing priest who saw the gifts God had placed in him. He took pity on the wretch Amr was and he became a ward of the Kyrkja. When he graduated from the Quadrivium, they thought any sinful and wicked ways were long behind. He was the model student and sought after for a prestigious career. The proof of a cure for wickedness.

And cure them they had, till the day Amr learned how deep the corruption of the men and women of the Kyrkja was. Greater than the sick dreams of his father ever could be! They had desired his skills and amoral purity to do the things that they were too afraid to do in service to the Lord. Sometimes, the shepherd must not only kill the wolves, but they also must slaughter their sheep in order to save the rest.

The black sludge now consumed his mind as he remembered what he was, and came back to himself in a flash.

"Malus fiat fiat manu," Amr muttered, his eyes no longer staring into the past.

"Sorry, I do not understand," Feles said.

The priest's long pause followed by that cryptic response disturbed him.

"Consider it my personal motto. My guiding star," Amr said pointing up to Polaris. "It means, 'If evil must be done, let it be by my hand'."

Feles shuddered. Amr could see Feles now understood that he would kill them both should he press further. The young Saami saw clearly what sort of monster this priest was better than anyone save Finn.

"So you would rather kill your dog rather than sell him?" Feles dared to ask.

Although the desire to murder the Saami was there, his necessity saved Feles' life. Amr gave a sigh of exasperation, "You help me up to that tunnel, and I shall consider it."

Feles considered his options and realized what he wanted most was to be far away from this supposed man of God.

"As you wish," Feles said softly. "As you wish."

40. VANITY REBUKED

Combat now thrilled Birgr like never before, dominating his desires with a sadistic glee. His mastery demanded bloodshed, for sparring was a distant echo of what he felt in that cramped overflowing chancery. To watch his victim's life escape its fleshly walls was an intimate sensation he never expected, and the lust to feel that again now overwhelmed his mind. He wanted more. Much more.

Dyrrvatn Kastali was being secretly flooded with men willing to join under his banner. Mercenaries sent by the jarls who would be cunning and capable. Birgr spent time with them all, listening to Sabino's counsel, spreading his influence over them with the Oracle's silvered words and choosing his own huskarls from among them. Once they had sworn their allegiance to Birgr and his designs, they would be given assignments that Sabino or the Lendmann Mother thought best.

The Lendmann Mother left Birgr largely to his own devices now. On a few rare occasions the Lendmann Mother would pick a man out of the lot when she came to inspect.

The first time, Birgr became upset at her meddling. Sabino tried to warn him to not challenge her. The rest of that day was obliterated from his memory save for abject agony. His mercenaries threw themselves into their sparring sessions and over time they craved bloodshed too. Any thoughts of fear or cowardice were melting away under the power of their new spiritual guides. Some caught on faster than others and exhibited similar miraculous extensions of power like the Ragnarites and Havarians. It was fortunate this underground temple was sturdy, for flashes of flame and blasts of thunder were not uncommon.

As Sabino suggested, Birgr christened these exceptionally powerful huskarls as his Ulfhethnar, from the Gamlehaven legend of the Wolf-Hides, the more feral counterpart to the berserker who had not seen in more than a century.

And the seven angels of the tapestry watched on.

Coppery hair flowing in a wind that did not exist.

Their faces now friendly to Birgr as they witnessed him best his men time and time again. Iron sharpening iron. Sabino showed him their actions before they moved, and bolstered his fleshly strength from beyond. It was child's play to intercept their moves and strike back. As the men's amazement grew, so did their worship of him.

"Greithr," Birgr said as one of his Ulfhethnar achieved a rare killing blow on him. "Good! All of you, good!"

He looked over the nineteen exhausted men who had failed to defeat him in a thirty minute brawl. "Much better this time. You have started to work well together." The praise raised the men's spirits as they considered their successes and failures.

"Now go and meditate on our training today," Birgr ordered with a gesture towards the altar.

"Jah, my Tign," the men said in unison. The word would be sedition to those who lived above. To call anyone but the family of the Visekonge by the honorific "Tign" was to guarantee a stay in the Crown's prison. But Birgr was the next Visekonge, in this the men had no doubt.

As the mercenaries knelt before the altar in silent reflection, a wooden clatter announced a late arrival. Birgr looked toward the steps to the mead hall and listened. The guard had let someone in.

"You are late. He will not be pleased," came the guard's hoarse whisper.

"I had no choice," the unknown man said.

"I pray it was worth the price," the guard replied.

The unknown man descended the stairs at a respectful pace, and revealed himself to be one who had been assigned to the University's Kyrkjaguard. Birgr held his grimace.

"My Tign," the man began and bowed deeply at the edge of the temple, "I come bringing news."

"Do not punish the man before you know the quality of his offering," Sabino advised.

"What is it?" Birgr asked, respecting the oracle's counsel.

"There is a conflict growing between the Ragnarites and Koenraadians over a dead priest." The man did not look up from his bow.

Birgr ground his teeth and squinted at the top of the man's head.

"Come with me," he said and walked to the opposite end of the temple. The man scurried after. Raising a finger to his lips Birgr focused on the man and frowned. He was still wearing his Kyrkjaguard uniform.

"You are being careless," Birgr said and tugged firmly upon the collar of the characteristic gambeson jacket he wore, drawing the man's attention to it.

"If I return soon, no one will be any the wiser, my Tign. Forgive me but I had to bring this news as soon as possible." The man's voice a hoarse whisper.

Birgr smiled genuinely. "Continue."

"There is a sectarian fight brewing between the Koenraadians and the Ragnarites. A Father Tuajaksson died and some outside inquisitor came in from nowhere and claimed it was murder. He seized the priest's home and all his belongings, despite no evidence of a crime, refusing the landlord his rightful chattels."

Birgr nodded, encouraging for more.

"This inquisitor went to Gud's Pisk and somehow managed to be granted authority in Dyrrvatn Kastali which means he will be reporting directly to the first inquisitor. The landlord went to his herrar at the University and demanded he be allowed to do his job. Even the dead priest's novice is fighting the landlord. That rogue inquisitor has been given his lead and is now claiming a heretical plot and possible witchcraft is happening in the capital!" The man's voice rose while telling the tale.

"Gently, gently," Birgr whispered as he put a reassuring hand on the man's shoulder.

Inside, he raged. Where did this outsider come from and why was he interfering? Birgr was sure he had left no clues, but neither he nor Sabino could be sure if they had missed anything, for that was the nature of all things missing. You never knew till it was too late.

"Have the landlord's petitions been successful?" Birgr asked softly.

"Only in part." The man returned to whispering. "The inquisitor has the house under watch night and day. A light is always burning in the window on the top floor. He is said to be reading and searching everything in that cluttered mess of a room. Who knows what had been hidden up there.

"Did you know that the dead priest was in charge of editing the Bok av Familiar? This at a time so prime for genealogies, it may have been a murder," the man asked, incredulous.

Birgr's eyes hardened by pure reflex.

"I... I mean..." the man stammered. "Someone might have wanted to alter the Bok av Familiar to gain the throne from the Sveinnaettir. A cousin or an uncle seeking to rise in precedence, inching closer to the Crown, my Tign." The man smiled and gave a sniff of a laugh at the irony. "Not that it matters when God is putting you there instead. The fools."

Birgr's lips contorted into a forced grin so abruptly it startled the man.

"This is true," he said and gave his mercenary a chuck on the shoulder as his eyes warmed at the thought. "It is good you took the time to bring me this information. Perhaps when the time comes we can exploit it and have the sects at each other's throats while we take our prize."

"My thinking exactly," the man sighed, relieved that his thoughts were aligned with his destined Visekonge.

Birgr shook his head and closed his eyes in gentle admonishment.

"Do not think. Do not presume. Just listen and obey," Birgr whispered, eyes boring into the other man's. "I need to think what this means and where we go from here. You will continue in your training and observation of this argument between the sects. Bring word of any new intelligence as soon as possible. Greithr?"

"Jah, my Tign," the man said, his voice suddenly weak and unsure.

"You said you had to get back? Go. I have things to do," Birgr said, dismissing him.

The man's steps grew steadier as he climbed the steps and exited the temple.

"What do I do?" Birgr wondered to himself.

"Let us go see what is really happening at the scene of our triumph," Sabino advised.

Birgr nodded to himself and walked toward the altar, sat down cross legged in front of it, hands on his knees, and closed his eyes and sighed.

With little effort, his soul popped out of his flesh and hung in the air above his resting body. The saturated colors beyond the veil were strong here, throbbing with with hazardous beauty that matched the emotions of the enterprise that now took place. He looked at his troop of men. Around them little spirits hovered, attending to their prayers and worship with caresses, whispers, stabs and bites. Some had a single larger manitou on them, others had a cloud of small gnat-like swarm of spirits. One of his Ulfhathnar was cloaked in a gargantuan shadow that even Sabino gave proper respect.

"Do you remember how to get there?" Sabino mocked.

Time and space stretched in an instant, the silver cord spooled out behind Birgr as he visualized his desire to be at the scene of the murder, appearing outside the chancery window in the warm evening air. The city bustled with life trying to finish chores before sundown. Golden light streamed through the thick air, drinking up the moisture from the ground and building gentle dark thunderclouds that popped up in the cooling sky. With a stutter of lightning here and there the clouds looked to give a quick downpour and vanish.

To the northwest a great light blossomed at the Domkyrkja as Vespers service completed. Angels scattered about the city in joyous praise, following the subjects of their servitude and protection as they returned home. Similar blooms of light could be seen from all the Kyrkjaplassen and every chapel where a service was held.

Birgr sneered at these distracting blooms. How complicated and arrogant the Kyrkja felt to him now. New blood under the Crown was not the only thing about to change. The Lendmann Mother and Sabino made sure Birgr understood the real goal of the lord of heaven, and as long as these niggling little distractions were dealt with cleanly, all would be settled according to plan.

He refocused on the window and listened.

Inside, the rogue inquisitor, who glowed with a dangerous fire, was flipping through the pages of yet another ledger. A tall stack of thick books rested at either elbow. A parchment spattered with scribbles in Latin that this Ragnarite filled from time to time with a worn out quill. He could all but hear the frustration of the man as he recognized the ring's symbol drawn on it several times in angry loops and aggressive arrows.

"Urban?" a voice came from behind the inquisitor.

"Jah?"

A small blond man with a jaunty mustache entered carrying a deep bowl of stew and a loaf of bread. Birgr recognized the food and saw deadly spirits crawling over it. This servant had used the same infested pot that he had witnessed the night before in the scullery.

"This should be interesting," Birgr thought to Sabino.

"It will not. Just watch," Sabino said disappointed.

"Oh, thank you, Jan," Urban said turning to take the food.

He set it on a scarce open piece of desk and gave thanks over the meal given. The deadly little spirits screamed in anguish and blew apart like dandelion fluff.

"See?" Sabino said to his disappointed pupil.

"Have we found anything new?" Jan asked.

"Not yet," Urban rubbed his brow and eyes, and Jan took the stack of books to Urban's left and put them on a table. "And with so many more to go. I feel like I have not begun at all. Every tome to the last cockeyed scribble in the margins. I must look."

"God bless you for all that you have done so far," Jan encouraged.

"I appreciate the support, but if I do not find something more than my own hunches... something that points to this conspiracy and soon, I doubt I will keep the support of the first inquisitor."

"Father Tuajaksson, God rest his soul," Jan crossed himself at the mention of his former master, "would have left something else. The assassin could not have found it all. I am still discovering things of his all over the scriptorium that might matter. Here are my notes for you," Jan added pulling out some folded papers from his hipbag. "Perhaps these will provide direction or give an answer."

"I pray for that hourly," Urban agreed.

"They have nothing," Sabino snorted.

"But two people are looking into this death that must be considered an accident," Birgr's voice was sour.

"I tell you, do not get involved," Sabino's warning was like broken glass.

A flock of small fae-like angels ascended the stairs in a zephyr of light, and a man's footsteps could be heard.

"We must go!" Sabino ordered.

The cloud of angels saw Sabino and Birgr outside the window and gave a musical shriek of warning. The slow steps ascending the stairs became a sprint as a man bounded up them.

"Urban! Jan?" the voice was deep and resonant. "What is wrong?"

A large man flew up the last flight of steps as the cloud of angels drew swords and began to advance like a swarm of deadly bees.

"Leave! Now!" Sabino ordered but Birgr was enthralled by the sight. With a glassy snap, Sabino vanished leaving Birgr on his own to suffer the consequences of his hesitation.

"What?" Urban asked, surprised by the commotion from Aske as he burst into the room, the half closed door slamming open, revealing a large Skaerslinger man, head surrounded by a halo of light and grace. The rays like spear tips stabbing at Birgr's soul.

"What is the matter?" Urban demanded, confused at first, but the deep fire Birgr saw in him now flared and his sword began to glow red as Urban's hand reflexively touched the pommel.

Aske's eyes flicked about the room before looking out the window. Even though Birgr had been sure he could not be seen, his certainty was collapsing. The Skaerslinger's eyes burned into him like a branding iron. Could he see beyond the veil?

"Foul Spirit, in the name of Jesus, I rebuke thee! Begone!" the man ordered. There was a split second when Birgr was about to laugh at such a phrase being used on him. Him! And by a Skaerslinger as well. Of all peop-

A giant wave of agony crashed into Birgr...

...

...blasting him back through the veil and into his own body. The force of his return to his flesh threw him backwards into his meditating men, scattering them like leaves in a gale. He slammed into the opposite wall of the altar collapsing a stack of unused pews and lay there, steaming.

His disoriented men ran to Birgr's aid, pulling the heavy pews off him, throwing them to the side without care.

When uncovered, Birgr began to return to his senses.

"What happened, my Tign?" his spy in the Ulfhathnar asked, his voice tremulous with rage that a blow had been struck against his Tign.

"I... do not know," Birgr said, voice weak but drawing strength from offended rage. "But they will pay for what they have done."

41. THE IMPORTANCE OF A NAME

Hunger now stalked them in their sleep. Mirjam dreamed of mountains of molasses kex. Leif dreamed of cheese. Declan saw visions of bacon while Solveig craved candied fruits. Finn wallowed in a nightmare banquet he could not eat. Inge dreamed of cooking for a king.

But Amr dreamt he was the food. Something horrible was chasing him through a dark winter pinery, broken chains on his wrists and ankles snagged on bare branches sticking out of the crusty snow. His bare feet cut by the ice left a trail of bloody footprints. Just out of sight his owner was running him down. Always a bush, or a tree, or a low rise in the way. When he could no longer run, he collapsed in the middle of a frozen lake with nowhere to hide, no shelter and too weak to run. The monster burst forth from the shoreline, its visage so horrible he woke.

Amr bolted upright breathing hard. The rest of his companions so exhausted they did not notice despite being piled around him. They slept on save for Feles who stood watch.

After two days of climbing down from the mountain and through the increasingly sparse woods into this plain brushland of rolling hills and boulders, they found the old Saami camp. From all evidence, it seemed that the Saami had moved out while they had been stuck in the heart of the mountain. Feles assured them there was no reason to worry, for he knew where the next camp would be. The migration would not begin till after the equinox, leaving them time to catch up.

"Everything greithr?" Feles asked softly.

"Jah," Amr said and realized something was missing. He looked around to discover what was gone. With all their camp gear lost, they had piled close together to conserve body heat. Not even a single blanket had survived so they used sheaves of grasses or balsam boughs to help keep warm. Were it not for absolute exhaustion, none of them would have been able to sleep through the chilly night.

"Dawn is breaking, Feles said, noting the brightening sky. The purple of the Girdle of Venus began to rise as the sun approached the horizon. To the west, the tops of the peaks had begun to glow pink.

Amr then saw Thyrnir stand up from behind Feles. The Saami gave the dog a gentle ear rub, coaxing a happy moan from him.

"Has he been with you all night?" Amr asked, looking at Bergamot wedged between Finn and Inge her head and paws propped up on her master's legs. A pang of jealousy went down Amr's spine.

"Jah. He came over soon after you were asleep. Been here ever since."

"Oj," Amr groaned and rubbed eyes that had not rested enough. Now too awake to consider sleep, his stomach growled.

"Since I am up, I may as well scavenge a little. What grows around here?" Amr said as he stood up.

"If lucky, we could find some cloudberries, lingonberries or mountain sorrell. Good chance it has been stripped clean by the passing herds, though." Feles considered Amr a moment. "You look shaken from your dreams. Why not stay here on watch and I will go scrounge about. I will fare better." Amr blinked again, his eyes unable to focus, then nodded, the motion thick and deliberate. Lack of food was taking its toll on him more than he thought.

Feles got up and went off into the dim morning, Thyrnir at his side.

Amr sat among the other sleepers as if the dream would come back at any second. Perhaps it was the dream's remnants tormenting him, but he could not shake the feeling that something was hiding in the low scrub and late summer grasses. Or was it now autumn? He could not tell anymore as he looked to the yellowing aspen on the eastern slopes.

When he felt awake enough, Amr stood up and surveyed the vacated camp. The fresh marks from the tipis were plain to see. The firepits were carefully covered over with cut sod. The light starved yellow and matted grass was returning to normal. Perhaps he could see about starting a fire, he thought. There was enough wood and tinder. With a task to keep him busy, he went to one of the firepits, removed the cut sod and felt the earth. The ground was no longer warm, leaving no chance for insulated coals to help.

The manual labor helped soothe his mind. By the time the sun broke the horizon, he had a frail little fire of twigs and grass building toward something more functional. The wind kept the smoke low for it was of good winnowing strength out of the mountains. The smell woke the others and one by one they came over to enjoy the heat that they wished to have been strong enough to make the previous night.

No greetings were offered, as they all numbly settled in around the fire.

"Where is Feles?" Finn asked, afraid to hear the answer. What might Amr have done if left alone with their new guide. His eyes remained locked on the fire in a trance born of poor sleep and hunger.

"Scrounging for something to eat," Amr answered.

"Good," Leif said in the same distant tone.

"I wish we had a pot and some water to cook with," Inge sighed. "Oh, for tea!"

"Or something to cook in the pot," Declan said.

"Oj, do not talk of food and drink," Solveig moaned. "I cannot bear the disappointment." Both girls were gaunt, having wasted away far more than the men. Mirjam was even more sickly, perhaps due to her near drowning. Declan was certain that if they did not find food and shelter soon, both sisters would take ill, and in this wilderness death followed close behind weakness.

"Then be thankful to the Lord," Feles said, returning with Thyrnir. Seeing the dog as the young Saami's companion was a shock to Finn. How had he not noticed that the dog was missing?

"What? Why?" Leif asked, confused at Feles' words.

"I have lived up to my namesake and have found us breakfast," he answered.

They saw his kyrtill was off, slung over his back like a sack.

"What did you find?" Amr asked greedily.

"Not only berries, I found an emergency cache! My family must have left it when I did not return. It is not much for all of us, but enough to keep starvation away." They all gave a weak cheer.

"By God's pickled gherkins, we are saved!" Inge exclaimed.

Feles opened up his kyrtil to expose the wealth of food inside. Several chunks of smoked caribou meat and a clay pot of fermented coltsfoot had been found. Feles had also collected a sizable amount of pale yellow cloudberries. It was enough for a few days rations for one person, or a single meal for them all.

Despite it being poor fare compared to what the Kronadottirs were used to, they ate with zeal and by the end of the meal, which was all too short, they felt much better.

Finn watched Thyrnir with a hard eye throughout the meal. Was this dog really Brother Trygve's Hawthorn? It still pestered his conscience. He looked down at the last bite of his caribou meat. His hunger desired it, but the need to know won out. Carefully, Finn hid it in his hand. Without a gesture and looking at the dog, he beckoned the dog.

"Hawthorn, koma."

Amr's head shot up to look at Finn.

"Koma Hawthorn," Finn said again. Now everyone was watching. The dog stared right at Finn who did not move a muscle, focusing his vision into the fire. "Come here, Hawthorn."

Finn thought furiously. "Remember your name. Prove me right. Redeem your master."

"What are you ta-" Leif began.

"Shh!" Inge silenced him. Leif glared at the friar for being shushed.

Hawthorn glanced at Feles for a moment.

"Koma, Hawthorn," Finn beckoned again still concealing he was the one calling. If it was Hawthorn, and he was free of Amr's sorcery, he would come.

Hawthorn stood up and walked over to Finn, tail swishing in slow rhythm as he walked to his name. Finn's eyes welled with tears and a smile emerged.

"Jah, that is my good boy, Hawthorn. Good boy. You remember Trygve do you not?"

The tail wagged harder at the name of his former master and the dog gave a soft whoff.

Amr went pale as milk.

"That is a good boy. Here, Hawthorn, here," Finn said and gave the dog his last morsel of food. The dog swallowed it without even chewing. Finn leaned forward into the fawn colored dog, silent tears rolling down into Hawthorn's furry flank.

"Good boy," he repeated while the rest stared in awe.

"What does this mean?" Feles asked, astounded by the scene and reaction.

"It means..." Friar Inge said rising to his feet and taking a dangerous step toward Amr, "this tjovekjakji son of a whore murdered Brother Trygve and stole his dog!"

"How dare you slander me!" Amr bellowed as he stood up to face Inge in kind. "I told you I found Hawthorn wandering in the pinery lost and without master."

"Was that before or after you murdered Trygve?" Inge shouted back.

"Mendacity! I had no idea whose dog this was! He was wandering, lost, north of Fjellporten!"

Finn's head shot up with that statement, a small grin passed over his lips and was quickly hidden away, for in that statement, Amr had just handed him the proof he needed.

"I cannot slander a man with the truth! Proven to be a murderer in the past," Inge roared back.

Leif and Declan jumped up and pushed between the men. Leif taking hold of Inge's shoulder, while Declan pushed Amr back a pace before blows were thrown.

"Brothers," Leif implored, trying to calm the two friars. Neither man would have any part of it, now shouting a tirade of accusations and profanities at one another. Declan was forced to hold the apoplectic Amr back while Leif lifted the no longer portly friar off his feet and turned him away in an effort to separate the two.

"Enough!" roared Leif. "This is neither the time nor the place!"

The two men of God became silent.

"Brother Finn," Leif said with regal agitation, "is this the dog of Brother Trygve as you claim?"

"My Tign," Finn said, "this dog was stolen from my fellow Havarian, Brother Trygve. The man Friar Inge replaced after he went missing. I long suspected that Amr had murdered him and taken his dog."

"You claimed that before. Why did the dog not respond to his name then?" Leif demanded.

"Because a demon had taken over the dog. A demon that the shrine had somehow cleansed from this animal thereby returning it to its rightful state." Finn's accusation was flat and hard.

"A demon? You are accusing me of witchcraft?" Amr shouted aghast. "Now that is beyond contemptible, Finn! Your hatred for me is so great you would create such fantasies for some pathetic revenge?" Amr foamed at the mouth.

"I would not," Finn said, standing and leveling a terrifying cold eye at Amr, "but you would."

"I have never been so offended in my life! I demand satisfaction by blood!" Amr fired back.

"You will have no such thing," Leif bellowed in that regal tone that echoed his father. "I rule here and we will not have a duel when every bit of energy is needed to survive. Now, as your Tign, I command both of you to forgo this quarrel till we are safe. Then take it up by whatever means you decide to finish your dispute, but not one second before. Am I being clear?" Leif looked at both men with imperious fury.

"Jah, my Tign," Finn answered.

"I shall obey to the letter," Amr agreed, shelving his damning evidence. He would be patient, very patient, till Trygve could be avenged.

Neither man's hatred dimmed from their eyes.

"What about Hawthorn?" Inge demanded. "You cannot hand him back to Amr."

"Will you take care of him," Leif asked. "You are a Havarian after all."

"Jah, you bet I will!"

"Then he is yours," Leif proclaimed.

"You cannot do that!" Amr exploded at Leif.

Now the Tronerving turned his own chilling gaze on Amr who showed no sign of intimidation.

"What do you mean by 'cannot'?"

"Thyrnir is my property."

"And you are mine," Leif said reminding Amr of where he stood in the hierarchy of life.

"I..." Amr broke off. His fists were clenched so hard they shook. "Jah, my Tign. I obey."

"And you best obey the spirit of my will and not just to the letter, or you will find out how great my wrath can be."

42. PREDATOR OR PREY

Days had passed since Birgr communed with Sabino and everyone's training suffered with the oracle's absence. His focus was out of control. His sparring was sloppy as opponent's actions were no longer exposed beforehand. Through force of will, he threw objects across the room or entangled them with the men's clothing. Even then, he could not best a room of twenty like he could scant days before. How much of his power had been because Sabino unchained his spirit, and how much was a service done by the oracle

Birgr still maintained the ability to project himself beyond the veil, like before, though he dare not go near that house again while just in the spirit. He also noticed that the little manitou surrounding his men now looked at him the same way a wolf watches a deer, waiting for it to become unaware. He prayed for Sabino's quick return.

Could the attack from that skeiturhuth have killed his oracle? Birgr laughed at the thought. But where was Sabino? He must be doing things of greater importance, but what was more important than mentoring the future Visekonge? Could that spiritual rebuke from the Skaerslinger have separated him from Sabino forever? Was this a more grievous wound in the spirit than he realized?

Remembering the Skaerslinger's affront infuriated Birgr afresh. His desire for revenge was most certainly justified. This foolish little investigation was a threat to the rebellion and must be ended. Meting out personal vengeance would be a pleasant bonus.

Birgr discovered that tracking the Skaerslinger was easy. Not only by his distinct appearance but by the deference people granted him. The citizens were not scared of him as should be proper, but gave way in a friendly manner as they would a favorite priest or guildsman. Birgr's prey walked at a leisurely pace for a large man, long strides eating up the streets and lanes, and he followed him on his daily chores for the inquisitor, tracking him like a migrating caribou, looking for the right place for an ambush.

But come nightfall, his plans were thwarted time and again. The Skaerslinger would vanish, and try as hard as he might, in the flesh or beyond the veil, Birgr could not find him. The frustration had become maddening.

The men began wondering about his absence, late arrivals and early departures from training and hobnob in the meadhalls. Seeing their leader wandering about the streets with an unknown purpose disturbed them even more, and Birgr knew it. His Ulfhathnar were needed to maintain discipline among the men in his absence. This distraction had to end, now.

Morning came with a hot dry wind that smelled of smoke and hints of autumn. It was an ominous portent after a week of frustration. Today, the skeiturhuth changed his usual pattern. He began walking toward the Toinnsjokanalen as he had done many times before. Birgr followed close for the streets were jammed with farmers bringing in large harvests from the fields. The smell of maize going to the mills filled the air and flecks of cornsilk drifted on the breeze as they passed in heavy laden wagons. All tongues were wagging on what perfect weather it was for coming to market.

Upon reaching the canal, the Skaerslinger did not turn toward the docks to join the stevedores for work, but crossed over. Was he on a new mission for the inquisitor? Birgr's stomach twisted at this but he continued to stalk his target. He began to pray silently for Sabino to return, desperate for his counsel and power.

Silence was his answer.

The western neighborhoods of the canal were set on a series of small rising ridgelines packed with simple houses and cottages. Tradesmen spilled into the streets with their industry and wares. Ahead, the Skaerslinger veered southwesterly toward the shore of the Dyrrvatn and the sawmills that crowded its muddy beaches. Their tall smokestacks belching dark fumes driven to the ground by the swirling wind, feeding a thick smog that came and went.

The Skaerslinger walked on. Every time he disappeared behind a billow of smoke or a cart Birgr's heart jumped, would his prey vanish once again? He breathed a sigh when he reappeared. Birgr's axe felt heavy in its sling. The meaty thump of the metal head bounced against the small of his back with every step, reminding him it was time to end this.

Smoke from the sawmills and blacksmiths that populated the shore obscured sight in a dim, burning fog that stank of ash and rot, bark and rust. The Skaerslinger entered a woodlot with cords of cut timber stacked in long rows. For the first time, Birgr considered the possibility this was a trap. He brushed off the thought with a smirk. The Visekonge's berserker might have a chance at besting him, but he was on the other side of the Union, probably in a grave or his body scattered by scavengers by now. The happy thought he was possibly in his father's dungeon entertained his fancy.

Then his prey did something odd.

The Skaerslinger scaled to the top of a row of logs and nimbly walked across the cords. Birgr took cover between the rows and continued to follow, getting closer as to not lose the trail. With so few people around, it would be hard to disguise his intentions if spotted.

Ahead, the big man leapt between the rows of logs, crossing toward the lake. Birgr's hair stood on end. He ran down the row in a desperate scramble and peered cautiously around the corner, he tracked his prey to the beach, and beyond that, a large pen of logs floated, pushed up tight to the shore in front of the sawmill.

Only a hundred yards away, a half dozen arks were beached. The floating shanties were partially disassembled, and their crude furnishings lay stacked on the shore. A gang of men tore apart the walls of the farthest one.

...And the Skaerslinger was gone.

How?

In a pique of fury, Birgr lashed out a foot at a large hunk of loose bark that shattered and spiraled away from him in disjointed hops. Was he hiding in the arks? Where had that skeiturhuth gotten to? Again he slipped away! Birgr decided to risk searching beyond the veil. He leaned against a stack of lumber, locked his knees and closed his eyes.

As he burst beyond the veil, the dismal scene of smoke and dim afternoon sun burst into terrifying rich color. The smoke became black and ominous, tinged with red, raining orange fireflies of ash. The sun was ringed with a gigantic sundog that blazed through half the sky with all the colors of dusk, or was it dawn? The cord wood dripped with filth and ichor as the manitou of the forest mourned the destruction of their domain, wailing and cursing the hands that felled their trees.

A voice from over the water cried out. Birgr looked out across the bright ripples and the jumble of black logs. In the middle of the log pen, his prey stood on a log as if it were dry land. That swarm of familiar warm lights flitted about him. But could they hurt him when not in the spirit?

"Come forth, oh servant of the most foul!" The voice was deep and strong. It tugged on his spirit like a hook in a fish. "You have tracked me for days and failed in your hunt. Thanks be to God for the Lord has declared that now is the time to end your suffering! Come forth and meet your fate!"

The taunt rankled Birgr. The lord was not with this child of the devil! No matter how many trappings of God he wore, he could never be anything more than a devil in the flesh. As Birgr readied to return to his body a voice called out far inland.

"Birgr, Son of Jakob!" came the cry. On the crest of the last ridgeline overlooking the water a wavering silhouette of a man danced like a mirage. It was Sabino! Birgr shouted for joy.

As if reading his thoughts, "Do not approach your prey! Come away and choose your battleground another day! You cannot win this fight!" Sabino warned.

Aid me then, and this will be over!" Birgr demanded.

"I cannot!" Sabino called, subdued. "Turn away!"

"Why not?" Birgr pleaded.

Sabino pointed at the sun, "I may come no closer." Then after a moment of hesitation, "You are disobeying the lord of heaven's wishes. I forbid you to do this!"

Birgr looked out at his prey again who's defiant posture angered him even more.

"Coward!" Birgr shouted at Sabino. "This is just one man!"

"He is bait. Have you forgotten so quickly what he did to us with just a word?" Sabino reminded him.

"I know you hear me, oh servant of the Devil!" the Skaerslinger called again. "Come forth and face me!"

Servant of the Devil? Birgr's pride was inflamed.

If you go, you will be punished! Even if you survive, you will regret the result!" Sabino threatened.

The seconds dragged by as he teetered on the knife edge of obedience or ending this threat to his destiny. With a snap, Birgr yanked his spirit back into his body. His eyes popped open, a sneer carved deep into his cheek. He muttered a curse so profane it would have curdled milk and strode towards the water.

"No!" Sabino shouted, but Birgr ignored him.

Rounding the cord wood, the world was gray billows of smoke with white ash and orange sparks sprinkling the log pen. Every step stoked the fire of his anger. With a spinning flourish, he unsheathed his axe from his back sling.

Using a half dismantled ark, he stepped out onto the shifting carpet of timber. The loud whine of the steam-driven saw cutting boards acted like his spirit's war cry as he searched among the ever shifting smoke. No one from the shore crew stopped him as they watched him stride out. Would he have to kill all of them? He doubted it. To them, it was just another settled feud.

Birgr's feet ran true and he walked back and forth among the smoke enshrouded logs seeking his prey, but not finding him. The trunks tottered and twisted under every step. The current of the wind-driven waves jostled them back and forth with dull thumps. How he wished he could look in the spirit and see through the vapor, but to lose his balance here? Tons of wood could crush his body. The thought of letting the Skaerslinger be smashed slowly between the logs brightened his bloodlust.

He reached the edge of the log pen constructed of a large cordon of slippery chains and rock posts designed to keep the logs from drifting away when the steamknarr cut their rafts loose.

The lake was strangely vacant of ships for the moment.

Where was that skeiturhuth?

"Who are you?" Birgr called out, turning back to face the log pen.

"I am Aske Rekkersson," came an answering call, from a direction behind him he did not expect. He scanned the curtains of ash and black smoke. "Who are you?" Aske demanded.

Birgr brayed a mocking laugh. Of course the peasant had no aettir. He was less than nothing. Possibly some orphaned brat that some soft hearted fool took pity on and now is a foolish lackey and maybe a thrall to that idiot inquisitor.

"Do you truly believe I would tell you when it is that very mystery that I must keep?" Birgr asked, and began hopping across logs at a near reckless pace toward the voice.

"You are no man of honor then," Aske taunted again.

Birgr gritted his teeth. A figure was moving in the smoke. He had him. Risking large hops across two and three logs at a time, Birgr rushed toward his prey, only to stare in amazement as an eddy of smoke revealed nothing was there.

There was a rush of rocking timber from behind. He turned to see the big Skaerslinger burst out through a bank of choking soot, his body and hair mottled with gray ash. A marking hammer swung at his head. Birgr ducked and the metal head whistled past his skull. Aske continued past with his bounding charge till just out of reach of Birgr's blind counterswing.

Both men stood at opposite ends of the same log. Birgr saw that Aske had no weapon, only timberjack tools. A cant hook in one hand and the short marking hammer in the other.

Birgr laughed.

"You expect to defeat me with those?" Birgr could not resist returning the taunting he had suffered. "Did your squa spawn an idiot devil?"

Aske did not answer, but seemed to take no offense at the insult. Birgr frowned.

"What puzzles me is how did a inquisitor manage to get skeiturhuth as a servant?" Birgr asked, seeing his prey woefully unprepared for the fight.

Aske remained silent, waiting for Birgr to act.

"What do you hope to accomplish with those simple tools knowing your god was sending you to face an armed warrior?" Birgr demanded, taking a careful step forward.

"The Lord commanded me to face you and bring no weapon," Aske's voice peaceful. "Look around." Aske gestured with his cant hook that seemed to push the smoke aside with his sweep, revealing for just a moment the log pen they stood on. "He has provided me with all I need to end your wickedness."

As Birgr's attention left Aske, he felt the world slide sideways. The log he was standing on spun under his feet, throwing him to the side. With a jerk and a stumble, he sprawled across three logs as the Skaerslinger spun the log. His furious glare at Aske was met by only a smirk of satisfaction on his foe's dark inscrutable face. Birgr reached out with his mind and gave the log that Aske stood on a mighty shove.

The Skaerslinger did not fall. He gracefully hopped off to land on the end of the log on which Birgr's arms and head rested. It hopped up sharply, striking Birgr in the face. Stars burst in his vision from the blow. The impact scraped his face with the rough bark, enough to weep blood. Aske's shoulders twitched in suppressed laughter.

With inhuman reflexes, Birgr came to his feet. Aske tried again to spin the log, but Birgr was ready for him and charged. A few swipes with the axe were parried by the cant hook, and Aske countered with the marking hammer.

Birgr's cuts grew closer and closer. In a split second, the Skaerslinger kicked water into Birgr's face. Aske pranced out of reach like a deer to gain a few yards of separation.

"You know little about log ponds. Move one log, the others are upset for they too must move," Aske lectured. "They are like people. Push one, you might never know who will move next."

Birgr risked a quick glance as the logs stirred. The log he pushed forced the rest into a new pattern that reformed with groans and thumps some climbing on top of others, rolling and grinding before finding their new buoyancy. Aske's log slid sideways while Birgr's moved back into the clear space which slowly began to cover over.

"Let us see if you can walk on moving timber," Aske taunted again, his feet as sure as a cat's.

As the logs filled in the open water, Birgr gave another loping charge from log to log, this time Aske did not wait for the attack but outran him on the timber to disappear into the smoke once more.

"If you are here to finish this for your god," Birgr shouted, "then let us have at it! We shall see who's God is true."

"All in His time," Aske said, coughing with a bad lungful of smoke.

Birgr made for the coughing, emerging on the log strewn beach, face to face with the partially broken down arks. From inside one of them came another cough. Like a hunting puma, Birgr slipped onboard. The roof was gone but the walls and bunk beds remained .

He entered the doorway swinging his axe. The sweeping blade struck nothing. No one was there. The doors on the entire row of the shanties were gone, and Birgr could see through the whole line of arks and out the end. Nothing could sneak out without him seeing.

He stepped through to the next shanty.

Empty.

Suddenly, there was the clunk of wood on bone and Birgr was knocked to his knees. A shrill Skaerslinger war cry came from above as Aske landed on his stalker. The loose rafter Aske had dropped on Birgr's head had done its job well, but was not enough.

Birgr found himself in a choke hold. Aske's massive biceps locked around his throat, axe clattered across the floor. With all his might, Birgr drove his elbows into Aske's kidneys. Hammering the sharp points into the Skaerslinger's kidneys, torquing hard.

When Aske's grip loosened, Birgr reached between his legs, grabbed Aske by the leg, and pushed off. The two men burst backward through the wall next to the door. The split logs flew apart like toys and the men landed with a large woof in the wet sand between the arks.

Aske no longer had a hold on him from the shock of the landing, and Birgr wasted no time in spinning around and started hammering Aske's face with his fists.

Their arms tangled as Aske fought to stop the blows. Neither was able to best the other's grapple. They rolled down into the shallow mud and sand of the shore. Birgr fought to twist the Skaerslinger's mashed face sideways and drown him in a few inches of dirty water.

Water filling his nostrils, Aske let out a frothing cry of fear and anger and drove a knee into Birgr's crotch. The blow flipped Birgr onto his back and the pair lay in a few inches of soot colored water facing the sky the crowns of their heads almost touching.

"Whatever manitou is in you," Aske gasped and snorted around his blood filled nose, "you cannot defeat the Holy Spirit, Praise God." He stood up, swaying while Birgr rolled into a tight ball.

The big man located the axe and the marking hammer on the floor of the smashed ark and took them. Aske cleared his mouth of all the blood from his mashed nose with a loud hawking spit. Breathing raggedly from his mouth, he turned to finish off Birgr.

Aske found himself nose-to-nose with this madman who grabbed his axe and smacked the flat of the blade into Aske's ruined face. Pain exploded as his nose broke.

The dazed Skaerslinger shoved Birgr, knocked him down and fled blindly through the line of arks.

"The Oracles of God guide me to my true power, skeiturhuth," he grunted and struggled in pain to get up.

Birgr followed him like an inescapable doom. He looked down the open doors and saw Aske rounding the corner of the last ark then bounding back out onto the log pond.

With a terrifying growl, Birgr pursued. Upon exiting the last doorway, he saw the frantic and unsteady flight of his prey. Smirking, Birgr launched himself toward where he predicted Aske would be in a superhuman leap. As he flew above the low hanging smoke, his foe danced back and forth trying to escape. He saw him stop to look back, confused that he did not see Birgr chasing.

As Birgr descended, he reached out with his mind and gave the log Aske stood on a swift pull, to beneath where he would land. The sudden shift sent the unbalanced Aske to the opposite end where he fell, clinging for dear life to the shifting log, trying to keep from rolling under the water.

Birgr landed hard. He plunged under the water up to his neck and popped right back out again. Aske gave a grunt of surprise as he was thrown high into the air, flipping end over end. Birgr smiled, riding the timber like it was a bucking caribou.

Aske landed hard on his back across a set of logs. His right shoulder twisted at a strange angle. He did not move. The whole log pen jostled about, a chain broke and timber began to escape through the breach.

Birgr strutted toward his fallen prey.

"That was a good fight skeiturhuth, but it is time to finish this. I have much left to do today," Birgr complimented.

Standing on two logs, he raised his axe to chop off Aske's head. "I cannot believe that a man with no training and only a timberjack's tools could have survived this long against me."

The Skaerslinger lashed out with his left arm. Before Birgr could act, the marking hammer smashed into his right knee. He screamed as it folded backwards, the head of the hammer coming away bloody. The mark of the Sveinnaettir sawmill stamped deep into his flesh.

"The Lord rebuke you, foul spirit," Aske snarled as Birgr, unable to keep his balance on his broken leg, fell between two logs catching himself before going under by wrapping his arms across them. His axe flew out of his hand and disappeared beneath the water as Birgr struggled.

His panic grew rapidly as every attempt to pull himself to safety made the logs rotate faster and faster. Their rotation acting like paddlewheels drawing them together with him between. Several tons of wood began to squeeze together, driving Birgr under.

With a gurgling scream, Birgr's left hand was crushed and he was trapped below the surface. The logs now formed a barricade blocking him from life-giving air. Shafts of sunlight glittered in the murky brown water growing more and more intense, his lungs burned for air as he sank. His heart pounded, useless arms flailed at the surface as the blackness reached up from the depths and claimed him.

43. SURVEYING THE RUINS OF HUBRIS

The Lendmann Mother Ulla stood patiently as her handmaid finished dressing her and applying the modest makeup for such functions. Her Kyrkja attire was much more plain than what she usually chose for court, but the goal was the same. A secret smile rested on her lips as she ran through the goals for the evening. If she played her cards right, capitalized on every advantage, the repercussions of tonight's feast would snowball. Mathilda lay on her bed watching the dressing ritual, prattling on about how pretty she looked and how she wished she could come along.

The doorbell jangled with hard, frantic chimes. A mere tremor of movement betrayed the Lendmann Mother's surprise. Matilda bounced up to her knees as her handmaid moved toward the door.

"I will go see," Mathilda blurted out. Before the Lendmann Mother could say a word otherwise, the girl threw herself off the bed to run out the door of her mother's bedchamber. "Finish dressing Mother," she called back.

The handmaid looked up at her Dame as her daughter was thundering down the stairs to see who was calling.

"Go on. Finish my jewelry," the Lendmann Mother commanded, her mind hours ahead, thinking of what information must be sprinkled about and who must overhear. She had to be careful for that first inquisitor could see through all deception and seduction. Then again, he was not her direct target of tonight's festivities.

Downstairs, the faint sound of many heavy feet rumbled about, then Matilda scampered up the stairs, all but diving into the bedchambers.

"Mother!" she gasped. "Come quick! It is too ghastly!" Her daughter's face was smiling in spite of her words.

"Oh, for the love of Heaven!" the Lendmann Mother grumbled and walked away from her handmaid who held the other earring. Matilda led the way downstairs to the dining room where a small crowd of strange men hovered around her table. They were all unknown to her. Common and filthy karls standing vigil over what was laid out on the table, hats off, heads bowed in prayer. An Anjar's hands pressed on a body. She strode into the room and the men parted in shock, none dared to look directly at the Lendmann Mother. The Anjar stopped his prayer and gave a low bow, arms spread and palms up.

A flash of yellow radiated on his right ring finger. Seven gold arrows radiating out in a field of onyx peeked out in the poor light. The hidden signet was revealed to her. She looked at the rest of the men with an imperious eye.

"Is he dead?" she demanded.

"No, Grevinne. He is not," the Anjar said, facing the floor. The rest of the men trembled at her voice. They had come at the Anjar's behest, carrying Birgr's body into this mansion, and now quaked in fear of the powerful Hirdwoman.

344

"He clings to this world for his skein has not run out yet," the Anjar proclaimed in the old manner of forbidden legends heard only as whispered tales that survived passage from the Gamlehaven despite a fervent attempt to stamp them out as heresy.

She gave a sharp nod. "Thank you, herrs, for bringing him to me. I will see to his needs now." She turned to her page, "Fetch my purse and pay the men in gold for their kind assistance."

The karls gasped in surprise at the generous reward.

"See to it you remember the kindness that has been given to you, and that you forget you ever saw this man brought low. That is the best way you can thank me and his aettir," she declared and held up a hand. "Now may the lord of heaven bless and keep you. May his angels follow your steps and grant you the boons you deserve for your service, Amen."

"And also with you," the men replied reflexively as if in mass and filtered out, taking a gold ertog, more than a month's pay, as their reward.

When the door closed, only the Anjar and her page remained, the stench of the workmen slowly dissipating. With deliberate ceremony, she held out her own hand to the Anjar, who kissed the seven radiating arrows on her own signet ring before standing at attention again.

"Where was he?" Her eyes swept over Birgr's ruined body.

"They plucked him out of the Dyrrvatn. He fell between the logs," the Anjar said.

"He is not breathing."

"He is, but it is shallow. I have placed him into a deep sleep that keeps the angel of death at bay for the moment."

"Do not be boastful of your own might. We both know from whence your power flows," she said in a sharp toothed rasp.

He winced from the rebuke "Forgive me, Reverend Mother."

"Mother, what are we going to do?" Matilda asked with that quivering excitement unique to girls of her age.

"There is nothing I can do for now. I have to leave for the feast," she huffed in irritation. "This could not have come at a worse time."

"You know the plans, my son. You know who he is." The Lendmann Mother picked up Birgr's ruined left arm. Looked closely at the obscene white pills of fat squeezed through the split skin of his fingertips and let it slap onto the table again with a sneer. "I leave it to you to fix the damage done and return him to us so all we have worked for does not come to naught."

The Anjar bowed deeply again. Sharp eyes fixed on her page who stepped forward awaiting her orders.

"Go and fetch six of Birgr's Ulfhathnar. They will not breathe a word of this to another soul. Have them empty out the temple. Then escort Matilda and our kind doctor there by the secret way." She turned to the Anjar. "Summon every power that we have to bring our Visekonge Berserker back to us."

The page bowed and ran to complete his errand.

"Your daughter is coming with us?" The Anjar was amazed.

"She is, and you will obey her instructions. The Oracles of Heaven speak through her and you will need their aid to mend this... this..." the Lendmann Mother never completed her thought. She looked at Birgr's battered body one last time and turned with a snort. "I do not have time for this. Fix it."

"As you command, Grevinne."

Mathilda's lips curled into a smile far older than she ever could possess and true terror crept into the heart of the Anjar.

44. AT THE RAGGED EDGE OF DISASTER

The cold misty wind whipped over the scrub land, tearing at the ragged clothes worn by the company of weary travelers leaving them shivering. They had walked for three days in miserable weather. Snow had begun to fall in the high elevations as winter rapidly approached. The caribou herds were easy to follow now, eating their way to the east northeast with more small herds joining together, almost ready for the migration south to their breeding grounds near the lakes.

It was impossible to hear over the hissing wind whipped grass, but every once in a while, they saw that they were being pursued. Not by the Wendigo or the Skaerslinger, but a much more common danger. A group of three or four white dots had begun following that morning. A polar bear sow with two or three cubs had found their trail and were closing in. But what worried them most was a sound that came from among them.

Mirjam had begun to cough.

It was a wet and rattling sound from deep within her lungs that promised worse to come if not attended to. Declan had given her his bearskin to help keep her warm, but this malady had gone beyond being chilled.

"There!" shouted Feles. His sharp eyes had spotted what looked like a set of pine trees set among some low cedars. "The windbreak. I see smoke!"

Their hearts beat the rapid rhythm of hope as they strained to see their sanctuary. "The herds must be on the lee side of the camp."

"Praise you, God," Inge breathed heavily. "Praise you for your mercy." He, too, had reached the edge of his endurance.

"We should be there in the hour if we push hard," Feles encouraged. "Then warmth and food for all of us in my father's tipi."

Solveig's dragging feet became tangled and she fell hard with a squawk of surprise. Declan rushed to her with Leif close behind.

"Are you all right?" Declan asked.

"No. I cannot feel my feet and I think I twisted my ankle," she groaned, eyes full of tears. Amr arrived, his expression was one of grim worry.

"What is wrong?" he asked.

"She cannot walk," Declan answered. "I will have to carry her."

"No!" Amr said, voice sharp. "I will carry her. We need your axe free if those bears catch us. How long has it been since we saw them?"

"We are only minutes away from safety," Declan protested.

"And how fast can a polar bear run? We have not seen them for hours now. For all we know they are only a hundred yards away in this mist! Your axe and skills as a berserker might be our only chance if it comes to that!"

"The friar is right," Leif said. "Of all of us, right now he is strongest after you, and you are our last line of defense. I can barely lift my own sword, let alone carry another. Much can happen in this short sprint to safety and every minute we wait, the chance we will not make it unscathed grows."

"Thank you, my Tign," Amr said, genuine relief in his voice.

"Do not think this absolves you of anything, priest," Leif warned. "Do that which you have pledged and let us get moving."

"At once, my Tign," Amr said and then helped Solveig up to one foot, and then boosted her up on his back.

"I am ready," he said settling her weight on him. She was so light, but in his state any more burden was almost too much. Softly, with every step, Solveig heard him chanting a prayer as they went on.

As they came closer, there was a loud yelp. Finn spun around and saw Bergamot holding up one of her paws. She was a pathetic picture. Loose skin hung off her bones, showing ribs clearly. He saw drips of blood on a thorny mat beneath her feet. As he rushed toward her, there was a dull crackling and hissing under the grass.

"Stop! Something is with us!" Finn shouted the warning. "Something moving under the grasses!"

"What are you sa-" and Inge went down in a heap, his leg wrapped in some sort of berry bramble. The sharp tang of juniper came to his nose as he stared in surprise. His boots had protected him from being cut by the thorns, but that was not what terrified him. The juniper was visibly growing!

"In the name of Jesus, begone, demon, and trouble us no more!" Inge shouted.

The plant quaked as if being shaken violently by its roots, and then went still.

Finn went to Bergamot and found three thorns stabbed in the pads of her paws. She could no longer walk.

"Greithr, Bergie... Greithr," Finn soothed and carefully pulled the thorns out. Her whines were soft and tired. "I will carry you."

"What is going on?" Leif called back, the wind tearing away his words. They had spread out too far. Someone was going to be lost if they did not stick together.

"Watch your footing!" shouted Inge. "The plants are moving! Something is stirring up manitou to infest the thorns!"

Leif cursed to himself and looked at Feles who had continued farther ahead, unable to contain his joy at being home. They were so close that Leif ached for shelter.

Finn hoisted Bergamot up on his shoulders like a yoke. He looked down the slope they had been following, and through a break in the low clouds and mist he saw something he did not expect. Near the horizon was the Kisiina Sea. She rolled in her white speckled glory, waves thundering in wild foam on her rocky shore.

They had made it, Finn realized, elated. With new life to his step, Finn moved on toward the windbreak of cedars. He watched for slithering juniper that might grasp at his ankles. Whenever he spotted it, he stopped and rebuked the plant till it moved no more.

"This is how our early explorers must have felt when they followed the lakes for the first time," Finn laughed as he remembered the early journals telling of trees that seemed to uproot themselves in the night and impassable thickets forming behind them as they went. He shuddered as he remembered the tales of what they called Morthin Glaepur or "The Killing Glens." Explorers would enter a thick heart of a forest to discover there was no way out, but predators always found a way in.

Just as quickly as it had struck, the juniper was behind them, and the path became clear. Farther ahead, Feles had reached the cedars and a joyful joik went up from the Saami as their lost son returned.

In a manner of minutes, the rest arrived at the Saami camp where Feles was giving orders fast and furiously. Bright red and dark blue clad men and women came out to attend to the injured and the ill. None of them could understand what was being said. It sounded like Noerrant, but was a dialect they had never heard.

Feles came up to Leif with a man who had seen far too many hard winters. His mustache thick and drooping to hide all but his lower lip.

"Herre Leif, this is my father, Ado, Chief of our Aettir," Feles said by way of introduction. "Father, this is Herre Leif."

Leif gave a polite nod and the man held out his hand in friendship. Leif took it.

"May the Lord bless all those who live in this place," Leif said.

"May Yahweh bless those who come in peace, Amen," Ado said. "Feles tells me his namesake has lived up to its reputation."

"Namesake? He said that before, but we did not understand," Leif said, curious.

Ado smiled at Leif and put his arm around his son's shoulder.

"Why he is lucky, of course!" Ado laughed. "We sent him out looking for lost caribou, and he came back with a Sveinnaettir of great importance."

"You know my face?" Leif was shocked.

"I do not, but I recognize the seal on your scabbard none-the-less, my Herre, and I know you are a person of importance if you have a family sword like this. Feles was only being polite," Ado explained.

Leif let out a bray of laughter at the foolishness of hiding his identity.

"Thank you, Feles, for your discretion," Leif offered graciously and gave a slight bow.

"My question is how do I address you, Herre? Deres Naade? My Hovding? My Greve?" Ado guessed.

"My Tign is the proper form of address," Leif admitted with a hint of embarrassment that caught him by surprise.

Ado's eyes became wide.

"My Tign? No. You must be playing a jest on me!" he said and laughed.

"My Herre, I would not do that to you. We have endured far too much to be playing games of such sort," Leif said.

He looked around and saw that Solveig and Mirjam were being ushered into a tipi with Inge while some of the Saami children were helping Finn take care of Bergamot's injuries and attending to the weary Hawthorn.

Ado stared at him still unable to believe who stood before him.

"What I would humbly ask of you, Herre Ado-" he stopped himself. "Is that how you prefer to be addressed?"

"It is as good a title as any, I suppose," Ado accepted.

"Greithr, Herre Ado it is. We would like to ask for your hospitality and aid. One of my sisters is injured, as you saw, the other is ill and we are all in desperate need of food, shelter and aid. May we find such things here?"

"Our hospitality is yours, my Tign, without question," Ado answered. "I would like to offer my sincerest condolences and sympathies for the loss of your father. We had only heard of his passing a few week ago by some seal hunters that sailed through."

"Seal hunters? Will they be back soon? We also need help in finding a ship on which we can purchase passage back to Mannvoenlandnaam."

Ado ran a quick calculation in his head and spoke to Feles in their tongue. Feles caught his meaning and with a "Jah, Papa!" he ran off.

"My Tign," Ado turned to address Leif again. "All these things we shall accomplish for you as best as our aettir can offer. We have had a long and successful season and have largess to spare. Life may not be like your palace, but we can treat you according to your station. All will be well."

"On behalf of myself, my companions, the Sveinaettir and all the Akiniwazi Union, I thank you, Herre Ado."

"Good. Now come and we shall help you get clean, even some new clothes, and you can tell us all about your adventure tonight at the feast."

45. IN DARK HALLS, A LIGHT SHINES

"Mother!"

The word echoed through the long dark halls of the Kronapalasset.

"Mother! Where are you?"

The hysterical cry bounced off the hard stone and wood, now punctuated by feet running on thick carpet over stone. No one answered. All the paintings were covered in heavy black cloth. Mirrors were concealed in the same manner. The Kronapalsset was dressed in deepest mourning.

No courtiers.

No servants.

No pages.

No thralls.

Not a single huskarl.

The palace was devoid of all life.

The shadow ran into the Crown apartments, shrieking the same word, searching every bedroom in turn only to find empty beds. Pale moonlight streaming through windows and open doors was the only illumination.

"Where are you?" the shadow howled as it fell to its knees at the end of the long hall through the residential wing and began to weep horrible wracking sobs of despair.

"Where is everyone?" it wailed.

Echoes were the only reply.

The night was endless and this shadow was frightened. It was then this dim figure noticed that there was another darkness growing in the darkest corner of the hallway. It too moved on its own. The frightened little shadow reached out toward the darkness.

"Hello?" it asked.

The darkness snapped at the shadow's hand.

It was hungry.

The scared little shadow ran.

"Anyone? Please! Help me!" the shadow begged sprinting down the long corridor. There was no response.

Ahead a door opened to the servant's stairwell. Darkness like oily smoke began to fill the hallway as if a fire was burning in the basement. The smell of burning wood and cloth. The stench of animal hair and feathers was strong.

The shadow turned left and ran down the stairs to enter the Sveinnaettir Court where all the private family functions were held by the Visekonge. Long bare tables of polished wood sat shining in the pale blue light. Chairs stacked neatly for the day they would be used again. At the end of the long hall, one of the grand entrances to the Court of the Statsraad was open a crack.

A flicker of warm candlelight peeked around the edges.

"Mother!" the shadow screamed again and was off like a shot. Behind it, the darkness flowed over the balcony like a deadly waterfall. The servant's doors blew open as it burst through, consuming everything it touched.

The little shadow hit the door to the Statsraad Court, knocking it wide, and entered into the most august chamber of the Kronapalasset only to find the hearth had gone out. The hearth that was never allowed to go cold, was full of cold blackened ash and cinders instead of the lovely warmth and light it had always provided in days gone by. Where had the light come from?

A giggle came to the shadow's ear. Startled, it spun around.

There on the throne sat the Visekonge, Gregor, with the Kronasonn, Olivr, in his lap. Attended on either side by two dimly glowing angels.

Neither paid attention to the shadow entering the room as Gregor talked softly with Olivr in words that the shadow could not hear.

"Father!" the shadow gasped. "Oh, dear Papa, you are alive!"

Gregor did not heed the shadow's voice.

"Papa, can you not hear me?" the shadow begged and approached the bottom of the dais in front of the high seat. The dark figure fell to its knees before the Visekonge begging him to see it there. The darkness gushed through the doors on either side of the dias and began to reach for the shadow like two waves of serpents that filled the court to the ceiling far above.

"Father, please! Hear me!" the shadow wailed. "Why will you not see me?"

"He cannot see you, for he has gone beyond," Olivr said without a trace of his retardation.

"Olivr? You see me?"

"I see you, Mirjam," the boy said, speaking her name correctly for the first time. The shadow that had concealed her ripped away like a tablecloth at becoming known by her brother.

"Save me, Olivr. Please!" begged Mirjam.

As Olivr got down from Gregor's lap, the Visconge patted the twelve year old boy on the top of his head and her brother stood between her and her father like a sentinel. Olivr looked at the darkness about to consume Mirjam.

"Get out of here," Olivr said in a commanding voice. Like whips, the smokey serpents were dragged back through the doors of the court and slammed shut like thunder. Angels materialized before them, standing guard in the court.

"Why did you hurt me, Mirjam?" Olivr asked.

"I did not mean to," she said. "I... Solveig..." she took in a deep breath and held it for a long time trying to collect her thoughts and then sighed.

"Then why did you go?" Oliver asked.

"Because I wanted to make Solveig happy, and making Mother angry makes me happy." Olivr looked down at her. This was not the simple boy she knew and loved. This was a new Olivr. Powerful. Thoughtful. Wise beyond his ability in the flesh.

"When Pader died, Mater had no one to comfort her but me."

"I know. I am sorry," Mirjam moaned.

"I needed you too, for I did not understand, and Mater was too hurt to help me."

"I cannot make things right again," Mirjam whispered cheeks wet with tears. She looked at her little brother, speaking with such intelligence yet remaining so innocent.

"How can you be like this?"

"I am Olivr's spirit. Here, I am everything I was meant to be if not for the feebleness of my cursed flesh. Here my mind is untainted by the corruption of the world. Free from the generations of curses put upon our family by our enemies and those in our family who bartered away their children's children's children's souls for power in the morrow."

Mirjam gasped at the thought.

"Is that why we have monasteries that pray for us?"

"It helps keep the worst evils at bay," Olivr admitted, "but because we are not in communion with God, we make others speak to him in our stead, refusing to pray for ourselves. Therefore, we suffer too. Much that could have been avoided has befallen us."

"Like what has happened to Leif, Solveig and me?"

"What has befallen you is due to your own will, Mirjam. These are the bitter fruits you have picked by your disobedience and now must eat."

Mirjam began to weep afresh at the reminder she was to blame for their predicament.

"And we know that all things work together for good to them who love God, and to them who are called according to his purpose," Olivr said.

"What does that mean?" Mirjam asked, voice hitching from her sobs.

"Even though you meant it for your own reasons, God has used your actions for His purposes and the benefit of those who love Him."

"Then why did Edda die?" Mirjam demanded.

"She died doing God's will. She destroyed a great evil. An evil not seen since the days of Noah. She died for God's glory as well as for all of you."

"Why is all this happening then?" Mirjam cried.

"I can only tell you this: there are many curses in this land. They are on both our people and the Skaerslinger. God is bringing all of Akiniwazi to a time of choosing where he shall separate the wheat from the tares. And from this harvest, a new nation will rise," Olivr proclaimed.

"But how?"

"Everyone must choose whom they wish to serve. God wants you to play your part in His designs, but He will not force you. It must be your choice to trust and follow Him."

"My part?" Mirjam wondered. What could the All Mighty want with her?

"What am I in the scheme of creation? I am just a prize for men to fight over," Mirjam bemoaned of her station.

"God has another plan for you," Olivr said and began to walk down the steps of the dais.

"What is it?"

"You must trust in Him first, then you shall see," Olivr declared brooking no negotiation.

The words chilled Mirjam.

"And if I do not?"

"Have you no faith in He who created you?" Olivr admonished. "Can you not see that by accepting His will without knowing you are proving that you have even a little faith in Him? You see miracles every day! Continuing to live through all your trials in the mountains, and yet you would not trust that He has your best interests at heart?"

"Do you know what we have suffered in the mountains?" Mirjam whimpered.

"I do. Pader has shown me in my dreams though I only remember them here. He watches and is very proud of you, Solveig and Leif. Proud at what you are becoming. Proud at what you will become. We praise God for the work that is happening through and around you."

"What work? We have been lost in the wilderness," Mirjam was frustrated with these cryptic answers.

"You have been in the furnace. Smelted like gold, continually skimmed for dross and all things that would find you wanting. But now, you are to be forged."

"Forged? What does that mean? Are we to be tortured?"

"You are molten. Without true form and intent. God now intends to forge you into the instrument of His divine plan," Olivr foretold. His voice powerful and reverberating. Musical but without melody.

"What is that to be?"

"Do you accept His will for you?" Olivr challenged.

"I want to know first."

"That desire is dross that He cannot work with. You cannot be forged into a tool of God's will till you choose to sacrifice your own desires to His divine and perfect will."

"I..." Mirjam choked on what she wanted to say. She was not even sure how she felt.

"How can I trust God to not destroy me?"

"None of us can. See me as your example. Here I stand in my spiritual body, pure and perfect. Not the feeble minded child you see in the world."

Mirjam's shame burned brightly.

"Choose now. Your time here is growing to a close."

"If I say I will do as God desires, may I say goodbye to Papa?"

"No," Olivr said.

Mirjam's heart broke.

She was beyond tears or pleading.

"You may say goodbye to Pader regardless of what you choose, but choose now, and accept the consequences of your choice."

Mirjam surged up from the floor and hugged Olivr with all her might.

"I will do as God asks for me. No matter what."

Olivr hugged her back. When they finished embracing, Olivr looked in her eyes, then rubbed noses with her as he cherished.

The court exploded into bright golden and white light as all shadows and darkness vanished. The dim eyes of Gregor became bright and saw Mirjam. She gasped in wonder and stood up, ready to run to her father who beamed at her from his high seat. Mirjam paused for a moment and looked at Olivr who wore an innocent smile.

"I will miss this time together," Olivr said with a hint of sadness.

"I will never be able to see you the same way again, Olivr. I love you," Mirjam whispered, kissing him on top of his head.

"I love you too, Mirjam," Olivr said, giving her one last hug and letting her go.

Mirjam slowly ascended the steps of the dias to her father. Gregor opened his arms for his willful and mischievous daughter and welcomed her into his embrace one last time.

46. HOOVES & CLAWS, ANTLERS & FANGS

The flap of the tipi opened to admit Finn and Inge. Swaddled in furs and blankets, Mirjam was attended to by the Saami's doctor and several of the women of the aettir including Ado's wife. Solveig sat next to her holding her sister's hand, her leg stretched out in a splint, tightly wrapped for her sprained ankle.

"How is she?" Finn asked, lowering the hood on his borrowed coat. The strong wind made the caribou skin tipi breathe like a living thing.

"Her fever broke a few hours ago," Solveig sighed in joyous relief.

"She should recover soon," the doctor said. "We stopped the illness before it dug in too far, but the poor dear is nearly starved. A few hours more and I may not have been able to save her."

Mirjam's slow breathing was a welcome sign after the last few days of coughing. Solveig wiped her sister's forehead as she sweated out the sickness.

"Praise the Lord!" Inge said. "We have much to thank you for, Doctor."

The Saami healer smiled. "It was God working through us, Father. Without Him, we could have done nothing but watch."

"How are you doing, Solveig?" Finn asked.

"I should be walking again tomorrow." Solveig sounded quite happy about that.

"It is miraculous that none of you are hurt any worse from your ordeal," the doctor said.

"Jah," Inge sighed and rubbed his belly which was now flat yet flabby. "I no longer retain my wonderful plump profile."

The doctor smiled.

"Are you eating well?"

"Absolutely," Inge boasted. "We all are getting the meat back on our bones thanks to your generosity."

"Good. You will need your strength. Tomorrow, we will start feeding this one more than just broth. She will be desperate for nourishment. Are you sure you must travel as soon as the next ship arrives?"

"We must," Finn said, his expression grim. "I would prefer to take extra time, but the season is closing and many lives depend on these three getting home."

A large gust of wind caused the whole tipi to bend and shake.

"With this wind, you will be in Mannvoenlandnaam the evening after you depart. Such a fierce breeze."

"I pray our kaptain and pilot will be expert at avoiding the ice," Finn said.

"Amen," agreed Inge.

The doctor rose up. "I believe she is in capable hands," he said looking at Solveig. "You have proven to be an excellent nurse for your sister," he beamed.

"Thank you, Doctor," Solveig blushed.

"Now if you will excuse me, it is time for my own supper," he announced and walked out the flap and into the windy night.

"Is there anything we can do for you, Solveig?" Finn asked.

"I would appreciate it if one of you would stay to pray with me. I do not know how to do it right, but feel it is time for me to learn to do this for myself."

Inge looked ready to burst with pride in her.

"I would be delighted to stay with you. Finn? Would you go pass the good news on to Leif and Declan, about Mirjam?"

"Of course."

"Oh," Inge caught him as Finn took hold of the flap, "Bring Hawthorn in for me, please."

"My pleas- uff-da!" Finn exclaimed, startled as the big dog shoved his way into the tipi, no longer content to wait even in the lee of the shelter. "Well, hello to you too, Hawthorn," Finn exclaimed and snorted a laugh. Hawthorn did not bother to look back, but made right for Inge who was settling in on the other side of Mirjam. Hawthorn flopped down.

Finn shook his head as he admired the quick bond Inge had begun to build with the dog. Not the same as Speedwell, but right in time, Finn thought.

"I shall be on my way," he announced, pulling the hood over his head, and venturing out into the harsh wind to find Leif and Declan.

Finn went back to Ado's tipi where Leif was being housed and scratched on the flap. No one answered.

"Are you looking for my husband or your herre?" a voice questioned from behind.

Finn turned to look and saw Ado's wife approaching with an arm full of firewood.

"My Tign primarily, but Herre Ado would do."

He opened the tipi flap for her.

"They are checking the herdsmen at the moment. The wind is making the caribou restless."

Finn pointed off to the sheltered side of the cedar trees as to ask the question.

"Jah, that way," she said and then ducked into the tipi with the wood.

Finn let the flap fall back into place and walked off into the dark and windy night. Ahead he could hear the constant grunts and honking of thousands of caribou. The animals had formed up into clusters tight to the ring of cedars using their own bodies and the trees to block the wind. Over this racket, the thunder of surf on the shore could be heard. Far overhead the clouds whipped by in long dark streamers against the sparkling blue of the heavens.

Finn saw several men and dogs on watch scattered about with an eye for any predators who might be seeking an easy meal. He walked from man to man going deeper into the herd till he found Ado, Feles, Leif and Declan.

"Brother Finn," Feles greeted him warmly and held out his hand. Finn took it, then Ado's hand.

"What news?" Leif asked.

"It seems Mirjam's fever broke and she will recover soon. Herre Ado, you have an excellent healer among your people. We are very grateful for your help."

The Saami chieftain nodded his head.

"By your leave, my Tign, I would like to go see Solveig and Mirjam," requested Declan. He looked at Finn with an expression that pleaded for him to take over as Leif's guard."

"Jah, go on," Leif said almost dismissively. "I will see you later." There was an edge to the statement that Finn had never heard before between the two men. Something bitter. He held his tongue as Declan walked briskly back to camp.

Finn noticed a bonfire on the shore casting a powerful orange light.

"What is that about?" he asked gesturing toward the blaze.

"Since you need a ship, we are keeping a signal lit for anyone able to come ashore. We use this method when we are courting trade. You never know what time of night a ship might be passing by, and in this land, a fire means people and profits to be made."

"I hear tell you trade with the ships out here."

"Jah," Feles said nodding. "From time to time. Whale oil, blubber, seal fur, walrus tusks and goods from the east." Finn cast his eyes out to the sea out past the long dark apron of the grasses and dunes. It sparkled in the moonlight.

Finn's tired eyes caught a glimpse of a swift moving white shape gliding over one of the dunes close to the furthermost herd.

"Perhaps we have more visitors?" Finn guessed and pointed.

Ado, Feles and Leif followed his finger. To either side, straggling a little behind, two more smaller white shapes appeared. They seemed to be approaching the herd at a slow trot and disappeared behind the dunes and grass again in a shallow gully.

"I do not think a ship has landed," Leif said as he scanned the shore.

"Then who could they be?"

The herd of caribou's honking cries grew and they began to move like a flock of birds avoiding a fox. Surging a little together, then stopping. Surging again and stopping, always away from the white shapes.

Feles yelled something to one of the other men in the Saami tongue while Ado kept his keen eyes sweeping the land. Another white shape was spotted to the south of them and then vanished behind a bank of brush.

"There they are!" Leif shouted as the three shapes disappeared into another gully. The white forms were closing in on the herd, pushing it toward the cedars till the whole mass of animals began pressing together as the herdsmen on the outskirts tried to control their animals.

"We need to get out of the way," Ado said head swiveling to track the herd's erratic flow. The four began to jog toward camp, careful not to spook the beasts more than they already were. Ado shouted orders ahead of them and the men sounded the alarm and the camp sprang into action.

The Saami came out of their tipis with a variety of items on which to make noise, from shields to empty cauldrons to bells and drums, and formed a line between the herd at the cedars. Women and children held up blankets to mimic a wall and watched the herd. The herdsmen struggled hard to ball up the frightened beasts, singing a joik to them in soothing tones helping to control them and stave off disaster.

The three white shapes plunged toward the mass of caribou which now churned and swirled like a pot set to boil. One of the outlying men scouted toward one of the shapes and relayed a report back through the scattered men no longer able to calm their animals as the shapes were almost upon them.

"Polar bears!" The word passed on like a wave on the water. The four men began to trot faster, fighting between the clusters of spooked caribou. Sharp antlers looked like the spears of a mustering army.

Then, just as they were about to reach the cover of the cedars, the bears struck.

With bellows, the polar bear sow and her cubs charged, and there was but one route for them to escape. Stampede through camp. Unable to control their animals, men tried to funnel the beasts away from camp. The giant pale terrors of the ice made their first kills, taking bites but leaving the carcasses where they fell then moving on to the next in a killing frenzy. They maimed whatever came within reach of their bloody muzzles, pushing toward the center of the herds while their prey swirled around looking for a bull to follow into the clear.

The Saami continued to shout and make noise with whatever they had at hand. Children holding up the blankets hid and braced for the impact of the herd.

Seeing their way barred, the caribou broke around the noisy screen sliding between the polar bears as they split around the trees. A few relieved cheers went up as the animals turned, wrapped around the camp and thundered past. But the polar bears came very close to camp before spears could be brought into play. A caribou, fearing the bloodsoaked sow more than the noisy line of blankets, burst through.

Women and children were bowled over as the terrified animal cut through the treeline and bolted through the camp, dozens more followed, knocking more and more down. Then hundreds. Those who could, climbed up into the branches of the cedars and any other high place that might withstand thousands of charging caribou. Others who could not find protection strong enough or climb into the trees succumbed to the thundering mass and were trampled by the sharp hooves. Finn and Leif began pulling several people into the branches of the tree they had taken shelter in. It rapidly filled to the point of drooping.

Finn could see tree after tree full of people escaping the horror. Others scrambled away from the surging river of animals as best they could. Desperate to see where Inge and the rest were, he scanned toward the doctor's tipi.

It was not hard to find them thanks to Declan's broad back and bearskin cloak. He had the limp Mirjam over his shoulder as he stood on a thick branch a few feet above the antlers as they rumbled by.

On the opposite side, he saw Amr dangling upside down by his legs, arms stretched out, clothes streaming like a flag in the wind with hands clasping hands with Solveig while Inge boosted her from below barely missing the trunk of the tree.

Finn breathed a sigh of relief as Solveig made it to the branch below Amr, safe from being trampled, but clinging to the trunk as the sharp tines of antlers flashed by only a little below their feet..

Inge jumped as high as he could and caught Amr's hands. With a superb effort, Amr pulled the larger brother up toward the same branch as Solveig.

A large bull stumbled and slammed into the trunk shaking the whole tree. Solveig's unsteady leg gave way and she fell. Amr, fast as a striking snake, grabbed her wrist saving her from certain death. Amr now struggled to keep both Inge and Solveig above the chaos of the stampede.

"No!" cried Finn impotently as Solveig flailed about ready to fall among the sharp hooves.

With a mighty pull, Amr tried to lift both up again, but could not. His legs once firmly hooked began to straighten an inch at a time, losing precious purchase. Again, Amr tried to raise Solveig up but his arms had become too weak. Declan shouted down something to Amr that was lost in the stampede's booming roll. Amr looked up, as if to see how much longer he had to hold on but caught sight of Finn instead.

In the dying light of the trampled and scattered camp fires, Finn saw Amr sneer, look back down at Inge who was flailing to get a leg over another branch with no success.

Inge looked up in surprise, perhaps at something Amr said.

Finn's heart stuck in his throat, praying against what he sensed was about to happen. As Inge vanished into the groaning mass of antlers and hooves, Finn's screamed his rage to the heavens.

47. AN ODYSSEY ENDS

Three days after the stampede, sails were seen on the horizon making for the shore bonfire. The camp was still in tatters, most of the men were out rounding up the scattered caribou while the women and children repaired their homes and prepared four new polarbear hides. The worst of the maimed were gathered into a large tipi for the doctor while the women tended to those less severely hurt. Too many lingered, clinging to fragile threads of life.

Inge was among them.

Although the angel of death fought mightily to claim him, God did not gather His servant unto Himself yet. Finn hardly left his side praying and keeping vigil over him, begging for him to awake.

Herre Ado, with Feles and the elders went to the shore to welcome the arriving ship. Leif, Declan and Amr joined them. The longship loitered off shore, the red and white stripes of its sails poking over the mist of the frigid sea till the tide came in, and then rode up high enough to be secure for the day.

A rugged group of hunters jumped into the waves and made fast the ship while the kaptein waded ashore and stood in front of his longship. Once secure, the men joined their herre and stood in front of the bow, waiting patiently.

The two groups stared at one another from beyond arrow shot with the ancient wariness of the mysteries that come from the sea. To Leif's eye they were a lean and hungry looking lot. Their kaptain's shock of wavy ruddy hair and thick arms gave him a mythical appearance. His beard was long and tied together with silver wire and beads. Although serious in temperment, the sailors quietly joked among each other as they took in the Saami.

Once satisfied they were real and not manitou, Ado raised his open hand high.

"Ho there!" he shouted. "What brings you to our shore?"

"Ho there!" the kaptein responded. "We saw your signal fire in the night and came to seek trade or lend assistance. We would not be averse to a good fight on behalf of those in need."

The hunters gave smiles and a low rumble of agreement.

Herre Ado said with a smile, "May God bless all those who come in peace," and offered a place to sit by the low burning bonfire. "Come and be warmed and let us speak in comfort."

"God bless all those who dwell in this place," the kaptein answered seeing there would be no fight today, then he and his men came forward and joined their hosts shaking hands as they met face to face. Food and drink were at hand and shared among them as everyone sat around the fire and enjoyed the warmth together.

"I am Kaptein Cai Gylfirsson Andvariaettir, and this is my ship, the Dristig Jeger, on our way east with a load of seal furs and walrus tusks." The glass beads in his beard bobbed and twinkled as he introduced himself.

"How far are you planning to go?" Leif asked.

"Home to Hvalrauga," Kaptein Gylfirsson answered.

That was little more than half way to the Sumarpalasset Leif calculated.

"Could you be persuaded to take passengers all the way to Manvoenlandnaam?"

"Manvoen...? Why would someone want to go there from here?" the kaptein blurted out surprised. "This close to winter, God would have to be very kind indeed to get the Dristig Jeger home against the wind after such a trip."

"How far away are we?" Leif's voice was sharp as a pick. The kaptein returned with just as sharp a gaze searching the face of the young man who questioned him. He took a pull off the jug of mead that had passed back to him and thought, frowning and raising his eyebrows as he calculated the fastest trip, and then handed the jug over to Leif.

"Twelve, maybe sixteen days. If tide and tempest are on our side, perhaps nine. This time of the year when the sea is warm, and the air gets cold, I would not pretend to think that it would be."

Leif took a deep drink and squinted at Declan. The berserker was entranced, staring into the fire. Exhaustion had finally claimed his focus. The horn was passed on to Herre Ado and he began the round again.

"Passengers I could ferry without issue. It is the return back to Hvalrauga that concerns me. My men and cargo might be lost sailing against contrary seas as winter comes in."

"Hvalrauga is not that far from Manvoenlandnaam."

"As the raven flies, no. I am still talking tide and tempest here! It may be only five days with normal sailing, but at this time of the year! Three weeks is most likely. And although the Witch of November may come to the lakes at predictable times, there is no timetable on the Kisiina Sea. We get week long gales and worse going into winter. And she never freezes up like the lakes do so you can forget taking a sleigh across her. She gets thick and chunky with boulders of ice like you never see on the lakes." Kaptein Gylfirsson spread his arms wide and sucked his teeth. "Like this. And, of course, there are always the proper bergs out there."

The hunters gave grunts of agreement with their kaptein. They all were ready for home.

"What if..." Leif chose his words precisely, "I offered to buy your entire cargo at twice your price upon setting foot at Manvoenlandnaam?"

A swift rumble of surprise went through the hunters, but Kaptein Gylfirsson was not moved.

"How will we reach home? Most of us have families we have not seen in four months."

"How long would it take a steamknarr to go between the ports?"

"No owner would dare risk his steamknarr on such waters at this time of year! No sailor would be a fool to step on her decks for such a voyage! Even if you hugged the coast, you would still risk ice near shore and then there are the storms that could pound you to splinters." The kaptein exploded, offended that some rich man would even dare to suggest something so reckless.

"But how long?" Leif persisted.

"It depends on too many things." He crossed his arms and glowered at Leif, trying to size him up.

"How long?" Leif watched the kaptein, but a sly smile slid over his face.

"In this season, the same as the Dristig Jeger could. Five days," The kaptein was growing tired of this game.

"But the wind would not be a factor then, and you could steam on despite a storm? Which means unless the storm was so severe they would have to put into a safe harbor, it would be five days no matter what. Not a gamble for precious time," Leif surmised.

"I suppose so," the kaptein conceded the point.

"But we would be short our ship. A problem I cannot have for next season," the kaptein rejected, shaking his head. "But this is foolishness. I am not willing to go along with such a mad scheme even for double my cargo's price."

"Then I would buy your ship once we reach Manvoenlandnaam."

One of the hunters spit his drink in surprise causing a whoosh of flame from the bonfire.

"Buy... my ship?" Kaptein Gylfirsson looked numb with disbelief.

"Or give you a new one to be delivered in the spring. How ever you would like to be compensated," Leif said, arms crossed and a grin cracking wide.

"Preposterous! Who do you think you are?" Then the kaptein burst out with a laugh. "I must say, my boy, you are one funny drengr to pull such a joke." The rest of the men roared at the jest. "I would not sell you my boat even if you were the Visekonge himself!"

The men's laughter grew into hysterical gales as the faces of the Saami froze, and Declan, who had been passively watching, gripped his saxe handle tightly. Leif watched the men enjoy their moment, smiling. One by one, the hunters and kaptein noticed the horrified expressions on their host's faces, and turned their focus onto Leif as he rose to stand before them, taking the lapels of his kyrtill and battered baldrick sash in hand. Deftly he twisted it around to reveal the Sveinnaettir Crown crest.

"Would you sell it to the Tronerving as an act of service to the Crown?"

The hunters were too thunderstruck to gasp. They took full notice of Declan as he stood, his saxe in hand, blade bare, and they realized the bearskin cloak was also clasped with the medal of his office as the Visekonge's champion.

"You are the Tronerving? Leif Gregorsson?"

"And on the way to my coronation. Will you chose to serve me, and be rewarded as the loyal retainers I know the Andvariaettir to be?

All the knees hit the sand as the men prostrated themselves.

"It would be an honor to serve you, my Tign!" the kaptein gasped. "Forgive your servant's words! I knew not who you were."

"Get up, man," Leif said, motioning to Declan to put his saxe away. I knew you were jesting with me like a real drengr, and a good sailor would protect his livelihood with his life."

His subjects rose up from their prostrations.

"I still require your help and will reward you as I said. Even if it takes my own steamknarr the Sjovinna to bring you home afterward with your ship in tow.

"As you wish, my Tign. We shall obey."

48. A BITTERSWEET & COMPLICATED FAREWELL

"I must be awake," came Inge's soft voice, "for it hurts too much to be a dream."

Finn gave a weak smile, blinking back his watery eyes, his vision shimmering.

"Tears for me?" Inge said giving a weak grin. "I am touched. You always were the sentimental one of us."

Finn gave a sad spasm of laughter. Inge's eyes were dull with pain, but still sharp enough to read his friend. His oldest friend, if counted correctly. Inge was a collection of shattered bones and bruised guts. He was a mad quilt of black and purple from where the caribou hooves had stomped him as he had cowered behind the cedar trunk that held the rest aloft.

"Is it as bad as all that?" Inge's question was not much more than a dim croak.

Finn nodded, for how could one survive all these wounds without an Anjar present?

"Good," Inge said with a puffy lipped smile. "I would like to go home to God and tell Him what I have been doing in the world."

"You cannot let my grief sit unmolested, can you?" Finn said, unable to keep the growing smile off his face.

Inge cocked a mischievous eyebrow over closed eyes.

"I suppose not. If I am not long for this mortal life, it is my privilege after all. This is how I choose to spend it."

A girl's relieved laughter caused Inge to open his eyes and raise his head but a little. Mirjam sat at the foot of the furs upon which Inge lay.

"I amuse you too, my Tign?" Inge said with some surprise, then lay his head back down. "Greithr. In times such as these, we all need amusements to keep up our spirits and dim the pain of our trials."

Finn was unable to speak.

"Have I been asleep long?" Inge asked.

"Three nights," Mirjam said.

"Then just like Lazarus, but funnier and with more bruises," Inge said and chuckled. He instantly regretted it for a broken rib pinched him painfully. "Oj!" he grunted. "Forgive me, Lord, forgive me. I did not mean any disrespect."

Mirjam laughed behind her hand at his irreverence. Finn shook his head.

There was a scratch on the tipi's flap. A second later, it flipped open to allow Leif, Solveig, Declan and Amr inside. Hawthorn's fawn head popped up from behind Inge and gave a low whine at seeing his former master. Amr narrowed his eyes at the dog. Solveig all but threw herself to Mirjam's side.

"We are going home!" she blurted out, Leif's mouth having just opened to speak. He gave a sharp look at his sister, rolled his eyes and hooked a thumb at her.

"Like the little herald said," he grumbled and kneeled down on his haunches next to Inge and laid his hand on the friar's shoulder. "We have passage on a ship."

"By God's armies of angels!" Inge said bursting with happiness, the shout causing all new pains to rattle around his body and he lay back with an arpeggio of groans.

"I look forward to familiar food and drink," Inge said.

"And sweets," added the overjoyed Mirjam.

"Thank you, Lord God," Finn whispered, bowing forward, touching his head to Inge's thigh.

"There is one small complication," Amr said. His face an inscrutable puzzle.

Leif's glance burned hot toward Amr.

"What is this?" Inge asked softly.

"You must stay behind," Amr said with the faintest hint of gloating.

Finn felt only cold. It radiated out from his gut like someone was pouring a glacial stream into him, leaving him numb from toes to his hair.

Mirjam and Solveig gasped.

Leif grimaced.

Finn slowly raised his head from Inge's leg, his eyes murderous. Inge saw it first.

"Finn? Finn!" he wheezed. "No, Finn."

Declan took hold of Finn as he turned on Amr.

"Not now, Brother," Declan whispered. "His day will come."

Amr inspected his fingernails for a moment, unimpressed with Finn's threatening glare and explained. "The kaptein does not believe Inge would survive the trip in an open decked longship. They have enough... meat... on board. There is no need to add more." He emphasized his statement by looking at Inge like a butcher at a leg of mutton.

Finn tried to lunge, but Declan had him well restrained.

"Get out of here you hellish bastard," Finn said.

Amr gave an exaggerated expression of false offense. Fingertips touching his chest, mouth hanging wide in surprise.

"Me? It was me who did the kindness of telling him the truth, Finn. In fact, it should be Inge who is most offended and hurt at being left behind in such..." he paused, looking for the precise word for how he felt, "august keeping."

Finn fought Declan's hold again, but the berserker's grip was iron. Leif stood up from his crouch. He looked at the ground for a moment, drew a long sniff and backhanded Amr, snapping his head sideways a fraction. The red shape of a hand appearing on the friar's cheek.

"That was cruel and unnecessary," Leif growled. "Get out."

Amr jutted his chin toward Leif, rolled his neck and gave a deep bow. His hands providing a foppish flourish to the act which stank of pure scorn.

"As my Tign desires, I obey," Amr said in a syrupy voice.

He backed up, rose upright with a prickly arrogance and let himself out of the tipi.

"My Tigns, Declan, would you leave me with Inge? I will be along shortly," Finn asked.

Declan gave him a supportive pat on the back as they gave the pair some time alone.

Inge recognized the forlorn look on Finn's face and frowned before the words came out.

"I am not going," Finn declared.

"Quit pouting. You are too going," Inge said as firmly as he could.

Finn's eyes widened with the insult.

"Pouting? I am not a child!"

"Then do not act like some hrodinefr brat." The tone was sharp despite the lack of volume. Finn was taken aback. "You see me. What would happen if a storm hit? I can hardly keep warm under all these blankets and furs and this big lummox resting half on me," Inge said and gave Hawthorn a rub on his ears eliciting a groan of happiness.

"You do not understand. Watching you fall almost broke me," Finn choked.

"Now you are being maudlin. What kind of a drengr are you? Be a man," Inge scolded. "Death comes for us all in due time. Nothing you can do will stop that." The sharpness was gone from Inge's words, but the authority remained.

Finn sat down again, crossed his legs and had a good sulk. Inge let him and rubbed the happy Hawthorn's ears. In time, Inge's patience ran out.

"Are you the elder of the two of us or am I? Why am I even asking such questions of you?" Inge let out a careful sigh, fighting hard to not cough. "Greithr, greithr. What is it that is tearing at your soul so much you have become a weepy old krone?"

"I am the one who broke the conditions of my skoggang. A death sentence now hangs over my head," Finn began.

"Which Leif commuted," Inge said over the complaint.

"Stuck on a trek through horrible demon infested lands and points known only to the most hearty of people, with someone who wants me dead... no, no. Not dead, tortured and then killed slowly by his own hands," Finn continued to whine.

"And from whom you are protected," Inge added.

"While preserving two girls unable to survive in such a place, nearly starving, almost eaten by monstrous weasels and almost frozen to death!" Finn ranted. "Oh! Oh! Then I must continue on, right into the very jaws of those same powerful men who had me convicted and sentenced to skoggang! Then, when all I wished to do was live out the rest of my days in Kynligrspiejl... look! Look at where it has gotten me?"

Inge waited patiently.

"All because I thought in my heart of hearts that God was calling me to do this. Now I do not even know! I have not felt God's presence or heard his voice clear to me in weeks! How do I know now that I made the right choice? Did I just go off to play the hero of the sagas and gather all the glory unto myself? Did I do this for political reasons? Personal pride? Why did I do this? How can I know?"

Most of this was shouted at the smoke hole above them. Bergamot, had remained asleep throughout it all but opined by letting out a squealing fart and kept on snoring.

"Taking his side, I see," Finn grumbled at Bergamot and began petting her gently.

It took all of Inge's willpower to keep from bursting out laughing. When he was sure he would not, he spoke.

"That was quite a display of self pity. Are you through yelling at God?" Inge asked.

"Jah." Finn's voice was spent.

"Good. Now can I explain how you can know?"

Finn just gestured for Inge to continue.

"It is simple. Do you believe we escaped all those dangers without God's help as poorly equipped and unready for such an adventure as we were?"

"Maybe?" Finn said.

"You think we came across Feles when the Wendigo was upon us by chance?"

Finn looked up. His features haggard.

"What about finding that cache of food that gave us the strength to reach the Saami?"

Finn gave a shrug of his shoulders. Inge gave a wry smirk and raised his head.

"Edda's sacrifice and our escape through the mountain? That was not God's doing?"

Finn now squirmed with the thought, and a new knife of sadness skewered his heart remembering Edda.

"But if that is not enough. I have one more proof for you," Inge said, laying his head back again. "Do you wish to hear what I call incontrovertible proof of God's blessing on you and His desire for you to do these things for His glory?"

"What?" Finn said, the doubtful devil on his shoulder cowered before the truth.

"Daniel."

The name was a punch, no, a kick to the heart by an oxen.

"If God was not moving heaven and earth around you, why did he send an angel. Your angel, mind you, before you. An angel who took on the trappings of the flesh, served demons and their children in secret just so we were able to escape, and then allow Edda a prayer of a chance to slay a Nephilim of ancient days?"

Finn now wept openly in shame. How could he have forgotten such clear evidence of God moving in his life?

"Would you like me to give you another reason to go with them to the bitter end, despite the price you may have to pay?"

"What could that be?" Finn looked like a drowning man, waiting for one last wave to finish him off.

"Amr," Inge whispered.

Finn's anger flared at the name.

"How could he possibly be the reason I would-" Finn ranted.

Inge raised his eyebrows and fixed his friend with a very knowing look.

"Oh..." Finn said, realizing what Inge was saying. "Without me," Finn started to say.

"That is right. They will be all alone in Amr's clutches. Do you think Declan or Leif could stand up to Amr? Does the ship have a priest?"

"I do not know. Would they dare sail without one?"

"They will need you, Finn. Now more than ever. They are still a thousand miles from the safety of their retainers and wealth."

"And you cannot help me," Finn said, nodding in sad acceptance of his fate.

Inge gestured to his broken body and gave a painful wheezing laugh.

"Perhaps in the spirit. In prayer, then." Finn compromised.

"Perhaps," Inge tentatively agreed. "I have been known to have a very long reach with my prayers."

Finn sat with Inge for a long time considering his dear friend's words.

"I will miss you, my brother," Finn lamented.

"We may still see each other once again before paradise," Inge said, a hopeful smile on his lips.

Finn gave a nearly imperceptible nod.

"Up," Finn said giving Bergamot a pat and stood. The big mastiff rose with a groan and a stretch.

"May God watch over you and send every angel he can spare to heal your broken frame." Finn's smile was sad but true.

"And all those He does not send to me, I pray He puts over you and blesses your very footsteps," Inge answered.

Finn turned to leave. He summoned Bergamot with clicks of his tongue, then took one last look at Inge as he held open the flap.

"Finn?" Inge said.

"Jah?"

"It may also be God's purpose that you witness or perhaps participate in Amr's just and final end," Inge suggested with a wink. "That should put a smile on your face."

Finn laughed in spite of himself.

"Perhaps so. Perhaps so." Finn paused a moment and fixed his biggest smile on Inge. "God bless."

And then he was gone.

AKINIWAZISAGA
Into The High Places

Book Three

LAND OF THE SEVEN FRESHWATER SEAS

AKINIWAZI

ENCYCLOPEDIA AKINIWAZI

Language

Nickames & Terms of Endearment

Elskling
[EHLSK-ling]
Darling

Kjaere
[CHEH-reh]
Dear or precious. Often "kjaere mann" for dear man or husband, or "kjaere kvinne" for dear woman. "Kjaere kone" means "Dear Wife".

Slang & Colorful Colloquialisms

Bacraut
[bah-KROWT]
Asshole

Fubrande
[foo-BRAHN-deh]
An insult; literally means "arse log". A piece of wood used below the horse's tail to prevent a certain type of sleigh from slipping too far forward when going downhill.

Fy da
[FEE-dah]
An expression of great disgust.

Gobermouch
Old Irish. A meddler and gossip.

Greithr
[GREH-thur]
Slang for agreement. Okay, all right, sure thing, so be it.

Hrodinefr
[ROWD-NEH-fur]
Snotnose

Lort'e
[LOR-tay]
A turd. Feces.

Oj
[OY]
"Hey,' "Oh" or "Oy Vey."

Skeiturhuth
[SKEE-tur-HOOTH]
Dirt (dung) skin. A nasty pejorative toward anyone of dark complexion. Saved mostly for Skaerslinger or Inuit descent.

Svikari
[svih-KAH-ree]
Traitor

Tambakkji
[tam-BAHK-yeh]
A cheap alloy. Used to describe a person you dislike.

Thu vethur
[THOO VEH-thuhr]
You bet. A phrase of agreement, or emphasis.

Tjovekjakji
[TEE-YOH-va-CHA-chi]
A thief. Literally "thief's cheek."

Places

Cities and Towns

Dyrrvatn Kastali
[die-err-VAH-ten kah-STA-lee]
Doorway Lakes Castle. The capital of Akiniwazi and its largest city located at the portage of the Athrflojt in the chain of the Faellgallervatn. It is located on an Isthmus between two artificial lakes, the Dyrrvatn and the Faellgallervatn.

Fjellporten
[fee-YEL-por-tan]
Gateway to the Mountains. Capital city of Wanishinabinoogiland, and site of the palace of Jarl Vilhoaettir the Towrnvilhoaettir.

Kynligrspiejl
[kin-LY-gur-speel]
Wondrous Mirror
A small town with a Havarian estate located on a large island in the middle of Lake Wanishinabinoogi. It also includes a Kyrkja bank that trades for the precious stones and metals found on the shores of the lake.

Mannvoenlandnaam
[mahn-VAIN-lahnd-nahm]
Promising Settlement
The first settlement in Akiniwazi set on the mouth of the Athrflodjt. Location of the Sumarpalasset.

Ulfshaugrstrond

[Oolfs-HOW-gur-strond]

Ulf's Grave Mound Beach

The Home City of the Kyrkja. It is the location of the Keldathing, the highest ecclesiastical court in all Akiniwazi. This is where the Cardinal of Akiniwazi administers and guides the Kyrkja and all its sects. It is located on the southeastern shore of Lake Neezhoday. Named after Saint Ulf, the founder of the sects of the Kyrkja, who is entombed there.

Dyrrvatn Kastali Locations

Blessath Borth Inn
[BLESS-ath BOR-ath]
The Blessed Table. A small inn in the Truartorg neighborhood near the Domkyrkjeplassen.

Domkyrkje
[dohm-HEER-hyah]
The name of the Dyrrvatn Kastali Cathedral, the first cathedral built in Akiniwazi.

Domkyrkjeplassen
[dohm-HEER-keh-PLAH-sen]
"Cathedral Plaza." The location of Dyrrvatn Kastali Cathedral. It is a circular plaza surrounded by seven avenues that radiate out throughout the city named after each sect, with the eighth being Haertak Boulevard. It is located in the center of the city near the north shore of the isthmus between the lakes of Dyrrvatn, to the south, and Faellgallervatn, to the north.

Haertak Boulevard
[HAIR-tahk]
"Conquest Boulevard" One of the rare bricked streets in the Akiniwazi Union. A memorial boulevard, lined with trees and statuary dedicated to famous jarls and every Visekonge. It reaches from the Visekongehagen to Domkirkeplassen at the center of the isthmus in which the city is built. This is more of the Hird and society boulevard, lined with rich shops, mansions and apartments for courtiers.

Kronapalasset

[KRO-nah-PAH-la-set]

Crown Palace

The palace home of the Visekonge and seat of all power in the Akiniwazi Union. Located in Dyrrvatn Kastali. Built in the center of the Kastaliplassen, which is a semi fortified trelleborg surrounded by government buildings and the hub for the eight main "spoke" boulevards in the city.

Kronaplassen

[KRO-nah-PLAH-sen]

Crown Plaza

The fortified neighborhood with all the services and housing for the Visekonge's palace. It is located in the middle of of the Dyrrvatn Kastali Ithsmus on a small hill allowing it to see the far shores of both Dyrrvatn and the channel to Lake Ishkode in the south and Faellgallervatr to the north which is the headwaters of the Athrflojt.

It is a double trelleborg measuring almost a mile in diameter. The outer perimeter is a circle of stone buildings filled with a variety of services and businesses connected to the operation of the government. These buildings act as an outer wall with gates that can be closed. The inner trelleborg style bailey is a relatively short stone wall and berm, which is 8 yards thick and filled with a network of fortified tunnels and chambers and is only 10 yards tall. The center of the large plaza is the Visekonge's Palace, the Kronapallaset, and four main outer buildings set in the pattern of the Jerusalem Cross. The complex has four main gates to the cardinal directions, with four secondary gates.

Statsraadplassen
[STAHTS-rahd-PLAH-sen]
Statsraad Plaza
The plaza where the manor houses and mansions of members of the Privy
Council and representatives of the jarls live when they are in the city.

Toinnsjokanalen
[tao-IN-sho-KAN-ah-len]
Two Lakes Canal.
Located at the thinnest point between the artificial lakes of Dyrrvatn and
Faellgallervatn and provide vital passage that crosses the watershed over
the isthmus of Dyrrvatn Kastali. It was an impressive feat of engineering
for its day, but has never become fully functional. Due to the nature of the
watershed, the locks to the Faelgallrvatn are often closed due to sediment
fill and slow currents.
The canal is now used mostly for Hird ship berths for quick access to the
Statsraadplassen,and freight offloading and transloading to the
ribbonroads and carts.

Truartorg
[TRU-ahr-torg]
Faith Square
A small neighborhood near the Domkyrkjeplassen.

Visekongehagen
[VIH-seh-KON-geh-hagen]
The Visekonge's Garden
A public landing and garden strip on the southern side of Dyrrvatn Kastali.
Used for more social events, popular with the Hird as a promenade.

Geographical Features

Amossonkanal
[AY-moh-son-KAH-nahl]
A great canal and string of locks in Mestrflosslidhaland to bypass the great waterfall and connects the lower two lakes for shipping. Named after its architect Herre Amosson.

Athrflojt
[AY-thur-flawt]
First River
This was the first river discovered in Akiniwazi. It has the oldest settlements and is the most populated area in the land.

Blawisflojt
[BLAW-ees-flawt]
Blue Ice River
This is the river that flows east southeast from Lake Wanishinabinoogi to the western shores of Lake Ogimaque. It is named for the frequent chunks of calved glacial ice that often float down its length.

Brestoeyane
[BRES-toy-YAH-neh]
Shattered Archipelago
Located at the confluence of Lakes Ogimaque, Lake Manitou to the south east shore where it connects to Lake Neezhoday's far western end. It is the most highly traveled and dangerous point for ships on the lakes.

Dyrrvatn
[DIE-uhr-VAH-ten]
Doorway Lake. An artificial lake that forms the southern shore of the Dyrrvatn Kastali Isthmus. It is connected to Lake Ishkode to the south by a short river and runs no deeper than twenty feet at its deepest point.

Eitrfjord
[EYE-tur-fee-ord]
Poison Fjord
A small concealed fjord on Lake Wanishinabinoogi.

Faellgallervatn
[FAY-el-GAL-ehr-vah-TEN]
Portcullis Lake
The Faelgallervatn is the lake that makes up the northern shore of the
Dyrrvatn Kastali Isthmus. It is an artificial lake, created to destroy demonic
sites of worship for the Skaerslinger and to bridge the Athrflojt to the rest
of the lakes, forming a new drainage path for Akiniwazi. The project was a
failure, but the lake is maintained. It is connected to the south by the
Toinnsjokanalen, which allows occasional water access between it and the
Dyrrvatn. It was also the site of the battle waged by Saint Ragnar and
preceded the discovery of the seven freshwater seas which allowed the
exploration of Akiniwazi.

Gamleverden
[GAHM-leh-VER-den]
The Old World
The name for Europe, Africa and Asia. Often also used for their traditional
homelands of Norway, Finland, Sweden, Iceland, Greenland and other
territories.

Grohstahyrmunnr
[GROH-sty-uhr-MOON-ur]
Cataract's Mouth.
The last bay before the cataract through the mountains.

Kisiina Sea
[kih-SEE-nah]
The sea that forms the northern shore of Akiniwazi. For many centuries the Kisiina Sea was clear and filled with ships coming from the Gamleverden. In 1266 AD came Fimbulvetr. For two years, winter kept hold, making for a stunted growing season and snow stayed all year round. The Kisiina Sea became an impassable slurry of moving ice flows and deadly storms.

Lake Bawajigaywin
[bah-WAH-jee-gay-win]
Lake Bawagii, as locals call it, is often envisioned as the temper tantrum prone little girl. She can throw up a fuss with the slightest wind and consistently freezes over. She is the southernmost lake and has the balmiest climate of them all. She is also the second to last lake before the Grand Cataract empties them all into the ocean. At her eastern shore, is a giant waterfall that no ship can survive, but over the centuries, the Forsamling have created their greatest engineering achievement: The Amossonkanal.

Lake Ishkode
[EESH-koh-day]
Lake Ishkode is the last lake before the Cataract empties out through the Grohstahyrmunnr into the ocean in an impassable torrent. Along some of its southern shore, hot springs, geysers and mud pots boil and bubble, heating the rivers that pour into her. This spirit of flame also seems to attack even the ships upon it, for more ships burn here than anywhere else. Her wealth in heat induced rarities make her a bounty of wildlife and fauna both on her shores and in her

Lake Manitou
[MAN-ih-too]

Lake Manitou's shape leaves few safe harbors for the heavy traffic and high population. Huge seas roll up and down its length with the winds, and her few bays are treacherous with winds and rocks are a danger to shipping. If that were not enough, the dead are even more restless here. There are islands that appear and disappear, ships that continue to sail but never reach port.

Despite the danger, Lake Manitou is the most populous of the lakes for she is surrounded by fertile farmland. At her northernmost point is the Confluence, a connecting point between her neighboring lakes, Lakes Ogimaque and Neezhoday. These three lakes are called the "Elder Sisters." Lake Manitou freezes completely over in only the coldest and calmest winters.

Lake Neezhoday
[NEEZ-ho-day]

Lake Neezhoday is two lakes in one. Her massive bay, Halfrhjartavagr, is almost a lake unto itself. Although not as big or as deep as Ogimaque, she can be just as violent and deadly. Between the eastern and western halves of the lake sit the Siloeyane, the largest chain of islands in Akiniwazi.

At her easternmost point, where Lakes Ogimaque and Manitou connect to her, is the Brestoeyane, a treacherous set of islands and the Confluence where both lakes pour their water into Neezhoday causing rogue currents and swells. These can sweep unaware ships onto the rocks and islands. The seasons and weather alter the flow giving the lake a "heartbeat" causing strange undulations of the water. Neezhoday also sports another large southwestern bay, the Erfithursandarvatn with treacherous bars, silting and cross currents. Lake Neezhoday has a strange tendency to freeze over only one half at a time. Only during the coldest of winters do both halves freeze over.

Lake Ninabemnibo

[NEE-nah-behm-NEE-boh]

Lying in the center of a low flatland swamp, Lake Ninabemnibo Is a lace of islands skirted in swamps and bogs. It is rich in peat and tars that ooze from the ground. The lake is riddled with over a thousand islands which makes it the perfect place for smugglers and vikings. Although it does not have big cities on its shores, it is peppered with small ports and villages, sometimes better known by their island name. Birds seem to be attracted to this land for it is rich in food. It is connected on its north shore by a long winding river that flows to Lake Ogimaque. It is fed by hundreds of streams and a few very small rivers that come from the rainy reaches of the South West ranges of the Ondeaandkorgfjall.

Lake Ogimaque

[Ohg-ee-mah-kay]

Lake Ogimaque is the largest, deepest lake in Akiniwazi. Even the fastest steamknarr takes over 3 days to cross her from end to end. Her shores are a rocky and foreboding mixture of ice, snow, rock, and sand in all seasons. She is not the farthest north of all the lakes, but she is the coldest but never completely freezes across, because of her size and power. Near the eastern shore sits Ogimaak Mikwam Island, an island regarded as holy ground to the Skaerslinger.

It is said that the demon Ogimaak Mikwam, the Ice Queen, rules the lake from a temple on that island and the lake takes on her personality. The lake is cold, violently tempered and never gives up what she takes. The surrounding territory is vastly wealthy in food and minerals.

Lake Wanishinabinoogi

[wah-nah-SHEE-nah-bih-noo-gee]

At the highest altitude, Lake Wanishi, as the locals call it, collects the runoff for the northwestern Ondeaandkorgfjall mountains. The lake is the first to freeze over, and the last to thaw. Ice often persists on her shores in the middle of summer. Isolated, with very few towns around it, she is the smallest lake, and it is always possible to see at least one shore at all times. Several glaciers calve into her waters, threatening shipping and keeping her waters almost as cold as that of Lake Ogimaque which she empties into through the Blawisflojt from her southern tip.

The mountains surrounding the lake have a powerful attraction, for they are rich in gemstones.

Neinnvanbjarg

[NINE-van-BE-arg]

No Hope Rock

A moderate sized island with a wood lot for steamknarr that ply the lakes.

Ogimaak Mikwam Island

[OH-gih-mahk MIK-wahm]

Island of the Ice Queen

This island is the claimed home of the demonic spirit, Ogimaak Mikwam. The Visekonge has assembled two fortresses with strong fleets of longboats to maintain watch on this spiritually active island. Forsamling ships are required on pain of death to stay clear of the island and never land on it. If they are to be wrecked on her shores, it is said captains will scuttle their own ships and die in the waves rather than be found there. It is thought that several thousand Skaerslinger live on this island.

Ondeaandkorgfjall
[OHN-day-and-korg-fee-ahl]
Evil Spirit's Basket Mountains
The series of mountain ranges that surrounds Akiniwazi to the east, south and west.

Silenoeyane
[sigh-LEN-OOH-yah-nay]
The Sieve Archipelago
A major island chain in the middle of Lake Neezhoday. It is very hazardous to ships as it contains many reefs, bars and other "pinnacles of doom." It is also subject to extremely strong currents as the waters of the upper four lakes drain through this point and combine with storm fronts to push water back and forth through their narrow channels and dozens of islands.

Vesterhavet
[VES-ter-HA-vet]
The Western Ocean
The name the Vikings ancestors of the Forsamling gave the Atlantic Ocean. Although, to the inhabitants of Akiniwazi, this is to their east, they still refer to it by its traditional name.

Political, Military & Miscellany

Akiniwazi
[ah-KEE-nih-WAH-zee]
Land of the Seven Freshwater Seas
Discovered in approximately 800AD by Vikings, it was considered a second Eden by many who explored it. Plants and game are plentiful, but wild. Domesticated animals and crops brought over to the land tended to not fare well, and most died off completely. It was discovered that the land was spiritually active, expressed by the belief that the veil between heaven and hell was thin. Prayer, worship and the gifts of the spirit gave spectacular manifestations by those who came to the land, as well as supernatural activity. In 1266 came Fimbulvetr, a period of two years that saw almost no summer, and the sea routes to the Gamleverden was blocked with never-ending icefloes and bergs. The mountains surrounding the land were also impassable mountains, cutting off the lands of Akiniwazi possibly forever.

Athrvorthfestning
[AH-thur-vorth-FEST-ning]
First Watch Fortress
The eastern fortress protecting the Brestoeyane from vikings and Skaerslingcr, and patrolling the waters around Ogimaak Mikwam Island.

Barskaborg
[bar-SKA-borg]
Taiga Castle
A chateau style fortress with a high stone tower and bridge that serves as the river gate on the Blawisflojt and the taxation point for travel between Lake Ogimaque and Lake Wanashinabinoogi.

Djevleportfestning

[DEE-yeh-vehl-PORT-fest-NING]

Devil's Gate Fortress.

The easternmost military fortification before the entrance to the great cataract into the eastern ranges of the Ondeaandkorgfjall and the supposed home of the Storm King, Ogimaa Nichiiwad, the demonic master of all Akiniwazi.

Sjuheilagdomen

[choo-HEY-lag-DOW-men]

Seven Saints Shrine

A shrine created to honor the seven sects of the Kyrkja and the man who envisioned the organization of the modern Kyrkja, Saint Ulf.

Sumarpalasset

[SOO-mar-pah-LAH-set]

The Summer Palace

The summer palace is where the Visekonge conducts business from Midsummer's eve to the end of August when they return to Dyrrvatn Kastali.

Towrnvilhoaettir

[TA-OHRN-vil-oh-EH-tur]

The seat of power for Jarl Vilhoaettir. It is a six story tower built in the middle of Fjellporten on a small hill. A mead hall known as the Jarl's Hall was built next to it for social gatherings, feasts, holidays, Things and other community functions.

Society

The Hird

The Hird is the royal structure of government in Akiniwazi that was formed in 1302 A.D. or 35 A.S., which stands for Ad Segregationem denoting the beginning of isolation from the world following the end of Fimbulvetr by Akiniwazi reckoning. It was the result of Visekonge Halmar Mikkelsson Sveinnaettir negotiating a truce between the warring jarls and ending The Aettirkrigen. This allowed for organizing a new aettir peerage that addressed many grievances of the clans and families and also formalized the aettir structure. This provided stability for tradition and new growth, hierarchy and a much smoother succession of power as time went on. The agreement was called the Halmarpakt and created the Akiniwazi Union which delineated the structure and territories of the land.

Lineage of the Sveinnaettir Dynasty

Halmar Mikkelsson the Uniter - Founder of the Akiniwazi Union

Axel Halmarsson the Peaceful

Boje Axelsson the Builder of the Palace

Cruim Bojesson the Crooked – Died/Assassinated.

Hrollief Ahlstrohm the Savior

Trigg Nyqvist the New Branch

Mikkel Triggsson the Fierce

Erick Mikkelsson the Resolute

Oysten Ericksson the Joyful

Wyck Oystensson the Clever

Vidar Wycksson the Bold

Gregor Vidarsson *Current Visekonge

The Statsraad

This is the ruling body of the Akiniwazi Union, created by the Halmarpakt in 1302. It consists of a fluctuating body centered around the thirteen lands of the Union. These are represented by the jarls directly or their designated factors and approved counsellors. There is a mutable extended membership of the Statsraad that serves at the pleasure of the Visekonge. These members are prominent members of the Hird as well as representatives of business owners and wealthy aettir, influential artists, philosophers and other educated men of the day.

The Statsraad have their own tables in which to manage the needs of the Union and advise the Visekonge. The Statsraad may overrule the Visekonge only with a unanimous vote of all the jarls, represented in person, and not by factor or counsellor. In this manner the bureaucracy of the government is delegated and managed.

The Privy Council

In addition to the Statsraad, each table is lead by a special advisor to the Crown known as the Privy Council. This consists of men chosen to personally oversee and focus the Statsraad members with the germane business of the bureaucracy. These positions include:

Chancellor – Highest judge in the Union and chief of the guard

Stallare Marshal – The general in charge of all the Crown's army

Admiral – Highest naval officer in charge of all the Crown's naval forces

Crown Chaplain – Spiritual advisor to the Crown

Minister of the Exchequer – Chief accountant and tax collector

Minister of the Wardrobe – Personal assistant to the family of the Visekonge and master of all the Crown household.

Coroner – Chief bureaucrat, Keeper of the Census and all Crown records, Curator of the Bok av Familiar

Aettir Peerage

Society in Akiniwazi is formed around the family structure, followed by extended family and clans which creates the political construct of the aettir. The aettir follow back to a common ancestor as is found in most feudalistic or monarchic societies. There are only thirteen dynastic aettir in Akiniwazi, all of which relate back to the nobility of the Gamleverden royal lineage, the sea captains who ferried settlers to live in Akiniwazi or a set of powerful men who became influential enough to take over power from those aettir that collapsed during the Aettirkrigen that began shortly after Fimbulvetr and ended in the Halmarpakt.

To solve the problem of new aettir and significantly more family lines, a new hierarchy of peerage was created to reflect the contributions of other aettir in the land. Often the origination of a new aettir was in the accomplishment of great acts or services to the Hird, the system is perpetually growing, which then leads to a hierarchy of the aettir, forming their own social structure as explained below. Once an aettir is part of the peerage, it can only be removed by the bloodline dying off or by being supplanted through marriage. In extreme cases, some have been stripped of their status for treason to the Hird.

There are considered six levels of aettir peerage in Akiniwazi. The highest is called the Hird, while the lowest is the Fellesaettir or "Common Aettir" that has no real organization or recognition. With the merits of members associated with them, they can gain status, and therefore common power among the Forsamling.

An aettir is recognized in its status and therefore grouped by the following:

Vapenaettir

[VAH-pen-EH-ter]

Crested Aettir

These bloodlines are allowed Heraldic crests and mottos in addition to possessing fiefs and lands as well as their colors and crests given due to great fealty and accomplishment to the Visekonge. Members of the klan are required to wear their heraldry at all special occasions and are considered the most senior of the families that do not possess a jarldom. They are often headed by a lendmann, herse or huskarl.

Landetaettir

[LAN-det-EH-ter]

Landed Aettir

These clans are allowed fiefs and lands as reward for service to the Crown or by their own enterprise. These were provided the privilege of recognized colors. They often were given much better titles and greater power as the Visekonge wished to rule in concert with the forming blocs of power. Any crest provided must be that of their patron jarl.

Fargeaettir

[FAR-jee-EH-ter]

Colored Aettir

Loyal retainers to the Crown or jarls are given the merit of aettir colors. Although they are given the distinction their own of heraldic colors, they take the crest of their patron jarl through which the merits were given.

Sivuaettir

[SIH-voo-EH-ter]

Paged Aettir

These are aettir who do not have land, colors or a crest, but nonetheless are recognized by the Hird in the "Bok av Familier" or "Book of Families" which is an official census and have their own pages in that book. These families can often trace their history back to the Gamleverden, which is part of why they are recognized as important families who immigrated by choice.

Fellesaettir

[FEH-les-EH-ter]

Common Aettir

These are unrecognized families by the Hird. They are known locally but carry no real political, legal or military weight. They are more or less a way to categorize families. This group of aettir often consist of Forsamling brought as thralls, exiles or from conquered lands by Denmark, Norway or Sweden. Those bearing Irish, English, French, Inuit or other non-traditional names and geneology are often treated like second class citizens by those in the other aettir.

Hird Titles (In Order of Precedence)

Visekonge
[VEE-say-KON-gay]
The Viceroy or Vice King. Addressed as "my Tign." This is the highest noble rank in the land. The original appointment was created by King Haakon IV of Norway through his youngest son, Sveinn to act in his stead in an effort to stabilize fractious jarls in Akiniwazi. The Visekonge is the defacto king of Akiniwazi but since the Isolation, it has taken on the actual mantle-ship of a King, but maintains the title Visekonge in respect to its origin, but no longer recognizes any other Earthly superior.

Visedronning
[VEE-say-DROH-ning]
Vice Queen
The wife of the Visekonge. Addressed as "my Tign."

Tronerving
[TROH-nur-ving]
Heir to the Throne
The eldest child, destined to be Visekonge. Addressed as "my Tign."

Kronasson
[KROH-nah-sun]
Crown son
Son of the Visekonge. Addressed as "my Tign."

Kronadottir
[KROH-nah-DAW-tur]
Crown daughter
Daughter of the Visekonge. Addressed as "my Tign."

Jarl

[YAH-rul]

An Earl. Addressed as "Den Aerefulle" (The Honorable) by introduction or "Deres Naade" (Your Grace) as a nonspecific form of address. Det Aerefulle Herre or Dame Ogimaque. This title was given to the heads of the 13 families that make up the Royal Hird. Jarls are always landed titles. There is one jarl per lake and major settled river system.

Jarlsonn

[YAH-rul-sun]

Jarl's son

The son of a jarl. Addressed as "Deres Naade" or introduced as "Den Aerefulle."

Herse

[HEHR-say]

A Baron and their land holding. Addressed as "Hovding" or "Hovdingfrue" (Hovdingfrue Tungloddr). The title used for the local representative of the Visekonge. It is usually a military title used more often with fortifications, it can also be the equivalent of a mayor or count to run an isolated territory that would be difficult to rule otherwise. They are more often appointed by a jarl and have an incredible amount of autonomy and power on his behalf.

Lendmann

[LEN-de-mahn]

A Count or Countess.

Addressed as Lendmann for either gender by using their given name after their title (Lendmann Ulla) or Greve (Male) Grevinne (female) are also common forms of address. Lendmenn run local affairs for the jarl or Herse. Often of an allied aettir (plural Lendmenn).

Huskarl

[HOOS-kar-ul]

House Man

An armed retainer or house guard with a limited number that accompany a member of the Hird. Unlanded nobility. They have two honorifics, sjef or meistari, depending on their function. A sjef is typically a leader of a group of soldiers, while meistari is used for berserkers and the ennobled title. Ennoblement is typically done for Huskarls who serve in a governmental capacity for the Hird.

Armann

[AR-mahn]

A courtier or Hird official. Although a member of the Hird and granted ennoblement, they do not have land but rather a royal office that is theirs as long as they are in position. Often this title is used for administrators of the Visekonge or in the Hird of the jarl. They have the right to command huskarls and Haulds. Given the honorific "Herre or Dame."

Hauld

[HAW-uld]

Ennobled Farmer or businessman. The lowest form of royalty but is not hereditary. Given for extraordinary service to the Hird. Allowed the honorific "Herre or Dame."

Forms of Address and Social Status

Berserker

[bur-SUR-kur]

This title is bestowed on champion warriors often blessed with great spiritual gifts for battle. Every jarl has one berserker whom he uses as his personal champion. This is a much sought after title among warriors in the army and the huskarls. As a sign of their station they are awarded the Bear Shirt, a cloak made from the hide of a bear, often with the head still attached and given a gold medallion denoting his patron. The design varies from jarl to jarl.

Traditionally, the berserker goes into a trance in battle and manifests most often as skin impervious to blades and fire. Other gifts manifest from time to time that vary with each berserker. The danger with the trances that these warriors enter is that they sometimes cannot control the fury that is unleashed and will kill friend and foe alike.

Dame

[Daym]

Mistress or Lady. A polite form of address toward a woman of superior position or status. Also used as part of honorifics for female Hird of unknown station.

Damer

[DAH-mur]

Plural form of address for a group of women.

Domari

[doh-MAH-ree]

A judge

A special sogumathr that also knows the legal code by oral tradition, and only used for criminal trials at a Thing. He is the final word on a legal matter. Although a domari is always present at a Thing, not all Things require their services.

Fredlause

[FRED-la-ohss]

Outlaw

A shunned person who is outside the law who has no protections, just like a wild dangerous animal. A person expelled from the protections of the law in Society.

Froeken

[FROH-ken]

Miss. An unmarried woman or maiden. Form of polite address to an unfamiliar equal.

Frue

[FROO]

Madam. A married woman. Form of polite address to an unfamiliar equal.

Herr

[HAIR]

Mister. Polite form of address to a man.

Herre

[HEH-reh]

Master or Sir. A polite form of address toward a man of superior position but unknown status.

Herrar

[HEH-rahr]

Plural for gentlemen or a group of men.

Karl/Kerling

[KARE-ling]

Free man or woman

This is the status of all people not under judgment of the law, or not a member of the Hird with royal status.

Meistari
[my-STAH-ree]
Sir (as in knight)
A term of formal address used exclusively toward huskarls or berserkers.

Niding
[NIH-ding]
Protected Exile
A conditional outlaw, someone who has been punished with skoggang or had his freedom or protection under the law constrained. A prisoner.

Sjef
[SHEHF]
Chief
The leader for a group of warriors. Sometimes an informal title of respect, similar to the term 'boss'.

Sogumathr
[SOH-goo-MAH-tur]
A Lawspeaker
The second highest ranking member of a Thing. Required to have complete oral knowledge of the law and the ability to speak on the behalf of the accused or victim in a trial or settle civil disputes and arbitration.

Thrall
[THRAW-uhl]
A slave
This may be a temporary status like an indentured servant.

Viking
[VY-king]
A raider, pirate, cutthroat, brigand
This term is a pejorative and insult, but also applies to those engaged in the actual acts of piracy, raiding and brigandage.

The Kyrkja

The Kyrkja [HERE-hyah] is an offshoot of the Roman Catholic Church by the proxy of several monastic orders that were active in Scandinavian lands at the time. This included the Benedictine, Franciscan and Dominican orders while influence and heritage from Carolingian colleges and Cistercian traditions are evident.

In 1266 and the beginning of the Isolation Era, being cut off from the Roman Catholic Church, they have gone off in their own directions to fit the unique circumstances of the land and their monastic traditions. Their stated mission purpose is to preach the Word of God to all those willing to listen and to protect those who request salvation. They have engaged in the spiritual war against the lords of the land and members of opposing Skaerslinger paganism. They war against all those who serve the demons and their masters. Each sect is organized around a set of gifts in the spirit or societal duties associated with those gifts to form a cohesive whole like that of the separate parts of the body of Christ.

Sects of the Kyrkja

Anjars (Anja)
Order of Charity, Healing
Colors – Red, Blue and Gold

Ankarites (Ankar)
Order of Preaching, Teaching and Ministry
Colors – Green, Black and White

Havarians (Havar)
Order of Preservation, Protection, Knowledge
Colors – Grey, Dark Blue and White

Koenraadians (Koenraad)
Order of Counseling & Wisdom
Colors – Brown, Red and Green

Ragnarites (Ragnar)
Order of Holy Warfare, Defenders of the Faithful
Colors – Black, Crimson and White

Sanaadians (Sanaa)
Order of Prayer and Prophecy
Colors – White, Light Blue and Dark Blue

Taitians (Tait)
Order of the Arts, Praise and Worship
Colors – Blue, Purple and Red

Things

Currency

The primary currency is the Silver Penning, with commonly recognized coin variations in the forms of Ertogs, Oeres and Marks. Coins can also be found in other metals such as gold and copper which have a variable value based on the local market. On rare occasions bronze and platinum coins have been minted. Although it is valued against silver, there is no universal standard of conversion and often devolves into haggling on what the participants need. In this manner gold is worth far less than silver in some areas, while in others far more. Silver is used as the baseline for precious metals in the Akiniwazi Union and the spot price set by the Crown banks.

Conversion Chart

	Penning	Ertog	Oere	Mark
Penning	1	10	30	240
Ertog	1/10	1	3	24
Oere	1/30	1/3	1	8
Mark	1/240	1/24	1/8	1

Trotes

Trade Notes

These are pieces of paper currency usually for large transactions backed by a specific commodity owned by the bank or company. The note itself is essentially a sophisticated I.O.U. that promises the issuer will keep on hand or provide in a timely manner the commodity backing the note. They help facilitate large scale trade between the lands and companies.

For example, a transaction may be purchased with for a specific sum backed by timber from a local lumber camp to meet payroll. This Trote can be taken by the purchaser and traded in for silver at any of the Crown or jarl banks. It may also be used to purchase other goods from a business or by anyone willing to redeem it for a large scale purchase at that amount. This cycle may continue till the Trote finds its way back to the original issuer, where they would pay the Trote in either silver or the backing commodity, or a combination of the two. If traded in to a bank, they are used between the banks in a similar fashion but never re-enter public use. The most common trotes are found for timber, peat, grain, fish, cut stone, building materials, bulk products like sand, manufactured items like glass, leather or paper. It is not mandatory to accept a Trote as payment, but is considered good manners if access to a bank or other repository of legal currency is possible.

Many a feud has started over failure to honor a Trote.

Gems

Precious and semi-precious stones are a fluid market often subject to the tastes of the buyer as well as availability. Cut gems are always worth something, though their value is wildly inconsistent, often applying their aesthetic value to its price. Set jewelry is worth the most but is even more inconsistent in value. The Hird and Kyrkja are patrons of lapidaries to help increase their wealth when provided with raw stones.

Food and Drink

Aquavit
[AH-kah-veet]
A potent liquor of clear to golden color. Strongly flavored with fennel, licorice or anise. Occasionally served from bottles frozen in blocks of ice.

Brennevin
[BREH-neh-vin]
An unsweetened liquor similar to schnapps. Sometimes spiced with caraway .

Clapbread
Small loaves of bread made from oats or barley.

Kex
[KEKS]
Cookies. Often made with cinnamon, molasses, ginger, nuts & dried fruits.

Switchel
A refreshing drink made with apple cider vinegar and water, often with honey, salt and cinnamon added. Used to make water safe and work in the fields .

Wastel
An expensive good quality bread made with refined flour.

Keeping Time & Canonical Hours

Time is kept in Akiniwazi on land in three hour blocks. If time is specifically known, it will be referred to as either the 1st, 2nd or 3rd hour of the period. (e.g. 7am would be Second Primae) Time after that is broken down by quarter hours at the most precise after that. These quarter hour delineations are are called early, mid and late (e.g. Mid Third Nocturne would be 2:30am).

Nocturne	Midnight-2am
Matins	3am-5am
Primae	6am-8am
Terce	9am-11am
Sexte	Noon-2pm
Nonae	3pm to 5pm
Vesper	6pm-8pm
Compline	9pm-11pm

Ad Segregationem
[AHD SEH-greh-gaht-seeoh-nem]
After Separation
All dates are commonly referred back to the date in which Fimbulvetr closed the passage to the Gamleverden through the Kisiina Sea in 1267 AD, trapping the Forsamling, separating them from their ancestral Viking homelands.

Miscellany

Karvi

[KAR-vee]

A small sailboat mostly used for fishing or shallow water. Rarely over 50 feet long.

Knarr

[NAR]

Similar to a viking longship, a knarr's draft is deeper, but is a far wider ship. It is a standard non-military vessel in Akiniwazi. They range from 100 - 400 foot long.

Skoggang

[SKOH-gahng]

A sentence for criminal activity. Literally meant "to go into the forest". It is a partial exile and shunning from society. Those who have been been given the punishment of skoggang are restricted to a certain area where they remain protected by the law, or a restriction on who may associate with him.

Steamknarr

[STEEM-nar]

A specific style of knarr unique to Akiniwazi that utilizes a steam engine and paddlewheels to sail. This class of vessel looks like a combination between a cog, caravel and sidewheel steamboat. Key features include multiple decks, often enclosed with a raised fore and aftcastle.

Thing

[TING]

An official gathering or trial, often presided over by an elder or sogumathr or domari.

Sport & Games

Knattleikr

[NOT-ly-kurh]

The most organized sport of the Akiniwazi Union. It is a modified version of the ancient game into a more organized competition. It is a combination of baseball and rugby. It can have unequal sized teams where players can come and go as they please. Games can last all day, ending because of dark, a set point score is reached or one team surrenders the pitch.

Stafurleikr

[STAH-foor-LY-kurh]

The Stick game (lacrosse) played by Skaerslinger. Sometimes used as an alternative to war. Death while playing is not uncommon and considered honorable.

Supernatural Beings

Azhikwe Ozheginguay
[AHZ-hee-kway ohz-HEE-gin-gway]
Azhikwe for short. The Spirit of the Screaming Faces. A demonic scourge of the Skaerslinger that preys on powerful men. It corrupts their spirits and through them their followers, thereby destroying whole groups of people.

Draugr
[DRAO-gur]
The animated dead. Corpses of animals or humans that are controlled by manitou.

Manitou
[MAN-ih-too]
A generic Skaerslinger term for spirit, demon, devil or ghost. Always evil spirit, devil or demon from a Forsamling context.

Ogimaak Mikwam
[oh-GEH-mawk MIK-wahm]
The Ice Queen
Second most powerful demon in Akiniwazi. Has a shrine on the largest island in Akiniwazi located in Lake Ogimaque.

Ogimaa Nichiiwad
[oh-GEH-mawk NEE-chee-wahd]
The Storm King
The most powerful demon in Akiniwazi. It is said to rule from a mythical fortress somewhere in the northeastern Ondeaandkorgfjall.

Wendigo
[WEN-dih-goh]
A demon of winter, starvation, cannibalism and madness.

MAP

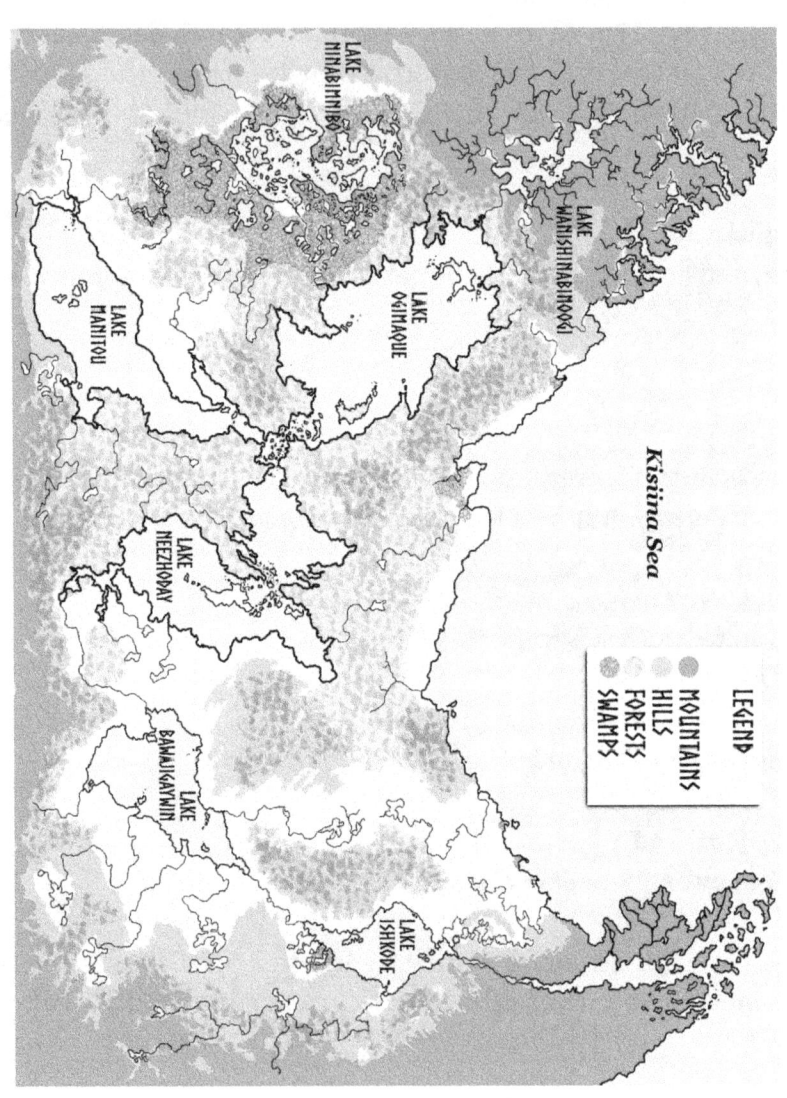

ACKNOWLEDGMENTS

I would like to acknowledge the contributions of the following people:

Editor
Jane Lambert

Alpha Readers
Torfinn Brokke, Francois Henning,

Beta Readers
Jeremy Dietzman, Ted & Jessie Genske, Matt Hurst, Sean McDaniel, Chris Nesbit, Ken Porter, Caleb Smay, Mike Tabor

A special thank you to
Austin & Judy Boncher, Dave Lawrence, Angie Grigaliunas and all the rest of my friends and family for proofreading, opinions, criticism and support.

Thank you all!

CPSIA information can be obtained
at www.ICGtesting.com
Printed in the USA
LVHW111351200120
644169LV00012B/471/J